*A STILL AND WOVEN BLUE*

RICHARD STOOKEY

# A Still and Woven Blue

A SAN FRANCISCO BOOK COMPANY/

HOUGHTON MIFFLIN BOOK

*Houghton Mifflin Company    Boston*

1974

First Printing  v

Copyright © 1974 by Richard P. Stookey

Library of Congress Cataloging in Publication Data

Stookey, Richard Phelps.
  A still and woven blue.

  "A San Francisco Book Company/Houghton Mifflin book."
  I. Title.
PZ4.S88135St  [PS3569.T646]    813'.5'4    73-21637
ISBN 0-395-18493-2                ISBN 0-913374-05-9

Printed in the United States of America


This SAN FRANCISCO BOOK COMPANY/HOUGHTON MIFFLIN BOOK originated in San Francisco and was produced and published jointly. Distribution is by Houghton Mifflin Company, 2 Park Street, Boston, Massachusetts 02107

*The title of this book is from a poem by Richard Wilbur.*

*The first Interlude is founded upon an early factual account by Charles Fletcher Lummis.*

R.S.

*To my father*

IF BRETHREN DWELL TOGETHER, and one of them die, and have no child, the wife of the dead shall not marry without unto a stranger: her husband's brother shall go in unto her, and take her to him to wife, and perform the duty of an husband's brother unto her. And it shall be, that the firstborn which she beareth shall succeed in the name of his brother which is dead, that his name shall not be put out of Israel.

*— Deuteronomy 25:5–6*

# ✥ Part One

*On the willows there we hung up our lyres.*
— PSALM 137

*1 NOVEMBER 1970*

*PETER*  T he road wound through tall pines down the hill to the crossing, then turned sharply left over the bridge. The river was low, gray rocks sticking out like fat fingers, and I could see fish shapes shadowed against the sandy bottom as I started up the other side of the canyon. Downstream from the bridge were two rusty carcasses, cars that had fallen off the road.

It was dry on this side, sagebrush and sandy red rock and a few scrub pines, but there was still some frost on the low places and I was careful. The road was steep and narrow; it seemed to cling to the canyonside more by willpower than by design. I kept watching for frost and hoping that nobody would be coming down.

There was a hawk working in the canyon below me now, and I watched it out of the corner of my eye, recalling that *Raptores* is the scientific name for hawk and a raptor is one who preys or plunders . . .

Suddenly he was on top of me — a radiator about seven feet high, close enough for me to read the *Peterbilt* written on it, air horn blasting, brakes hissing. I don't know what I did, but then he was past me and I was still on the road and he was yelling as he disappeared around the corner down the hill.

I pulled off onto a wide shoulder and turned off the engine. My heart was beating piledriver strokes as I lit my pipe with shaking hands. While I was sitting there, wondering what had kept me both out of his way and out of the canyon, another one came screaming around the uphill corner and past me down the road. It was empty, with the trailer piggyback on the tractor. The driver didn't look older than twenty, but he sat there calm and sure of himself, full of purpose and coordination.

On the other hand, they don't have to act like they own the road either.

I sat for a few minutes watching the hawk. It seemed I could almost see his goldfoil eyes peering down into the canyon as he hung there, buoyed steady on the rising air. Then all at once he turned and, slipping sideways, sailed far off down the river.

I stopped for gas in North Yancey, serving myself at a single pump in front of the old sandstone hotel. Then about a mile outside of town I turned off and, following the directions in his letter, took an oiled gravel road to the east through a flat but narrow valley rimmed by low mountains. The floor of the valley was a bright frosted green color and there were clumps of conifers here and there, representatives sent down by the bordering woods. The mountains rose more steeply on the south side, and I could see the blue smoke of cabins set along the border of trees, probably near the river. A mile or so further up was the lumber mill from which those gracious trucks had come. Then finally after about five miles the valley ended abruptly and the road wound into a steep wooded canyon. Here the river appeared again alongside the road, but it was smaller now, a series of gentle slides and falls between deep pools ringed by mossy boulders. It was all ferns and moss and icy water, a primeval coolness.

Exactly one mile up the canyon, just as he had said, was the yellow mailbox. I turned onto his road, one lane of good gravel, and wound steeply up a tributary creek. Soon the woods became less dense and I seemed to be driving up to the sun out of a dark pit. Then, very suddenly, I was at the top and in a meadow clearing perhaps a quarter-mile square with the creek running

*4*

through it. The cabin was against the trees at the far side, and I could see his red stocking cap.

He, Merlin, stood grinning, his tanned cherubic face bright in the sun, as I drove up and parked in the graveled place beside the cabin to which he pointed me. I turned off the engine, opened the door, and took his hand.

"Ah," he said. "My learned counselor."

"It is I," I said, getting out. "The very same."

I always cooperated. We had played this game for a very long time.

"And your journey?" he said, affecting solemn interest. "It was pleasant, I hope."

"A delight, sir. An exquisite diversion. And your health?" I continued to wring his hand with mock solicitude.

"Vigorous, my lad — due no doubt to the Spartan tone of my existence in these high mountains, which you must have noticed already." An elaborate gesture, palm upward. "And if I might boldly inquire as to your own . . . ?"

The rules were simple. Any number of inane inquiries and responses was permissible — until the health of the guest was put in issue. From that point it was strict ritual. "Failing rapidly, sir," I said. "It is the dread lumbago." I hobbled dutifully as he moved with high concern to my side and helped me up the steps of the porch.

"That is a very pity. And you so young." His long face brightening by degrees until: "*However,* it so happens that even as we speak there reposes in my medicine cabinet a prime remedy for that precise affliction. It is a bitter nostrum, but its effects are beneficial in extreme cases."

"How kind of you, sir, not to mention generous. This attack has been unmerciless."

Clucking sympathetically, he pointed me to a chair on the porch.

"I will stand, sir, in anticipation of your safe return," I said. "I have been sitting a time."

"That you have. And as you wish. And to be sure, to be sure." He did a little jig as he ducked under the drape of burlap hanging over the doorway and disappeared inside.

I leaned on the porch railing and looked out over the clearing. About fifty feet from the cabin the creek ran slow and flat between willow-clotted banks. The sun was dropping fast toward the brim of forested hills, and fingers of shadow extended out into the meadow. Near the far wall of trees, where the road entered the clearing, a doe with a fawn made her way through the creek and bounded splashing, back legs pushing, up the bank. After a little hesitation the fawn followed, and they moved together into the forest. The doe seemed a little lame.

Suddenly from inside the cabin there came a bumping sound, followed by one of breaking glass. Then a florid curse. Apparently the Spartan tone of Merlin's existence had not improved his manual dexterity . . .

He burst through the burlap and pushed by me to the table, the bottle in his right armpit and two jelly glasses in his hands. Setting the glasses down with exaggerated care, he then plucked out the bottle and put it precisely in the center of the table.

"Did you break anything I might want to inherit?" I said, sitting down.

He smiled wanly. "Lost a good soldier," he said. "Fortunately there was another eager to take his place in the line." He poured standing, then settled into his chair.

We talked — or rather he talked — until dark. He was full of North Yancey stories, impressions of the characters who frequented the bar of the hotel. He did them all — man, woman, and child — but the favorite, the undisputed favorite, was a certain garrulous individual whom he had dubbed The Constable. Holding his tongue in his cheek to make the tobacco wad, Merlin performed The Constable:

"Now you may not believe this, being a city dude and all, but the other day I am driving down the road minding my own business when right at the Bloomfield turnoff there is this nigger girl, standing there all by herself just as pretty as you please. Well, being a gentleman I stop, and she up and asks for a ride. Well now, I ain't too sure about that because what would people think, if they saw me driving down the road with a nigger girl in the car, I mean. It just wouldn't do. Well, so I just up and tell her that, in the politest way I can, of course — but then right away she up and says, 'Oh no, I ain't no nigger gal, no, sir, I'se from . . .' and she names one of those Caribbean islands, I forget which . . ."

Arching his eyebrows in puzzlement, his tongue making the tobacco chew . . .

"Haiti?" I said, cooperating.

"No." Rubbing the point of his chin . . .

"Puerto Rico?"

"No . . ."

"Jamaica?"

Merlin's eyes sparkled as he sat up straight in the chair, full of constabulary outrage. "Hell no, sonny. I didn't even let her in the car!" Gales of constabulary laughter, complete with knee slapping. Spit. Sigh . . .

We sat in the smiling silence and watched flickering dark shapes wheeling and veering over the surface of the creek. "Them are bats," Merlin said. "Keep your neck vein kivvered."


Later, inside, he cooked on the woodstove while I sat with a drink and watched. The cabin was as I had expected, spare and neat. It was a large single room with a bathroom attached, apparently an afterthought. Against the far wall were his narrow bed and a small bookcase filled with newspapers. Against the near wall, in the kitchen part of the room, were a round oak table and two cane-bottomed chairs. Between lay a spotlessly clean expanse of bare wood floor.

I, at the frantic request of his agent, had asked him about his work — charitably assuming that there had been some — and now he was babbling energetically as he clanked about amongst the iron doors and lids of the ponderous stove. ". . . And so you may tell our swarthy friend, the Smyrna manuscript merchant, to rest easy and keep shut. There is something simmering, but I will take my own time with it."

"He is used to that," I said. "It's just that like the rest of us he doesn't quite know what to think. As you would have learned if you had read his letter, he's worried that you might have decided to quit, to end your days in romantic but unproductive solitude. I couldn't reassure him because I don't know what you're doing up here any more than he does, and since you're not telling . . ."

And lo, now he was a prizefighter — dancing around the room on his toes, shadowboxing. "Me retire? Still got the wind, don't I? Eh?" A quick combination. "Legs like India rubber, sweetie." Patting his thigh. "Hands like greased lightning." A wild flurry — then a groan. His hand on the small of his back, he hobbled to the stove.

"And so what should I tell him?" I said to his back. "I have to tell him something."

"Tell him to go to hell," Merlin said, rattling his stovelids.


It was after dinner — when he had cleared away the remains of the thick venison steaks that he had somehow managed to obtain out of season without even owning a gun — that he told it, his Baptist story. The coffee and bourbon were on the big oak table between us and he had been quiet a long time, picking his teeth with a broomstraw and staring vacantly at his glass, his bald head shining brilliantly in the light of the gas lamp. I knew what was coming, and I waited patiently, obediently, while my cup of whiskey-laden coffee breathed its aroma up to me. He had done this so many times — tried his ideas, his visions, out on me — that I had almost come to expect it, had almost given up wishing that he would see the futility of it all and stop, stop trying to wring from me some reaction that is not there, will never be there.

I am at bottom a practical person, a person not given to fanciful associations. I have satisfied myself about this.

"What do you know about the Baptist?" he began. "John the Baptist."

Now, as always, I did not resist. There was no use resisting. "Nothing," I said. "I mean he baptized Jesus in the river, that's all. Is that what you are writing about?"

He continued to stare at the flickering bourbon as he spoke. " '. . . And straightway coming up out of the water he saw the heavens opened and the Spirit like a dove descending upon him, and there came a voice from heaven saying *Thou art my beloved Son, in whom I am well pleased.*' "

For a moment I said nothing, then: "Who is it talking to? The voice I mean." He, Merlin, looked up at me as if I had said something astonishing. I was just trying to get clear what happened.

"I think the Baptist might have wondered too," he said quietly.

"What?"

"I think maybe he wondered too for a minute who the voice was talking to, because before then maybe he wasn't too sure about the whole thing. Maybe before then he had even thought that he might be the One himself, that one day God might just come and say to him, 'Okay, John, it's you.' But then that was all settled. The dove was on Jesus, and God was talking to the guy with the dove on him."

Merlin took a cigarette out of his shirt pocket and lit it. The smoke swirled up into the level of darkness that lay above the light of the lamp. "But then," he went on, "maybe the Baptist didn't really believe it then either, even though the dove had made it plain enough, because some people say that he had to ask Jesus himself a little later. But that was afterwards, when Herod

*9*

had put the old guy in the slammer for shooting off his mouth too much."

"I didn't know he was in jail," I said. "But I do know who Herod is. He is the bad king. No matter what Bible story you want to talk about, the bad king's name is always Herod. Herod is the one who is killing all the boy babies and then his daughter, Herod's daughter, finds Moses in the bulrushes. And then a few thousand years later Herod is at it slaughtering innocents again, and Mary and Joseph and tiny baby Jesus have to keep out of his way. And then thirty-three years after that Herod gives the okay to nail him up. So I know all about Herod. He's the bad king."

The booze must have been getting to me. I had begun to talk like him now.

"That is a pretty good summary," Merlin said with a wicked grin. "There is not much I can say to improve on it except maybe to note in passing — and purely by way of embellishment rather than contradiction — that it was *Pharaoh's* daughter. But that was in another country . . . and besides, the wench is dead . . . It might not hurt though to add also that the Herod in the manger story is old Herod, Herod the Great, and the one in the crucifixion is one of his sons and the one we are talking about — Herod Antipas. Aside from those minor points . . ."

I put on a hurt look. "Well," I said, "even if there was more than one, they were all of them bastards."

"Maybe," he said slowly — and then he was lost again in the glowing whiskey. I waited, obediently, and finally he looked up at me. He was done with frivolity now, ready to get on with it. "Old Herod, who gets credit for massacring innocents and little else, was by the standard of the day a great and creative king, a builder of harbors and aqueducts and temples to the measurements of Solomon. He was also a tragic hero, Lear and Othello in one. But that is another story. It was one of his sons I meant — Antipas, who got a piece of the kingdom when the old lunatic was finally still, who got Galilee and Peraea. The whole thing was still under Rome, as it had been before, but still

Antipas was in some sense a king — with a king's prerogatives. And it happened that in his kingdom there lived a beautiful and proud and ambitious woman. Herodias was her name . . ."

"Wait," I said.

He looked up smiling. "Yes, she got her name from the old man too. She was Antipas' own niece in fact; but you can't let that bother you. Everybody was related to old Herod. He spread his seeds."

"Okay," I said.

"Okay. Now Herodias was already married and had a daughter, but her husband lacked the ambition necessary to keep her happy and she did not discourage Antipas. She became his queen, and she brought her daughter with her. Unfortunately Antipas already had a queen in good repair, namely the daughter of the King of Arabia. She went packing, and her father commenced to plot revenge, a revenge which . . . but that is another story too."

"I was hoping you might say that," I said. "I am having enough trouble now." He ignored me and filled his glass again. "I'll take it your way from here on out," I said, pushing my glass toward him. He poured me an inch, then set the bottle down without a sound before he went on.

"Anyway, at this time our friend the Baptist was preaching and baptizing and crying out in the wilderness east of the Jordan. He was drawing pretty good crowds, too. It was getting to be the time when the scriptures said, or some people thought they said, that the Messiah would come and set things straight. Everything else fit; it was the darkness before the Light. And then here comes the Baptist and some of them started to say that here is the Light. He, the Baptist, did his best to talk them out of it, but he never did convince some of them — and maybe, just maybe, he didn't ever quite convince himself either . . .

"But there's no need to bother ourselves about that. The important thing is that the Baptist started to build up a pretty good following — and Herod Antipas started to fidget. A rebellion

*11*

was all he needed now. The wolves were already snapping all around him — the insulted Arabian king was massing his forces near the border, looking for an opening; Agrippa, Antipas' spendthrift nephew, was currying favor in Rome, looking for an opening; the Roman governor Pilate was unhappy with Antipas and would welcome an opening . . . A rebellion was all he needed now, the wolves would all spring at once.

"And so Antipas was not surprised — rather he simply acknowledged the arrival of an anticipated crisis — when the news came that the Baptist was speaking out against his marriage to Herodias, when the word came that the multitudes on the riverbank were being told that God's wrath would once more be turned upon the nation of Israel if the adulterer Herod Antipas did not return Herodias to her husband and come to the Jordan to wash his soul . . ." By now Merlin was speaking only to himself, his roughly resonant voice filling the room as he gradually put aside the disguise of vernacular banter and took up that convoluted language which always lay just beneath it. His eyeglasses flashed in the gaslight as he continued to gaze into the amber liquid in front of him. I kept still.

"It was a difficult problem. Antipas agonized over it as, early those cool mornings, he paced the terraced roof of his modest palace within the citadel Machaerus, high above the pewter waters of the Dead Sea. What, he asked himself, would his father have done — the father who had built this jagged fortress to guard his eastern flank against that same Arabian king who now plotted war once again? Would Herod the Great have disposed of the Baptist summarily, taking the risk that his influence was already significant enough to make execution an open invitation to civil disorder? Or would he have ignored him for the moment, taking the risk that the Baptist, if not nipped in the bud, would become more than an annoying pest? Might he even have made some gesture of repentance — short of returning Herodias, of course (even David, who not only took the wife but also arranged the demise of the husband, had not had to do that) — in order to keep the madman quiet? As the sun behind his back revealed itself above Arabia to set aflame the wild western peaks of Jeshimmon, Herod Antipas, Tetrarch of Galilee and Peraea, searched his blood for the answer.

"Herodias herself, in spite of what some have said, really had no strong views on the subject. True, the Baptist had said some rather extreme things about her in the course of his denunciation of Antipas, but such things from the mouth of a lunatic Peraean agitator were nothing to concern oneself about. Whether the madman lived or died, it was all one to her — and if Antipas wanted to make some absurd show of contrition, well, that was his affair . . .

"And then one bright morning Antipas came down from his sunrise broodings with the answer: politician that he was, he would choose all three alternatives so that he would not have to choose any one of them. He would stop the offending mouth without courting disaster, yet he would leave open the possibility of a future . . . arrangement. The Baptist was placed in prison for safekeeping.

"But Herodias . . . didn't I say that she was noncommittal, nay, unconcerned, about the fate of the Baptist? What was it then, I wonder, that led her to him when he was safely lodged in the prison at Machaerus? Perhaps, perhaps . . . I think that at first perhaps it was simple curiosity, an uncomplicated desire to confront one whose powers of fascination were sufficient to transfix the masses — indeed, whose powers of fascination had already by then proved sufficient to hold the attention of the troubled king himself during the long afternoon audiences that had become a regular event in his private chambers. Perhaps . . .

"The regal Herodias and her maiden, swathed in green velvet, led by the leering jailer down the long stone passageway, stopping before one of the massive doors, going in . . .

" 'Some say that you are the Promised One, Baptist. What do you say of that?'

" 'I say that I am not He.'

13

"Yes, and so perhaps it was just curiosity at first. Perhaps it was not until she saw him, the electricity still crackling out of those perpetually astonished gray eyes, his wild independence manifested not in the rude contempt she had expected but rather in a kind of distant courtesy — perhaps it was only then that she resolved to break him, to tame him, to show him that the holy fire did not make him more than a man. But — whether then or later — the resolution was made . . . and so one evening her maidens bathed her and perfumed her and clothed her and she went down into the prison again. Alone. And found him . . . sitting on the cold floor of his cell, those eyes staring fixedly at the far wall, those eyebrows contracted into a frown not of outrage but of concentration so intense as to require a physical effort to sustain it. And she, Herodias the queen, went in, stood silently before him . . . He continued to gaze as if at something thrust between them until, slowly, his face seemed almost to melt as he lifted his eyes to her face.

" *'Why have you come here?'*

" *'I have come to comfort you in prison.'*

"There was no expression on his face as he looked up at her. Her black eyes held his gaze as she pulled the ivory pins from her hair and let it fall in loose perfumed curls down her back, as she unfastened the velvet cloak and let it fall to the stone floor — and stood before him in a fine chemise. There was no sound but her restrained breathing and the soft clicking of palm trees in the courtyard. The Baptist gave no sign, made no sound, as she quickly dropped the linen garment around her ankles and stepped out of it, one short step toward him. The moon had risen now and it shone through the cell window upon her nakedness — smooth narrow shoulders, full olive blacktipped breasts, gently swelling thighs where they bordered the combed triangle of silky hair . . . And now, suddenly, she breathed deeply, her body swelled and relaxed, rose and fell — and there was the clicking of the palms in the soft wind. But still, still the Baptist gave no sign, made no sound. His eyes remained yoked to hers — and thus they stayed, like figures in a frieze, until . . .

" 'Will you have me, Baptist?'

"The great maned head dropped into his hand with a small sound. A sob? Then, slowly, he raised his face again to hers, then past hers . . . she saw the cords in his neck tighten — and then he was bellowing the few measured syllables in a voice strident with rage.

" 'Jailer! Take this slut from my cell!' "

The sound drained from the cabin room. Merlin was still, his hands folded on the table, interlaced fingers. He seemed to tremble a little as the gaslight glinted on his forehead. I got up and went to the sink. When I turned on the water it made a hissing sound, like dipping a horseshoe.

"I am writing about that," Merlin said after a long silence.

"I never heard it that way," I said. "I thought that . . ."

"I just made it," he said.

"Right. But what really happened? Didn't . . ."

He smiled at me, that tolerant closed smile I had seen so many times before. "I made it," he said quietly. "That's what happened."

I turned away from him and began to wash off the dishes, the water hissing in the sink. Through the window I could see the great orange moon pushing up over the trees like a submerged balloon.

"And what do you think about that woman?" Merlin finally said.

"I don't believe her," I said.

"No. You don't." He spoke it as if he was assenting to a self-evident proposition.

I ignored him. "I don't believe that women are as conniving and ferocious as you make them," I said. "But maybe I have known different women than you have."

"Maybe," he said without looking up. He filled his empty glass again, then was silent for a long time. I could hear frogs outside.

I finished the dishes and sat down again. "There is more to it though," I said. "A woman that you made, let alone a queen, wouldn't let him get away with that. She would have him pay."

He smiled up at me. "You do know me, Peter," he said.

"But she couldn't just tell Antipas then, just say okay, kill him now. She had had her chance before, before the king came down from his terrace that morning with the answer, before they went out and got him and clapped him in the dungeon, before he started bending the royal ear in those afternoon interviews. Now that she had acquired a reason she couldn't just . . ." I heard my voice trail off as I looked up at his face. He was staring at his glass again — the amber liquid seemed to have drawn all of the light in the room into a single glowing spark.

"No," he said slowly. "She couldn't do that." He was silent again for a moment before he went on. "But the next day happened to be the birthday of Herod Antipas, and in the evening a feast was to be held in the great hall to celebrate the event. The proper dignitaries were all assembled — cunning Jerusalem Pharisees on country holiday, overpolite Roman bureaucrats, tiresome Smyrna Greeks — yes, they were all there, patient vultures distinguishable only by their respective plumages. But one seemingly indispensable reveler was to be absent. Herodias the queen had sent word to Antipas that her monthly pains were upon her and that she would stay in her rooms undisturbed until they abated. In her place she sent Salome, her daughter by the forsaken husband."

"Seven veils," I said.

He went on as if he had not heard me. He had not heard me. "Salome was at that time only sixteen years old, but her character, like her body, was fully formed and gently ripening like an avocado in the sun. She was not so complex as her mother — she had none of her mother's ability for plan and design, for deliberation. No, she was not that way at all. She simply let life break over her and then bathed in the wash. She was . . . she had . . . a story is told that once when Salome was fourteen years old she was traveling with her mother in Egypt and one day, as they neared the city that was to be their destination for the night, they saw camped just outside the walls a band of young shepherds, members of a savage and despised nomadic tribe. Perhaps they had sold their flocks in the city, perhaps . . . They had wine, and their drunken shouting and singing rang through the evening as the caravan passed them and went through the city gates. Salome, taken to a palace in the city, retired early to her room. Then she covered her rich garments with a coat which she had stolen from a servant and, slipping out of the palace into the cackling streets, walked through the gates to the firelit camp. There she sang and danced for the astonished youths until the morning star appeared — and then, as their astonishment gave way to drunken confidence, suffered repeatedly what they mistook for rape . . .

"And so what she did she might have done without her mother's counsel — if it were not for the price exacted: that was the mark of Herodias. Thus it must have been that on the afternoon of the birthday feast Salome, smooth and quick as a bird, had curled quietly at the foot of the queenly bed and listened without argument or interruption while her mother, pale and drawn as if she had just finished a difficult birth, commissioned it. And yes, Salome might have wondered — but she did not question. For whatever her faults, Salome was admirably devoted to her mother.

"And it was easy, so easy . . ." Merlin, again impaled upon the glowing spark of bourbon, was nodding a little now. But I had seen that before — he could talk for hours yet. "Imagine the dance, my . . . imagine the dance, Peter. The girl Salome modestly asking her stepfather if she could soothe the pain of her mother's absence by dancing for him, he smiling through his wine, nodding as she rises from the pomegranate- and grape-strewn table to leave the hall — then she returning after a moment, standing before him wrapped from heels to head in a purple velvet cloak, motioning to the musicians, dropping the cloak . . . her smooth hard body in the costume of an Alexandrian dancer, sparkling coins above, full diaphanous skirt below — then the first slow movements, the soft ringing jingle of the clashing coins, the expert motion of her body as the clangorous music increases, builds . . . (his lidded eyes shining now, browsing upon her steady and suggestive gaze, her surprisingly luxuriant breasts moving smoothly beneath the spangling coins, long firm legs moving smoothly) . . . increases in tempo and fury until her torso no longer attempts to keep the rhythm but begins a whipping, shaking movement from the hips, arms held out straight, the flesh of her bosom and shoulders vibrating with the frantic clangor of the coins as she moves deliberately toward him and then slowly shaking descends with bended legs before his sitting figure until her reverberating breasts are at the level of his eyes, close enough to touch, shimmering, jarring, tinkling, sparkling, quivering, the music clanging loud, loud . . . and then silence as she pitches forward into his lap. Her body slick with sweat, her soft panting . . .

"He carried her easily to a small room, her face pressed against the heavy beating in his chest. In the great hall the feast continued; in the small room the feast began . . . and finally he slept. She waited half an hour, then rose and dressed herself in a proper linen gown before she waked him gently with a *'My lord, you must return to your guests. It is your birthday.'*

"He obeyed, following her light steps back to the hall. There at length he rose to speak. *'My stepdaughter has pleased me profoundly this birthday night. Profoundly. She shall have her wish of me, up to half my kingdom.'* Salome sitting smiling like a quiet sparrow . . . *'Speak your wish, my dear. It shall be granted if it lies within my power. Speak!'*

"And then that small voice, home from the convent: *'My lord, I wish the head of the Baptist.'*

"A silence so deep . . .

"The face of Herod Antipas was a bruised cloud as he sank back into his couch, his eyes closed tight. He was motionless for a long moment . . . then a slight movement as if to question her — then he sank back silent again. A still silence, profound. Profound . . .

"And suddenly he was standing — and the sound of his cup clattering on the stone floor supported his voice, full of screeching rage, as he bellowed at the chancellor, '*You heard the wish, you drunken fool! Fulfill it!*'

"And Herod Antipas, Tetrarch of Galilee and Peraea, stumbled sobbing from the hall . . .'"

Merlin rose from his chair and poured the last inch of whiskey from his glass into the sink. The water hissed as he rinsed his glass. "It was brought directly," he said, "on a silver charger — and was placed gently among the pomegranates and figs."

"What's that?" I said.

"What?" He turned back toward me, his glasses flashing in the light.

"A charger. What's a charger?"

Merlin sighed. "It is a plate," he said. 'A large flat . . . plate."

We went directly to bed, I on the floor in his sleeping bag. As I fell spinning into sleep I could hear his voice, softly: "And how is your mother?" But I was too far down to come up for that.

It had been six months then — half a year since that rainy Wednesday in April when he had come home quite sober at two o'clock in the afternoon and had announced that he was leaving, that even after twenty-six years he was leaving, that even though he was sixty years old he was leaving, that even though she was fifty-eight years old and would be alone in that huge empty house he was leaving (she, my mother, Clarissa, her right hand with the emerald wandering up to her temple to sweep away a strand of gray-blond hair as she told it: how she had been laying the cards at the kitchen table, watching the rain come down straight, and the cards had been bad for him — the seven, the nine of spades, a dark woman — when he had come running up the back stairs soaking wet and she had just managed to say, "Why are you home?" before he was shouting at her, he who never shouted at anyone, drunk or sober, shouting, "I have to *go!* I have to go *now!*") . . . and yes, half a year since on that same day he came through the straight rain which turned to snow long before he got to this place, this place that he had then owned unknown to her, to me, for who knows how many years before, this place to which he must have come before during the numberless unannounced disappearances which had made their marriage, if it could be called . . . and six months, half a year too since he had ventured beyond the caramel stone of North Yancey into his old world, or had received anyone from that world into this new one — me, of all people, with my simple and starkly explicit instructions ("Read all mail, answer that I can't be reached, deposit all checks to Clarissa's account less two hundred a month general delivery North Yancey, NO VISITORS"), his only contact with the outside . . . and yes, half a year too since his hitherto prolific pen had yielded a word for publication (the letter from his agent that I forwarded returned unopened with his childlike scrawl across the envelope: "I said only checks") .

Then suddenly, unexpectedly, one steaming September afternoon his letter had come to my office in San Francisco — that long, strangely talkative letter written and addressed in dull pencil which, in two small sentences near the bottom, had softly summoned me, had obliquely commanded my presence. "There are fish up here, my boy, who are longing to make your acquaintance. Do not wait too long to extend the barbed shank of greeting in their direction."

And I had come. In spite of everything, neither of us could really doubt that I would come . . :


After breakfast, while he washed the dishes, I went down to the creek to see if anything was rising. It was fine water, long flat pools strung like beads between the riffles, and there were not enough willows to cause any real difficulty in casting. I saw only one rise, a big fish taking a gnat with a soft sucking slup. I made a mental note of the place, noticing that I could reach the rise easily by standing at the head of the riffles below. On the way back to the cabin I saw the doe again, the lame one that I had seen the evening before. The fawn was not with her this time.

Merlin was sitting on the porch in the sun. There was a pot of coffee on the table and a cup for me.

"And how did the waters seem to your practiced eye, Isaac?" Merlin said.

"Fishy," I said, sitting down. "I'll have a cup with you to compose my mind."

Reaching inside his flannel shirt, he produced a half pint. He took off the cap, then poured into my cup from the bottle with his left hand while he poured from the coffee pot with his right hand. "This ought to steady you," he said.

"I didn't know that you had taken to carrying it with you," I said.

"You can't be too careful," he said. "There is always the possibility of burglars."

It was a fine bright morning. A light frost lay sparkling on the meadow like a shower of crushed glass. I took off my wet shoes, propped my feet up on the railing, and leaned back in the groaning chair. The aroma of coffee-bourbon rose from the cup in my lap and mingled with the smell of pines. I closed my eyes, the warm sun on my face, and tried to think of nothing, to turn off my brain. There was no sound but the creek when I listened for it, no sound at all when I did not listen . . .

"Who did he kill?"

I opened my eyes, dropped my feet from the rail, and straightened up in the chair. "Who?" I wasn't sure what he was asking, I wasn't quite back yet.

"Your murderer. Who did he kill?"

Ah. I had told him in a letter, and again at dinner when he

had mentioned it, that I had taken an assigned appeal, a murder case, by way of diversion from my steady diet of estates and securities issues and corporate reorganizations. Jacob Morse, who one cold San Francisco night took it upon himself to . . .

"A Chinese whore."

Abruptly, Merlin stood up and looked out toward the creek, his back to me. He said nothing for a moment, then: "And you will be his lawyer then. You will defend him." It was not a question, yet not quite a statement. His voice had a peculiar edge.

"No," I said. "Not really. He has been defended . . . he has already had his trial with another lawyer. The jury said guilty and then they said death. My assignment is to take the appeal, to try to convince the Supreme Court that there were legal errors in the trial and that he should have another one, another trial."

Merlin continued to stand with his narrow back to me. I could see his shoulders rise and fall gently as he breathed. Finally, after what seemed a long time, he turned. His face seemed a little pale, a little . . . confused, as he sat down again and took a sip of coffee from his cup. "Were there any legal errors?" he said quietly.

I shook my head. "I don't know," I said. "I haven't really got into it yet." He looked out over the silently sparkling meadow.

"Your interest in my humble affairs is flattering, sir," I said after a moment. "In days of yore you never evinced such interest."

Suddenly he seemed to relax a little. "I have some interest in murderers," he said smiling.

"So I have noticed," I said as I got up.


A slight wind had come up by the time we got down to the stream — Merlin with his old telescoping steel pole and a cottage cheese carton full of worms, I in full fly-fishing regalia. He led the way to a narrow grassy bend where the water cut deep under the near bank. "This is my place," he said. "You can have the rest of the stream." He sat down on a rock and started rummaging for a worm in his carton.

I worked downstream with wet flies. The gentle quartering wind was perfect, just enough to make it difficult for the fish to see me, yet not quite enough to hinder my casting. I caught my first after about five minutes. He was deep behind a rock and I saw him come up to take it, then scramble down behind the rock again to sulk. I coaxed him gently until he came to the surface, a spinning knife flashing in the sunlight. Finally he was tired and came to the net. I carried him up into the grass — eleven inches of rainbow, bright red and blue and silver, still strong as he struggled against the air. I took him in my hand and, holding my knife by the blade, hit him once behind the head with the handle, a wet socking sound. He continued to struggle so I hit him again, harder this time. He quivered and was still. I picked some grass, wetted it, and made a layer at the bottom of my creel. Then I slid him in, beautiful and fat, all red and blue and silver.

Working on down, I caught six more in less than an hour — none as large as the first, but all bright and firm and strong like him. A limit would have been easy, but I wanted to start back to the city early. I sat down on a rock and gutted the fish, laying them in a neat row on the grass. The wind moved quietly in the willows.

When the fish were cleaned I put them back in my creel and started back upstream to meet Merlin. Soon I saw his red cap behind a screen of willows just down from his pool. He was on to a fish, a big one to judge by the bow in his rod. I didn't want to bother him so I moved to a place where I could watch. He was horsing the fish badly, but there was no danger of losing it unless he pulled the hook out, because the old leader he used was so heavy. Finally he worked it over to the undercut bank and, kneeling and leaning over the edge, peered down at it. He was perfectly still, the cords in his neck tense with looking, for what seemed a full minute — then, suddenly, he straightened his back and pulled up strongly on the pole, arching it over his head. The fish came out of the water like a wriggling rocket, sailed straight over Merlin's head, and landed in the grass behind him near a little feeder ditch.

It was a big one, a German brown of about twenty inches with deep red, almost maroon spots of color along its dark sides. The hook had come out, and as the fish flopped in blind violent bursts, bending its body double in the air, it moved toward the little ditch.

I ran out from behind the willows and stumbled toward the fish. Merlin had dropped his rod and was coming toward it too — or I thought he was coming toward it until I felt his eyes on me. Then suddenly he, his eyes, seemed somehow to be asking questions of me, questions that were utterly meaningless in the violent emergency of the moment but that nevertheless seized me, held me. With locked glances we faced one another from opposite sides of the furiously writhing fish, like a statue of two wrestlers about to grapple. Thus we remained for an interminable instant, our inertness a kind of counterpoint to the frantic thrusting motion at our feet . . . until at last I wrenched myself away.

Dropping to my knees I made a movement toward the fish. It escaped me and, flopping now with a little less vigor as the overloaded air began to suffocate it, moved toward Merlin. He took one short step — then with a calm and deliberate motion he kicked it into the feeder ditch. The fish lay still in the water for an instant before it thrust with its tail and, churning up a great cloud of mud, scrambled down the shallow ditch to disappear into the stream.

Again I was seized in that terrific stasis, crouched on hands and knees in the grass like a pointing bird dog while my almost languid gaze played over his booted feet. Then the vacuum of loss in my throat gave way to the swelling ball of anger in my stomach and I was shouting, screaming down at the boots.

24

*"God damn you!"*

The sound of moving water slowly filled the empty silence —
then Merlin's voice was above me, calm and flat:

"He has already, it seems."


As I drove south out of North Yancey that afternoon it
occurred to me that he had not even mentioned why he wanted
me to come.

# ✢ Part Two

*The novelist's skill consists in the choice of the
present moment from which he narrates the past.*
— JEAN-PAUL SARTRE

*MERLIN*   **T**he ocean: a silence beyond sound, a being beyond presence, a power beyond force . . . That Christmas night it was a black velvet thing insinuating upon the beach — then withdrawing with a deep solid clattering over seaward beds of smooth slingshot stones. Cottages huddled on the headland under the weight of moonbruised clouds, long-legged shorebirds piped their doleful song . . . and the wrinkled tops of these wrinkled feet stared up at me as I, rapt in contemplation of my own profundity, put their wrinkled bottoms one before the other down the night sand . . .

The dog's growl, a deep dry rumbling from somewhere in his chest, stopped my wrinkled mind and feet together. He was directly in front of me, about ten feet away — a massive, thick black-and-brown Doberman, tiny pointed ears, tiny pointed eyes. I stood frozen, my limbs tingling with fear, until slowly, silently, he began to circle me, to walk in premeditating measure around the spot of sand into which I seemed to have struck roots — then I was turning, facing him as he silently circled and, before I really realized it, talking. ". . . And so you see, dog," I heard myself saying, "so you must understand that my awkwardness in your distinguished presence is not the result of distrust or ill will. Rather, I must attribute it to my upbringing, my private deprivations. You must recognize, my noble friend, that I was never

*29*

fortunate enough to have a dog when I was a boy, and so never have I known the joy of chasing over grassy lea and bosky woodland to the cadence of a gaily wagging tail. Nor, sad to tell it, have I been granted the companionship of a cheery canine in these my later years — so that the pleasure of sitting before a crackling fire with the faithful friend of man recumbent at my slippered feet, this too has been denied me. Rather, my experiences have ever been limited to chance encounters with members of your species, or with aromatic evidences thereof. I have, for instance, been bitten by several dogs, but never have I held a grudge for what I consider the manifestation of natural instincts. Moreover, I have on occasion been introduced to dogs when I have paid social calls upon their masters, if you will excuse the gross inaccuracy of that expression. At such times I have always been delighted when the gracious friend of man leaps up to me in enthusiastic greeting and slobbers all over my suit. Very friendly meant. And later in the evening at the festive board I have always been touched to see the noble creature sitting quietly by his master's side, trustworthy eyes turned upward in devotion as he follows every movement of fork from plate to mouth until the master, noting the inconspicuous presence, drops some morsel — a small chop perhaps — in gratitude for past services well and truly rendered. Not to mention of course the many times I have listened with interest while your attentive brethren howled the night away in honor of a penned bitch . . .''

On I rattled, around he circled — I turning like the ungreased hub around which he revolved, like a babbling child swinging a weight on the end of a string . . . so that I did not really hear the whistle begin but rather merely came to notice it among the elements of the mechanical exhibit in which I was participating: a clear high silver whistle that seemed to reverberate through the night with the joy of purity. The dog immediately sat down on his haunches in the sand and I saw over his shoulder a slight figure in a navy peacoat, then heard a deep smooth female voice saying, somehow saying, "Heel, Ludwig." I felt a laugh gathering in my bowels amongst the terror but successfully stifled it. The dog went to her as she walked toward me. Her smooth face like a pecan nut cradled in the upturned collar of the coat . . .

"I am so sorry," she said. "He is trained, he was just holding you." Her voice like polished teak . . .

"That is a distinct comfort," I said with more than a trace of acid. Then, to pierce the resulting silence, more kindly: "I love dogs, ever since my days as a postman."

She laughed then, a soft almost hoarse laugh. "I am sorry," she said. "I would have kept him with me if I had thought that there might be some one else on the beach. I did not expect, tonight . . ."

Then she was done with apology. For a moment she looked up at me with a dreadful brazen candor, then she said, flatly, "You are Merlin Carson."

Her black hair piled, pinned with ivory . . .

"I did not know that my infamy had preceded me to this place," I said. "Are you a creditor or an anthologist?"

Again she laughed that soft throaty laugh. "I have read some of your books."

"I am flattered," I said. "I had thought that only members of my immediate family . . ." And we were walking, going her way — the stars suddenly kaleidoscopic now, the velvet sea glowing now, and I blathering anew of dogs, birds, beaches, revolutions, revelations, epiphanies . . . sputtering on and on and on while she listened inscrutably intent, an occasional soft chuckle set in her receptive silence like a small fine jewel.

When years later we came to the cement stairway leading up from the beach she stopped and turned toward me. There was a strange self-satisfied smile on her face as she said, "Good-night, Merlin Carson." Just that. And then I found myself saying, "Good-night" — just that — to the back of her coat as it moved up the stairs, the dog close behind. Then my voice was calling: "Wait. What is your name? You know *my* name, I ought to know *your* name." The coat stopped, and the dog — and she

*31*

turned, the streetlight at the head of the stairs lighting up her face. She seemed to hesitate a moment, then:

"Good-night, Merlin Carson."

And she was gone.


I was in the city then, working in that little apartment over the pet store. It was a good place, warm and comfortable and secret — furnished with extra things from the house, Clarissa's house. There was a narrow bed, an overstuffed chair, a kitchen, even a little fireplace for rainy afternoons . . . I remember standing at the window with a small glassful, the fire burning gaily as I watched the people below in the streaming street — old men running from awning to awning with newspapers held stiffly over their bald heads, grand ladies from Pacific Heights emerging from their chauffeured limousines like butterflies from cocoons and sweeping majestically into Madame D's cluttered antique store on the corner, girls in uniform blue sweaters and plaid skirts walking home from school in little clots, talking excitedly together but still, at nine years, holding their umbrellas just so . . .

And the other afternoons too, those crisp autumn afternoons when the world seemed immersed in crystal — down the stairs to the street, into the Depot for a quick platter of oysters, then off — leaving the clucking shops behind me and striding strongly up past tidy apartments filled with mistresses and poodles, up, up, then over the top and down, down, the cable chuckling clamorous in its slot beside me in the street, the ships in the bay moving past the old island prison like great waterbugs as I shuffle down beside houses with brimming window boxes to Beach Street and the cable car turntable and at last the bend of bay . . . stringy old men in bright rubber caps swimming endless laps in the lagoon, walruses in training . . . the click of bocci balls amid the rattle of Sicilian tongues . . . the hot dog stand by the seawall ("A cup of black coffee please." "How about some french fries too, honey? You need some fattening up." Flame red hair piled high, the look of perpetual astonishment firmly in place. "No, thank you, just a cup of black coffee today." And her beige Coupe de Ville at the curb — the most successful hot dog stand in history. "You ought to take cream with it, honey. Black is bad for your stomach." "I'll just have a cup of black coffee today if it's all the same . . ." "Don't get smart with me, mister. My husband is right out in back.")

Perched on the seawall, a grizzled old pelican waiting for winter . . .

*PETER*    **I** was home at ten o'clock. I held the elevator door while a blowzy blond and her drunken friend stumbled past the doorman and made their way inside. He, with lipstick on his collar, was almost asleep on his feet. I asked her what floor and when she answered with a vapid grin he looked up at me, stared menacingly, and then put his head back on her shoulder. They got off at eleven and went slurring off down the corridor. "But you don't have to be at work until nine, honey," I heard him say.

When I opened the door to my apartment Mother was there ironing in front of the television set. "You must be the most punctual person in the world," she said.

"It is possible," I said. "What are you doing here?"

"I thought you might need a few shirts ironed," she said.

"Sure you did. Do you want some port?" I opened the closet door and put my fishing gear inside, taking the package of fish out of the creel.

She had not heard me. It was an old movie from the fifties — women in ridiculous suits with padded shoulders. "Do you ever iron your fingers, Mother?" I said.

She straightened up and smiled at me, then went to the television set and turned it off. "It was just an old movie," she said. "Would you get me a little port, Peter? Just a little." She showed me with her fingers. "It has been making me dizzy . . ."

She went on ironing while I put the fish in the refrigerator and made the drinks, her port and my double martini. When I came out and set the glasses on the coffee table she turned off the iron and went into my room with the shirts. I was slumped on the couch, my head against the back, when she came out again and, walking almost gingerly it seemed, crossed to the couch to sit down beside me.

"A long trip," she said.

"Brutal."

She picked up her glass, then put it down again to sweep a strand of gray-blond hair from her face and secure it with a pin. Then she folded her hands in her lap and looked straight at me. I closed my eyes.

"Did you get any fish?" she said.

"Seven," I said. "One good one."

"Oh, good," she said. "I'll take them and freeze them. You can come over next week."

"You eat them yourself. I brought them for you."

She seemed to hesitate a moment, then: "All right, Peter. Thank you."

I slouched in the silence and breathed deeply, already feeling the martini in my bones. After a few moments I heard her move to pick up her glass, then abruptly put it down again on the table.

"Don't make me question you," she finally said.

I sighed, then slowly sat up and took a long swallow from my glass. "Okay," I said. "He is fine, in radiant good health. The sun has given him some color. He says that he is working — I doubt it. He is drinking about the same or maybe a little more. The answer to all of your questions is no. No, he isn't coming home, no, he didn't say how long he was going to stay, and no, I didn't find out why he went up there in the first place."

She smiled up at me — that small smile tinged with terror that came upon her whenever she talked about him now. Again her hand went to her forehead to capture a falling strand of hair. She dropped her eyes, still smiling that smile.

"Well . . . well, he wanted to see you about something. What did he want to see you about?" Her voice was pitiful, confused.

"I never found out; he didn't say." I got up and started toward the kitchen. "There's nothing else to talk about that we haven't talked to death before, Mother. Nothing has changed, everything is the same. I'm going to bed. Stay in the other bedroom tonight and I'll take you home in the morning. I have an early appointment at the prison."

She looked up. "At the prison? Wait just a minute, Peter. I want to talk to you. Just a minute." She hesitated, then: "The solitude . . . does he seem affected by the solitude?"

I knew that we would quarrel. I had tried to get away, to avoid it, but now the strength was lacking. I heard my voice whining, barking: "Solitude? Affect *him*? How could solitude affect *him*? How could he be more solitary on his mountain than he was when he was here? The all-seeing eye moving among us, *experiencing* us. He is no different now — just as self-centered and self-contained and hermetically sealed as he ever was, just as puckish and charming when it suits his fancy to be so, just as much of an overbearing bully when that's how he happens to feel. No, Mother, your darling Merlin is still the same — still, in the words of that simpering critic, 'A universe unto himself.' "

She drank her port down in one swallow, stood up quickly, and went to the ironing board. She stood with her back to me, trembling with anger. "You don't have to come home and tell me what Merlin Carson is," she said in a tense whisper. "I asked you how he was . . . how he looked. You can keep your evil venom to yourself."

I stood up and went over to her. She was still trembling as I put my hand on her shoulder and spoke to the back of her head in a quietly pleading voice. "You are my mother and the widow of Arthur Carson. Let that be enough now. Let it be done."

She would not turn. "Good-night, Peter," she said softly. I did not move until she added, "Please." She was crying.

I went into the kitchen, took the bottle of gin from the sink-board, and went to my bedroom. As the door closed behind me I could feel my stomach tightening into a sour knot.

*MERLIN* ✢ **T**hat day . . . it rained. There was no wind. I stood at my window and listened to the counterpoint of the cackling fire against the drumming steady thud of rain falling slack against the street. People standing waiting in front of awninged shop windows, the roaring hiss of a bus pulverizing water into a wake of swirling dirty mist . . .

I went to the bed. I slept. I dreamed . . . riding Lady up toward Big Canyon. Autumn, a gentle wind rattling the red and yellow leaves of the aspens as we move up the old log drag toward the spring. Lady walking fast as she always did, always wanting to trot, me holding her back into a fast walk, talking softly to her as the trees moved rattling by . . .

The door was knocking . . . someone was knocking on the door. I put my feet on the floor and said, "Wait a minute," as the clouds of sleep, all red and yellow, dissolved in the sound of slack rain. Only Clarissa knew about this place, what would Clarissa . . . I went to the door and opened it.

Her face, a pecan slick with rain. Soaked black hair falling over her eyes.

"Come in," I said.

I led her to the fireplace, then went to the bathroom for a towel. When I came back she had put her dripping coat on the easy chair and was standing with her back to the fire taking pins out of her hair. She took the towel from me, and I sat silently on the bed as she scrubbed her mass of black hair with it.

"How did you find this place?" I said when she was done.

She looked at me for what seemed the first time since she had come in. Her smile was almost smug. "I have known for a long time that you were here," she said. "I saw you on the street after . . . that night, and I followed you." She leaned forward from the waist, letting her hair hang straight down to the floor like an inkfall — then swiftly she straightened up and, her hands at her temples, tossed it over her head to tumble lightly down beyond the small of her back. Then, grasping it like a thick rope with one hand at the back of her neck, she took her pins, small ivory ones, from the mantle and commenced to put them in, one by one, over her ears. Her dark hands — small, narrow, well-kept . . .

"You followed me," I said, as if to myself. She went to the chair by the fireplace, sat down, and began to take off her shoes.

"Yes, and then I saw you again and followed you again until I was sure that this was where you worked. You live somewhere else." There was a note of triumph in her deep voice.

"My wife might dispute with you about that," I said.

She had taken her shoes off. Standing again, her back to the fire, she raised her arms and, hands working at the back of her neck, began to unbutton the white blouse.

"May I inquire what you are doing?" I said.

She stopped and looked at me with a puzzled expression. "Taking my clothes off," she said. "They are soaking wet."

I wince to recall my indignation. "Indeed they are. But you can't, I mean, you can't just take them off and sport naked before the fire. Whatever opinion you might have formed of me in the course of your . . . researches, you can't just come in here and . . ." Mercifully I stopped, impaled on her unbelieving eyes. "What is your name, please?" I finally said.

She ignored the question. "Well then," she said, "do you have a bathrobe or something?"

"Yes. Well?"

"Fine. Well what?"

"What is your name?"

She smiled, warmly this time. "My name is Betty Chen."

"Your name is Betty Chen," I said. "There is a robe in the bathroom." She followed my pointing finger and disappeared through the doorway.

I sat on the bed and numbly watched the water from her coat soak into the upholstery of the chair. The story about Giacometti came to me: hit by a Paris taxicab, lying in the street almost unconscious with pain, thinking, "Finally, finally something has happened to me!" The water spread like an inkblot down the back of the chair . . .

She came on silent feet and stood in front of me, the shoulder seams of my flannel robe drooping to her elbows, the hem at her ankles. Her face was pouty, insolent, as she said: "You can look now. I am proper for you."

I snorted to my feet and went to the window. The rain had stopped now and galoshed people were stepping gingerly over the drying streets, furled umbrellas hooked over their arms. "You must allow for the Victorian sensibilities of an old man," I said. I could hear her low voice laughing softly as she arranged her clothes on the chair in front of the fire.

When I turned she was sitting at my writing table. "Would you like some brandy?" I said. She smiled yes and I went to the kitchen. When I came back she was smoking one of my cigarettes and reading something that I had been revising. "Is this your work?" she said.

"Yes, it is," I said, betraying some proprietary annoyance.

"Your handwriting is very messy," she said.

I put her brandy on the table and went to stand in front of the fire. She went on reading, her brow knitted with concentration. Finally she looked up. "I don't understand poetry," she said. "I like it, but I don't understand it. I just like the way it sounds in my head."

"You understand more than you think," I said. She smiled

vaguely and took a sip from her brandy. There was the sound of the fire, a bus passing in the street. Then I heard my own voice, magisterially: "Now."

"Now," she repeated, looking at me straight then dropping her eyes.

"Now," I said again. "To what good fortune do I owe the honor of . . ." I hesitated, expecting some kind of answer, some kind of volunteered explanation. There was none. She looked intently at her small toes.

"Well?"

She glanced up quickly, her face full of annoyance. "I am trying to think what to say," she said. She blinked her eyes once, then resumed the examination of her toes.

"Well, is there something I can do for you?"

"I suppose so," she said without looking up.

"Well," I said after it seemed evident that no further details were forthcoming, "well, what is it you *suppose* that I can do for you?"

There was an almost tranquil expression on her face as she looked up. "I want to stay here with you for a few days," she said.

I was moderately prepared for any of a number of replies. That was not one of them. I went to the bed and sat down — then amidst great clearings of my throat I commenced to sputter. "You want to stay here? But no. No. I work here, this is my office, Miss . . . are you Miss or Mrs.?"

"I am not married. I am Betty."

"You are Betty . . . but no, no you cannot stay. Why should you want to stay? No, that is impossible. Absolutely."

I was a bit unhinged.

She was silent, her broad face vacant of expression as she gazed into the fire. Then, with an abstracted quickness, she moved to put out the cigarette. The robe . . . her breasts were small, high and firm, but she might have nursed a child . . . and I was on my feet again, bolting terrified toward the window again. My voice against the pane was a strident wounded whine.

"Now this is madness! Really, really I must get back to my work! What do you want with me?"

There was no answer. The sound of the fire filled the silence until I turned again. She had drawn the robe up about her neck and she looked at me with a startled, confused expression. The question must have lingered on my face, for after a moment she said, softly, "I just told you."

Frustration, overlaid with strange feelings of exhilaration, brought a great sigh from me. Fast upon it, fanning up the muscles of my stomach, was a crabbed sullen anger. I went again to the bed, sat down slowly and, leaning forward, folded my hands between my knees. My face must have seemed to plead with her.

"Let me start somewhere else," I said. "I have seen you once before in my life — last Christmas on Carmel Beach in the middle of the night. It was a chance meeting; your dog was at the point of devouring me and you rescued me from him. You had on a blue navy peacoat. You were — you are — very pretty, and the circumstances of our meeting were romantic. I was quite thoroughly drunk, taking a barefoot walk after midnight in order to ventilate my brain after a withering scene with my wife in the stuffy cottage we had rented to escape the city for a few days. After you rescued me we walked along the beach. I jabbered like an idiot and made a pass, or the nearest approximation thereto of which I am capable — even when drunk. You properly bade me a firm and polite goodnight and left me where I had started — beached. That was it. The next morning I had an enormous headache and a sullen wife.

"Now today I am scribbling and muttering in this little place which nobody knows about, or I think nobody knows about — and you come, dripping like a kitten. You promptly announce, number one, that you found this place by following me or scenting me out with your dog, and, number two, that you want to stay here . . ."

Throughout this tirade she had watched me with wide eyes,

her left hand clutching the robe under her chin. As if to break her gaze I got up now and, continuing the sermon, went to the kitchen for some whiskey. "To the first of these declarations I have to say that I resent it a little, I mean being tracked like some kind of a possum . . ." At this point my speech was garnished with a profane exclamation as I dropped a glass into the sink and broke it. I got another, poured, and went back into the living room. She had not moved, and her eyes were fixed on me again as I went to the fireplace and turned to face her.

"As to the second thing, I am still too astonished to know what to say. I work here. I am a rather elderly married man. I am too poor to afford a mistress. I am too busy to take an apprentice. I . . . what can I say?"

She continued to look at me for a moment, then dropped her eyes. In vain I waited again for her to say something. Then, sighing again with that strange combination of frustration and exhilaration, I returned to the bed, put my glass on the floor, and once more folded my hands between my knees. "Where do you live, Betty?" I said quietly.

She looked at her fingernails. "I don't live anywhere now," she said. "I used to live in a hotel on Stockton Street."

"When did you move from there?"

"This morning." She took a sip from her glass, then put it down on my desk. On my papers.

"Did you live there alone?"

There was an edge of contempt on her voice as she said yes — as if she was disappointed in me for thinking that the answer could be so simple.

I was not daunted. "Well, then why did you leave?"

"Because . . . people could find me there," she said in a voice that was almost a whisper.

"People could find you there," I repeated. She nodded her head slowly. "What people? People who want to hurt you?"

She got up quickly and, with one hand at her throat to keep the robe closed, went to the window.

"People who want to hurt you, Betty?" I said again.

*43*

"Yes . . . in a way," she said coldly to the windowpane. Her narrow back was tense — a pouting child in her father's bathrobe. I knew she was going to fly at me, strike out at me, before long — but I pressed on. It seemed to me I had that right.

"In what way, Betty? Hurt you in what way?"

She was silent.

"Betty?"

Then it came. Her burnished cheeks were glowing with anger and impatience as she whirled around to face me. "Oh, why do you have to go on like that?" she hissed.

My voice was calm, measured. "Because I am still trying to find out why in hell you have come here. Don't you think I am entitled to know that?"

"Entitled?" Her eyes were wide with disbelief. "Why should you be *entitled* to anything? I am a gift, don't you understand that? When someone offers you a gift you either accept it or refuse it. It is really so easy — keep me or send me away!"

She jerked her eyes away from me and took a quick step toward the fire. Her foot caught in the hem of the robe — and suddenly she pitched forward and fell in a heap on the floor at my feet. Then before I could move she was on her knees — tearing the robe off, throwing it — and then it was in the fire and she was standing straight in front of me, her eyes flashing with fury. I jumped up shrieking like a madman and ripped the blanket from the bed. Throwing it over her rigid shoulders, I caught her, covered her, held her — but then she was not trying to escape any more. She huddled small against me as the tears came hard . . .

She sat curled at my feet, wrapped in the blanket like a sick cat, as we listened with heavy silence to the rain, to the splatting sound of it falling slack again from awning to pavement. The ticking of the clock, the hiss of a passing bus . . . My brain wandered far, to other places, other times — leaving in the husk only enough of me to notice after what must have been hours that the streetlight outside my window had come on. Startled, I looked down at her — nestled on the rug, the blanket tucked up under her chin; her sleeping face seemed made of deeply glazed pottery.

I stood up slowly, took my coat out of the closet, and went home to Clarissa.

*PETER*  ✣  The guard left me in the yellow room. "He will be down right away. Push that button for me when you are done." The yellow steel door rang shut with a solid finality. I looked at the small black button beside it and was comforted by a vague sense of relief.

Or rather I was in half of the room. The whole thing was perhaps thirty feet square, but it was cut in half by a glass partition which extended from the ceiling down to a wooden counter which projected into both halves of the room. On the counter were twenty black telephones, ten on each side of the glass. Small wooden partitions attached to the counter made ten small booths. There were chairs, ashtrays — and strong white fluorescent lights.

I sat down on one of the chairs and waited. There was a hole, a pipe-cinder hole, in my new coat. Annoyed, I waited, fingered the pipe-cinder hole and waited. The light was too bright. I was going to have a headache.

After what seemed like fifteen minutes a yellow steel door on the other side of the glass opened and a guard led in a tall pale man wearing thick spectacles. He was perhaps fifty years old; it was difficult to say. His head, massive and oblong, was crowned with sparse sandy hairs, cut short, which stood up straight from his scalp like pins in a pincushion, and from his long stringy arms hung a pair of grotesquely large hands which brought to my mind the russet-coated orangutan at the zoo. Yet for all that, there was a strange grace about him, a certain lightness in the way he walked.

At first the tall man did not look toward me — he was engaged in sober conversation with the bull-terrier guard, speaking down into the gradually reddening face until its owner turned abruptly and went to a chair near the far wall. Then he, the tall man, smiled in my direction and began to move uncertainly toward the counter and the glass wall, his great hands held loosely out in front of him. The warden had mentioned his eyes but I had not thought that . . .

I glanced quickly at the guard. He was leaning back in his chair against the wall, his face spread with a stupid grin which then became open laughter as the tall man stumbled on a chair and fell heavily to his knees. The man, Morse, remained thus, on his knees, while his smiling mouth moved to form some words for the guard — then he grasped the counter, pulled himself up into a chair, and finally sat facing me. I picked up my telephone, then looked up to see his lips moving as he talked to the glass wall. I heard my own voice piping, "Pick up your . . ." and then trailing off as my glare brought the guard to his feet. The porcine face reflected disgust as he shambled to the counter, forced the telephone into a great loose hand, and turned again to walk to his accustomed chair.

"Mr. Carson?" The high reedy voice seemed to come from a great distance.

"Yes," I said. "Right here." I looked straight into his face, his long smiling face. The thick lenses magnified his eyes, but out of focus, so that they seemed to swim in their sockets like oysters on a plate. I found myself watching his mouth as he spoke.

"You are my first visitor here, Mr. Carson. I have never done this, with these telephones I mean. But we are all right now."

"Yes," I said. Then, after an uncomfortable silence for which I

47

somehow felt responsible: "Your guard seems a nice enough fellow."

I watched his mouth widen into a grin. "Oh — Kling, you mean. He is a prince. Terrific sense of humor."

"Terrific," I said. Then, as another long silence began to yawn before us: "Shall we get right down to business, Mr. Morse?" He nodded and folded those enormous hands before him on the counter.

I shuffled papers for a moment, then began it — explaining the process by which we were to test the validity of the judgment against him, the judgment reflecting the jury's dual determination that he was guilty of murder of the first degree and that he must pay for it by inhaling lethal gas. "You have the letter from the Clerk of the Supreme Court telling you that the court has assigned me to represent you on your appeal. My job is simple — not particularly easy, but simple, uncomplicated. I review the trial record, then I decide whether something that happened at the trial — or something that did not happen but should have — adds up to a legal error which might have affected the outcome of the trial. Then I write a brief to the court setting forth what I think were these errors. The attorney general then writes his own brief trying to answer my arguments — trying to say that what I have said was an error was not really an error, or that even if it was an error it did not affect the result of the trial in any significant way. Then I can write another brief answering their answers if we decide that that is necessary. Finally, when all of the briefing is done, the court sets a date for oral argument and I get up on my feet in front of the seven of them, the seven judges, and try to convince them . . ."

And through it all he sitting politely silent and, holding the telephone in one great hand like some ridiculous toy, stroking his cheek with the long palplike fingers of the other. I found that I could not look directly at him as I spoke — his eyes, those immense, softly swimming eyes, seemed somehow to threaten me, to seek to envelop me . . . and I found myself speaking to the back of my own compact and manicured left hand.

"Do you understand that?" I asked, looking up at his face again when it was finished. "Do you have any questions about it?"

"No," he said. "It was very clear. I am sure that you will do the best job that can be done for me." He hesitated a moment, then: "But can I ask you a question that has nothing to do with this?"

There was a trace of exasperation in my voice as I said, "Of course."

He produced an ingratiating smile, showing his long teeth. "Are you any relation to Merlin Carson?"

It was like a fist in my face. I felt a sigh escape and, with it, the strength seemed to drain from my body as if a plug had been pulled. Then suddenly all of it was there together: exasperation turned to incredulity by a question so far removed from the immediate business of preserving the life of or at least postponing the death of the questioner; the old accustomed resentment rising, surfacing ("You wouldn't be related to the famous poet would you? How exciting it must be to be so . . . so close to him!") ; the old accustomed desire to correct, to set the record straight; and now, floating far, far below, some new frantic confusion — all of it roiling together within the seething instant before I could finally form the old accustomed simplifying response, spoken with effort, softly, patiently . . .

"He is my father."

A smile of amusement spread over his face like sunlight. "You don't say," he said through it.

"I do say."

"You do say." And then all at once he was softly chuckling, his head gently bobbing up and down.

I waited a moment, watching him in astonishment, before I said, "I await your convenience, Mr. Morse."

In the silence he seemed contrite. Then he spoke carefully, his great hands folded on the counter. "I am sorry, Mr. Carson. It is just that . . . it is such a coincidence that you should be his . . . his son." He hesitated, then his face brightened again. "I mean, I have been a . . . a fan of his, you know? But you may not believe that somebody like me could be interested in . . ."

"I can and do believe it, Mr. Morse — and I am sure that my father would be flattered. But, if you will excuse me, that is not what concerns us, you and me, right now." I was curt, business-like. "To put it bluntly, what concerns us is a matter of life or death — *your* life or death. These people are not kidding you know, that little green room downstairs really exists — they really do put people in there and kill them. And if we are not successful on this appeal your ugly little friend over against the wall will take you down there one morning and strap you in the chair and the little pellets will fall in the bucket of acid and you will be dead. It is that simple. And that is why, Mr. Morse, we must keep our minds on business; that is why you must devote your whole being to listening to what I say and answering what I ask. When we have won a new trial for you we can talk about poetry." I let it sink in a moment before I added, "Do you understand that?"

"Yes, sir," he said quietly, his eyes swimming down toward folded hands.

"Okay," I said with a note of forgiveness in my voice. He smiled wanly down at his hands and I went on. "Now, I have not finished studying the transcript yet — that is the typewritten record of your trial — but I have noticed that you put on no witnesses, you did not testify yourself and no witnesses testified in your behalf. Is that correct?"

"Yes," he said.

"Was that your decision or your lawyer's?"

He looked thoughtful. "Well, both," he said slowly. "There was nobody who could testify for me, and as for me, myself . . . well, the lawyer said that if I did, it would hurt more than help." He smiled up at me again. "Anyway, I had nothing to say. It was pretty clear . . . what happened."

"Yes," I said, fighting off a chill. "I am reading the tran-script." His head was bowed low over his hands now. I waited a moment, then: "Did you see a psychiatrist?"

He looked up. "Yes," he said. "The lawyer sent one. We argued for a while and then he left. The lawyer said that his report wouldn't help us."

"What did you argue about?"

"My mother," he said smiling. "You know psychiatrists."

"Yes, I do," I said. "Does the lawyer have that report?"

"I suppose so."

It was enough for the time being. The headache had begun, at the back of my neck. "Okay, Mr. Morse," I said. "I will come and talk to you again when I have finished the transcript and have got that report from the trial lawyer." I stuffed the papers into my briefcase, then looked up at him for a hurried good-bye. The eyes, his eyes swam up to meet me . . . I sighed, somehow knowing the answer before putting the question.

"Morse?"

"Yes, sir."

"Your eyes. Could you see . . . before?"

"Yes, sir. This is just since . . . since that night you are reading about in your transcript." He smiled wistfully down at his hands.

"And the doctors — what do they say?"

"They don't know. They have given up. At first it was just a little, a little haziness beginning the morning . . . afterward. Just the last month or so it has been more and more. I can almost notice the difference day to day now."

I said nothing.

"It will soon be done," he went on quietly. "Now I see only shadows, only dark and light." Raising his face again, he brought a long bony finger up to the heavy lenses. "I will be glad to be rid of these," he said. "They hurt my ears."

There was nothing to say. I was pushing my chair back to get up when I heard his voice again in the phone.

"Mr. Carson?"

"Yes," I said, sitting down again.

"Can I ask you another impertinent question? About your father I mean?"

"I suppose so." My voice was tired, flat, drained. The headache had moved up to my temples.

He groped for the words. "Well . . . I don't know how to say it. I mean what does he . . . your father, what does your father think about my case? I am, you know . . . interested to know what a great writer might think." He smiled at me innocently, blandly, his eyes like oysters on a plate.

"He doesn't think anything about it," I said. "Not as far as I know."

"Did you tell him about it?"

"I told him the bare facts, that I had been assigned to represent you and so forth. He seemed interested but he didn't say anything." For some reason I suddenly felt anxious and confused — a memory was struggling to reassert itself.

". . . but he didn't say anything." He repeated my words, his face bright with smiling. "Maybe he will say something later."

"Maybe," I said. The memory had escaped — now my body was heavy with exhaustion. "Good-bye, Mr. Morse. I will see you in a few days."

I put the telephone in its cradle and stood up. Morse got slowly to his feet, and as I pushed the black button I could see through the glass that he had begun to laugh again.

*CLARISSA*  **A**nd yet something will not
let me hate you, Merlin.
Why is that denied me?
  Do you hate me, Merlin? Do you?

*JACOB MORSE* ✥ **I** remember coming in from Albuquerque.
It was raining. I watched the lights, all colors reflected in the
drops on the window. It looked like a different town, not the
same town at all.

"How long did you say?" the hippie kid that was driving said.
"How long since you were here?"

"Just about thirty years," I said. "Since the war."

"I wasn't even born," he said.

"No. It was a long time ago."

They let me off near the bus station and I started in walking.
The rain was coming down pretty good but my big army coat
kept me dry. I turned on Market toward downtown. The side-
walks were full of people all stacked up with packages pushing
and shoving and cursing. There were old Salvation Army ladies
with wrinkles around their eyes ringing little silver bells. Car
horns and Christmas music blaring at each other. I cut up Grant
to get out of it. I never remembered that many people on the
streets before. Not even on VJ.

That end of Grant was the same, only it had got richer now —
more stores with big howling silver plates and smooth fur coats
looking out at you. And a better class of people shoving you.
Big mean-looking mick bulls with blue and purple veins in their

earlobes prowling around and looking to vag you if you don't keep moving. I did, heading on up toward California. I figured that if I made it up past there and then headed down I would get to where I knew my way around a little better.

When I got into Chinatown and turned down Washington I could see those big new buildings down toward the waterfront sticking up in the sky like castles. I kept on heading down. Those little Chinese grocery stores that never seem to close — they were the same at least. But when I got down to Columbus and looked around . . . it was gone. The Settlement, disappeared like it was just imagined in the first place. No, there was some of it left — the iron grillwork arches that used to be full of lights; there they were, standing dark and forlorn in the rain. But the rest . . . the street was dark, deserted, where all that had been. The old buildings seemed almost peevish, like they were sick and tired of looking at the same dumb expression on old faces peering up at them through the rusting arches.

I stood on the corner and scratched my head. Up toward Broadway was a lot of lights and noise, as if that was something now, but I headed on down toward the waterfront, or what was left of it. Some of the alleys were the same anyway, and I knew where I was going. Stepped on a drunk in a gutter, but he was picked clean.

I turned the corner onto Front. The place was still there. The name was changed and it had been fixed up, but it was still there. I went in. The same bar in the same place — it seemed to look even bigger, darker, and heavier. Just that many more years of beer, blood, and tears rubbed in. Everything else was different. The old brass hat racks were gone, the spittoons; and there was a rug on the floor. There were a lot more elbows on that bar before too. But that was the war. I sat down and made myself at home.

I don't know how it got started. I was minding my own business and drawing something and somebody asked about it and then I think it was some longshore mick started in spouting off.

55

Anyway, it was all arms and legs for a while and then I read the label on the bottle just before it hit me. Good-night, sailor.

I remember waking up, the sun coming in through her red and white checkered curtains. She was standing by the window in a silk dressing gown, her back to me as she watered the flowers in the window box. I watched her through the fog for a long time — her little narrow back, long black hair brushed straight, the silk making different textures and shadows as she moved. Finally she turned. I didn't recognize her, but somehow it seemed that I had seen her face before. She wasn't an Indian, but maybe she reminded me of some . . .

"Hi," she said. I heard my voice saying something just as I went under again.

Then it was night, neon lights flickering through the window, the checkered curtains making shadows on the wall, the heavy shape beside me in the chair turning into an old Chinese woman who said, "Wait, you wait," as she got up without a sound and went out the door . . . then the old Chinaman standing framed in the light of the doorway, the crone fluttering behind him like a moth.

"You go 'nother room, she got 'nother room you."

I got up slow, feeling the big bandage on my head. "Down hall," he said, wiggling his finger at me. I followed his slithering feet down the hall as the crone darted back into the room behind me like a nighthawk with a bucket. He went around the corner, then stopped at the door of another room.

"She come in morning," he said as he switched on the light. I was asleep again before he closed the door.

I woke up careful. Out of the bare window I could see the stained cement of another building. A window with old curtains like green gauze, a fire escape with a yellow cat sleeping among empty flowerpots. Clouds, fluffy gray and white, were being pushed through the sky by a wind that howled a little as it blew between the buildings. I sat up slow, swung my feet out, and perched on the edge of the bed. The bandage was like a turban on me.

I was in some pajamas but I could see my clothes hanging in the closet. I crept over there, holding onto the sink, and found my wallet. The money was still there, seventeen dollars.

I had just sat down on the bed again when she knocked on the door and came in. She was wearing the same dressing gown, green silk with a high collar, but she had on long silk pants now too and little black slippers. Her hair was pinned up high on top of her head.

"What's this about?" I said. "You don't owe me anything." She smiled, a smartass kind of smile that I seemed to remember from somewhere.

"Sure I do," she said. "You gave me a beautiful picture." She kept on smiling that smile while I went from confusion to puzzlement and then . . .

It was the little slant whore in the bar.

"You already paid for that," I said.

"It's worth more than a kiss," she said.

"I'll collect the rest when I feel better." I put my hand up to the bandage.

"Maybe," she said.

She went to the window and opened it, then turned and came back to me. "Now hold still," she said, starting to take off the bandage. I kept quiet while she did that and then washed the cut. She seemed to know what she was doing.

"I don't have any money you know," I finally said.

"Yes, you do, you have seventeen dollars. Will you please hold still?"

Then she was done washing it. "Want to see it?" she said. She helped me up by the arm and took me to the mirror over the sink. It was a nasty one, about three inches long across my temple. "Twenty-one stitches," she said.

"Nice job," I said. "Did you do those too?"

"No. A friend."

I kept quiet again while she squeezed it out with a sponge and then put on a new bandage. The wind howled between the buildings. The radiator turned on, started to bang a little, then went hissing along.

"Well, I am obliged to you," I said when she was done. "What's your name?"

"I already told you." That smile again.

"When?"

"Monday night."

"And what's today?"

"Wednesday. Christmas Eve."

"And what did you tell me?"

"Betty," she said, then turned away to wash out the old bandage. There was the sound of the water, the sound of the wind. Her little body, all hard corners in green silk, bent over the sink.

"Well," I said finally, "I can pay for this room and be on my way."

"You ought to stay quiet a few days," she said. "You lost a lot of blood. You ought to stay here a few days." Her voice was low and deep over the sound of the water.

"I can't. You know how much money I have."

"Want a job?"

"What?"

She wrung out the bandage and put it on the towel rack, then closed the window and turned back to face me. "You stay here and rest until Friday. Then help the old man with the mopping and cleaning up in the mornings until you find a job. This room and five dollars a day."

"How do you know I don't have a job?" I said.

"Just guessing."

There was a knock at the door. She went to open it and the old woman came in with a tray of hot food. They talked Chinese a minute, then the old woman gave her the tray and went out again.

"Okay?" Betty said, putting the tray on the little desk.

"Okay."

She smiled her smile, then walked quick to the door and opened it.

"Merry Christmas," she said as she went out.

*PETER* ✠ **S**ometimes now I think I can almost remember him. He is leaning over Mother's shoulder, smiling down as she holds me in her arms. Black hair just a little gray on the sides, pipe held tight between his bright teeth. He smells like smoke, smoke and wool. Then Mother turns and he is gone.

Of course it is the pictures, the pictures of that one week — but sometimes it seems I can almost remember . . .

It was my seventh birthday. The cake was done and we were all sitting around the dinner table, Merlin and Mother and I. "Your mother and I have something we want to tell you," he said. "Something we think you ought to know now." I remember looking from one face to the other — Mother watching me through narrowed eyes, Merlin contemplating his fingernails as, hesitantly, he began it . . . *Arthur George Carson. Born Shambip, Utah 1906. A.B. Stanford University 1931. J.D. Stanford University 1933. Married Clarissa Rowe Jenkins, San Francisco 1932. Wharton Wharton and McAllister, Attorneys at Law, San Francisco: Associate 1933–1938, Partner 1938–1943, Military Leave 1941–1943. United States Army Air Force 1941–1943. Killed in Action, Pacific Theater, April 8, 1943.*

And then it was done. The house silent as an empty church as, again, I looked from one face to the other — from his closed face to her pale anxious face and back again. "But you're still my father now, aren't you?"

His wan smile as, looking at her, he nodded yes . . .

But no, not yet done — for there remained those long foggy summer afternoons, blue and pink hydrangeas brushing softly against the windowpane as she sat darning socks on her ebony egg, her long pointed fingers working with inevitable sureness, her sensible shoes flat on the carpet as, softly, she told it . . . told of that rainy Christmas Eve when he, all blue eyes and black hair, stood on the train platform and kissed her as the train started to move shuddering and he turned and ran to it and was gone, gone to the airplanes, leaving her with tears coursing down her powdered cheeks and a tiny swelling in her belly . . . told of that one small week in the spring of 1943 when he returned, his breast resplendent with the evidence of valor, to find two where there had been just one, a family where there had been just a wife . . . and yes, told of the visit, the grave colonels . . .

Yes, of course it is the pictures, the yellowed photographs that she kept in that leather-covered cigar box in the sewing table, that she would hand down to me, one by one . . .

But sometimes it seems I can almost remember him . . .

*JACOB MORSE*  **I** stayed in my room that day and the next. The old Chinalady brought me food and changed my bandage once, and I just slept and drew a few things. Then it was Friday and I went downstairs to find the old man. He knew all about it and right away set me to work with a mop. At one I was done. He gave me the five and said to come down again the next morning.

I went out. It was Stockton Street, a good long way from the bar. She must have brought me in a cab.

I walked down Stockton to Washington Square, then down toward the Wharf to get something to eat. Everything was changed, parking lots where all of the places I knew used to be. I had a crab and a beer in a place I didn't know and then started walking down the Embarcadero. There were some old guys fishing off one of the wharfs and I watched them until they left, their wet gunny sacks bulging with fish. Then I went back to the hotel.

A week went by. I got up early every day, had some breakfast at the place on the corner, and worked for the old man until noon or so. Then I would take off and walk until dark. It was cold clear weather, waiting for the next storm, and everything was bright and sharp. Those new skyscrapers poked up fat and shiny in the brittle sunlight. Alcatraz, standing empty out in the bay, seemed close enough to spit on.

One morning I asked the Chinaman. "Oh, she be back soon," he said. "She visit sick friend." He gave me a wink and a nod and started in with his little cackling laugh. I turned my back on him and rinsed the mop out in the bucket until I heard him slippering off down the hall.

It was Monday night she came. I had been asleep a few hours but I heard her come in, then felt her breath on my face as she slid into bed. Her little body was firm and smooth like a peach. Afterward I slept hard and dreamt of red buttes in the desert, riding through them on a spotted pony.

In the morning she was gone, but there was a note on the mirror. "You have a day off. Meet me in the lobby at ten."

It was another bright clear day. We walked down to a place on the Square and had breakfast. She looked fine, like a young girl almost, with a striped scarf around her neck and blowing behind her. I had shaved anyway, and it was warm enough to leave that lumpy overcoat behind. We might have been a father with his college-girl daughter — if it wasn't so obvious that I couldn't be her father. I asked her how old she was. She said thirty-five. I looked at her again and it was possible. You can't tell with them.

It was a pretty expensive place. She said she was buying and to order anything. I said that she must make a pretty good living at it. She didn't sound angry when she said she did, only a little annoyed that I had to bring it up. After a minute she looked over at me and said, "You don't have to start that already."

I kept quiet and pretty soon she was smiling and talking again. I drew on the place mat while she went on about Carmel, where she had been with her sick friend. She liked the ocean, all the birds and rocks and everything, and she said she walked on the beach with her friend's dog for three hours every day.

"You ought to go down there to draw," she said.

"I don't go anywhere to draw," I said. "I just draw where I am."

She was quiet a minute, then she scooted her chair around to look. "It's an old guy I used to know," I said. It was Hector Manygoats.

"An Indian?"

I nodded. "An old Navaho. Down where I used to be."

She looked at it hard for a long time, then finally up at me. "Why aren't you there any more?" she said.

"Well, there was this beautiful Indian maiden and we were very much in love, but her father . . ."

"Okay," she said smiling.

There were some kids playing football on the Square. She watched them out the window and stirred her coffee. I drew Hector and watched her out of the corner of my eye. Pretty soon he started to look like her — I wasn't concentrating too well. Her face was firm and smooth like a young Indian's, but the color was brighter, deeper, rosier. There was a pouty line to her lips even when she was not being that way, because she had learned to keep them closed over her big top teeth. Big eyes for a Chinese, small pointed nose. I watched her careful, hard — to remember.

"Do you sell your drawings?" she said after a while, still looking out the window.

"Sometimes. When I need the money I sell them, when I need the heat I burn them."

She looked back at me hard and quick. "That's criminal," she said. She was serious.

"I've been called that before," I said. "By several judges."

She looked confused, as if I had brought up something she wanted to find out about but she didn't want to let go of the other quite yet. She decided not to let go. "You should at least keep them," she said. "They are very good, you know, very . . . compassionate."

"That's a nice word," I said.

But she wouldn't be put off. "Will you give them to me instead of throwing them away?"

"So you can get rich while I freeze?"

"Will you?"

I gave up. "Okay," I said.


We walked down to the bay. The old chocolate factory had been turned into fancy shops and we looked in the windows. There was an Indian kid with a guitar and a sign by his turned-over hat. "For the Alcatraz Indians" it said. I put in a quarter and asked him what an Alcatraz Indian was. He said that they had captured Alcatraz from the government. I said sure but then I asked her and she said that they were out there, a hundred or so of them. I asked him why they didn't capture the financial district instead, but he wasn't amused and finally she pulled me away by the arm. I couldn't stop laughing. "It's like a school of sardines taking over a cannery," I said. She sat me down by the fountain until I was better. We watched the seagulls, the boats in the bay. But Alcatraz was there too, and whenever I looked at it I started in again.

Finally she said she had to go. I put her on a bus, then walked down to the hot dog stand and got some coffee. There was an old guy sitting on the seawall like a baldheaded bird. I sat a little ways from him and drank my coffee. Two old farts on a fence.

When I finished the coffee I got up and headed back up toward Beach Street. The Indian kid with the guitar was sitting on the grass having hot dogs and beer with some of his friends. There were two Navahos, one a bad-looking fat one with a long jagged scar in front of his ear. The kid whispered to them and as I went past the bad one asked me if I wanted to have a beer. I walked over to them and took the beer that the kid handed up.

"Nice day," I said, taking a long swallow.

"Not so nice out on the Rock. It's cold." The bad Navaho talking, a big chip on his shoulder.

I smiled big at him. "I'll bet it is. Wait until it starts raining."

"You have a big mouth," he said.

"Pretty big," I said. "Where are you from?" I wasn't pushing.

"Alcatraz." He was pushing.

We looked hard at one another for a minute, me smiling big — then he started to get up.

"Keep your fat behind on the grass or I'll cut your other ear off," I said to him in Navaho. His face seemed to dissolve as he sat back down. I drank the rest of the beer in a gulp and put the can down on the grass.

"Thanks for the beer," I said to the kid.

They all watched me as I went up the hill.

*MERLIN* ✠ **I** put the bag down and opened the door with my key. She was sitting in the chair by the fireplace — her hair piled, pinned, her face calm and smooth and bright above the simple whiteness of her blouse.

"Good morning," I said.

She smiled softly and looked me up and down. "Good morning," she said. "Good morning, Merlin Carson."

"I have brought your breakfast."

"Thank you," she said as I carried the bag past her to the kitchen. She did not get up.

"Don't worry," I said from the kitchen. "I am a good cook."

"I won't worry," she said quietly.


I was astonished to find that I could work with her there. When her breakfast was done I would go to my table while she rinsed off the dishes, and before she was done and installed with her book again by the fireplace, I would be immersed in something. Sometimes I would look up and be surprised to see her there, sitting still and straight and quiet like a tranquil cat, her legs tucked under her. After a moment she would raise her eyes and then, with a little smile, drop them to her book again. Soon it would be noon and she would get up to make the coffee while I built a fire for the afternoon. Then there would be a few minutes with our coffee before she stood up and, rinsing out her cup in the sink, went to the bed. She seemed to fall asleep immediately, the big green afghan tucked up under her chin, and I would go back to work. Always she was asleep, so still, when I left in the afternoon.

It was all so regular, so ordered — as though the violence of that first mad afternoon had set up an equilibrium, a softly tensioned polarity to which each of us had submitted, surrendered, while we waited for the forces to dissipate, to disintegrate into a new, less fragile configuration. Our smiles were soft, our talk muffled, our questions few. We lived patiently, we waited . . .

I would watch her sleeping — her smooth polished face seeming not to breathe, her shining hair pinned. She seemed like a doll, so small, so delicate and fragile . . .

One afternoon I finished early and, getting a small bourbon from the kitchen, went to the window to watch the schoolchildren coming home. The fog was marching in over Pacific Heights, the sun drawing light wisps like strands of cotton candy from the rolling mass. If I were a musician, I remember thinking — only a musician could do that, say that . . . and then all at once the sound was there pressing around me, against me: a high, sustained vocal scratching that somehow was in the room before I heard it, that somehow had gathered itself to its full terrible momentum before I could turn and . . . She was sitting up on the bed, her round black eyes the same shape as her round mouth and both the same shape as the sound . . . and I had to break away from it, the sound, its grip on my shoulders like an outraged hawk, before I could run to the bed and, holding her, talking to her, push her down. And then there was just her breathing, her hard fast breathing as I put the afghan over her again and sat on the bed with my awkward hand on her cheek until finally she was quiet.

When I thought that she had gone back to sleep I slowly stood up. Before going back to the window I glanced down at her once more. Her eyes were open, on me.

"You are good, Merlin," she said.

She closed her eyes again and in a moment was asleep, breathing evenly and quietly as if it had not happened.


The nights were long. I would waken in the dark and, lying still in that ponderous oaken bed, watch the trembling shadow of a branch on the wall until it dissolved in the morning light. I turned it over in my mind, fondled every side of it with the fingers of my brain — and always it ended in the same feeling, the same conviction: that it was cruel, outrageously cruel, her coming now. And I thought of that man I had read about in the newspaper — the man who, after spending his life in prison for some crime of his youth, and after finally being released when all his hairs were gray, had after three days of freedom robbed a grocery store and allowed himself to be caught so that he could be returned to the imprisonment which, after so many years, had become his comfort, his security, his peace. ("That's my home," he had told the judge. "Just send me home . . .") Yes, I too was guilty of an early crime, I too had suffered imprisonment — and now that freedom loomed in the darkness of my age I too feared the wrench of attaining it, the deracination that it would demand. It was as if my imprisonment, like his, had earned me the right to continue it — to insist that I be left in peace to sit in my cell and patiently go on filling my looms. And yet, I thought, somehow I am entitled to this — it has come late, but it has come, and perhaps on the other side of that wrenching, that deracination . . .

One morning just before the light I slipped back into sleep. I dreamed of a whale, a great ancient whale. I seemed to travel along beside him as he went, to gaze into his placid eye as he ploughed plunging through a gray polar sea, waves breaking into icy spray across his grizzled chin as he drove through them. Somehow he seemed to know me, to acknowledge my presence as we moved along together — me smoothly, as if blown by the wind, and he powerfully driving. Once he sounded, and then there was only the expanse of gray ocean, only the cutting wind . . . until suddenly with thrusting flukes he hurled himself spouting through the surface, thrust his body entire into the air for an endless tick of time . . . and then fell crashing back to resume his plunging course. Again I moved along beside him, again that great round eye seemed to greet me, acknowledge me, and I was filled with joy as we went, as we went. But then, then, suddenly the sea was calm, warm and flat and calm — and I, only I, was stopped, arrested, hopelessly becalmed. As I watched in anguish, the great whale turned his back and swam slowly away from me into the bright sun . . .

The sun was coming in through the window. I could hear Clarissa stirring in the next room.

*CLARISSA* ✤ **H**ow often I think of them now, the days before . . . when I was yet a child, a beautiful golden child, and he had hair as black as jet . . . They swirl in my brain like a cloud of swallows, those days . . .

That bright morning on the Lyell Fork, camped at the foot of the glaciered mountain, the ice an inch thick in the pots — he making the fire, his pipe tight in his white teeth, and teasing, chuckling so warmly, happily, as I begged him to get into the sleeping bag again, to warm me again . . . as he had warmed me so well before the sun rose. His eyes watching me, his soft mischievous look . . .

We went up the mountain that day. There was a little flat clearing hollowed out like a bowl there just under the glacier where the water came down all icy and the river began. He took out his cherished rod, the one Peter has now, and his flies — trembling with impatience to catch his first golden trout, his hands trembling as he strung the line through the rings. I could not watch him; I never could when he was so . . . intense about something. I walked to the far end of the little flat bowl, just where the water came down out of the glacier, and the sun was so warm there, so warm beside the great ice glacier, and I could see his fishing line moving against the sky, far away against the sky, and I lay back against a rock in the sun, the warm sun, and I slept . . .

Until he was there beside me, his face composed but a little pensive at the corners of his eyes as he showed me the beautiful spotted fish, still supple and bright, and told me sadly, so sadly, that no, it was not a golden trout, as beautiful as it was, no, it was not a golden trout, we must not be high enough for a golden trout — and then his eyes relaxing, brightening, as we brought out the lunch, the good St. Helena wine that tasted like smoke . . . and the sun so warm, so warm as he . . . took me again there . . . under the glacier. Only the mountain would be watching he said, only the mountain . . .

And then coming down, the great stag and two does looking quickly up at us with wide frightened eyes before they sprang crashing into the forest . . .

Only the mountain . . .

*JACOB MORSE* ✤ We got on good then. Every day she would meet me in the lobby at one and we would go out for what was her breakfast and my lunch. Everybody seemed to know her. Wherever we went there would be somebody. We get on a bus and the driver asks her whatever happened to somebody or other, a kid driving a milk truck stops in the middle of the street and holds up traffic for a block while he shoots the shit with her, a withered Mexican lady with two canes comes out of a grocery store and they hug and kiss on the sidewalk in front of me while I look at the buildings. Every day something like that. I asked her about it. She said it was simple; she had never lived anywhere else.

"But this isn't any small town," I said. "There are a million people here."

"It's like a small town," she said. "Every day I see somebody I went to school with — or their kids or their parents. It's like a small town in a lot of ways."

"And you like that?" I said.

She looked at me with a sad smile. "It's very nice," she said. "But sometimes you need a place to hide."

One day when I came down to the lobby she was there kind of dressed up. She asked me have I got a tie and when I said no she said something to the Chinaman and he went and in a minute came back with one. Her eyes were all sparkling. "It's a surprise," she said. I put on the tie and we went out.

We had an enchilada at the corner and then got on a bus. It went out California, way out, and then we got off and got on another bus. That one went south by some nice houses and then we were in the park. We got out in front of the museum and she led me by the hand past a pool with a statue of an Indian kid playing a flute to some lions. Then we went inside. The signs said "van Gogh Exhibition" and there were a lot of people.

"Do you like him?" she said as we walked along. "It's the last time the show will be in America; they will take it back to Holland then."

"Do I like who?"

She stopped and looked at me, her forehead wrinkled up a little. "van Gogh," she said.

"I never met him," I said.

"Are you fooling me again?"

"No," I said.

She took my hand again and pulled me past the crowd of people to a little table in the corner with a sign that said "Members." She showed the lady at the table a card that she had in her purse and we went in a door to where the pictures were. The crowd was there again. Everybody was in a line moving past the pictures and there were some special ladies telling us what the pictures meant and how this van Gogh was feeling when he painted them. We got in the line. The light was too bright and there were too many people.

"I won't say anything," Betty said. "The paintings will say all that needs to be said."

We came to the first bunch of pictures and the first lady telling us. She pointed at the pictures and read to us from some letters that van Gogh had written to his brother. I watched Betty's face as she listened. Her eyebrows were pointed with attention and she held her lips tight closed so that her teeth wouldn't show.

74

"Well, what do you think?" she said when the first lady was done.

"Fine, just fine," I said.

She looked at me straight and then we walked to the second lady. van Gogh wasn't feeling too good when he did these, the lady said. I could see what she meant. The people were starting in to push a little to get a better view. I was starting in to sweat.

We stopped in front of a picture of a room with just a bed and a chair. It was my room in San Tomás. The chair, the bed, everything was in the same place. The morning light — there was no two ways about it.

"Where was that room?" I asked Betty.

She turned to me with a serene smile on her face. "Beautiful, isn't it? So ordered, peaceful — monastic almost."

"But where is it? Where did he paint it?"

"Provence," she said.

"Where?"

"France. The south of France." She was back to looking at it, her eyes shining with excitement.

She could have been wrong. The lady was there, just about to start her speech. I asked her. Same thing.

"Didn't you believe me?" Betty said.

"Yes. No. It looks like a place I used to be."

"In France?" she said.

"No. I never been in France."

She turned back to the picture — then we were pushed along again by the line, along and around a corner. There was another big room full of pictures, the same bright light. The guy behind us kept pushing his binoculars against my back. I was getting a headache.

Then there was another lady talking. Vincent, which was what they all called him, was feeling worse than ever now. There was a picture he made of himself with a bandage tied around his head. The lady said that he had cut off his ear to give it to a whore. I looked at Betty. She could feel my eyes on her; her face got hard and she looked straight ahead. Then I looked back at the picture while the lady went on to something else. You poor crazy bastard, I thought, how would you like to be standing in this line with me? You wouldn't have lasted this long. The face came up out of the canvas, begged me to get him out of there . . . but then the guy was poking me with his binoculars again. I turned around.

"Do you mind?" I said. My head was pounding by now.

It was a little Jew — bald head, red eyes. "I am *trying* to hear the docent," he said real feisty. He meant the lady.

"Well, would you not poke me with that thing?"

He wasn't going to answer. He looked away and then started pushing past me to where the lady was talking. As he went by I grabbed his arm and squeezed it hard. He stiffened and started in to whimper a little and then everybody was mumbling and Betty was there pulling me by the hand toward the door. I let the little sonofabitch go and went with her. As we passed out the door some guards were going in to see what was the trouble.

Then we were out, walking fast past the kid and the lions, then a little farther and into an oriental garden place. She was mad, trembling mad. "I should have known better," she hissed at me. "I should have known better than to bring you at all."

"Yes, you should have," I said.

She was quiet, smoldering, as we walked through some little paths between pools and bridges. Everything was quiet and careful, little bamboo fences and stone birdbaths. Then there was a little covered place with tables and white-faced girls dressed up in kimonos. I asked her could we get something to eat there and she said only tea and cookies. We sat down and they brought some to us.

"This is Japanese, isn't it?" I said to her.

"Yes." She was still mad but a little better.

"I was here a long time ago I think, in the war. But it was different then; it was Chinese."

76

She smiled a little and looked at the goldfish in the pool. "First it was Japanese," she said. "But then during the war the Japanese were bad and they made it Chinese. Now the Chinese are bad and it is Japanese again."

I kept quiet a while, just looking at the goldfish with her. She was getting better but I didn't want to rush her. Finally her face was softer. She took a bite from a cookie and smiled at me. It was okay again.

"Do you see those little trees that look just like big ones only small?" I said, pointing to one.

"Yes," she said. "They are bonsai."

"Well, they have some of those bonsais where I used to be, only different. Way high up on the mesas, on the sides of dry hot canyons and along the ridges, these little trees all wrinkled and wizened but old, full grown — two or three hundred years old. And you can be walking along in a grove of them and see right over the top, like you were in an airplane. And then in October people go up there all together to get the nuts, little nuts like a coffee bean that come out of the cones. The kids run around underneath like squirrels and somebody gets an old broom and beats the nuts down from the trees. They get big sacks full, to last all winter. When you warm them in the fire at night there's nothing smells so good. Anyway, these little trees . . . we call them *piñones* though, not bonsais."

She sipped her tea and looked out at the little trees. "Where is that?" she finally said. "This place where you were."

"New Mexico," I said. "New Mexico and Arizona."

"And that's where the Indians are? And the room that looks like van Gogh's?"

"That's right."

"Are you going back?"

"Maybe," I said. "Not right now."

She smiled at me, a soft warm smile. "But maybe you'll take me there sometime?"

"Maybe," I said.

*MERLIN* ✤ He always needed me; that was the root of it.

I cannot remember when it was different, when it was not the same. To each of us was given something. The ideas, those great, grandiose, daring, outrageous ideas which could take an endless, dusty, buzzing summer afternoon and miraculously transform it into an adventure of waterwheel factories and fortresses impregnable against Indians and bears and cunning traps for snaring feral cats and tiretube slingshots cocked by a mule for propelling boulders over the pond and over the barn to fall rattling into the orchard — these, the ideas, were his. They lurked behind his smooth inscrutable forehead like fish in flat water, always two when he needed one. And mine — the something that was mine? It was there too, always: that crucial something that the idea needed to make it live — sometimes the soft tale to get Mother out of the kitchen long enough, sometimes the wheedling that it took to talk an uncle or a neighbor into loaning the vital part, often just the plain hard work that stood between his conception and the delicate finishing touches of which only his hands were worthy. But they were always there, his part and my part, like the halves of a cracked coin — one half perhaps more polished than the other, but both nevertheless fitting together exactly.

And yet, and yet I expected that all that would be gone, dissolved, when I came back. During the ten years that had passed since that January morning in 1931 when I picked myself up out of the snow and walked past Father's still-clenched fists to the gate and down the lane to the road — during those ten years I had stumbled through my twenties and into my thirties in a world so far removed from his that the possibility of any remaining point of contact seemed more than remote. His world — that had been a simple projection, an extension, of the succession of triumphs which had begun long before that January morning, a succession which had led him remorselessly through college to law school to a good job and a big house and a fragile, blooded wife. Mine, mine had been a succession of a different kind — a succession of drafty trains and steerage cabins and occasional jails and too much liquor and not enough food and reams of nonsense scribbled in cold hotel rooms and on sunny terraces. He had continued to flourish, I to dissipate.

No, I told myself, the jagged edges would be worn smooth now, they would not fit at all . . .


I remember the morning that the telegram came. The sun warming my defenseless head as I sat on a damp bench in Mexico City and watched dour distinguished old gentlemen taking their morning promenade while pigeons flew like swirling scraps of torn paper around the empty cupola of the bandstand . . . the beautiful boy from the hotel, shining black hair falling across his eyes, coming across the street with it, holding it out to me with a shy smile, then turning quickly to run with flying hair back across the street . . . me holding it awkwardly like the summons that it was until the boy had disappeared again behind the tall carved doors of the hotel, then opening it, glancing at it quickly, and shoving it into the pocket of my coat. The pigeons like swirling scraps of torn paper as I stood up, as I said out loud, "Yes, it is time for this to be over now."

But the prodigal son was not in time. The train was somewhere in the middle of Texas when he, on his way to some other place, dropped in for a dream. He was sitting in a straight chair reading his Bible — the worn leather-covered one with brass on the corners that had sat unopened on the shelf near the stove for the ten years preceding my abrupt leave-taking. He looked up at me, his face a hundred years old. "I am so glad you could come, Merlin," he said. "I am reading your book you see; it is really quite good." But when I reached out to touch him he was gone — only the Bible was left on the cane seat of the chair . . .

Too late. Too late. There was more anger in me than grief — anger that he had not waited. I told it all to the closed cedar coffin, then went outside to walk under the swirling stars . . .


He, Arthur, took care of the business that had to be taken care of. I stayed on — mostly because I didn't know what to do next. I would take a lunch and a horse up toward the dry farms, ride until I was hungry, and then spend the long fall afternoon under the cedars with a book. When I came down in the evening Arthur would be there and we would sit on the pondbank with bottles of beer and talk in low voices about the gathering war.

Arthur was less forbidding, less pompous than I had expected. He was the big-city lawyer, there was no mistaking that; but underneath the veneer there was much that I recognized. There was no condescension, no talking down to me — somehow he even seemed remotely pleased that, all of the shouting past now, I had become what I had become. "You are what you ought to be," he said one day. "It is good to be what you ought to be." He asked questions, then listened with an interested but quizzical expression on his smooth face while I answered them.

Physically he was as handsome as ever — his head of black hair, so thick and heavy that it made me wince, had taken on just that bit of gray around the temples that would spell reassurance to a worried client. He wore glasses now too, little rimless ones with fine gold earpieces, but they lent him a scholarly air that was entirely becoming. His hands, the rough hands of a farm boy when last I had seen them, were now soft and manicured — the simple flat wedding band seemed to speak solidity, establishment, control. Only an unfortunate habit he had acquired, that of touching his face too much, betrayed a vague edge of anxiety.

I had been right in some ways, wrong in others, about the effect of those ten years upon us. The total dissimilarity of our respective experiences made us rather distant and defensive at first — I had been right about that. But in a way the effect seemed beneficial too, for that very dissimilarity tended to sweep away what was left of the syndrome of dominance and deference which the difference in our ages had imposed upon us as boys. That kind of thing seemed to be rooted in common experience, in the feeling that the elder has already seen and experienced everything that the younger is seeing and experiencing — and when that feeling was no longer supportable it seemed that the structure crumbled and we were left as equals. Just as I could not very well sit with an ironic and knowing smile on my lips while he told of sitting in a private dining room and negotiating the settlement of a ten-million-dollar lawsuit, so the sneer of superior experience could not cross his face while I told about getting out of Pamplona just in time and walking over the mountains with a Basque shepherd into France. These were, yes, different worlds, and the inhabitant of each was entitled to the quiet respect of the visitor, a respect that could not exist within that boyhood arrangement of rank and command, of inspiration and instinctual response.

Or so it seemed to me. It only remained for me to see how I could be wrong about that too — how that vast shoal of common experience which lay beneath both our worlds could still in some strange way cause the old relationships, the old ties and tensions, to raise themselves up and struggle for recognition . . .

It was the last afternoon. We had decided to try to start up the old Model T flatbed truck which had stood on the pondbank for nobody knew how long. We cleaned the plugs and turned it over and miraculously it started, spitting flames and sparks out the tailpipe when it backfired. Finally we got it running fairly smooth and Arthur decided that a trip to the head of the creek was in order to celebrate our success. We telephoned Martin and Glen, Uncle Lyman's boys, and asked them to meet us up there in a pickup in case we needed a tow.

We set out clattering down the lane and turned up the road. By the time we passed Larkin's place there were three dogs after us. Arthur's face shone with happiness, blue eyes squinting in the wind in spite of his spectacles. "We'll make it!" he shouted at me over the din. "We'll make it!" He retarded the spark a little to make a backfire and sent the dogs scrambling into the sagebrush.

And yes, we did make it. After we coasted down into the flat just down from the spring and he turned off the engine, we sat smiling in the silence a moment and watched the afternoon breeze ruffle the cottonwoods. Then we climbed down and walked slowly toward the spring. It was all changed now — but we had been prepared, warned. After Father had had to let it go for taxes in the thirties the county had kept it for a picnic area, and now there were barbeque pits and tables and trashcans under the trees where we had spent so many carefree hours. The spring itself, where the creek came out of the mountain, seemed smaller, less . . . miraculous. We did not say very much — there were too many memories hovering around us to say very much. We walked along side by side, our hands in our pockets.

We were heading back to the truck to wait for the cousins when he saw it, saw them. He stopped and stood still a moment, looking, then reached up and passed his hand over his cheek. That old look, or almost that old look, came over his face.

It was swings, old rusty swings. Evidently the county or someone had put them up for the children to use on picnics, but beer and heedlessness had backed cars into them and now it was just the frames standing empty and rusted and twisted on the dusty flat like two great insects with broken forelegs.

"You know," Arthur said quietly, "we could fix that." He rubbed his cheek again. "There are two good legs on that one and two good legs on the other one. That's enough for one. Then we could hang a swing with ropes and a board . . ." His face was tense with concentration.

"It would be a lot of work," I said. "The legs are rusted onto the crossbars."

"Not so much work," he said. "Think of the kids when they come on the next picnic." He turned his face to me, looking hard to see if it was still the same, if he could still . . . infect me.

"We owe it to this place," he said in a hushed voice.

I found a rusty pipe, maybe originally a part of the swings themselves, in the sagebrush and we backed the truck under one of them in order to get close enough to hit the junction where the pair of straight legs joined the crossbar. Arthur took the pipe, climbed up on the bed of the truck, and started beating at the junction while I held the legs steady. His face had that look I remembered so well, that intensity and determination which had worked so many wonders before my eyes — and yet it seemed that something was different, something was changed: yes, yes, it was that vague expression around his eyes, an expression which spoke almost . . . desperation, as he swung the pipe high over his head and brought it down hard against the junction. The clanging echoed against the steep bluff across the creek.

I was surprised at how quickly it came. We laid the V-shape of the two straight legs on the ground and then tipped the crossbar with the two twisted legs until it, they, tumbled over into the brush. Arthur was pleased. "Nothing to it," he said with a grim smile. "A piece of cake."

We had just begun on the second one — had backed the truck underneath so we could knock the broken legs off and put on the straight ones — when the cousins came. They had brought some beer and we sat on the running boards of the old flatbed while Arthur explained what "we" (which now included them) were doing. Martin listened with a perplexed expression on his broad face. He had brought his deer gun and he wanted to shoot it at targets on the bluff.

Arthur of course would not be dissuaded, would not be deflected. It would only take a minute, he said. He assigned two of us to one broken leg and one to the other and then, climbing on the truckbed, started beating on the junction with the pipe. Martin stood aside with his hands on his hips for a few minutes, but then he gave in and joined me at the leg to which Arthur had assigned us.

But this one did not come so easily. It was rusted solid on the crossbar and, besides that, the crossbar had been flared out with a hammer to hold the legs on better. Finally Arthur told me to take a turn hitting with the pipe, and then each of the others took a turn. After fifteen minutes or so Glen broke the rust loose — but the flare was still there. We twisted the leg piece to get a better hitting angle — the sleeve to which the legs were attached making a horrible rending squeak as it turned on the crossbar — but still the flare was too much. It was impossible with the tools we had, simply impossible.

It — the mutiny — began with soft and cautious suggestions. We were all subject to the instinct of obeying Arthur. The cousins were five and six years younger than he, not just three like me, and the idea of questioning his judgment in a situation like this would simply never have occurred to them in the years before Arthur left to go to college. During those years Arthur was the undisputed foreman at work and leader at play and they, why they were nothing but sniffling kids who followed him around with adoring eyes and were grateful for every opportunity to hold a tool. But that had changed now. They, both of them, were men now — men with families of their own whose judgment was no longer considered as worthless by everyone as Arthur was accustomed to consider it. What is more, they had gotten out of the habit of automatic obedience.

It was Martin who started it. "I'll tell you what, Arthur," he said. "Glen and I will come up here with some tools next week and finish this up for you. Let's have another beer now and shoot the gun."

Arthur, swinging the pipe again, went on as if he had not heard, making a grunting noise each time he hit. "It might be coming," he said. "I think it's coming."

It was not coming.

"Well, what do you think, Arthur?" Martin said, looking up at him. "We'll come up and finish it next week."

Arthur did not answer; he just seemed to hit a little harder. Then all at once Martin had let go of his leg and was standing with his hands on his hips watching the three of us. I could see the disgusted expression on his face. If Arthur noticed at all he did not show it.

But then Glen too, overwhelmed by his brother's bravado, had stepped back. "We could do this in five minutes with some cutting oil and a hacksaw," he said. "Just cut off the flare and it would be done. We'll come back next week, Arthur."

He couldn't ignore it now. With one final fruitless blow Arthur stopped hitting and looked down at them. Everyone, all of us, knew what would have happened twenty years before — but that, that instinctive facility for cowing us, was gone now, and in its place was a pitiful look of outrage and confusion and unbelief all rolled together. Then after an instant that look had passed, dissolved, and he was looking straight at me. "You take the pipe, Merlin," he said. "It's starting to come."

We all watched Arthur drop the pipe on the truckbed and climb down. My hands were still on the iron leg as he walked over to me. He pushed me aside a little roughly and, taking one leg in each hand, turned his back and waited for me to climb up on the bed. "Go on," he said.

For a moment I was still. Martin and Glen, both with hands on their hips now, stood watching me through narrowed eyes. I wondered, I wondered — could they know what was happening now, what was really going on? I doubted it. Part of it, the surface of it, they could understand. That was the simple question of authority, of not being bossed like boys when they no longer were boys just because the somebody who was doing the bossing had got into the habit a long time ago and didn't seem to be able to break it. But the rest of it, the thing that lay beneath that question of authority — that they could not understand; no, could not even have been expected to understand. Arthur's project was nothing but nonsense to them, it was just not something that you sweated away a Sunday afternoon doing. And well it might have been nonsense to them — for they had stayed here, they had not gone away. They had never had, never would have, the need to let their minds wander back to this place while their bodies sat behind a desk in San Francisco and watched the blowing summer fog out the window, or slouched in the drafty compartment of a train pulling into Vienna in February. Who could have explained to them, who could have made them understand how absence and frustration and anguish and meaninglessness and aimless reminiscence could turn this patch of sagebrush and cedars and jack rabbits into a land as holy as that pitiful strip between the Jordan and the sea? No, it would all seem nonsense if someone were to tell them, explain to them, how after a long enough time living in memories the idea of actual physical return to this place could take on an aspect of pilgrimage — one element of which was a relentless unreasonable impulse to reassert one's "belonging," to somehow convince the land itself by leaving a physical mark, a monument: Kilroy was here.

"We owe it to this place," Arthur had said.

No, no, they could not have understood, could not have been expected to understand . . . and as I stood watching Arthur's tense back, his hands on the twisted iron legs, I wondered too how much of it he understood, how much of it he had brought out of the murky depths of impulse . . .

I will not forget his face, the look that spread across it as I climbed onto the truckbed and took the pipe in my hands — vindication struggling with gratitude, and these with abject entreaty . . . until the confusion made him turn and look away. I glanced at my cousins, at their scornful faces, then raised my eyes to the junction and brought the pipe up over my head to strike. But then, just then, the idea came — the answer.

I lowered the pipe again to the truckbed. "What do you think of this, Arthur?" I said. "We need a rope and some wood for the swing anyway. And we need some more beer. I'll go down in Martin's truck and get them and bring back a sledge and a hacksaw and some oil. You guys shoot the gun."

The cousins were silent. I watched the top of Arthur's head as he shuffled his feet in the dust for a moment. Then finally, slowly, his face came up to me. The smile was calm, smooth — but dark and cloudy eyes betrayed him as he said, "Okay, Merlin. Okay."


And so some of it still remained — the something that was his, the something that was mine. The jagged edges of our broken coin were smoothed a little, bent a little — but they still fit; they still fit.

And the next morning we were on the train back to San Francisco . . . and his Clarissa.

*JACOB MORSE*  She asked if I would do some drawings of her. I said that I would, that I usually drew things by just remembering them, but anyway I would if she wanted. We went up to her room. It was the first time I had been in it since that morning when I woke up. All fresh flowers and linens and new paint and a nice rug. I noticed that she had a print on the wall of that picture of van Gogh's room.

"Is that new?" I said.

"Yes, I got it yesterday." She smiled her smartass smile.

"What's that other one?" I said. There was a bad painting of some ocean surf on the other wall.

"My daughter did it," she said.

"Sure," I said.

I told her to sit in the chair by the window and read a magazine. I sat on the edge of the bed. I wasn't used to that kind of thing and it was hard to get started, but it turned out pretty good after she got interested in the magazine and forgot that I was there.

When it was done I showed it to her. She just smiled at it and propped it up on her dresser.

"Shall I take my clothes off now?" she said then.

"Do you mean for me to draw you?"

"Yes," she said, wrinkling her eyebrows.

"Whatever you want," I said. "This is not exactly my line."

I sat on the bed and watched. Her face was full of mischief but somehow determined, concentrated, as she quick took off her clothes and threw them in a pile in the corner. I felt a rise coming on but was able to turn it off. She was all business.

"What shall I do?" she said.

"Do what you want."

"You're supposed to pose me," she said.

"You seem to know more about this than I do."

She puckered her lips and thought a minute, then went to the chair and, putting one foot up on the seat, took the pins out of her hair so that it fell down straight. Then she took her silver brush from the dresser and, keeping her right foot on the chair, started in brushing her hair. "Is it all right if I am moving like this?" she said.

"Sure."

I did my best, concentrating on her back and her little square behind. She kept on brushing.

"You don't have to keep that up," I said. "I mean you can quit now, I'll remember the rest." She stopped brushing and I kept on drawing.

"Can I watch you finish it?" she said. I said why not.

She came over to the bed and, jumping up behind me, knelt with her hands on my shoulders. I could feel her breath on my ear, and in a minute the rise was coming on again and I stopped drawing. "Let me finish this later," I said, reaching my left hand back to touch her place.

"No!" She squealed like a hurt hawk and jumped off the bed, then ran to the closet and put on that green silk thing, buttoning it up to her chin. "You finish that now!" she said. "I want to see it!" Full of mischief, but at the same time determined, determined. She stood by the window while I kept on with it. "A good job too!" she said, shaking her finger at me.

When it was finished I stood up and took it over to her by the window. She looked at it a long time without saying anything, then walked over to the dresser and put it alongside the other one. She stood looking at them both while she unbuttoned her robe with one hand; then she quick looked away from them and walked back to me at the window. My hands were inside the robe as she kissed me hard and hot. "Those are worth more than a kiss too," she said, pulling the checkered curtains.

A long time afterward we were quiet on her sweet-smelling bed, listening to the moan of the afternoon foghorns. Two dark petals from the rose on her dresser had fallen on the handle of her silver brush.

"You will draw me again, won't you?" she said from far away.

"Maybe," I said.

*CLARISSA* ✣ When, how, did that end . . . and the other begin? Was there a point, a cusp, a divide?

It is too easy, too easy to choose the end of his school, the beginning of his law practice — for there were other mountains, other glaciers after that; after that still his eyes would watch me and he would surprise me . . . ambush me. No, it was later, years later, after it had begun to wear its mark into him — later, when he would come home late, late, his face gray and flat, and talk of his business until I had to get up and leave him to get him to come to bed; later, when early in the dark morning half-way between waking and sleeping he would turn to me in bed and hold me tight, tight for a long time, burying his face in my neck and making pitiful soft whimpering noises; later, when there was the airplane and his eyes began to shine for it as once they had for me, when he would gravely tell me of the release (his word, his dear word) that he felt when he broke through the clouds and (his words again) the sky seemed to stretch beyond the sun; later, when — perhaps, who can say, perhaps reacting to (submitting to?) all the rest of it — when I demanded and got this house, this heavy squatting imperishable house where my things, my mother's things and her mother's, can surround me, comfort me, protect me; much later, when he would sit alone in

*91*

his study for hours and pore over those maps and letters and dusty government reports — those memorials to his frontiersman grandfather and that forsaken land that he had tamed for sons to quarrel over; even later, when he began to want a son . . .

How suddenly, how swiftly that came upon him! After years of meeting my soft suggestions with abrupt words about living our own lives before we took on another, after years of barely tolerating the presence of children in company and afterward congratulating himself for having the wisdom to avoid that burden — after all that to be so suddenly consumed by a passion for fatherhood, a passion for an heir, never for a moment dreaming of course that it could be other than a son in his own image, never for a moment considering of course that there might be a little girl who would sit with me in the sunroom and have tea in her great-grandmother's cup . . . And yet perhaps, perhaps that was the reason, the reason for his sudden haste: that he felt it slipping from him, his . . . power, and he thought that if that was to be he would make his heir before it was gone. Yes, perhaps . . . for by then, by the moment of his resolve, it was indeed slipping from him — and I was using all of my resourcefulness, physical and mental, to nurse and nourish that remnant which stood between him and guilty despair. Yes, and perhaps in his secret heart he might even have thought that that resolve, besides providing him with his heir, might unlock some vigor reserved for the . . . the intended use of those organs, a vigor which might linger . . . How could he, how could we have known that by virtue of its very urgency that act of resolve was itself to be the final trauma?

Yes, and then my resourcefulness was not enough . . . and the dark descended behind his eyes.

It is like a play: Merlin making his entrance now — eyes sparkling, tongue twinkling, bumping into furniture and tripping over rugs and dropping dishes with Chaplinesque fervor . . . The audience is amused but curious — what part might this funny little fellow play? What part indeed.

*MERLIN* I knew what she would look like — even if I had not seen his pictures I would have known. Long neck, golden hair, fine skin, a startled patrician expression — it was all there, everything her pedigree bespoke. She simply turned out to be a little more of what I had expected. I had not thought that eyes could be so blue and bright, skin so soft and clear, fingers so long and graceful. She seemed too perfect, too fragile to be real. I could not imagine her going to the bathroom to do anything but wash her face.

She seemed suitably convinced of my divinity. Arthur had given her the two slender books that Europe had wrung from me, and she had read them with infinitely more care than they deserved. She would ask me questions in that respectful tone which she had learned in her finishing school, then listen with porcelain hands folded on her lap — twitching her nose a little when the brilliance of my answer was too much to bear with tranquility.

Mercifully, she was soon cured. There were only so many questions that even the most resourceful mind could think of to ask about those adolescent screeds, and when she allowed me my head and I began to perform, she showed signs bespeaking latent humanity. While Arthur watched in amazement, a bemused smile on his Olympian lips, she would fold her arms in front of her and laugh until the tears came. "You had better stop, Merlin," Arthur would say. "She is going to hurt herself."

They tried to give me one of their baronial chambers upstairs but when I talked them out of it, pleading susceptibility to drafts, they let me have the little maid's bedroom off the kitchen. It was close to the back door, which facilitated nocturnal prowling, and had a view of the garden in back. I would sit at the little desk in there after breakfast and write letters or read while she worked in the garden. Sometimes I would go out and help her, doing what I was told with good will, but usually I preferred to stay inside and watch as she dug and snipped and pulled in her ponderous gloves and dainty yellow bonnet. She, who looked like such a stranger to labor . . .

In the afternoons I would take their insufferable dachshund on long delicious walks. It was late October, and the heat of Indian summer had given way to crisp bright days that reached in the windows with crystal fingers to tug me outside. Often I would go up past the big old tile-roofed school on the hill above the streetcar tunnel and watch the children playing in the yard at recess until a burly woman with white hair drawn back in a bun emerged from the building carrying a brilliantly polished hand-bell and with doleful peals summoned them back inside. Then I, we, would walk down the hill past the library and through the neat business district that seemed to have been disgorged from the mouth of the tunnel — past the abusive macaw perched outside the pet shop, whose dislike of the dachshund rivaled my own in intensity and surpassed it in articulation, past the ice-cream store where brawny youths in peppermint-striped shirts manfully scooped before the bright round eyes of boys with damp nickels, and then finally, benignly, to that dark oasis with the ring on the door for tying up mobile sausages, where amidst the good fellowship of certain rude peers I would not infrequently take a glass of refreshment, or perhaps even two on feast days rating double of the first class in my pocket missal.

And thence erratically would I home, Clarissa and her perpetual coffee filling the frothy hours until Arthur, gray with carking care, crunched his elegant Chrysler down the gravel drive . . .

*JACOB MORSE*  **I**t was time for me to find a job. One day at breakfast I told her so.

"What for?" she said. "You already have a job."

"I need more than five dollars a day," I said.

"Maybe Wing will pay you more if you need it."

I looked hard at her across the table. She turned the look right back at me. "I think I understand now," I said.

She was quiet, just kept looking at me that way for a minute. "Well, what's wrong with it?" she finally said.

"You know what's wrong with it."

"There's nothing wrong with it but your stupid ego. If you have a job you won't have time for . . . what's important." She dropped her eyes.

"I begin to understand a lot of things," I said.

She looked at her coffee cup. Her face was closed and clouded. "Write me out of your fucking fairy tale," I said, getting up.

The next day she took me to see Carl. He didn't like the idea, but he needed somebody and when she put on some heat he folded. She was worth too much to him.

"I don't like it, Betty," he said. "But if that's how you want it . . ." He scratched his belly. "Are you sure you know how to mix a drink, buddy?"

I started to work nights with him. It didn't take long to see why he needed somebody else. He was all the time on the telephone, handling that part of it, and when he wasn't on the telephone he was jawing with somebody over the bar. Some nights he wouldn't mix ten drinks himself. The girls would come in sometimes, Betty too, but it was always just to check something with Carl and then off they would go again. They all had apartments where they did their actual business — Betty's was a classy penthouse one on Green Street. It was big business, big money. I kept my nose out of it and worked like a bastard.

"I don't know how you do it," Carl said to me one night after I had been there about a month. "It doesn't seem to bother you a bit."

I told him it was easy, she had her business and I had mine. "Yeah," he said, "but it's one thing to know about it and another thing to watch somebody, me for instance, lining up tricks for your girl every night." I didn't say anything and he went back to polishing glasses, his hands fluttering like birds. After a minute he looked up at me again. "You're a strange guy," he said. "I don't think I like you." I just smiled — and then the telephone rang again.

With Betty and me it was about the same. We still had breakfast together most days, and then she would drag me somewhere to see something or we would take a walk. It was all right, easy and relaxed. She seemed to have eased off on those big ideas of hers — she didn't ask me to draw her any more at all, and when I would do something and give it to her she would just take it with a little smile and stuff it in her pocket. It was all right, easy and relaxed — but every now and then I would catch her looking at me with something in her face I didn't understand.

Then Jenny came home.

I went down one Sunday morning and they were there together talking to Wing. "You have two of us to take out this morning," she said. "This is my daughter." My face must have been something to see, she started in laughing and told me to sit down. I did.

"You never told me, is that what I'm supposed to say?"

"But I did," she said with her smartass grin.

Jenny was about eighteen then. She was big, six inches taller than Betty, with long slim legs. Her face was that same oval shape but somehow less oriental-looking than Betty's. Her hair was cut short with little curls around her ears, and she had big round insolent eyes that looked at you like she was about to suck you in. I was done for; it was like somebody had hit me with a hammer.

I walked them down to the Square, one on each arm, and we had breakfast at Mama's. Jenny sat across from me, and I watched her while Betty told it — that this was her last year in some fancy girls' school in Arizona, that she would be here a week for her Easter vacation, that usually they stayed together in Carmel on her vacations but Betty wanted her to meet me, that she was an art student . . . Jenny sat quiet, eating with small deliberate bites while Betty went on. Now and then Betty would ask her a question and she would answer in a tinkling high voice that seemed too small for her. Then when her food was done she patted her mouth with the corner of her napkin and, putting her elbows on the table, rested her chin in the palms of her hands so that the long fingers, covered with rings of Indian turquoise and silver, pointed up toward her incredible eyes like a tulip opening.

After breakfast we walked up Columbus to see Carl. The place was closed but he was always down there Sunday mornings in his little office in back. I had one on each arm again, and everybody on the street was watching us. Jenny, stepping beside me like a long-legged antelope, was careful not to brush against me as we walked. The sun was warm; a little wind off the bay blew the curls around her ears . . .

Carl let us in. He was surprised and kept bumping into chairs.

He kissed Jenny like a big hairy bear, then went behind the bar to make us a big Ramos.

"I've known Jenny since she was a baby," he said to me. "I'm almost like her father, isn't that right, honey?"

"Yes, Carl, almost," she said in that tinkling voice.

He poured the drinks and then put his hands on the top of the bar. I looked at the wiry black hair growing up to the first knuckle of his stubby fingers. "I can't believe my eyes," he said. "When did I see you last, two years ago?" Jenny smiled at him and nodded. "You were getting pretty then, but now . . ." He looked over at Betty. "I just can't believe my eyes," he said to her.

They started in talking about her school, Betty in the middle telling it while he asked questions. I watched his hands, the hairy backs of them, as he moved them from the top of the bar, folded them on his stomach, then put them on top of the bar again. They seemed almost to dance, to play, as he moved them back and forth like fluttering black birds.

". . . And so what happens when you graduate in June?" he was saying. "Do you and Betty have a college picked out yet?" They told him about a scholarship she had won to study with some famous painter in Mexico.

"I see, I see," Carl said. He turned to me. "Have you seen her paintings? Beautiful. Beautiful."

"No," I said. "Not yet."

"You will," Carl said. "You will see what I mean."

"I'm looking forward to it," I said.

He gave me a careful look, then turned back to Jenny. "Whatever you try you will succeed in," he said to her. "Your mother will see to that." One hairy hand lay on Betty's for a second, then quick flew up to join the other on his belly.


We walked back toward the hotel. "I'm not working this week," Betty said. "We'll stay here in the Green Street place until Tuesday, then go down to Carmel until Sunday. Why don't you come down Friday for the weekend?"

"Carl won't let me," I said.

"Carl will let you," she said.

"Okay." I looked over at Jenny. She smiled a quick smile, then lowered her eyes.

At the hotel Wing called a cab to take them and Jenny's baggage up to the apartment. I said good-bye in the lobby and went up to my room. My brain was buzzing like a hive of bees.

*CLARISSA* ✛ **I** have tried, oh, how I have tried, to winnow and sort my feelings, what were my feelings them. Then — that was almost thirty years ago now . . .

Merlin was always there, of course. Sometimes he would go out in the afternoon to visit his literary people, and once or twice in the evening, but most of the time he was there — reading his everlasting newspapers in the kitchen, writing letters in that forlorn little maid's bedroom which he insisted on having, helping a little in the garden sometimes, even walking the dog when the weather was nice. Not that he was underfoot, he would never be that — but he was there, he was about.

And yes, it would be foolish to deny that I found him rather mysterious and exciting and awesome. He was, after all, a poet, an actual poet who had written two actual books of poems which had been published with hard covers. Besides that he had traveled, had seen all of the places that I had only read about, had had experiences and adventures that were beyond the reach of my schoolgirl imagination. But still that was not all, there was that something else too: as childish as he was in so many ways, still he had that certain way about him, a vague kind of recklessness, a self-contained heedlessness that was to me rather deliciously naughty and wicked, that made me feel almost giddy . . .

I must not forget that I was only twenty-nine years old, that my husband was . . . ill.

We began to talk in the afternoons. I would make a pot of coffee at five and we would talk in the kitchen before I started to make dinner. Or rather he would talk and I would listen — because I was not Arthur, who was not only his big brother but someone who was used to talking himself. No, I was only Arthur's youngish wife, who not only had become good at listening but also had had no experiences that could interest one so worldly; and yes, also because his talk was, is, a sort of natural phenomenon like a sunrise or a cyclone which one simply experiences as a spectator, marvels at, so that even when one wants to add a word or hazard an opinion one keeps still for fear of . . . spoiling it, flawing it. Yes, and he would talk at first of Arthur, of their days in that fabulous land in the Utah desert, but then later not so much of that (for that soon became reserved for the evening and Arthur and the bourbon) as of his experiences and adventures during the ten years that had passed since that shrouded argument with his, their, father that had sent him (as he said it) riding the rails to Portland and beyond. The years in New York, the years in England and Paris and Spain — he wove it all like a tapestry before my eyes until it seemed that I could almost reach out and touch it. And as those afternoons passed, one after the other, it seemed that slowly, imperceptibly, my quietly ordered San Francisco life became smaller and smaller . . . until all at once it was less than small, all at once it tasted faintly bitter in my young mouth.

I must not forget . . .

I was ready to play my part now. Each of us was ready. But the script — the script still had to be provided.

*MERLIN*  &  He, Arthur and I, began to talk at night. After dinner she would retire to the kitchen, leaving the coffee pot with us, and he would go into his study and bring back the bottle of Old Fitz. Then, as the single overhead light flooded over the big round table, we would push the bottle back and forth between us until the night was old.

We had a lot of remembering to do, a lot of reconstruction. But somehow it was more than that too — if only because each had an access to the other's mind that had been denied before. The layers of reserve, propriety, contempt, fear, adulation, which the difference in our ages had deposited and which had kept each from the other's contemporaneous impressions — all these layers were now peeled away. Events, people, all had a roundness, a depth, which they all seemed to have lacked when they were actually experienced, and soon we found ourselves witnessing with astonished eyes a train of new events, new people — and yet not quite that, not quite new either; rather almost a mirrored *déjà vu* wherein the vision following the happening had more reality, more substance than the happening itself had had, as if the experience had provided the suggestion necessary to fruition in the image. And yes, it was out of this world, this strange procession of images more real than reality itself which would rise up every night over that heavy dark table — it was out of this world that his . . . conception sprung.

I remember the night that it began. We had been talking about old Harlow and had been caught up in one of those convulsive spasms of laughter which from time to time overtook us and reduced us to temporary imbecility. It was the moment afterward, when there was nothing left of it but heavy breathing and the wiping of reddened eyes — I remember looking up at him through my tears to see if he was going to start again . . . but that strange abstracted look was there instead. His voice seemed to come from far away.

"And we are the last," he said.

Suddenly I was sober. I had no idea what he was talking about, none at all. "What?"

"Of our line," he said. "The last of Grandfather's line."

But that was not so, I said. There was Sister Julia's big family right up in Sacramento, there were all of our cousins — our father's brothers' boys — and their families.

"That's not the same," he said in that same faraway voice. "It was our father, not the others, who bore Grandfather's spirit, his soul. We, the three of us, were our father's sons. Walter is dead, and you and I have no sons. We are the last, Merlin — it will die with us."

Then, while I sat in silent astonishment, that voice began to talk of things that were no longer our shared experiences but rather were the fruit of a project that must have occupied him, possessed him, for a very long time. Most of it, most of the things he spoke of I had heard something about — from Father or someone else long ago — but Arthur knew everything about them, everything, much more than Father or anyone else could have known, or if they had known could have communicated. Great pieces of letters, books, reports, came looming up and hovered over the table as that voice droned on — describing, re-creating Grandfather's departure in the long wagon train from Kansas, the wearying voyage across the plains with a seemingly delicate and obviously pregnant English wife, that first winter in the dugout near the creek . . . He knew everything: the names of Indians that Grandfather had fought and killed and befriended, the exact location of stockades and cabins and houses and barns long since disappeared, the entire organization of the Federal battalion that had settled in at Camp Floyd in the late fifties to keep the Mormons loyal. He quoted from memory great pieces of Grandfather's letters to General Johnston about the grazing privileges the army assigned to itself — and the general's letters back; about the time one of Johnston's soldiers had had the bad judgment to hit with a rifle butt a hired man who, after meditating upon the affront for a time, then proceeded to snipe the soldier dead when he, the soldier, was on parade in Salt Lake — and the general's letters back. It all came welling up out of him without effort, without searching, as though he had lived with it so long now that it was more than memory, more than recall. I sat silent, dumb, like a man watching a geyser.

The hours were small when he pushed himself up from the table and trod up the stairs, leaving me to wrestle in my narrow bed with the residue of that . . . *tour de force*. Because no, it had not been, had not ended up being, a simple recounting of interesting family facts, the sort of thing that one interrupts in midstream with a "Say, Arthur old boy, you really have hit the books on this stuff, haven't you?" No, it had been something else, something else entirely — it had been a re-creation grounded not in the mere knowledge of old documents but rather in the casting of himself backward in time until it seemed to me, to him certainly, that he had actually walked in the dust behind Grandfather's wagon, had actually stood trembling in the stockade and listened to the howl of frenzied Indians, had actually hollowed out the dugout by the creek with his own fingernails, had actually walked beside Grandfather and our father the twenty-five miles to Camp Floyd and confronted the general himself when the soldiers began to harvest our hay for themselves . . . But why? I asked myself. Why had he of all people undertaken this? He had never been an historian, had never within my memory even shown an interest in the frontier exploits of Grandfather and his feuding sons. No, Arthur had always been the one to change the subject, the one who was more interested in finding a better way to do something than the way that they had done it — and yet now . . . now he was possessed, obsessed by it. I had no answers when the predawn gray released me into sleep.

Yes, and there were three more nights of it, three more nights before he came to, came back to, his . . . point. Each began as before with that aimless antiphonal reminiscence which had been all, enough, before — but now that had become an overture, a prelude, a mere means to transport us to the point, the shelf from which he would launch himself out. Memory became no longer enough for him: now he would go into his study and come back laden with the maps, the neatly bound volumes of letters, the government reports, the albums of newspaper clippings. Lovingly he would spread them out on the table and show me, guide me, his long manicured fingers pointing, gesturing, dancing over the precious papers as he put it all together, breathed life into it before my ever more astonished eyes. I sat silent, attentive, like a student watching a virtuoso — and let it happen.

And yes, finally it did happen. Slowly, imperceptibly, my curiosity about his motives withdrew before the force, the overwhelming thrust of it. His commitment, his total immersion, was communicated to me and I became, like him, infected with it, swept up in the eddies of blood and time which swirled in the wake of his compulsive eloquence. This was mine too — this heritage of grandeur and vision and boldness and conviction and action. I, we, had withdrawn from it, turned aside from it into the miasma of introspection and self-doubt — but here it was, our own blood speaking out to us through the mists of time.

And so I was prepared, as a patient is prepared for a surgical operation, by the time he finally came down on the point of it. The single element in me that might have been deficient was now nourished sufficiently to play its proper part — and it was time to cut.


"I want to prolong this, extend this," Arthur said. "I want a son."

It was still quite early that night. She, Clarissa, had gone to bed right after dinner and we had just begun to dip into the bourbon. He was going away on a business trip to Los Angeles the next day.

"Make one," I said.

He looked straight into my face. "I can't," he said.

Then he told it, short and blunt, the part about his . . . inability. I listened quietly, watching his white smooth face in the light, his lips moving rigidly like those of a marionette. Then, as he circled nearer, I felt a chill beginning between my shoulder blades which grew in intensity as the realization began to invade me, the realization of what he was about to ask. Finally he paused and, running his fingers over his cheek, said it:

"I need you, Merlin. I need you to do this for me. You are the only one . . ."

The chill became a gentle shudder as I stood up. I walked into the kitchen with my glass and filled it with water from the tap. When I came back he was sitting still as a stone in his chair — his face in his hands, that smooth mane of gray-black hair glistening in the light.

"That's crazy, Arthur," I said to his back. "That's complete madness."

He said nothing for a long time. I stood still and watched his back until it began softly heaving.

"I'm desperate, Merlin," he said in a muffled voice. "You have to help me, Merlin."

*JACOB MORSE*  **I**t was like some demon had got inside me; it gnawed at my guts like a rat.

That night at work Carl watched me out of the corner of his eye as I went through the motions. "What's wrong with you?" he said. "Don't you feel good?"

I told him it was just a toothache.

"You ought to have it looked at," he said.

"I will if it's not better tomorrow."

"You still ought to have it looked at," he said.

I told him I would walk home. When I got to the hotel I still wanted to walk and I kept on up Stockton toward Nob Hill. It was cold — the fog seemed to go right through my clothes to the bone — but I kept moving. When I got up to California there was a cable car and I got on. There were some kid sailors who had had a little too much giving the operator a hard time, and I went inside, slid the door closed, and sat down alone. Then the sailors got off and it was just me and the conductor and the operator down to the end of the line on Van Ness.

"You going back with us, bud? This is the last run," the conductor said.

"No, I'll take a bus back," I said as I got off.

I headed down Van Ness past the auto agencies. The British

car place was all lit up and I stood for a while looking at the Rolls Royces through the window. Then I went on down to Turk, crossed the street, and headed up the hill. I knew where it would take me but I didn't seem to care. The demon was gnawing at my guts.

The housing projects squatted like prison tiers on my right, a little park stretched out dark and cold on my left, as I walked fast up Turk Street, waiting. There was no one on the street, but I could hear the high cackling sound of a woman's laugh coming from somewhere way high up in the projects. The wind tormented the fog through the trees at the far end of the park as I kept on, kept on, kept on — then turned down a dark side street. Brooding Victorian tenements crouched on both sides of me now. I walked around a burned mattress on the sidewalk and kept on, waiting.

Then the car was there beside me, an old Chrysler full of darkness.

"Hey man, whatcha doin'?" the voice said.

I kept on walking; the car kept on alongside me. "Taking a walk," I said.

"He takin' a l'il walk," the voice said, and then I could hear the shadowy laughing of the others inside. "It's a luv'ly evenin' for a walk."

I kept quiet, kept walking — the car still right beside me. Then a back window rolled down and there was another voice. "We thought you might be lookin' for somethin'," it said.

"No, just taking a walk," I said.

"Jes' takin' a l'il walk," the first voice, the driver, said. There was more laughing.

Then it was the second voice again. "We thought you might be lookin' fo' a l'il black stuff," it said. There was no laughing. I could hear my footsteps on the sidewalk.

"I wouldn't mind," I said.

They started in talking all at once. "He woont mind! He woont mind!" Then it was the driver again.

"Well, man, this is yore lucky night. Yes, sir, yore lucky night."

I kept on walking; the car kept on alongside me.

"L'il Jimmy heah, he got a sistah who'd be jes' right fo' ya. You like nice big squishy black boobs, dontcha?" Laughing. Then another voice.

"You like a nice smooth black ass, dontcha?" Laughing. Another voice.

"You like a nice slipp'y black cunt, dontcha?" More laughing. I kept on walking.

Then it was the driver again. "Why dontcha stop walkin', man? Jimmy's sistah is jes' right fo' ya. We'll take you right on ovah, man."

I stopped. The car stopped. The laughing stopped.

I went to the window. The sour smell — whiskey, pot, sweat . . . them — came out at me. Two in front, three in back, the driver looking up at me smiling, the others hushed with waiting, their eyes glowing like yellow coals in the dark.

"That's bettah, man. That's bettah. You don' needta worry 'bout us. We yo' friends."

Silence, a dead silence, as I looked at them, one by one. So I would know.

"C'mon man, hop in. Coley, let the man in," the driver said.

The rear door near me opened and a tall broad one got out. I saw the front door on the other side opening too as I said, "I'll keep walking."

"Oh no, man, you gotta ride," the driver said — then somebody had me by the arms and the broad one pushed his fist in my stomach and I was in the back seat and we were moving.

"Check him," the driver said, and they started through my pockets. The breath of the big one was enough to knock me out. "We don' wantcha to hurt us, man," he said close into my face. I got an arm free and put the heel of my hand under his nose. He knocked it away and then they had my arm again and he hit me hard in the stomach.

"Cut it out, Coley," the driver said. "You gonna get yore turn."

They held my arms tight and I could hear their breathing,

smell it, as we turned up Fulton. The fog swirled around the streetlights like cotton candy.

"How 'bout it, Jimmy," the driver said over his shoulder. "Yore sistah goin' be ready pretty soon?"

"Oh, she ready," said a high voice over near the window. "She 'bout ready now. An' she reel anchus fo' it — reel anchus."

*CLARISSA* ✠ **I**n what deep and hidden recess, in what murky cavern of his brain must he have hatched it? Where did he find that diabolical capacity? Was it simply what had by then become his lust for fatherhood — simply that fate had provided him with a means for passing on his precious and unique blood by throwing upon his shore a bearer of that blood who could be persuaded to part with a few drops? Certainly there was that . . . but perhaps there was more. It was almost as if he wished upon me a guilt to match his own; as if he would thus create an equilibrium of guilt, sustained, supported, by the living presence which was to be the innocent badge of both its evil elements; as if in that way he could capture me, hold me, imprison me . . . Me, in whose face he could see the gray smile of resignation locked in a death struggle with the bright laugh of liberation, he would consign to a grim fulfillment. Me, whom he had now relinquished the idea of keeping in joy, he would keep in guilt. And so perhaps after all it was an act of love — if appropriation can manifest love. And so perhaps that is why such massive outrage came to be . . . compassion? Pity?

But that (the compassion, the pity) came long afterward. First the players had to speak their lines; then the playwright, betrayed, was obliged to take up a role himself — but not before the *ingénue* had begun to improvise . . .

I remember Arthur getting up early that morning, the sound of him shaving and dressing and moving about in the bedroom as I lay between waking and sleeping in the canopied oaken bed. I must have fallen back into sleep, but then his smooth handsome face was high above me, watching me, watching, until my eyes were open and he was bending down to kiss me long and long in the dark. And then his voice in my ear, so strangely hushed: "See you Thursday night. Take good care of Merlin." Just that. And I was asleep again . . .

At breakfast Merlin was even more uncommunicative than usual, if that were possible. I was not concerned, and when he went out soon afterward without announcement or farewell I was left alone to spend the brilliant fall morning in the garden. The air was clear and sharp as I gathered the chrysanthemums, all breathtaking gold and white and yellow, and brought them into the house in a basket. I put them in vases, six vases full to overflowing, and set them out, upstairs and down. The house glowed with them. As I dressed to go downtown for lunch I thought how wonderful it would be to come back in the afternoon, my face tingling with the chill, and see them all glowing there in my rooms.

And yes, indeed they were there when I returned at five — but so was Merlin.

I had never seen him really drunk before, and at first I was a little frightened. But then, little by little, I relaxed — for although I knew that he was somehow different, it seemed that the drink had just made him more of himself. He was very courtly, winsomely gallant, as he helped me off with my coat, took my packages, and announced that the coffee was ready. My best cups and napkins were laid out on the kitchen table, and as he poured he inquired diligently about my lunch and my afternoon. I tried to answer, to tell him, but in a moment he was off and babbling — something he had seen, the lunch he had had, Lord knows what else. The drink, something, had put him in rare form. I sat dumbly smiling as he gathered momentum, then felt soft laughter rising as he reached his stride, describing how he proposed to clean his brain by washing it in a clear mountain stream. Gesturing wildly, chattering like a jay, he took an imaginary saw from his pocket and began to cut neatly around the circumference of his skull just above the ears. Then, removing the cup of bone and placing it gingerly on the table, he gently lifted the brain out, holding it at the sides with both hands, and placed it in the stream at his feet. His face glowed as he explained how the impurities, the madnesses, would soon be washed away and the brain would glisten white under the clear flowing water. Then, reaching down to lift it carefully from the stream, holding it up for me to admire in its new purity, he put it on a convenient rock to dry in the sun for a moment before he snatched it up, popped it back into his head, and replaced the cup of skull with a pat. A smugly satisfied smile lit his face as I dissolved into laughter . . .

An unlikely beginning, an unlikely prelude . . .

I remember no words . . . perhaps there were no words. I remember the touch of hands, the drawing near. I remember too my strange lack of resistance, the first blush of astonishment swiftly drowned in a calm sense of foreordination. And his eyes, I remember his calmly troubled eyes as he led me softly to the small dark room, as he undressed me softly while I stood weeping on the cold floor, as he kissed me softly and let me down on the narrow bed, as he took me softly . . . softly burst inside me. And yes, then I remember his breathing, his soft sobbing, as he lay beside me afterward . . . the ticking of the clock in the kitchen, my mother's clock . . .

And it was never to be again.


Why, why then did he have to explain it, tell it? What reason could he have had? There was no need, after all. Arthur could have told it later, as he had planned. Besides, I asked nothing, I did not even say what he might have expected of me: *Merlin what is to become of us, what will we do now?* No, there was none of that. I knew all that I needed to know, for the moment at least — that he would go now and would not take me even if I would leave it all and go with him. Why couldn't he leave it there then, why couldn't he let it be for the moment an interlude of simple mutual weakness, simple mutual lust, simple mutual betrayal? But no, he could not, he would not. It had to be laid bare, all of its demented machinery had to be exposed . . .

Sitting on the bed stiff like a bird, his face bland, drained, telling it — justifying his betrayal. No, not the simple betrayal (weakness, lust) through which we would have been bound in mutual guilt; no, not even really the cruel betrayal of me which his participation in the hideous design had wrought — no, neither of those: rather it was the betrayal of Arthur he would justify, the telling itself. "He wanted to explain it to you himself, to make you see himself, but I can't let it be like that now. You have to know before I go, so that you will be able to face him, so that you will not have to live in guilt until it suits his convenience to tell you . . ." Justifying, justifying, his high concern that the simple but now only apparently mutual guilt be lifted from my shoulders masking something that somehow seemed more perverse than the scheme itself: an insane insistence that an accounting be rendered, that the accounts be clearly stated. O Merlin, how I hated you then, how much more than I hated the demented architect himself did I despise you, your bland face blandly telling it, establishing it, stating it — not hoping or perhaps even desiring that your own part be pardoned, your awkward position understood; not expecting or perhaps even asking that your apparent weakness be recognized for strength, your apparent lust for competence, your apparent betrayal for loyalty; not regretting or perhaps not even realizing that you were coldly stripping from my weakness lust, betrayal, the comfort of mutuality and laying them at my feet as tools freshly used; no, none of these — rather, simply setting it forth in a precise manner so that the debits and credits were clear, so that there would be no mistake, so that if there was to be condemnation it would be for the proper crime. O Merlin, how hideous you were . . .

And how foolish. For even then, even after my icy fury had sent him and his cardboard suitcase in pathetic retreat down the garden stairs, there would have been time to . . . wash myself. But no, by then my mind had already hardened around that darker, more reckless revenge . . .

I remember the cab driver's face as I gave him the address, the look of troubled confusion as he labored to accommodate the house from which I had emerged, the coarsely rouged and lipsticked face I turned to him, and the destination I demanded. His eyes were on me in the mirror as we moved through the sparkling night up Portola Drive and over the top. The city below us was littered with jewels. Far far out in the bay the ships lying at anchor seemed like children's toys on a glass table, their small lights flickering like dying stars . . . The cab turned up Front Street and stopped in front of the place. The driver avoided my eyes as I paid him, then left me standing alone on the curb.

I was not afraid. Rage, anguish, that palpable thirst for vengeance which had brought me here — all were now fused into a calm and sinister efficiency as I went in and sat on a stool at the end of the bar. It was as though I had been varnished, encased in clear plastic: the brittle blue light, the drooling leer of the bartender, the harsh music of the juke box — all struck against that outer coating, played upon it like a spray, but nothing reached inside . . . to touch me.

It seemed that less than a minute passed before he was there beside me. Tall, thin, young, his fine yellow hair cropped short, his long long face smiling, his pale green eyes shining — his uniform, like a little boy dressed up. My painted mouth talked and smiled. My hand, coated in plastic, was cold and still as he took it, as he fondled it in enormous fingers like a tiny bird. Blue in the light, his fingernails were like fluted shale, high cliffs stretching up from the meadow to the sky . . .

I dressed in the dark and left him there sleeping. The night clerk did not look up from his newspaper as I moved through the sordid lobby and out into the street. It would soon be light. The vegetable men were loading their trucks at the warehouses, talking in rapid Italian. They stopped to watch me as I passed, and I could hear their dirty laughter fill the silence behind me.


Yes, and then it was that day, and until the evening of the next. I was alone in my house, peacefully, calmly alone. I went through the rooms polishing the dark woodwork, rubbing it to a low warm luster. The chrysanthemums, yellow and white and gold in their vases, seemed to mock me — but gently, and I let them stay; yes, even let them watch as I took out all of my mother's silver then and laid it out on the round table: candlesticks, platters, bowls, all of it ranged there like a glistening army. Then as evening began to gather outside I poured a glass of port and began, polishing each piece carefully, lovingly. It was late when I finished and put it all away, each piece in its place. The port had made me sleepy, but I made a little supper and ate it before I went up to bed. It was warm under the feather quilt, and I remember my strange contentment as I sank into sleep . . .

Poor Arthur, poor, poor Arthur. What did he expect to find when he returned? A distraught wife recounting with anguish her cruel rape at the hands of his beloved brother? A contrite and guilt-ridden wife tearfully revealing her moment of intoxicated indiscretion? Perhaps a cunning and restrained wife seeking to conceal her shame? And Merlin, what were any of these wives to say about his sudden departure? The distraught wife and the contrite wife — yes, they might say that he had fled before the wrath of his elder could descend. But the cunning wife, what was she to say? That he had been called away to a poets' convention? That . . . well, that Merlin was just that way, the rascal? Poor Arthur.

I was sewing in the parlor after supper when he came. He closed the door quietly behind him and I could hear him hanging his overcoat in the hall closet before he walked toward the kitchen. I called to him and he came through the dining room toward me, his face smiling and calm.

"Where's Merlin?" said Arthur as he kissed my upturned cheek. His face prepared to register unbelief . . .

"Gone, of course."

The prepared look displaced by one of pitiful confusion as the "of course" did its work . . .

"Sit down," I said.

Then it was my voice, flat, calm, droning almost, seeming to move like blown smoke through the light of the single table lamp, telling it — my rage still sufficient then to tell it all, to tell of the mission accomplished, of the confidence broken, of the sordid revenge that would put it all to naught . . . his face contracting, seeming almost to fall in upon itself as I told that, as I said it: *the first sailor I could find.*

Then the silence as he took out his pipe and lit it, the smoke moving like blown words through the light of the single table lamp . . .

"Go, Arthur," I said. "The child will be mine."

*MERLIN* ✤ Sometimes in the dark now I can hear our voices. It is as if that night they were caught in a great fishbowl, an enormous globe which materializes in the room and presses cold and smooth against my ear. Never are there any words — it is just the sound of the voices: the querulous whine of my own voice, the low smooth steady assertion of his. At first the questioning voice dominates, attacks, and the other seems to withdraw before it, to back and hedge. But then the other begins its slow advance, relentlessly pushing, pushing, until the higher voice can only squeak, can only quibble helplessly — and then there is only the low voice asserting, asserting, asserting, until finally it fades into merciful silence. I lie sweating in my bed until it is gone, until I am retrieved by the heavy sound of my own breathing . . .

I never presumed to divine the consequences. Somehow, in fact, it almost seemed that the consideration of consequences was irrelevant to, or at least ancillary to, the decision — if it was a decision at all. What had been foregone was now simply declared, acknowledged — not really through a process of creative argument but rather through the simple relentless exposure of elements that were already there, like nuggets under rocks — and so as I sat with that strange numbness in my limbs and watched the light glint on the lenses covering his eyes, the idea of consequences seemed more a matter of curiosity than of importance.

I would have to depart, that was clear enough; would have to dissolve again into the aimless life from which I had come. The vague thought, maybe even hope, that these weeks would somehow extricate me from all that had now perished — but strangely, I found my deepest heart and soul greeting its demise with joy and relief. Also, of course, I would not see them together again, but there too I found less cause for concern than for jubilation. Him I could meet from time to time in secret places, and she was no loss at all. And then there was the child, the contemplated fruit of this premeditated madness. Arthur seemed awesomely confident about that, I thought — but even if he were right, even if that hasty encounter would get him his heir, what would that be to me? Would I ever want to see it? Even perhaps someday to claim my share in it? No, no. Impossible. There were already others, surely more than the two I knew about — they had never evoked even the slightest curiosity from me. Why should it be different now?

Yes, there were consequences like that — sober, rational consequences which seemed to some degree capable of prediction. I weighed them, examined them, accepted them, and put them aside. And yet when that was done there were still the others: the unnameable unforeseeable consequences which would ineluctably rise up like bubbles of gas from this . . . corruption, the inevitable afterclaps which would continue to reverberate in the dome of my life long after the event itself had passed into silence, the invisible concomitants which with sure stealthy vengeance would seek me out and settle upon me like dark birds of prey. What was I to do with these? Was there no way to defend myself against them, no way to confuse their approach? I could not hide, that much was clear — but was there no way to fight? The only answer that these questions evoked was a dull gnawing terror . . .

But wait: did I not say that my concern with possible consequences was not really a concern at all but merely a matter of curiosity? What of this talk of terror, then? Strange it is, yes, very strange indeed, that one can be possessed by terror and yet possess it: that one riven by stalking dread can yet take that very dread in his hand and examine it, turn it over in the light — and then, accepting it as his own, calmly lay it in the traveling case alongside his razor and comb . . .

Arthur's letter, seven neatly typewritten pages that crackled when you held them, found me in New Orleans five months later. The war had come by then, had sucked us up into its vortex of chauvinism and hysteria, and everything seemed changed, transformed. The newspapers screamed and raved, radios howled from open windows, people muttered together in little clots on streetcorners. Waiters in cafés suddenly could not take your order without apprising you of some new lunacy. I hid in my room behind a livid web of wisteria and blessed my murmuring heart.

It, his letter, was a paean of joy from the South Pacific. Out of that dark scheme, out of my inexplicable betrayal of it, and now out of that insane war, had risen his salvation. Yes, she had confronted him with it when he returned two days afterward from Los Angeles — had impaled him too upon that palpable profound rage and sent him too fleeing out of range like a terrified animal scrambling down the flank of a stirring volcano. And yes, there had been weeks when, living alone in a hotel, he had hesitantly touched the skirts of suicide. But then the war, the glorious war had come to rescue him. In spite of his advanced age of thirty-five they had taken, accepted him — not to fly the fighter planes reserved for beardless boys, but at least to fly those lumbering transports from one steaming island to the other. The wand of meaning had touched his life . . . No, no, he did not mention Grandfather, he did not mention that at all. But he did not need to, it rose out of those typewritten lines like a perfume.

Then, near the end of the seventh joyous page, treading quietly in the train of that hymn of martial redemption, came one soft and careful paragraph that told it, that softly spoke it:

her failure to conceive, his renewal, their corporate joy. The child was due in late September — his child, their child, his . . . heir.

I sat silent and watched the bees in the wisteria, wishing vainly for the strength to believe.

*CLARISSA* ✢ **T**hat Christmas Eve — no, of course I did not plan it that way. How could I have planned it? No, it simply happened — and then it was a fact, a fact to deal with as best I could . . .

I remember his face, his smooth handsome smiling face peering through the rain at me over that mountain of packages. The collar of his Army overcoat turned up, the bill of his Army cap pulled down. We, the two of us, standing dumbly there for a long moment until either I remembered that I had to ask him in now or he decided that he would not wait for me to remember and came in himself to dump the packages beside the tree . . .

Yes, of course I had invited him. Whatever had gone before, whatever were to be the ineffaceable scars of what had gone before, whatever were to be the inevitable fruits of what had gone before, whatever . . . he was home from his training and was to leave for the Pacific the next night. And it was Christmas. But that was all. There was no other thought in my mind. None.

And so when that strange vague timidity began to dissolve in the candlelight at dinner, I could not really have expected to see it replaced in his eyes by that soft shining look I had almost forgotten. But then, you see, it was clear, determined: what had happened, what was happening, what would happen . . . It had to be. What to do with it, about it; well, that was for another time . . .

I remember his face afterward, his quietly joyful face as he sat on the edge of the canopied bed beside me and looked smiling out the window into the rainy night. And so this at least has been returned to me, it seemed to say. Yes, and perhaps I should have left it there, should have let that be enough, should have resisted the desire, the need to make it more — to make him completely whole. Perhaps, perhaps . . . but I could not resist, would not resist, did not resist; it seemed so right, so necessary — almost as though by simply saying it, stating it, the impossible transmutation could come to pass and all would be undone, all would be whole. Yes, he should have this too now, I remember thinking, he must . . . and so I gave it to him: said it, stated it, and then watched the realization flow over his face like morning sunlight over a mountainside.

"Then this, tonight, might be . . . might have . . ."

"Yes, Arthur," I said. "Yes."

*MERLIN* ✠ **I** stayed on. The bright New Orleans spring of '43 became a blazing summer, and that a breathless autumn — but still I stayed, walking gingerly in the eye of the everlasting war. When one morning an amorphous lump of prose began to grow like a fungus from the end of my stubby pencil, I was not at all surprised. I let it grow for the sake of curiosity, to see where it might be headed, but when the winter rains began and, in spite of three hundred pages scrawled on yellow lawyer's tablets, my curiosity remained undernourished, I put it all in a suitcase and resumed a long-neglected study of primitive burial rites.

It would not be long . . .

And no, it was not long, not long at all before that luminous April evening came when I returned from a ramble to see the corner of Julia's telegram under the door. I remember the strangely calm sense of fulfillment, of completion, of relief almost, as I went in and gingerly laid it in the center of the round table, then went to sit by the window with a long whiskey. It was fully dark outside when I stood up and, taking my penknife from the desk, cut open the top of the envelope. The message was so short — it seemed that it ought to have taken more words to say it . . . I laid it back on the table and went out to have dinner.

Two days later her, Julia's, letter came. Again it seemed that there should have been more to say. A C-47 full of jeeps and Marines, somewhere over the Solomons, too many Zeros, too many too fast. Nothing left to bury. And that was all.

But no, not quite all. If there was anything to find consolation in, dear Julia said, it was that he did not die before he had seen his son. ". . . *But perhaps you don't know about that yet either. I know how you and Arthur were about writing. A fine big boy, nearly ten pounds I would guess, was born last August 6. Peter Lyman (for Grandfather) Carson. Clyde and I went down and brought them home from the hospital. Then early in March Arthur was able to come home at last on a short leave. I talked to him on the phone and he seemed so happy, so proud. I am sending along a little snapshot I took of the baby and Clarissa just after we had brought them home. You will see that the little darling is a real Carson . . ."*

*JACOB MORSE*  **C**arl came to get me. "I told you not to walk home," he said.

"It wasn't good judgment," I said. "When can I get out of this place?"

"The doctor said I could take you now. You have to come back tomorrow for them to look at your head."

The nurse brought my clothes and I got dressed. My head was swollen round. We went down to his car and started home.

"Betty's waiting for you," Carl said. "I called her."

"Why did you do that?" He didn't answer.

It was raining and the evening rush hour was just starting. It took us half an hour to get across town. He stopped in front of the hotel to let me out. "Come back to work next Monday," Carl said. "Rest your face a few days and then Betty wants you to come down to Carmel for the weekend. He looked straight ahead at the windshield wiper going back and forth.

"Okay," I said. "And thanks."

I was about to open the door when he reached over and put his hand on my arm. Then he turned and looked me in the face — his putty nose right in front of me, those mournful black eyes. "Don't screw them up," he said. "Don't do it." I looked at him for a second, then got out and closed the door.

126

Betty was with Wing in the lobby. "I got mugged," I said. "That's all."

We went up to her room. The two pictures were still there, that one of van Gogh's on one wall and Jenny's on the other. I sat on her bed while she talked. It was like sitting where I was and looking at where I had been and where I was going.

"So now at least you can come down with us tomorrow," she was saying. "The sea air will heal your face up in a day."

"No. I have to see the doctor tomorrow. And I have something else to do too. I'll come Wednesday."

She looked like she was about to say something, then thought better of it. "Okay," she said. "We'll meet you at the train Wednesday night."

"I'm going to bed," I said, getting up.

She didn't answer. When I closed the door she was watering her flowers again.

*MERLIN* ✥ It was a cold bright December day. The wind on my face bit like rocksalt as I stood on the spraystrewn deck and, warming my hands on a cup of bitter coffee, watched the gulls bickering in our wake. A big tug with four garbage barges in tow shouldered past us and pointed its padded nose toward the Golden Gate.

When the engines eased off I walked carefully to the bow, holding the handrail as I went. I could see men in overalls lounging and smoking on the slip, waiting to take the mooring hawsers. Then the deck shuddered as the engines went into reverse and a boiling white surf led us in until we groaned to a stop against worn pilings. I walked through the door into the cabin and, putting the full cup of coffee on the counter, went down the stairs.

The streets were swarming with Christmas shoppers. I caught a streetcar up Market Street and sat behind the motorman. We inched through the traffic, picking up more burdened people at every stop. The motorman stamped his foot on the bright brass button on the floor that rang the bell and deftly manipulated the two levers, one with a round wooden handle worn silken smooth by a thousand pairs of gloves. At Civic Center the traffic thinned and we moved up the hill to Duboce, then down again past the palms of Dolores to Church before we started the long gentle climb to the tunnel. Then the lights switched on and we plunged into the darkness like a rock down a well. I counted the dim lights set in the wall of the tunnel until I lost track, then I closed my eyes and waited for the other end to come.

The little shops of West Portal were resplendent with ribbons. I got off the streetcar and walked the half block to the pet store. The macaw was still there, insolent as ever on his wooden perch by the door. I gave him a cookie and a curse and shuffled down the street to the corner.

Stanley looked hard at me, then dropped his rag with a slap on the bar. "I'll be damned," he said. "Where have you been?"

"Out of town," I said.

"Out of town for two years?"

"That's right," I said. "Do you have anything to drink here?"

He brought a bottle and two glasses and started talking at me. Nothing had changed, nothing at all — except for the war. He had lost his oldest boy at Bougainville.

"I'm sorry to hear that, Stanley," I said. "I met him once at the ball park, do you remember?"

"Yes," he said. "I remember. That was the day Bailey hit a grand slam."

I got up to go. He reached over and laid his hand on my sleeve. "I heard about your brother too," he said, squeezing my arm once. "All of the good ones go."

"That's how it seems, Stanley. Only the old ones and the sick ones are left to run the world."

I walked out into the light and headed up the hill, then across Portola. The big houses set back from the street behind their smooth lawns looked unruffled, impregnable — as if nothing, no, not even a war, could affect their monumental composure in the smallest degree. Hedges stood square and strong and steady along the driveways, azaleas huddled brightly under enameled windowsills, small silky dogs peered out from French Provincial living rooms. In the park across the street small boys were playing a rough game of football, their new shoulder pads shining in the brittle sunlight.

I stopped in front of the house. Nothing had changed, nothing at all. The broad front of dark wood and stone was like a brooding forehead glaring down at me. I walked slowly up the flowered path, mounted the steps, and lifted the massive brass knocker.

All was silence. Then slowly, deliberately, the great paneled oaken door moved open and her face was there, a deep and placid pool. We stood looking at one another for a long moment before she spoke — softly, evenly.

"So here you are."

"Here I am," I said.


Yes, there I was. There I was. Eight months had been enough, eight months of ugly drunken scenes and muttering friends and cold jails. And yes, now I had submitted, had meekly bowed my head and submitted . . .

It was not that I had been taken by surprise. After all, I had been patiently waiting behind my wisteria — waiting for them, the Furies, to seek me out. No, I was not startled by their arrival — it was just that I did not anticipate such resourcefulness, such imaginative cunning. I could not have conceived it — not in my wildest flights of fancy, not in my blackest episodes of drunken lunacy — and yet there it was, a cold, hard, solid fact. How I cursed Arthur! How I cried out to his treacherous spirit, cried out into the nameless void into which he had departed! He could not do it! He had to come back, to save me, he *had* to! The gall, the pure brazen effrontery of it, drove me wild. I raged like a wolverine in a trap, howled like a hound on a chain . . . but there was no answer — not even the malicious chuckle that I always half expected.

And she. She! What hold could she claim on me? Had I not told her, exposed the whole thing to her? Did she not have the opportunity to scuttle it at the outset? Of course, of course. It had been her own choice, her own cold and deliberate choice. When she and her astonishing icy fury had sent him scurrying, was she not then in the same position, or potentially the same position, as she was in now? Of course, of course. She could not complain, she could not really *expect* anything now!

It was so simple, anyone could understand it. Even a lawyer or a lawyer's wife could understand it. I was an agent, a factor, a mere stand-in who had entered into a contract on behalf of his principal. But then the principal had had the audacity to die, to let himself be killed. Now was I expected to fulfill the contract, pay the debt? Of course not. The notion was outrageous, not to mention legally indefensible. Anyone could understand that. *Anyone!*

. . . Until one dark brooding day I lay on my back counting the cracks in the ceiling of a squalid cold Chicago room and suddenly, abruptly, it was done. My howling rage was spent, drained, and in its place was only a small pitiful whimper:

"Will you let me be now? Will you be satisfied if I do this? *Will you?*"

*JACOB MORSE* ✥ There was time. I got up early and went down to breakfast, then jumped on a bus. The stores were just opening when I got downtown. I bought two sketchbooks, big expensive ones, and was back in my room before ten.

It was like they were all waiting inside me, waiting to get out. My hand flew over the paper as they came pressing in, bickering over their places in line. I remembered everything, everything, and pretty soon the sheets covered the bed, the floor, like the leaves of a shedding tree. There was Walpi, the view along First Mesa from Tom's house, not a building out of place, not a stone forgotten — but before that was done Rosa and her little brothers were tugging on my coat, their dark round faces shining out at me, one in front of the kiva playing in the dirt, one with Tom on the bench in front of the house, another with that one-eyed dog — and then those were almost done but the snake dancers were crowding in, their song humming in my ears as I watched my hand make their faces, their headdresses, their docile pets . . . old Sammy . . . the view far away west to the holy mountain of kachinas . . . Edgar, his long narrow legs running . . . But then I had to, had to turn away from those Hopi voices, because the others, the Navaho voices were stronger now, insisting . . . and it was the sing west of Tuba City, women standing on a knoll watching the races, men in the steam baths, Henry Yazzie squatting by the fire and handing up a biscuit to Lucy — but Lucy wanted to be seen closer then, her wise eyes begging for a color that I did not have, her breast all shining with turquoise and silver and coral . . . but then I put her aside, so that she would not watch me, accuse me — and already Chinle was there, Albert smiling through missing teeth under a dusty black cowboy hat, caravans parked under the cottonwoods, Hector Manygoats' farm in Canyon de Chelly at the foot of the trail to White House, Dorothy Ramirez . . . Then, before I knew that there had been a change, it was Taos, the old men calling like loons from the tops of the pueblos as we wait, as we wait . . . Tony Nacio dressed up to go to Santa Fe . . . Blue Lake . . . and Brent, dear old young Brent, her sky blue eyes shining behind the web of wrinkles as she lures you through her studio into the pastel disorder of her room and sits you on the flowered bedspread for coffee, her tinkling laugh as she tells of the "enormous Texans" who have taken all of her fishing holes, her solemn mouth as she talks about that writer who would have lived if he had stayed . . .

At nine Wing came with some soup. "You should eat when you are hurt," he said. "And sleep." He looked down at the pieces of paper spread out all over the floor and the bed, then turned around and went out the door when I did not say anything.

I stopped to drink the soup. It would not wait much longer, I knew that. There were so many other things to do but it, it would not wait. My mind wanting to forget it just seemed to make my hand want to remember it more. I picked up the other pictures and piled them in a corner. Then I opened the second sketchbook and let my hand remember . . .

# �֍ INTERLUDE

*JACOB MORSE* ✛ I was in the house drinking with Santiago when it came, a shrill high whistle that seemed to be a bird or an animal until it began to repeat the same tune again and you knew it was a pipe, a flute. I stopped talking and listened.

"It is the Brothers," Santiago said, looking up at me.

"What brothers?" I said.

He stood up. "Come on," he said.

It was a cold night. The stars were bright; they seemed to be sprinkled on the sky like chips of a broken mirror. There were still patches of snow on the ground, and the mountain stood up white above us. We stood in the doorway and listened as the whistling song drifted down to us from the canyon that went up from my little hill. "Get your coat," Santiago said, and we started up the narrow trail into the canyon. Starlight and snow were plenty of light.

We wound up through the chaparral, me running sometimes to keep up with his lurching gait. After a few hundred yards we stopped and listened, then he led off into a side canyon and up onto a little ridge. At the top he stopped. "Get down," he said. "And don't say anything." We squatted down and waited as the whistle came closer — down the side canyon. Now there was another sound with it, a heavy swashing sound like buckets of water being thrown against a wall.

They came around a big rock and passed just below us. In front was the one with the pipe, a small reed thing that he pointed down at the ground as he played the wailing song over and over again. It was Diego, the guitarist from Bluewater. Behind him twenty feet or so two others that I did not recognize were carrying gas lanterns — and behind them, walking with a strange slow jerky step, was the one who made that other sound. Over his head was a black bag like the hangman puts on you, and he had nothing else on but a pair of loose linen pants. His feet were bleeding a little from the frozen rocks, and in his hands he had a braided yucca whip, which he brought up over his head and down on his bare back every time he stepped forward. The rear of his pants was red with blood. Then, back of him another twenty feet or so, came another man dressed just the same, with just the hood and pants. Over his shoulder was a big timber cross, the end crunching along over the rocks and snow maybe fifteen feet or so behind him. He staggered once, but he didn't fall.

I could hear my own breathing as they went out of sight. The sound, the sounds floated back to us, then seemed to disappear as the parade went on up the main canyon.

"Those are Brothers," Santiago said, blinking his big eyes at me.

"Your Brothers?"

"Yes," he said.

"Why?"

"*Está cuaresma*," he said. Lent.

We walked down the path to the foot of my hill, then he said he had to go. I watched him go down into town, then turned and went inside.

The next day there was no one else in the cantina so I asked Lupe. She spit on the floor. "The devil is in them," she said. "They will burn in eternal fire." I asked her would they keep it up all the way to Easter. "They have just begun," she said into her dishpan. Then she wouldn't say anything more. I ate quiet by myself while she went out to do something in the back. Then when I was just leaving she came in again.

"Your friend the crazy little hunchback is one of them, you know," she said.

"Yes," I said. "I know." She spit on the floor again and I went out.


It was a good time to stay home and keep my nose out of it. I was busy doing some prison pictures and there wasn't much reason to go into town. When I did have to go in for something I could feel the tenseness, a kind of expectation in the air. Everybody seemed to talk in a lower voice than usual, to smile less than usual. When I would see a bunch that I knew talking on the street they would say hello back but then they just seemed to wait for me to leave. I got the message quick. That was fine with me.

Santiago was irrigating for Baca and I didn't expect to see him again until Friday. I was just going to bed Thursday night, though, when I heard him knock on the window. He had a bottle.

"I can't come tomorrow," he said. "I have something else, something that I have to do." I got the glasses while he sat down. He had been drinking already.

Some of the pictures I had been working on were on the table and he started looking through them. I sat quiet and watched him — his high ridged forehead all wrinkled up as he went from one to the other, his big eyes red in the gaslight. Finally he looked up. "It is not good to keep men like that," he said.

"No," I said. "Not good."

He went back to the last picture, Cartwright clubbing an Indian with the butt of his shotgun. "I would kill him," Santiago said, pointing with an unsteady finger.

*139*

"You probably would," I said. "Or he would kill you."

He didn't answer. Picking up all of the pictures, he turned them over face down on the table and filled our glasses again. Looking at them had made him mad. He drained his glass and put it down hard.

"They couldn't keep me there," he said. "I would climb out, I would dig a tunnel with my fingernails, I would break the walls with my head!" He slammed his fist down on the table. I smiled and grabbed the bottle before it fell.

"Don't you believe me?" he said. He was pretty drunk.

"I believe you. They would just kill you, that's all."

"No! No!" Suddenly he was all excited. "I would kill *them!* *Them!* I am a *man!*" He held his hands out to me over the table, the fingers spread wide apart. "Don't you see these hands?" he shouted. "I have killed many men with these hands, *many!*"

He was silent for a second, his hands still held out over the table, then he looked up at me with a pleading kind of look. "Don't you know what judo can do to a man?" he said. I put my hand out to touch his shaking fingers, but he quick grabbed my wrist with his right hand and started to squeeze. I looked over at him but he had dropped his head and was facing down at the table. He was strong; all of his strength was in his arms and hands. I stayed still, didn't try to escape, and looked at the top of his head, thinning black hair barely covering the hogback ridge that rose from his forehead — until slowly he brought his face up. When our eyes met he all of a sudden let my wrist go and put his head down on the table, then started in with a shuddering kind of sobbing.

"O my sweet Lord! O what you suffered for us, my sweet Lord!"

I sat quiet and watched the heaving of his twisted back. For a few minutes there was just the sound of his crying — but then, just as he seemed about to stop:

"O my sweet Lord, forgive us! We want to make satisfaction to you!"

I stood up and went out on the porch. His sobbing came out to me through the open door so I went down to the end of the porch where I could not hear it so much. It was another bright clear night. The moon was bright and full; it lit up the hillside like day. I lit a cigarette and breathed the cold air.

I had just thrown away the butt of my cigarette when he came out on the porch and walked over to me. His face seemed calm but his eyes still did not look right. "Brother," he said, and took my hand. I held his hand for a second and looked down into his face. "Brother," I said. He took a cigarette from me and sat down on the stairs. Neither of us spoke for a long time.

"I will be going for a few weeks," he finally said.

I asked him where.

"Guam," he said.

I nodded and was quiet. He was breathing hard again.

"There are some people there who have to be got out. They are keeping them way deep in the jungle, in a stockade. I am going in there with the Marines to get them out."

"It will be dangerous," I said.

"That is why I have to go. It will be dangerous, very dangerous, but I am the only one who can get them out of there."

"When do you leave?" I said.

"Tonight."

There was another long silence while he looked out at the white mountainside. I stood behind him and waited until finally he turned and looked up at me again with those red wild eyes. "I could kill those men so easily," he said. "I could take a Thompson machine gun and shoot pebbles off a wall, that is what I could do, what I did." And then he was sobbing again, his face in his arms as he sat on the stairs. "Ay, but how I hated the slap of the bullets hitting their bodies! Ay, how I hated that sound . . ."

I stood quiet until it was done. Then he stood up and took my hand again. "Brother," he said.

"Until then," I said. "And good luck."

I sat on the stairs in the moonlight and watched while he

shuffled down into town, dragging his short leg a little more than usual. He stopped at Mateo's and leaned heavy on the fence, then went on and was gone.

The next night, Friday, the sound came again from up the canyon. I quick put on my coat and started out. I knew what I would see but I wanted to see it anyway.

They were up the side canyon again and I went to the same place where we had watched them. The moon was bright again and there was really no need for the two lanterns they carried. This time there were four hooded ones behind the lanterns. The first two had whips and the third had a cross that looked a little smaller than the one before. Santiago was last. Piled on his bare back, and lashed to it with a rope, was a pile of buckhorn cactus the size of a bushel basket. He seemed calm, almost unconcerned, as he shuffled along behind the cross, but the back of his linen pants was bright with blood.

I crouched quiet until they went around the corner. Then I went home.

I saw Baca in the store one day. "Is he still working for you?" I said.

The old man smiled under his bristly gray moustache. "Yes," he said.

"He hasn't been up to see me."

Baca smiled again, a knowing little smile. "It is the season," he said, turning his back and walking away.

"I don't have to tell you anything," Lupe said. "You will see it, and then there be no need to tell you anything."

"What will I see?"

She snorted and went back to her dishes. I took a swallow of beer and looked out the window. Baca and some others were standing talking in front of the store.

"Is Baca one of them?" I said, not expecting an answer.

She snorted again, then spit on the floor. "He is the Elder Brother," she said.

"Mirabel?"

She spit on the floor again.

I named the three others I could see through the window. Each time she spit. I got up and went out.

Finally it was Holy Week. I heard the pipe every night now, sometimes close to my house, sometimes far away, but I never even went to the window to look. That was their business, whatever it was.

Thursday afternoon I went down to the store like always. As I walked down I could see little knots of people gathered on the hill that overlooked the graveyard — holy ground, they called it. When I got to the store it was shut tight. I waited a few minutes, and when it looked like nobody was going to come I walked up to where the people were. There were some I didn't know — quite a few of them — but a few that I did know. Everybody was squatting with their backs against the adobe walls of the little houses and smoking cigarettes. There was some scowling and whispering when I came up, but that stopped when Mirabel's old uncle waved at me and I went over to where he and his wife were sitting.

"How does it go with you?" he said.

"Fine. With you?" We shook hands and I sat down with them against the house.

"Those people won't bother you now," he said. "They didn't know you."

I thanked him and gave each of them a cigarette. We smoked and sat in the brittle sun, leaning our backs against the little adobe house. "They come soon," Mirabel's old uncle said.

In about an hour they came. We heard the pipe first and then the swishing and then they came over the ridge and headed down toward the graveyard. Behind the piper this time there were five or six women singing hymns in high cracked voices. Then came six in the black headbags and calzoncillos — four with whips and two with crosses. There were others too — Baca and some of the others I had seen talking together on the street. They walked alongside the naked ones like attendants of some kind. Santiago was not there.

Next to me I heard Mirabel's old uncle's wife mumbling with her rosary — then others around me were doing the same thing, their hard fingers fumbling with the beads.

The parade filed into the graveyard. The four with the whips kept it up, the piper and the women kept on piping and singing, as they wound through all of the paths. Then all of a sudden the parading stopped and they started in going to each grave and praying there, the six in headbags crawling on their knees. At one grave the one who had carried the smaller cross spoke to Baca and Baca started in kicking him in the stomach and chest with his boot. The man didn't complain or resist, and when it was done he crawled with the others to the next grave. I asked Mirabel's old uncle. "He was not kind to his sister," the old man said.

Finally they all kissed the big wooden cross in the middle of the graveyard, the women too, and they took their whips and crosses and headed out again, singing and piping up toward the ridge.

"Where are they going now?" I said.

"*A la morada,*" the old man said. I was going to ask him what that was when I remembered it — a sullen little stone hut without windows about a quarter-mile up the canyon, backed up against a rocky bluff and overlooking the grain mill. I had asked Santiago about it once. "We have our church there sometimes," he had said.

The parade disappeared over the ridge, and then pretty soon we couldn't hear the pipe any more. The wind had come up; women nursing babies huddled in their shawls as it whistled through the rooftiles. But still no one was leaving. I stood up.

"They will come back," Mirabel's old uncle said up at me.
"Two times more."

"I must go," I said.

"I understand."

"I have been ill," I said.

"I understand. You will come tomorrow?"

"I don't know. I have not been well."

"I understand," he said.

I gave him two more cigarettes and started down the hill,
feeling a hundred eyes on my back — then all of a sudden I
stopped and, turning to face them, walked back to the old man.

"Have you seen Santiago?" I said.

"No," he said, then he quick looked away.

I turned again and walked down the hill into the town.

It was just getting dark that night when the boy came. I heard
the knock and when I looked up his face was pressed against the
window. I went to the door. "Come in, boy. You are Mirabel's
son, aren't you?" He nodded yes but kept standing in the doorway, his eyes flashing under a shock of thick black hair.

"I said come in. What do you want?"

Still he did not come inside. "Don Ramón wants you to come,"
he said.

"Don Ramón Baca?"

He nodded yes and was quiet, just watching me with those
bright eyes.

"Why does he want me?"

"I don't know."

"Is it about Santiago?"

"I don't know."

I sighed and put the newspaper down on the bed. "Where?" I
said.

"The house of Chavez."

"Don Ireneo or Don Manuel?"

"Don Ireneo."

I sighed again. I didn't want to get into it. I had seen enough of it.

"Do you come?" the boy said.

"Yes."

He turned and ran down the stairs. I shut the door, then went to the window and watched him running down the hill until he was gone. I got my coat and started out. It was cold and the wind cut. There was no one around and very few lights on in the houses. Mateo's dog barked at me as I went by, and I saw a face come to the window and look out, then disappear again.

When I passed the cantina Lupe was just closing her door. She asked me where I was going and I told her.

"Haven't you seen enough yet?" she said.

"Baca sent for me."

Her face darkened and she was quiet a second. "Oh, you poor man," she said as she closed the door.

I went on down the hill, then headed out east toward the big house. I could see their old cars and wagons huddled around the front gate. There were some lights on in the kitchen but I could hear singing coming from somewhere close by. I followed the sound to a little adobe chapel set in behind some oak trees on the south side, then turned and went back to the house. Don Ireneo's cook was in the kitchen alone. I knew her but she looked scared when she saw me — like she was trying to figure out how to get me out of there before somebody found me. When I told her that Baca had sent for me she still looked a little confused but she let me in anyway. She gave me some coffee and then we talked a little while she worked.

In a little while I heard the sound of them coming back from the chapel, then the thump of boots in the hall as Don Ireneo and Baca led the six hooded ones inside and into a room across the hall from me with a big rough table and some chairs in it. The windows of the room had been covered over with black cloth. When Don Ireneo came into the kitchen he didn't seem surprised to see me and greeted me in his usual warm but kind of distant way, always as if he had something a little more important on his mind. He seemed almost apologetic as he made little tries at conversation and helped Emilia arrange the food on three big trays. I could hear Baca talking quiet in the room across the hall, then he came out again and went down the hall. Don Ireneo was talking to me about something and I just caught a glimpse of Baca leading another hooded one into the room and closing the door behind him. Then in a minute he, Baca, was in the kitchen. He nodded to me without smiling and then started to carry the trays, one at a time, into the room where the hooded ones were. When he had carried the third one in I heard him telling them to put a handkerchief in the keyhole. Then he closed the door and locked it with a big key which he put back in his pocket.

From outside came the sound of the people leaving. Then Mirabel and the other helpers came in the house and filed into the kitchen. Don Ireneo talked with them about things like water and the weather, while Emilia and her daughter took coffee and cups into another little eating room adjoining the kitchen on the south side. Then it was ready and Mirabel and the others started to go in. When they had all gone in Baca came up beside me. "You will honor us by joining us for coffee," he said, pointing to the little room. It wasn't a question. I went in in front of him and took the chair he pointed to. The others came in after us and took chairs along the sides.

Don Ireneo put his head in the open door. "Is everything satisfactory?" he said to Baca, who was still standing up by the door.

"Fine. Excellent."

"I remain at your service," Don Ireneo said, and closed the door. Baca did something with the doorknob, then sat down at the other end of the table facing me. Mirabel poured the coffee and everybody started to smoke. I sat quiet and waited.

"Thank you for coming," Baca said after he had lit up his cigar.

"I am honored," I said.

"It is we who are honored."

I nodded thanks and waited. Baca stroked his moustache with a short square finger and looked at a spot behind me on the wall. His eyes were cloudy, tired, and his hand holding the cigar twitched just a little as he brought it up to his mouth and then blew a cloud of smoke out over the table. Somebody moved a chair and coughed.

"We are not pleased to have to call you here," Baca finally said, still looking at the spot on the wall.

"I am not pleased to be here," I said.

"It is not good but it is necessary."

I nodded and waited again while Baca took a sip from his cup. Then he looked straight at me for the first time. "Do you know that your friend Santiago Ramirez is one of our brotherhood?" he said.

"I have heard that."

"And do you know what that means, what it . . . involves?"

"No."

"But you have some idea." He was stroking his moustache again.

"I saw the parade today," I said.

"And did that . . . offend you?"

"It is not my business," I said.

Mirabel snorted and moved in his chair. A thin smile was on his face as he looked out the window toward the oak trees. Baca glanced quickly at him, then lit his cigar again and blew the smoke out over the table. "You might be wrong about that," Baca said.

I didn't say anything. I could hear the fat one, Blanco, breathing alongside me.

"Do you love your friend?" Baca finally said.

"I don't know what that means."

"Would you fight for him?"

"Yes."

"Would you take care of him if he was sick?"

"Yes."

"Would you help him to do something he wanted to do?"

"That depends on what it was." Mirabel was smiling again.

"Would you prevent him from doing something that might harm him?"

There was a heavy silence. Blanco had stopped breathing.

"No," I said.

"Would you prevent him from killing himself?"

Another silence.

"Maybe," I said. "Are you going to get to the point soon?"

Mirabel started laughing, then stopped quick as the old man's wicked glance hit him. The others coughed and moved in their chairs.

"Very soon," Baca said slowly. He stroked his moustache some more, and his thick gray eyebrows pointed up like tents as he looked at the spot behind me.

"You have said that you saw the procession today."

I nodded yes.

"Do you know what will take place tomorrow?"

"I suppose you will burn one another at the stake," I said.

Nobody laughed. Baca gave a great sigh, and now Mirabel was looking at him with something like worry on his face.

"You don't understand any of this, do you?" Baca said to me in a tired voice, looking straight at me again.

"No," I said. "Especially I don't understand why you have to mix me up in it. It is your business. It is Santiago's business if he wants to do it. It is not my business."

Baca's eyes seemed to pull in under his eyebrows — and then Mirabel, the worry still on his face, was talking at him fast. "He is right, don't you see that? He wants nothing to do with this. Let him go home. We can do it ourselves; it is a special case." But then all of a sudden the old man was shouting at him:

*"He has been named!"*

Mirabel closed his mouth and slumped down in his chair. His eyes were dark as he stared out the window toward the oak trees again.

Baca's hands were twitching more than a little now as he put his cigar in the ashtray. He closed his eyes and rubbed the eyelids with a thumb and finger, then looked up at me again with a tired face. "I will say it quickly," he said. "Tomorrow there will be a . . . representation of the Passion of our Blessed Lord. Your friend Santiago Ramirez was among those who offered themselves for the honor, the honor of . . . playing the most important part — and the choice has fallen to him. It is necessary however that another give consent, and he has named . . ."

"Wait a minute," I said.

". . . he has named you."

"Wait a minute. I am not in on this."

"You can refuse to consent," Baca said in an excited voice.

"I am not in on this at all." I got up and started for the door. "You are all crazy," I said.

Nobody moved but Baca. He stood up fast and was standing in front of the door when I got there. His eyes were like red coals as he looked up at me. "Do you consent? Do you?"

I stopped and stared at him a second, then put my hand on his scrawny shoulder and pushed him hard out of the way. He fell on a chair and crumpled against the wall. Then Mirabel was up with a knife, and chairs were scraping as the others got up. I quick grabbed the doorknob but the door was locked. It was going to be tough. I picked up a chair — but then I heard Baca yelling from the corner.

Mirabel stopped short and put the knife on the table. The others stood still while the old man picked himself up from the floor and walked slowly past me to the door. Reaching in his pocket, he took out the big key and turned it in the lock. Then he looked up at me with a calm tired face.

"Go with God," Baca said.

I walked through the empty kitchen and out into the night. There were cyclones of stars.


I was about halfway up the road into town when I saw the little trail leading off toward the mountain. I had never noticed it before and didn't know where it went, but before I could stop to think about it I was moving off through the chaparral. Pretty soon it started to go up and I was climbing hard up the side of the mountain, all silver in the starlight. But then, just when it seemed that I was headed up into the snow, all of a sudden the trail turned and leveled off and I was swinging along the mountainside behind the town.

The moon had come up now. Down below, the houses of the town looked like they had been scattered on the hills by some careless boy. I could see my own little house huddled in the shadows against the hill — but when I came to a fork leading down that way I kept on to the left. An owl flew up from the trail and muffled its way into a stand of cedars, bats went tumbling past my face. I floated along, a long-legged ghost in the moonlight.

When the trail finally started to go down I realized where it was headed — but I didn't stop, I kept on. I didn't care.

I didn't recognize the mill at first. I had seen it only in the daytime, from the road down below — and with the wheel groaning and creaking as it turned under the spout. Now, as I perched on the high point and looked down at it, it seemed smaller, less . . . important. The wheel stood silent, locked, as the little stream gurgled down the canyon in its own bed. I stood quiet and looked down at it for a long time before I raised my eyes to the other side of the canyon.

The morada squatted under the brow of the bluff like a big stone toad. I thought of those stories where you have a dragon that you have to give a maiden to every year or it will eat up the town. Yes, this was its time, the morada's time — it almost seemed to know it, to say it, as it glowered down on me, its stone sides breathing in and out. It would get its maiden, it seemed to say. Nothing, nobody, would keep its maiden from it.

"Fuck you," I said out loud as I started down.

I gave the mill a wide berth to avoid the dog. There was a little stone bridge a few hundred yards upstream and soon I was working up through the brush on the other side. It was bad going — there was no trail and more than once I took an icy branch across the face. Then I was almost there. I stopped to breathe and looked up at it crouching there on the little flat. There was no one there; I knew it, sensed it, but still I went the last few yards as quiet as I could — until I was standing in front of the heavy door. The air was full of evil, as if the holes in the unchinked walls were big oozing pores. I stood a long time and looked at the keyhole, then turned away. It was locked, I decided.

Walking up to the other end of the little flat, I looked down the road leading up from the town. They would come this way, I thought. Santiago would bring his cross this way. I could hear coyotes far up the canyon as the wind blew against my back. For the first time I felt cold.

I turned back again toward the morada. The two crosses were leaned on their sides against the back wall, the crossarm on the big one as high as the roof. I went to it, put my hand in the crotch, and tried to lift it. It would not come, so I went down on one knee and put my shoulder to it. It came slowly and then I was standing up with it over my shoulder. I took a few steps and heard the end of it chugging over the rocks behind me — but then I heard something else. Somebody was coming up the road in a wagon.

I tried to move too fast; I could feel it getting away. Then my feet were going in the wrong direction and I could feel it heeling over on top of me. It seemed to hang in the air while I scrambled to get out from under — then it came down on me like a stone. I felt my leg give, then I lay quiet.

There was more than one of them — I could hear their voices over the creak of the wagon.

Somehow I got out from under it. My leg was hurt pretty bad but I hopped on it anyway and then started crawling up the bluff behind the morada. It was steep; I went on all fours until I heard the wagon come up — then I lay quiet again. Their voices came clear now, and I heard the sound of the key in the door-lock. They both went inside, but after a minute one came out again and then I heard him call to the other one.

"Maybe it was a cow," the other one said.

"Maybe."

The beam of the flashlight poked in the brush on both sides of me. I could feel my heart beating in the hurt leg. Then they went to the other side of the morada and I couldn't hear them anymore. I breathed again for a minute.

They came back to the big cross. "I bet it was a cow," the one said again. Then I heard them both struggling as they loaded it on the wagon. When it was on they went back in the morada and closed the door. In a few minutes smoke started to come up out of the chimney.

I started up the bluff again. The leg was beginning to stiffen already and it sent a shot up my back every time I stepped on it. I kept on as best I could, but after half an hour I wasn't more than a hundred feet above the morada. The leg was getting to be too much for me. The wind was starting to cut.

Then the cave was there, an opening in the rocks about four feet by three and covered over mostly with brush. In the moonlight it looked as deep as a well, but I could see that there was a level place for a few feet anyway. I wondered for a minute who I would be sharing it with, but there wasn't too much choice — I couldn't go any further on the leg and if I stayed out the cold would eat me up. I stuck my head in far enough to get out of the wind and lit a match. There wasn't much to see — a fairly level rocky place for maybe six feet and nothing but blackness beyond that. I crawled in and pulled some brush in after me to cover the opening.

The leg was a little better when I had moved a few rocks around and laid it flat on the ground, but the cold was bad even out of the wind. I sat there shivering and waiting for the light to come. Morning seemed a long way off. I tried to think of other things, warmer things. I thought of the South Pacific, a long time ago, the ship moving over the water like a water bug in quicksilver, the whole world a dish of warm smooth water under that burning eye . . . I thought of summer in the cornfields, lying on my stomach between the rows and watching the ants . . . and then I was asleep.

Maybe the sound of the pipe woke me — anyway, it was there and as I looked out through the brush I could see that the sun was high. My leg was swollen up now to twice its size just below the knee, but the ache was just a dull thudding thing even when I moved it a little to go to the opening. I stuck my head out and looked down the road. They were just beginning to come up. I moved the brush around a little so that I could see out better.

The parade was big this time, and besides there were maybe a hundred people standing along the road waiting for them to pass and then closing in behind to follow them up. Behind the piper and the hooded ones were fifty or so women and kids. One old woman carried a big crucifix, another had a statue of Mary, and there were some others with pictures of saints. The women sang along with the pipe, the same song that had been at Don Ireneo's chapel, and every fifty feet or so they fell down on their knees in the road and prayed, the little kids holding on to their mothers' black dresses. There were more of the others too, the hooded ones. Maybe six had whips, and there were two more with burro loads of buckhorn cactus tied on their bare backs. As they came closer I could see Baca and Mirabel and the others walking along beside.

Right behind the piper came the big cross — and Santiago. He looked small and broken, but he carried it easily, his bare hump wedged under the crotch. He was hooded like the others, but there was a little crown of wild roses on his head. There was no limp, no staggering, as he dragged the huge thing crunching over the stones up the road. He seemed full of some patient steady strength.

Finally they came to the morada. Baca and another one took the cross from Santiago and laid it flat on the ground. Some others took the piles of cactus off the other two and laid them against the side of the building. Then they all went in and closed the door — Santiago and the hooded ones first, then Baca and his people. The onlookers, who had followed the parade up, sat down on the hillside and took out their cigarettes. I could see a few people I knew.

The women and children had gone to a place in front of the door of the morada and were on their knees singing again. The words of the song, still the same song, drifted up to me: *"En una columna atado hallarás al Rey del Cielo . . ."*

I pulled my head in and sat back against the wall. There was a little trickle of water coming down from the ceiling of the cave toward the back. I watched it wind through the stones, then come out on the floor in a little stream that went winding off into the dark. After a while I crawled over and washed my face, then drank a little. It was good, cold and sweet. My pant leg was getting tight so I took my knife and slit it up to the knee. The swelling was a little bluish and the skin was hot when I touched it. I washed it with the water, then sat down in my place again to wait.

The singing kept on, the same song over and over as the minutes became an hour, then an hour and a half. The wind had started up again a little and sometimes the words would be blown away, but then there they would be again, floating up to me: *"Ay, mi dulce dueño, desagrabiar te queremos . . ."* I listened to the song and the wind, I watched the trickling water.

Then they were all mumbling and I went to the opening again. Two of Baca's helpers were digging a hole at the foot of the cross. The singing had stopped and the sound of the pick echoed up and down the canyon. After a while Baca came out and looked at the hole. They stopped digging and he went back inside. Everybody was standing now, waiting. The wind blew their coats and dresses as their fingers fumbled with their rosaries. An old woman started in to moan but nobody seemed to notice her. A dog pissed on the corner of the morada.

Baca and Mirabel led him out. He was limping a little,

dragging his short leg, but he seemed calm like before, easy and calm, as he walked by himself over to the cross. The old woman was groaning louder now but nobody paid her any mind. Santiago laid himself down flat on the cross, his arms extended out the crosspiece. Baca came over and said something to him, then something to one of the men who went back in the morada and came out with a new hemp rope. Suddenly the wind stopped. There was no sound but the moaning of the old woman as Mirabel and the other one took the rope and started to lash Santiago's arms to the crosspiece — but then, all of a sudden, there was Santiago's own voice, a hoarse sob:

"*Not with a rope! Ay, how you disgrace me! Nail me! You must nail me!*"

Mirabel looked up at Baca and said something to him. Baca shook his head slowly from side to side, then Mirabel dropped the rope and stood up straight. Baca kept on shaking his head and one of the others went over to Mirabel — but then Mirabel had pushed the other one away and was stooping over again to grab the rope. He looped it three or four times around the arm, then put his boot on the timber and cinched it hard. Baca looked like he was going to move or say something, but he stayed quiet and still while Mirabel went quick over to the other arm and did the same thing. Hard. Santiago didn't move or cry out, and then Mirabel went to the legs, cinching it again like he was loading a mule. Then it was done. Mirabel went to the edge of the crowd and stood there stiff and sullen.

Santiago was like a crumpled rag doll, his arms and feet turning from purple to black, as they lifted the cross and dropped the end of it into the hole with a chunk. Then, while two of them held it steady with ropes, they filled in the hole with rocks and dirt. Finally it would stand there alone and everybody stood back in a little circle. The wind had come up again, and little spurts of dust blew around the foot of the cross as they stood looking up.

After a few minutes Baca turned and went back into the

morada. When he came out he walked straight to the cross and, reaching up, made a long cut in Santiago's side with a flint knife. If Santiago felt it he made no sign — but the old woman, who had been just moaning to herself for a while, started in to wail like mad as the blood came coursing down over his calzoncillos. "Blood and water!" she bawled. "Blood and water!" Nobody paid her any mind. The dog pissed on the corner of the morada again.

I pulled my head in and closed my eyes. There was hardly any feeling in the leg now and I was a little dizzy. I crawled over to the water and washed my face again. It was better then and I sat up against the wall. The wind whistled past the opening of the cave, making a sound like the old woman. For a long time I watched the water trickling down through the rocks, a long, long time. Then all at once the wind had stopped again . . .

"O God! I die!"

I quick went over to the opening. There was a crowd around the cross but I could see three working fast with shovels and picks. Above them Santiago's hooded head hung limply down on his chest, his black arms stretched out like an owl on a barn door. The old woman was screaming now and two other women had gone over to her. Then the cross came down, flat on the ground, and Baca was there with his knife cutting the ropes. The crowd pressed in and Baca's men tried to keep them back. Then Mirabel bent down and picked Santiago up from the cross like a wet scarecrow and started toward the door of the morada. Other women had started to moan and scream and everybody was milling around like ants as Baca and the others went in and the big door slammed shut.

All of a sudden the wind started in howling. One of the heaps of cactus piled against the morada moved across the flat and stopped up against the cross as some people turned and started down the road toward town. Others stayed clustered at the door on their knees. After a few minutes Mirabel and two others came out and started in lifting people to their feet, telling them to

*157*

leave. Finally they went, little black knots of them strung out down the road, and the three went back inside.

In twenty minutes there was nobody on the road. Only the wagon and mules standing on the other side of the morada showed that anyone was there. Across the canyon the mill had started up, and when there was a lull in the wind the creaking sound of the wheel came across to me. The sun had fallen down behind the rim of the canyon. I went back inside the cave and lit a smoke.

It was almost dark when I heard them coming out. They brought the wagon around to the door and went inside again, then Baca came out with two others. He carried the bundle himself, the blanket sewn shut, and staggered with it to the back of the wagon. There he let the two others help him put it in. After a minute Mirabel came out and stood beside the wagon while the old man locked the door. Then they all got in the wagon and drove lurching and creaking down the road. I watched them until they turned and headed off into the dry flats north of town.


I will not forget the face of the old man at the mill, his dark, round, unbelieving face as he opened the door, as my hand slid down the doorframe and I crumpled at his feet . . .

# ✠ PART TWO

*(resumed)*

*MERLIN* ✠ Ah Clarissa, my dear, wise, cunning Clarissa, may the great silent God have mercy on our souls! How we have sinned, against heaven and each other, against others and ourselves, in this pitifully tangled life!

If only there had been bitterness, that patient, enduring, resigned bitterness that we both surely expected — then it would have been so much easier, so much simpler. Then it could have been what it was meant to be: a firm compact, a solemn simple vow with terms clear and direct. Then there would have been duties and responsibilities, rights and liabilities, burdens and benefits that we could have grasped, comprehended, assimilated. But no, no, that never came, that saving bitterness would not come. Instead, instead . . . what can we call it? An insidious affection, a smiling friendly devotion which not only lacked the sheer convenience of gall but also would never quite be transmuted into that other bundle of emotions and attractions to which the word love is attached. And so we endured, so we persisted — so many years, my dear, too many years.

No, no, it was not the child that bound us, that held us. At first, of course, at first, when his needs involved us both, when his very being stood for so much, was the reason informing it all — yes, but that passed so quickly, so quickly: it seemed only a moment before we had submerged him in that myth, that cruel lie that propriety, convenience, perhaps even a perverse respect for the deluded dead, had engendered. And then what was left, what remained to bind us?

Not that I was unwilling, not that my assent to the lie was grudging — no, I could never claim that. It was as much of fatherhood as I wanted, as much as I could sustain. And after that seventh birthday, after that horribly surrealistic business meeting at the great round table, after his small face had looked up into mine (". . . but you are still my father now aren't you?") — yes, after all that was painfully passed I sensed the grave and heavy mantle of fatherhood lifting from my shoulders . . . and I rejoiced; I did rejoice. And yet still it was somehow strange — to watch him, see him, as I was metamorphosed from father to uncle. For it was not a thing to be immediately accomplished by grave and awful announcement. We did the same things as before, went to the same ball games, fished the same streams — and yet slowly they took their toll: the long murmuring afternoons he spent with you in that oppressive sewing room, the cautious questions put to me . . . the vision grew, waxed, until one day those questions had become the questions of a prince asking his regent about the fallen king. Then, then, the metamorphosis was complete. I had become Merlin, and he began to think about the law.

Was that not the time, my dear? Was that not the point at which we should have taken stock, reassessed it? Then, when the myth had eaten away his need, my fatherhood; then, when the contract had been performed, the debt discharged? But no, no, we did not. The inertia of it had become too great — and we continued, persisted, endured. And, yes, I watched through confused and dazzled eyes while you, with what seemed almost a dogged determination, transformed yourself into an old woman of forty years — while you pottered aimlessly in your garden, while you sat in your Queen Anne chair with your sensible shoes flat on the rug and crocheted doilies, while you gathered your cherished objects about you like an ornate shawl . . .

Ah yes, your objects, your beloved things! Your chiming clocks and overflowing cedar chests, your polished silver and old pewter, your china dolls and china dishes and china teacups and china figurines and china vases, your crystal decanters and crystal goblets and little crystal salt dishes with spoons and droll crystal dogbones for laying carving tools on, your Belgian lace and Irish linen and Basque embroideries, your Turkish rugs and Italian tapestries, your array of lemonsmelling furniture — and yes, your house, your vast, solid, squatting, imperishable house! What a strange comfort they gave you, they give you! How you fondled them, polished them, cleaned them, rubbed them, scrubbed them — wallowed in them!

I have never forgotten the vaguely bemused expression that crept over your face that night ten years ago when I sat across from you at that same great round table and told it, tried to explain it. For once you had nothing to say, for once there was none of your soft insipid wisdom to blunt and blur my words — you simply sat quiet with that look on your face and let me go on until I was done, then you simply stood up and went to bed without a single word. Were you angry? No, I don't think so. You knew that I was right; your silence acknowledged that I was right — but somehow you had known it all before and did not care. Yes, and as I sat alone afterward in that pool of light and drank myself into a sullen stupor, somehow it was *I* that was angry, it was *I* that raged: How could you accept the truth of what I said and yet remain so serenely unmoved? Was there no remorse? No guilt?

But nevertheless I *was* right, nevertheless it *is* true! You were, are, have become, precisely what Arthur was in that anguished and desperate time which spawned our woe. He had his imperishable family, you your imperishable objects — and yet each is the same: each speaks an unspeakable terror in the face of inevitable death, each manifests a stubborn refusal to deal with life in the context of that contingency which is our very essence, each is the hysterical reaction of a chess player who has been quietly informed that the board will be overturned and the pieces upset before he has finished the game. Do I, did I, sound like an embittered philosopher my dear? Name it what you will, but throw no stones unless you can deny it.

For you remember Arthur only too well. You remember his maps and scrapbooks and letters and reports — you remember his insane preoccupation with self-perpetuation, that preoccupation that finally reached such an intensity that it was willing to seemingly contradict itself and accept a brother's blood. And you know too the soil in which that deadly plant sank its roots — that nameless unease, discomfort, that emptiness which possessed him in spite of, perhaps in a way because of, his material and professional success. Something was missing, he felt; something was absent. "Is this all there is?" he asked. "Is this all there is? Do I simply go on doing this until I die? *Until I die!*" But no: there was something else, something that the finger of death could not touch, something . . . imperishable.

And you, my dear — can you really deny it? That deadly plant has rooted itself in you too. Your answer has been different, and yet the same. Death will only get a piece of you, isn't that so? For you have your cherished objects about you, guarding you, protecting you, comforting you. They seem almost to share their permanence, their immutability with you, do they not? Sometimes it seems that you can almost hide among them, obfuscate yourself among them, does it not? They have become — let us say it plain — almost *a part of you,* have they not? A part that will endure forever! A part that death cannot reach!

They say that we can't take it with us — but why should we want to take it with us? How much better it is — don't you agree, my dear? — how much better to leave it here. For we know nothing of that other place. Perhaps, just perhaps, it may be an endless void, an emptiness so vast and wide that we can never find our way out. Well, then let us remain, let us leave behind that portion of us that can remain — so that we will not be . . . forgotten.

But it is all folly, dear Clarissa, all nonsense. Do not be so deluded. Death will come and unerringly find you and remorselessly pluck you out from among your beloved objects like a burr from the wool of a lamb — and then he will scatter them, your objects, over the earth like seed wheat in the sower's hand. There will be nothing left, my dear, nothing! Before the mountain pinyon broadens its trunk an inch you will indeed be . . . forgotten.

But would you interrupt my lecture? And by accusing me? What have I to do with your delusions?

*What indeed.*

*Do you really wonder that I have looked for safety, comfort, warmth elsewhere? Do you really wonder that I have sought some permanence and continuity in my things when this life has been sucked so dry by your foolish posturing and absurd fatalism? Was there really a need to turn it all into that tragic charade of Fates and Furies? Was there?*

*Of course I did not expect that you would return to me, to the child, filled with visions of domestic contentment. You had lived too long in that other way for that to be possible. But neither did I expect that the years would bring no bending, no softening in you. Our need, the boy's and mine, was real. We were ready to give all that we could — including the freedom that you . . . required — if only some little warmth, some little (yes) love would return to us, to feed us, sustain us. But no, your Furies and Fates would not hear of that — they would allow you to go through the motions that some absurd notion of duty, of liability, seemed to have enjoined upon you, but they would not permit you to involve yourself in our lives, to give even the tiniest part of your precious self.*

*I shrink from even mentioning that other thing — that ultimate resolve of yours. How foolish of me to think that that too might pass, might dissolve in the years . . . How absurdly grave your face was that night — when you made the . . . announcement. I remember thinking only that it was premature, that it*

165

*was so wrong to try to reason it all out at the beginning. There would be time, there would be years to learn whether, after what had gone before, the . . . emergency of our legal union would ripen into all that marriage implies. There was no need, as there had been no need that night two years before, to spread it all out and decide all of the issues. But no, then as before it had to be done, then as before you had to do it.*

*Your voice could not have said, "I have taken this matter under consideration and . . ." No, it must have been just your face that said it, your grave, concerned,* principled *face. But your voice did say the other words, the judgment. "Platonic," it said, again and again, as if by repeating the word its implications would become more clear to me. They were clear enough, dear Merlin — but it all seemed so premature.*

*Did you never love me, Merlin? Did that foolish vow never bite, never bind?*

*And you ask me what you have to do with my delusions.*

No. No. No. I cannot allow it. That is all beside the point. You must play the cards that are dealt to you, that is the point. You must not hedge your bets on the hope of leaving some mark, that is the point.

Besides, you have given a completely wrong impression. It was not like that at all.

*O Merlin, you poor, poor man.*

*JACOB MORSE* ✣ **I** made the four-fifty train, the pictures in a big manila folder under one arm and Wing's ragged suitcase in the other hand.

Betty had told me to pay the few extra dollars to sit in the club car so that I could stretch my legs out and have a drink or something to eat. It was way up at the front of the train. I walked down the platform past the string of double-decker commuter cars that they would cut loose at San Jose. Guys in suits with umbrellas and newspapers pushed past me, hurrying to get a good seat. In some of the cars guys were already sitting around tables, their coats and ties off and somebody dealing the cards. Guys my age — I might have taken their money in the hold of some bucket in the Pacific thirty years ago.

An old man in a white coat was waiting outside the club car. He looked like a Samoan — long kinky gray hair. "Yes, sir, just call me Brownie," he said, taking the suitcase. I said I would keep the folder and he waited for me to climb up the steps into the car.

It was pretty swell company. There was just a refined-looking old couple sitting at one of the tables and a fiftyish lady with diamonds around her neck in one of the sideways chairs. I took one of the chairs across from her and put my folder down on the floor. Brownie came and asked if I was going all the way to

Monterey. I said I was. "If you need anything, you just call Brownie," he said.

Just before we started up a man and a lady with two young girls came in. The girls were blond, seven and nine maybe, and they had on matching blue party dresses with petticoats that stood out straight from their waists. I watched them walk by giggling and then jump into the benches at the table across the car from the old couple. Their parents clucked at them to calm down and put some packages on a chair.

We started up then, and right out of the yard we went into a tunnel. The lights in the car were on and I could see myself in the window across the aisle. My face didn't look too bad now, only like a mule had kicked it in a little on the left side. We came out of the tunnel and then went through some more short ones and pretty soon we were going along past the garbage dumps south of the city. The garbage trucks were like little red boxes out by the shoreline, and there were clouds of gulls boiling around them like flies. I picked up a magazine and started in looking at the pictures.

After a while Brownie was taking orders for drinks. The lady with the diamonds ordered a double scotch and I watched her smoke a cigarette while she waited for it. She had old hands, big swollen knuckles, and she left lipstick all over the end of her cigarette. Brownie brought the drink and called her by name. She smiled pretty at him, like a little girl — then saw me watching her. I went back to my magazine.

Brownie came and I asked for a beer. When he brought it I said to have one himself. He looked at me strange, like what was I doing in that car anyway, then smiled and said he would a little later. I watched him strut on down to where the old couple was. The king of the club car.

"Are you an artist?"

I looked up. It was the lady with the diamonds. She had a nice smile, just like a little girl.

"Pardon me," she said. "I saw your folder. Are you an artist?"

"No," I said. "An architect."

168

"Oh. I thought you were an artist." She smiled again, then quick took a sip from her glass and looked out the window. She would have known what to say next if I was an artist.

"It's the same sort of folder that artists use," I said.

She looked back at me gratefully. "Yes, I thought it was," she said. "My son is an artist."

I told her that I had once wanted to be an artist too and she started in to tell me about her son. It was too bad about her hands; the knuckles were like mountain ridges. She didn't have any rings on them so as not to draw attention, but she could have worn gloves if she wanted. I liked her.

Pretty soon it was dark. We were still going along through the commuter towns. Every few minutes we would stop and I would see the wives sitting waiting in their station wagons, then we would start up again and go through the corridors of buildings. I could see the road sometimes through the buildings and we were going faster than the cars. Then we were in San Jose and the train shuddered a few times while they cut loose the commuter cars. We were the last car now, just the engine and a chair car and us.

Then we were going along through open country, rolling hills and little towns. We were right beside the road for a while and we still went faster than the cars. The two little girls had moved to chairs just across from me and were slouched down reading magazines. They had blue ruffled pants on under their petticoats. Then the younger one decided she was bored and started in to tease the bigger one. Finally the bigger one had had enough and called to her mother, who was still at the table. "Mommy, make Christy stop bugging me," she said. The mother came over and took Christy back to the table. "She thinks she's so smart," Christy said to me as she went past.

The lady with the diamonds was still talking to me. She would talk about something for a while and then when it petered out pick up a magazine until there was something else that she wanted to talk about. She had a daughter who wouldn't settle down; she talked plenty about that. And the war, how we should get out of it, that was good for half an hour or so. "I like to keep up with the times politically," she said. I said I did too, it didn't pay to be behind the times. Then she was asking me did I go to Carmel often and did I have a hotel.

"No," I said. "My wife and daughter have rented a house. They are going to meet me at the station."

She looked just a little disappointed. "That's nice," she said, and looked out the window again.

Pretty soon Brownie came and said that her supper was ready. She went with him to a table down at the other end of the car. I went back to my magazine and watched the little girls playing with paper dolls until she came back. I asked her how it was. She smiled that little-girl smile and sat down. "Oh, Brownie takes good care of me," she said. Then we talked some more about her daughter who would not settle down.

After about an hour she said that we would be there pretty quick. There were some lights and she said that was an Army fort. I could see some barracks on one side and what looked like a shooting range on the other. Then she pointed way out to the right where the lights stretched out around the bay. She said what point it was by name, point something, and then we were slowing way down and starting into the town.

Everybody put on their coats and was waiting for the train to stop. The youngest little girl was asleep and her father was trying to decide whether to wake her up or carry her. "You've got packages," I said to him. "I'll carry her." The woman looked over at me without smiling, then turned back to her husband. "Why don't you just wake her up?" she said to him.

Then the brakes were squeaking and I could see the station platform up ahead. They were there, the two of them standing close together under a light. I waved.

"Is that your wife and daughter?" the lady with the diamonds said.

"Yes, it is."

"You are very lucky," she said. "They look like two sisters." Her voice was soft and breathy.

The train stopped. She quick stood up and held her hand out to me. "Good luck," she said. "I have enjoyed talking to you. And I won't forget what you said about my daughter." I stood up and took her hand. It was cold, and I could feel the lumpy ridges of her knuckles.

"Thank you," I said. "You are very nice." She smiled that surprising smile once more, then quick turned away and followed the little girls and their mother down the aisle.

"Did you have a nice trip?" Brownie said to me at the door. I said I did and gave him a dollar.

"Mrs. Willis is a very fine lady," he said.

"Very fine."

He took my arm and came up close to me. "She's worth twenty million," he whispered in my ear.

I nodded.

"You know the family. Oil."

"Sure," I said. "Sure."

He gave me a nod that said well there you have it, then he stepped back and said a little too loud, "It has been a great pleasure to serve you, sir. Until the next time."

As I picked up the suitcase and walked toward the two of them I could hear him talking loud to the old couple. "Not too bad a trip, was it, Mr. Phillips?"


They had a car, a big new English one. Betty opened the trunk and then watched with a sad kind of smile while I put the folder and my suitcase in. "Some drawings for Jenny?" she said.

"Yes," I said. "A few."

She closed the trunk with a thump and we got in the car. Jenny was already sitting alone in the back seat, her feet curled up under her. Betty started the car and in a minute we were going fast up the long hill out of Monterey.

"I didn't know you could drive," I said to Betty. She just smiled and wrinkled her nose at me. "And whose car is it?" I said.

"You are very curious all of a sudden," Betty said.

I shut up and looked out the window as we dropped down the other side of the hill and into the town. The houses were like expensive old cabins, all shingles and stones. I could smell the ocean as we went along under the trees in the fog. Then we were pulling into a long gravel driveway with flowers blooming along the sides.

"Is this it?" I said, looking at her.

"This is it." She was laughing to herself as she got out.

It was a big elegant house, all made of those smooth stones that you find in the bed of a river. The stones were inside too, in the big room downstairs, and there were gas lamps on the walls like in a castle. You could have driven a team of mules through the fireplace — big iron pots in it, black hooks and chains and arms.

"You are too much for me," I said to her smartass grin.

She led me up the stone stairway to the bedrooms, then pushed open a big oak door and turned on the light. "This is yours," she said.

There was a big bed with a canopy over it. The roof of the room was sloped with the beams showing and there was a little bay with a green soft chair. The window was small and was made of diamond-shaped pieces of glass with black metal in between them.

"There is the bathroom," she said, pointing to a door next to the dresser. "Wash your horrible face and put your things away and then come down. We'll have drinks by the fire." She turned to go out, then stopped by the open door. "Why didn't you go to the doctor like you said you were going to?" she said.

"I didn't have time."

She smiled that sad secret smile, like when I was putting the folder in the car — then she turned again and went out, shutting the door quiet behind her.

I put down the suitcase and went to the window. The limb of an oak tree was right outside and the garden was below me in the fog. I could hear the ocean now, the breakers hitting the beach down the hill, and I knew that I would be able to see it when the fog cleared in the morning. There was the groaning sound of a foghorn, far, far away.

When I got downstairs they had a fire going. Betty got up and poured some whiskey over some ice for me, then went back to her deep white wicker chair by the fire. Jenny was stretched out on the couch like a lioness in the sun. She had on a long blue silk blouse with red and yellow flowers on it and some smooth sand-colored pants. I looked away from her and went to the chair across from Betty.

I took a swallow of the whiskey. It was smooth and expensive. Betty, slouched down in her chair, watched me with a wicked grin on her face. "Is this all yours?" I finally said.

She was full of mischief. "What do you think?" she said. Her eyes were bright by the fire, her face like old copper.

"I don't think anything," I said. "I wouldn't be surprised though. Is it?"

"How could it be mine? I live in a little room in a cheap Chinatown hotel." She was having a good time with me.

"Come on," I said. "Is it?"

She laughed that low laugh of hers again — but then all of a sudden her face was serious. "Of course it's not mine," she said. "Nothing is mine." She smiled a hard quick smile, then looked away from me into the fire.

"It belongs to a friend," she said after a long silent minute. "When he goes away I use it — the house, the car . . ." Her smooth face was still as she kept on looking into the fire, that mass of hair piled up high on her head like a fur hat, the fingers of one hand playing with the buttons of her blouse.

"That's nice," I said, to say something. Then, after another silence: "How often do you come?"

She seemed to revive a little, moving in her chair and looking at me again. "Two or three times a year," she said. "Whenever Jenny comes, and then sometimes I come alone."

"What do you do?"

"Oh, everything," she said, smiling now. "Walk on the beach, go on picnics, shop in the stores. Jenny paints. There is a lovely studio in back."

It was an excuse to look at Jenny. She had not moved, had not said a word, since I came down — now she just glanced up at me and smiled agreement to what Betty had said. Her long legs stretched almost to the end of the couch, her silver rings glowed in the firelight as she rested her head in the long fingers of one hand.

"Is it a good studio?" I said. "I mean is the light good?"

"Wonderful," she said in her tinkling voice.

"We'll show you in the morning," Betty said. "You might become a painter here."

"Not likely," I said, looking back at her. "That takes money."

Betty did not answer; she was looking into the fire again. Then all of a sudden she got up. "But you haven't met the man of the house yet," she said. "Would you like to meet the man of the house?" Her eyes were bright, full of mischief again.

"Might as well," I said.

I got up and followed her through the dining room and kitchen toward the back of the house. At the back door she stopped. "He has broad shoulders and lovely eyes," she said, watching me.

"Go on. Go on."

She opened the door and made a little whistle. A big black and brown dog with shoulders as promised ran through the door and, eyeing me, started rubbing against her legs. "This is Ludwig," Betty said.

"What?"

"Ludwig, Ludwig — like Beethoven."

"Oh. Sure."

She took my hand and held it down to the dog. He looked up at me through calm brown eyes and sniffed. "You can pet him now," Betty said. "He knows you." The dog stood quiet while I patted his head. He had jaws like a bear trap.

"I guess you can pretty much pick your friends with him around," I said.

"That's right." She started back toward the living room. The dog followed behind her, and then came me.

Jenny hadn't moved from the couch. The dog went straight to her and she reached down a long hand to scratch him under the chin. "It's a good Luddie," she said as he sat down on the rug by her.

We talked about the dog. He came with the house too, belonged to the friend. Betty showed me how he minded her — got the newspaper, gave it to me, went to the kitchen, came back, all when she told him to. His chest and shoulders seemed too big for his behind, but he had a lightness about him like a good heavyweight. I was glad to be on his side.

Pretty soon Betty stood up. "I get up early here," she said. "You two stay down and have another drink."

I looked at Jenny. She was staring into the fire, smiling a vague smile. She made my throat hurt.

"No," I said. "I'm worn out. We'll have a drink tomorrow."

Jenny looked over at me, still smiling but maybe just a little bit puzzled. Not disappointed or offended — just puzzled. I stood up as Betty turned and headed back toward the kitchen. "Bed, Ludwig," she said, and the big dog followed her out.

"You show me your studio tomorrow," I said to Jenny. "I'd like to see it."

She did not look at me. "Sure, you'll like it," she said softly.

I started up the stairs. "Well, good-night," I said.

"Good-night," said her little high voice behind me.


I sat by my window and waited. Wisps of fog moved through the tree outside. The foghorn moaned over the booming of the surf. Then I could hear them coming up the stairs and walking down the hall together, talking low. Two doors closed and it was quiet again. I got up from the chair and went to the bathroom to take a shower. When I got out and grabbed the towel I could see her sitting in the chair smoking.

"Where did you come from?" I said.

"Next door," she said without moving or turning around.

"I thought you were going to bed early."

"It *is* early," she said.

I put on the robe and went up behind her. There was perfume in her hair and it was down, falling down her back. I put my hands alongside her ears and my face in the hair on top of her head. She did not move, but I could feel her start, jump a little, then relax.

"You are a wicked woman," I said into her hair.

"No," she said in a soft low voice. "I am good."

I went to turn off the light and then came back to her. She stood to meet me and opened my robe with her hands. I could feel her little hard breasts against my chest, her hands like busy birds on my back, then fluttering to the front and moving up my thighs.

"Now," she said.

And after a long time she had had them all and lay there just softly smiling, moving with it, and I began the smooth strong charge — and it was like a bulldozer pushing snow over a cliff . . .

*MERLIN* ✛ The old Chevrolet, top down, swept up along the tidelands road at an even sixty-two. To our right, in the little wooded tide channels, an incredible variety of shore birds played and hunted in the morning light. On the other side of the road fishermen sat in canvas chairs and meditated upon cosmic issues while pretending to watch the tips of their planted poles. Ahead lay the junction — and the highway to the mountains. It was the fifth day.

At first she had been reluctant, unwilling to dislodge herself. "I am fine here," she had said. "I am fine here now like this and soon it will be better and I can go." Still I had no idea of what the "it" was that would be better, still that remained a vague unspoken presence between us — but by then that had become almost incidental to me, for I had begun to fear that she would leave, disappear, before it was time: before that placid equilibrium into which we had settled had truly run its course and something new, whatever that might be, had replaced it. And so I had pushed her, persuaded her — thinking that up there at least she would have to ask me if she wanted to leave, would have to expose herself to what I could summon up to say. We needed more time, I had told myself. I needed more time.

At last she had agreed, submitted — and now, now she sat with catlike contentment, narrow hands folded on her lap, as we sped past the gently turning windmills of flat valley farms, then up over the vast glistening plane of water which the spring-bursting river had spread, then down off the causeway to cross the turgid river itself, and then, Sacramento behind us, finally began the long gentle climb toward the foothills and the mirage of blue peaks beyond. It was not until we turned off the main highway and rose into the first fragrant pine woods that her pecan face began to betray the deep joyful agitation that prompted my question.

"Have you ever been to the mountains before, Betty?"

She turned toward me, glowing with wonder. "No," she said. "Never."

"Never?"

"Never."

"And how old are you?"

"Thirty-five years old," she said in a wistful voice.

We did not speak again during the two hours of hard driving that it took to reach North Yancey. The snow was gone now, melted by the late rains, but the red earth was soaked to capacity and officious rivulets crossed the road here and there with their treacherous burdens of mud and clay. Just beyond Cragen's Crossing, where the road up the north side of the canyon takes that bend to the right, I hit a slippery spot and just got control of the car when one of the log trucks came by going the other way. I felt a clammy chill from the draft as he passed.

We went through North Yancey without stopping and turned off up the long valley just as the sun kissed the rim and dropped below it. I told her that we were almost there. She gazed straight ahead and smiled, running the fingers of one hand over her dark soft cheek. Then soon we were at my turnoff and headed up the gravel road. As our rate of climb overtook the plunging sun there was light on the tops of the trees, and when we came into the clearing the cabin, standing splendidly against the darkening wall of pines, was bathed in a pool of fading sunlight that dissolved as we approached.

I pulled up by the porch and turned off the engine. "Is this it?" she said, her face glowing.

"This is it."

She was silent for a moment while her eyes, wide with wonder, feasted on the sky, the stream, the woods, with a voracious joy. Then suddenly she sprang from the car and was out and running toward the creek, hopping as she took off first one shoe and then the other. "You go in," she shouted back at me over her shoulder. "I will come in in a minute."

"You can't!" I called as I got out and took a few halting steps after her. "That water is like ice! The mosquitoes . . ." Her white blouse flew into the air as she disappeared behind a clot of willows and was gone.

Sighing, I turned slowly, walked over the soggy spring earth to the back of the cabin, and headed up the short trail to the tank. Everything was in order there. When I turned the valve at the bottom of the tank I felt the jarring rush of water down the pipe, and as I walked down toward the cabin again I could hear the sound of running water inside. I unlocked the door, turned off the water at the sink and tub, and sat down in my chair by the table. It was just as if I had been gone for a day, rather than two months. The dishes lay shining in the drainer just where I had left them that icy January morning before I locked the door and walked through shallow crunching snow to the Chevrolet, then bechained. There was no dust, no cobwebs — only the windows, streaked with the grime of a rainy spring, betrayed my absence. That sense of well-being and self-sufficiency which always accompanied my arrival stole over me once again as I stood up, fixed the burlap curtain over the doorway, and went to the cupboard in search of something with which to suitably honor another successful opening.

The fire was softly roaring in the great woodstove when I heard her light steps on the porch and looked up to see her pushing through burlap into the room, underclothes in her hand. Tiny pools of water formed around her feet; her nipples

*179*

showed wet through the white blouse. "Come over here," I said. "I seem to do nothing but dry you off."

She came to the stove and put her back to the heat as I went to the bathroom to get a towel for her. Then I filled my glass again and sat at the table while, once more, she began to dry her mass of ebony hair. Once more I watched in silence, once more I was caught up in that task as if it were the most profoundly important work in the round world . . .

"You can't be that mean," she said suddenly. She was looking at me straight, gripping her hair with one hand behind her head.

"What?" I was startled by her earnestness.

"You can't be *that* mean and musty, you stern old man." She was content to smile at my confusion.

"What?"

"I am soaking wet and this is the only warm place."

Her gently taunting voice seemed to echo as I felt my mind dive, swoop like a gull, then right itself as if on some stable underlying current. "No," I said, summoning up the smile of a patient tutor. "I am not *that* mean and musty. Rather than send you to the cold bathroom I will take some air on the porch."

As I rose and moved grimacing past her outthrust tongue to the burlap door and out onto the starbesieged porch, my mind was tumbling like a fireball . . .

It seemed like hours afterward, hours of whispering water and screeching crickets and sighing willows, when she came out through the doorway and, filling my glass from the bottle, sat down at my feet on the stairs. Her hair was in a long thick braid down her back now, and she was wearing the clothes that I had bought for her, the Norwegian sweater, the beaded moccasins.

"There is some brandy for you in the cupboard," I said.

"No, I am fine. Just the air is enough for me." That unnerving playfulness had passed from her and she was almost grave now, lips held firmly closed in a small secret smile as her eyes continued to sparkle with the novelty of her new surroundings.

*180*

"Do you like it here?" I said, watching her.

The smile broadened. "Yes. Yes, I do. It is like an island."

I did not answer; rather I simply continued to watch her, absorb her, as she sat with her arms clasped around her knees and breathed deeply in and out, her nostrils trembling a little with each breath. Finally, finally I had to look away — I lit a cigarette and gazed blankly out into the night.

"Do you come here often?" I heard her low voice say after a few moments.

"Yes," I said. "Several times a year. This is my refuge, my aerie. I come here to work out my poisons."

She was not looking at me; no, she was staring up into the sequined sky with the intentness of a stargazer. And yet that smug look seemed to steal about her mouth as she said, "And your wife, she must enjoy it here too."

When I did not answer she suddenly turned away from the sky and looked boldly at me. "Does she?" she said.

"My wife has never been here," I said into the night. She looked away again, the smug expression now in complete possession of her face.

"Then this is a secret place," she said in a hushed voice.

"Yes."

"Only we know about it, you and I." It was spoken as an affirmation.

"Yes."

She breathed deeply once more, then abruptly stood up and went inside. When she came back she had the bottle of brandy and a glass. "If you are going to drink, so am I," she said. She sat back down on the stairs, poured about two inches into her glass, and lifted the glass up to me. I tapped it with my own, then watched while she drank off about half an inch.

"There is no need for that," I said. "I always drink. It may not be good for you."

She looked up at me impishly. "Is it good for you?" she said.

"Yes, it is," I said. "It is my friend. It sharpens my vision and gladdens my heart."

"Well, it is my friend too, then. I want to be with you, where you are."

"I cannot guarantee that you will get there that way."

She laughed her low hoarse laugh, then drank off another half-inch and set her glass back down on the step. "We shall see," she said. She leaned back against the post and shut her eyes. The gaslight coming through the window made flickering shadows on her dark face as she said, "Now tell me a story."

"A story? I said. "What kind of a story?"

"Any kind. I just want to hear a story."

"Don't you want to eat some dinner first?"

"No, no," she said. "I'm not eating, I'm drinking. I need a story." Eyes closed, she smiled up into the brilliant sky.

"Who should be in this story?" I said.

"You," she said. "When you were a little boy."

"That would not be interesting to you."

"Yes, it would — and all your brothers and sisters."

"I only had one brother," I said. "Two when I was small but only one after I was ten. And one sister."

"Well, then, your brother. A story about you and your brother."

Screeching crickets filled the silence. I watched her hand go down to the glass again and raise it to her mouth. Her eyes remained closed as she took a tiny sip and then slowly lowered the glass back down to the step.

"I can tell you a story about two brothers," I finally said.

"Yes," she said. "Two brothers."

"These were twin brothers, not like my brother and I."

"Twin brothers," she repeated to herself.

"Yes, and one was tan and smooth and fair, a quiet man dwelling in tents, his mother's very darling — while the other was red and rough and shaggy, a man of the field, a skillful hunter whom his father loved because he ate of his game . . ."

Why it was that story among all stories, even that story among all those comprehended within that awesome book which begins at the beginning and ends with Joseph in his coffin in Egypt —

why it was the tale of that great hoax that came into my head I shall never know. But then, as the wind moved gently through the willows, suddenly I was telling it: that mythic tale of fraternal supplantation and maternal guile, of individual outrage justified by racial necessity, which seemed, seems, to contain within it all stories, all tales, as a crystal prism contains all colors; my cracking voice intoning it into the clamorous night as she, Betty, sat still and silent, her eyes softly closed, her lips forming a joyful but enigmatic smile as her head lay back against the railingpost. Once, perhaps twice, her dark narrow hand went down to search out the glass on the step — but then, as Rebekah's deceit approached its necessary fruition, she drew up her knees and laid her shadowed head upon them. And when at last the pitiful cry of Esau came whispering from my lips and I had cleared from my throat the half-sob that, inexplicably, always trod in its wake — then I knew that she was asleep, deeply, irretrievably asleep.

"Have you but one blessing my father? Bless me, even me also, O my father!" the crickets screamed into the swirling stars.

Hours afterward I rose from my chair and with the strange dull steadiness of inebriation lifted her weightless body from the stair. She was a sleeping child as I carried her through the burlap and, laying her gently on the bed, took the beaded moccasins from her feet and covered her with the feather quilt. I stood for a long time and, as I had done so many times before, watched the soft rise and fall of her breathing, the imperceptible movement of her delicate nostrils . . . then I turned quickly away and stumbled out through the burlap onto the porch.

The moon had come up, a thin crescent like the clipping of a silver fingernail in the brittle sky. As I leaned on the railing, watching it, nameless disquiets struggled together in my breast, tugging and pulling within me until finally, with a heaving sigh, I sank back into my chair. Then, incredibly, as the great pine forest softly roared around me, my astonished cheeks were wet with tears.

*JACOB MORSE*  **C**ome on, get up."
She was shaking
me, sitting on the edge of the bed in a coat and slacks and shaking me.

"What for?" I turned over.

"We're going to walk Ludwig on the beach. Get up." Pulling on me.

"It's still night."

"It's almost seven. Get up." She started in pulling the blankets off.

"No, no. I'll get up."

"Okay, you had better," she said. "Coffee's ready downstairs. If I have to come up here again you are in trouble. Deep trouble." She shut the door behind her and I could hear her going down the stairs.

I washed my face and put something on. When I went down she was in the kitchen looking at the newspaper and drinking coffee.

"Where's Jenny?" I said.

She looked up. "Hah. Jenny gets up for lunch. She's still growing." She poured some coffee for me and I drank it. I wasn't awake yet, and the coffee tasted strange, too hot, as it went down.

"The world is a mess," Betty said after a few minutes. She put down the newspaper and stood up. "Let's go."

The morning was clear, just a breath of cool wind moving in the big trees as we walked down the hill to the beach. In the daylight the houses, set back amongst their trees and flowering bushes, seemed even grander than before. Most of them were not big, but there was a certain distinguished feeling about them, a kind of quiet, careful gentility. In one yard an old woman in a gray plaid skirt and rainboots was working in the garden already, a straw hat pulled down low over her spectacles. I nodded as we went by, the dog behind Betty like a black and brown shadow, but she looked away and went back to her snipping.

Just before we got down to the beach there was a big grove of eucalyptus trees with a house in it made of those same smooth round stones but with a tower jutting up like a castle. I asked Betty. She said it was the house of a dead poet.

"I met a poet here last Christmas," she added after a minute. "A live one."

I looked over at her calm shining face. "Did he write you a poem?" I said.

"He might have. I should check on that."

We came to the road, then went down a cement stairway to the beach. The sand was cold and the wind cut a little as we walked down to the shore. When we reached the water she said something to the dog and he ran off up the beach. We followed, and every few minutes he would come back and wait for us — then take off again when she spoke to him, churning up the sand behind him as he ran. There was no one else on the beach that I could see.

"This is what I like to do," Betty said. She looked happy, her hands stuffed deep in the pockets of her coat as we walked along. The wind had loosened a strand of her hair and it blew across her face. "I would like to do this every day," she said.

"Why don't you?" I said. "You could live down here." I

almost said something about her being able to find the business but I kept it back.

"I would have to give up too much," she said, tucking the strand of hair behind her ear. "You can't have everything at the same time." She looked at me straight like that was supposed to mean something. It didn't, and I looked away.

Now there was another dog way down the beach, a black speck running back and forth near the water. Betty whistled and Ludwig came running back and walked behind her again. There were some birds, little long-legged white things that ran in and out with the surf, and the other dog was chasing them. As he came closer we could hear him bark, high and sharp. It was one of those square little dogs that you see on the scotch bottles. Ludwig looked tense and nervous but he kept on walking right behind Betty. We could see the little dog's master walking toward us up the beach now, an old guy in an English tweed cap smoking a long cigar.

Then all of a sudden the little dog was on us, coming in after Ludwig like a goddam kamikaze. We stopped and Betty said something to her dog and then he just stood his ground, growling but still. But the little one wouldn't take the hint — he kept on coming in and then going out and coming in again. I was yelling at him but he didn't pay any attention, and then finally he just came in and gave the big dog a good bite on his back leg. Ludwig yapped once and started after him but then Betty said something to him again and he stood still.

But then here comes the little one again, with visions of the kill no doubt. As he ran past me I planted a solid kick hard under his chest and sent him spinning out into the surf.

Now the old man was running and yelling. He went out to his dog and pulled it dripping and shivering from the water, then came charging back at us just like the dog had.

"Just what do you think you are doing, sir?" he screamed at me. He had an English accent.

"Saving your dog's life," I said.

186

"What can you possibly mean by that?" He had his face close enough for me to see the red veins in his blubbery nose.

"Suppose we had let this dog go," I said. The old guy sputtered but didn't say anything to that.

"Your dog bit him," Betty said. She knelt down to show the bite on Ludwig's leg.

"There was still no reason to kick him," the old guy said. "You could have chased him away, I was coming as quickly as I could." Betty looked up at me.

"He needed a kick," I said.

That set him off. "He needed a kick!" he screamed. "You need a kick yourself, sir!" His face was all red as he looked up at me for a second, then reared back and fetched me a rattling kick in the shin with his tennis shoe. I was a little stunned, then I sat down in the sand holding my shin and started in laughing. The old guy stood looking down at me like I had gone plain crazy, but I couldn't stop. Finally he got tired of standing there — he turned around and stamped off back the way he came, the little dog still dripping and shivering under his arm.

"This dog had better not be damaged or you will hear from me," he said over his shoulder as he went.

Through my tears I could see Betty standing quiet with her dog and looking down at me. Then the laughing had stopped and there was only the sound of the waves and the tiny figure of the old guy way up the beach.

"You are the strangest person I have ever known," Betty said with a severe kind of smile.

"Oh, come now," I said — and then I was laughing again.


We drove for lunch to a place that was like a big covered patio, with an open fireplace in the middle and little booths on the edge where they sold paintings and jewelry and things. There was a counter where you got your food, and then you took it to the table yourself. We sat by the fire and they talked about

Piscino, the painter in Mexico who Jenny was going to study with.

Jenny was all in blue, flared pants and a sweater with little silver buttons up the front. She slouched in the chair across from me and looked around the room while Betty did most of the talking. Every once in a while she would add something in that airy little voice and then Betty would be off again talking about highlights and masses and motions. The kid at the food counter was watching Jenny — a smartass Italian punk with curly sideburns. I caught him at it and glared at him until he went back to his meatloaf. Jenny saw it; she dropped her eyes and smiled when I looked at her afterward. Betty . . . you never could tell what Betty saw.

When the coffee was done Betty stood up. "Well, my dears," she said, "I cannot waste all of my precious time with you."

I asked her where she was going.

"I have other engagements, other commitments — strictly confidential. You have to see the studio and then look at that big fat folder of drawings, I have to keep my previous commitments. You are both sturdy, you can walk home."

Before I could say anything she was prancing out the door. I looked at Jenny. "She doesn't mean that she has a . . . a date, does she?"

Jenny smiled. She knew what I meant — for the first time I was sure that she knew all about that. "No," she said. "She was teasing you. She is going to see her aunt."

"She has an . . . ?" I stopped myself. "She has an aunt everywhere," I ended up saying.

"Yes." Jenny smiled vacantly out the doorway.

I watched her and was quiet until my cigarette was done. Then I got up. "Well, should we do as we were told?"

She gave me a quick smile and, gathering her legs from the seat of Betty's chair, stood up. It was like watching a fawn get up from a meadow — the same feeling of surprise when she actually made it. But then she was up and, blessing the greasy punk behind the counter with a glance, went out with me into the sun.

The wind blew the curls around her ears as we started out, hands stuffed in our coat pockets. She kept up with me easily — long loose graceful strides that took her floating over the ground like a giraffe. There were blossoms on the trees, and now and then she would stop without a word and look at one while I waited, then quick set off again, giving me a surprised little look when I caught up with her.

"You will wear an old man out," I said.

She laughed her tinkling little laugh. "I don't think so," she said.


She wanted to see the drawings right away. I got the folder from the bookcase and took them out, laid them out in three rows on the floor in front of the couch while she stood behind me watching. She didn't say anything, but when I stood up her eyes were round with looking.

"Do you want a drink?" I said. "There's a lot to look at." She shook her head no without looking at me. I left her there and went into the kitchen for a beer. My throat was dry and I couldn't keep my hands still.

When I came back she was sitting on the couch, elbows on her knees, face cradled in her hands, those long fingers with turquoise rings making a tulip as she looked at the one at her feet — Lupe at the cantina. I sat down quiet in one of the wicker chairs and drank my beer.

A long time had passed when she finally turned her eyes up on me. "Wow," she said in a soft voice. I made a stupid grin and she went back to them. It was going to be okay.


We were out in her studio. It was just like in the movies — easels and brushes and rags and skylights and canvasses stacked in the corner. She showed me some that she had done. There were one or two that I liked and I told her so.

"Do you think there is some hope then?" she said. It was all different now; her eyes watched me close.

"Some hope? I mean how should I know? I'm not a painter." She got an amused look on her face, then quick turned to put the canvasses away.

"Well, okay," she said when she was done. "Would you like to try it sometime?"

"Try it?"

"Painting. Would you like to try painting?"

"Maybe," I said. "I'd rather watch you, I think."

She made a quick smile. "Tomorrow, then."

"Tomorrow."

When we went inside Betty was back — standing there in front of the fireplace looking down at the drawings on the floor. She seemed startled, confused, when we came in the room, and she went right upstairs to change her clothes. When she came down, though, she was all right, smiling and bubbling over with chatter.

"Of course I kept my appointment," she said to me with a sly grin. "I always keep my appointments."


The next day, Friday, Betty woke me up early again. When I came down she was at the kitchen table with coffee like before, but her nose was in a book.

"You've given up newspapers?" I said, pouring my own coffee.

There was that same startled, faintly troubled expression on her face as she looked up. "Yes," she said in a vague way, and closed the book.

"This is that poet," she said. "The one I met on the beach last Christmas." She pushed the book over to me. *Meditations on Decay* it said, and then the name of the guy. It was a funny name, like a magician or something.

"I'm not much on poems," I said.

She looked serious and wrinkled her nose. "You ought to look at it, sometime when you can be alone with it," she said. "His honesty is terrifying."

I didn't know what that meant. "Sometime," I said, getting up.

On the beach Betty was quiet, subdued. There was a storm building offshore, tall black clouds gathering over the ocean to the south, and the wind blew strong against our backs as we walked along, the dog running out in front of us again. A line of pelicans flew north before the wind, just skimming the tops of the whitecaps as they went. Finally we turned, Betty not having said ten words, and walked with the wind pushing against us back to the cement stairway. The tower of the dead poet jutted up against the darkening sky like a blunt gray finger.

When we got back to the house Betty took her book and curled up with it on the floor in front of the fireplace. I made a fire and then left her there while I went up to shave. When I came down the dark mood had somehow left her. She went singing out into the garden to get some big yellow flowers, then started in clanking around the kitchen while I read old magazines by the fire. By the time Jenny came down at eleven-thirty there was a beautiful spread laid out on the table — omelettes and cold meats and cheese and some German wine that smelled like moss. Just as we sat down the rain started in pouring out of the black sky — but we were like an island of spring, all yellow flowers and wine that smelled like moss.

Then lunch was done and we were there with coffee and Betty was saying that she would be gone again that afternoon.

"Your appointment book must be pretty full to go out in this weather," I said.

"Packed," she said with a wicked grin. She went upstairs for her coat and then we heard the car start and she was gone.


The rain came down straight and hard for half an hour, then it started in to hail. Jenny and I had more coffee while hailstones like marbles clattered on the roof of the house and bounced crazily off the skylights of her studio in back. The yellow flowers left in the corner of the garden took a beating — in a minute they were flattened, their heads on the muddy ground, their stems all crooked and broken. I watched Jenny watching it, her face troubled and tight until it was over.

"Well," I said, "it has let up. Are you going to teach me to be a painter today?"

"Okay," she said, looking hard at the bright straight flowers on the table.

We went out through the littered garden, crunching the ice on the path as we went. She closed the door behind us, then plugged in a heater and put on a starchy brown smock over her blouse. I sat smoking while she got everything ready.

"You look like a painter, that's certain," I said. She smiled without looking at me and kept on with it, washing this and moving that.

"Okay," she finally said. I went over to the easel and she showed me some things, how the colors mixed and all that. Then I tried it. It was fun, but the brush kept getting away from me; I kept wanting to hold it wrong. I could feel her breathing next to me.

Finally I gave up. "You paint," I said. "I'll watch you, maybe I'll learn better that way."

She took down the canvas I had been messing with and put another one up. "I just started this the day you came," she said. It was an orange and a pitcher of water that were sitting on a table over in a corner of the studio. Bright colors.

"There is something wrong with it," she said.

It was the tablecloth. "Maybe it's the tablecloth," I said. I got up to show her and she handed the brush to me. "No, no," I said, giving it back. "I'll just tell you, I don't want to ruin it." I stood behind her and pointed, telling her, but then I had to quit. Her ear looked like something to eat.

"You have the idea," I said. "You can't paint with me looking over your shoulder." She smiled up at me, almost a shy smile, but didn't say anything. I went back to my chair.

Pretty soon she was into it deep — deep enough to make me disappear. I could look at her hard now. She held her lips like Betty did when she was concentrating on something, tight and kind of puckered, and she wrinkled the top of her nose just the same when the going was ticklish — but somehow that great calm placidity never left her, that feeling that nothing, no not even the painting she was so caught up in, was more important than being aware of and enjoying the pure experience of being herself. Those round black eyes never narrowed with effort, they only seemed to get bigger, deeper, rounder — and yet at the same time more threatening, more likely to swallow up whatever they lit on.

All of a sudden I couldn't sit still in my chair. I reached in my pocket for another smoke. She jumped a little, then smiled at me.

"I broke the spell," I said.

"Yes," she said. "But it isn't any good anyway. It isn't drawn right to start with and the things which should have some weight don't have any."

"The things aren't sitting on the table," I said. "They're touching the top of it but they're not sitting on it, not pressing down on it."

"You draw it," she said, bringing me a tablet and pencil. I did it quick, just a few strokes to show her.

"That's it," she said when I was done. Then she was looking at me with a hard bold kind of smile. "Why don't you teach me to do that?"

"Teach you? I can't teach anybody. Your teachers at the school, that painter in Mexico — they can teach you, they know something. I'm a bartender who scribbles on tablecloths. I can't teach you."

"You know more than they do," she said without taking her eyes off me.

*193*

"You are making fun."

"No, I'm not," she said, turning away. She started in washing the brushes in the sink. For a long time there was only the sound of the water.

"Besides," I finally said, "supposing I could teach you something, a day or two wouldn't be enough."

She didn't answer. I listened to the sound of the water and watched her back moving as she worked on the brushes. Then all of a sudden she had turned the water off and, straightening up, was turning toward me again. Her face was spread with that look of vague kindliness which says nothing at all, but her lips were moving.

"Mama's here," the tinkling little voice said — and the car was coming down the driveway.

*MERLIN*  ✠  The sound of running water woke me. I looked up at the ceiling until I realized where I was, then glanced over at the bed against the wall. It was empty, the quilt thrown back. Sun streamed in the window over the sink and warmed my feet in the sleeping bag.

I had an epic headache.

She came bustling out of the bathroom, dressed and scrubbed. "You are awake," she said. "I was just going for a walk."

"Go ahead, I will make some breakfast," I said, the sleeping bag still zipped up to my chin. She bent down and kissed my smooth pate, then was up and out the door.

I lay still a few more minutes before I unzipped and struggled to my feet. It was really a wonderful headache. After putting some water to heat on the little gas ring, I shuffled to the bathroom.

"The juice is going to kill you," I said to myself in the mirror.

When I came out the water was boiling merrily. I put five tablespoons of coffee in and stirred it good. When it smelled right I turned off the heat and let it sit a few minutes before I put in a cup of cold water to settle the grounds.

I filled my cup and went out to sit on the porch. The sun was just beginning to hit the stairs and I sat there in a helpless daze, willing the weakness to depart as the smell of coffee drifted up into my face. There was not a cloud. At the far end of the clearing the old lame doe was feeding by herself in the sun.

After a few minutes I saw the slight figure of Betty come out of the willows near the stream, way down, and start walking slowly toward the doe. She had her hand held out in front of her as if she had something to eat. The old doe raised her head to look and stood completely still for a surprisingly long time while the childlike form moved toward her — then she turned abruptly and hobbled into the forest. Betty stopped and watched, then started back toward the cabin. I got up from the stairs and went inside.

The ham was sizzling on the gas ring when she came in. I gave her some coffee and then started the eggs. She was a bit pensive.

"I see that you met Mazie," I said.

"Who?"

"Mazie. The old doe."

She smiled a little smile of understanding. "Oh," she said. "Yes." She resumed the wistful examination of her coffee cup, then after a moment looked up again. "She has been hurt, you know. She can't run."

I shook my head. "She has been like that for three years. I am always surprised to see her again every spring. She must be tough."

Betty looked down again at her coffee, the steam rising up to her musing face. "Does she have any fawns?" she asked after a moment.

"Last year she had one for a long time, but now it's gone." I turned the eggs and went to the cupboard for plates. "When the fawn is not with her she is always alone."

"Always alone," Betty repeated. She took a tiny sip of coffee, then put her cup down again and looked out the window.

"Watch out," I said. "The food cometh."


She did the dishes while I shaved. Her mood was gone — I could hear her singing, a little off key, over the sound of the running water. When I came out she had made the bed too and was unsuccessfully trying to fold up the sleeping bag. I shooed her away from it.

"Do you know what I want to do today?" she said when I had finished folding the bag. "Take a far hike."

"A far hike, you say."

"Yes, a far, far one. With a lunch and everything."

"That can be arranged," I said.

There was an old wicker fishing creel in the corner. We filled it with necessities and started out, heading up toward the ridge. She was in front, starting strong, and I hobbled along behind with the creel. The woods were wet and soggy and I was glad when we rose up out of them onto the sunny slopes above.

I came around a bend and she was waiting for me, sitting on a sunny rock. "I wish I had my dog," she said as I came puffing up.

"You mean Ludwig?" I said, collapsing on the rock beside her.

She looked surprised and put her hands on her hips — then she remembered. "Oh, you do know Ludwig," she said smiling.

"Yes," I said. "Noble beast."

She wrinkled her nose at me. "Well, anyway, I wish I had him," she said, starting up the path again.

We made the ridge in about an hour — even with her stopping to wait for me every few hundred yards. There was a mass of rocks on top and we climbed up among them by way of a convenient cleft apparently designed with an old man in mind. Then we were at a little level space beside the topmost rock. The narrow valley stretched out below us like a great footprint in the forest; white smoke from the mill evaporated in the frosty blue sky. Far down, a little south of the tip of the footprint, the buildings of fabled North Yancey were huddled like gravestones in a French churchyard, their tin roofs glinting in the sun. I thought of Roncesvalles, a long time ago . . .

"What a lovely calm place," she said. "It is like a fairy tale land where knights fight on horses." I nodded and kept silent, catching my breath, as she climbed up the highest rock, the copestone. Then she was up and standing straight, her narrow body outlined against the sky.

"I am at the top of the world," she said. "I am the highest one."

I found a cigarette and sat down, watching her. It was true. She was the highest one, in a country where knights fight on horses.

"Your realms are vast, my queen," I said in the most sonorous voice I could muster.

She turned toward me, smiled graciously down on me. "I owe them all to your great wisdom," said her low smooth voice.

"Merlin lives to serve you," I said, inclining my head.

I watched as the smile dissolved from her face like white smoke in the sky. Slowly she came down from the pinnacle, slowly walked over to sit beside me on my rock. Her tiny feet were like a child's next to mine, her tiny beaded feet . . .

"Let's not play that game any more," she said softly.

We opened the creel and spread our lunch out on the rock. There were three hawks working above the pine hills across the valley, and together we watched them while we ate. We were silent — that breathtaking mastery of air and sky, too wonderful even for Solomon, rendered us blissfully dumb as we dabbled in our pickles and cheese. Now and then I would turn from the hawks to watch her watching them — her lips held tight over her teeth, her eyebrows knitted with concentration. Somehow there seemed to be something more in her face than wonder; she seemed almost to be questioning those lethal soaring shapes, demanding some answer from them.

How strange, I thought — how strange that I still knew so little about her. Six days we had been together, bound in that gentle spell of silence: six days that were like a hushed interlude in our respective lives, an interlude that — although it could not last, could not endure — still showed no sign of that disintegration which would necessarily lead either to a new arrangement, a relationship capable of growth, or to . . . nothing. Who was she? Out of what time, out of what history had she stepped into this transitory silent vacuum? What had been her dreams, her events, her loves? What had been the faces, the personalities, that had shaped her? And yes, how strange, how very strange, that I could ask these questions of myself, in the abstract as it were, and yet not feel the slightest urge to put them to her. Somehow, wonder was enough. Was it that I feared, no, sensed, that with illumination would come that inevitable disintegration, the demise of our fragile polarity — and that that disintegration would indeed lead to . . . nothing?

It was in the fen of these ruminations that my brain was wallowing when I noticed that she was up again, standing above me and looking intently down at my face. Then her voice was speaking: "You are a great poet . . . ," it was saying.

"This is true," I said, interrupting her. I marveled at the rapidity with which my mind had returned to the solid ground of repartee. She, however, did not smile.

"You are a great poet; you should be able to tell me. What does it mean to be free?" She looked at me straight and hard, as if she really expected an answer. I struggled to come up with something, a bone to throw.

"It is very simple," I said. "To be free is not to be bound."

She looked away again, searching out the hawks. "Is that how you tell what something is, by saying what it is not?"

"Sometimes I do," I said. "Especially when I am drawn into philosophic disputation without prior warning."

Smiling faintly, she scuffed the toe of her moccasin on the rock. "Okay," she said. "But can you ever be not bound? Can you ever do anything freely, because you want to, without forces pulling on you and making you do it?"

I scratched my head. "There are always the forces," I said. "Being free is knowing what the forces are and deciding which to submit to and which to resist. Being bound is not doing that, but submitting to the strongest one just because it pulls hardest."

Her lips were pursed with contemplation as she looked at me again. Then, just as it seemed that she was about to say something, her face relaxed into a demure, almost girlish smile . . . and then suddenly she had turned and was headed alone down the rocky cleft. I watched her until she disappeared around the bend, then I picked up the creel and started down after her.

*JACOB MORSE*  I was in my room, snoozing in the chair, when she came in.

"Get dressed," she said. "You're taking Jenny out to dinner."

"What's wrong with you?" I said. "Why don't I take you both out to dinner?"

"I have an appointment."

"Oh, come on and stow that," I said. "Jenny told me about your aunt."

She didn't look too surprised, only a little annoyed. "Well, she's sick. I have to go over there tonight."

"Fine," I said. "We'll stay home and then all go out tomorrow night."

She didn't blink. "No. I've made a date for you with somebody."

"Screw that," I said. I was pissed. "Do you know I get a little tired sometimes of you booking up my life for me?" I got up off the bed and went into the bathroom for a drink of water. When I came back she was glaring at me like a smithy forge.

"Will you listen a minute?" she said. "Just a minute? I took two of Jenny's paintings to a man we know who has a gallery in town. When he saw them he bought them on the spot and invited us to dinner so that he could see her again and tell her about it himself. I accepted, but then I went to see my aunt and she needs me tonight. Now won't you just do this for me, just this?"

"What's wrong with tomorrow night?" I said.

"He has something else. I've already called him and he expects you to bring her now. Won't you do this for me, just this?"

She had me. "Okay," I said. "But I don't like it. You could have asked me first."

She sighed and went to the door. "Go down and make me a drink while I tell Jenny to get ready," she said.


We took the car; Betty said she would get a cab. Pretty soon we were going through a guarded gate into something named a forest on the signs but which was really just a big park for millionaires to have their houses in. The rain had stopped and it had turned almost warm. Jenny was in a long white brocaded kind of coat that buttoned up the side all the way to her neck. She opened her window a little and the wind blew her hair as we drove along quiet in the dark. Way back from the road you could see the lights of rich houses in the trees.

After a while we went down through a golf course and then into a kind of driveway where they had a guy to park your car. My new suit felt kind of wrinkled on me all of a sudden but I got out and went inside with her. There were ladies in furs, chandeliers hanging from the ceiling.

We stopped at the place for coats and she started in on all the little buttons. I stood there all fidgety, waiting, but I didn't think I should ask to help with them. When she was done I took the coat and gave it to the lady along with the overcoat that Betty had found for me in the friend's closet.

When I turned around Jenny was smiling at me in a well-here-I-am kind of way. It was a soft white skirt that went to the floor, a low knitted blue thing on top, and a pearl on a blue ribbon around her neck. I wasn't going to be a leering old man so I smiled back at her face and gave her my arm in good fatherly fashion — but as we walked to the bar there was that dryness in my throat again.

Smith was waiting for us, smiling through porcelain teeth and thick glasses. He looked Jenny up and down like she was some kind of a valuable statue, then took her hand and sat her down at the table. "I am very pleased to meet you," he said to me when she introduced us. Heavy on the very. Then the waiter was there and he was ordering, giving instructions about some drink I never heard of. The waiter knew him and listened good.

When the waiter was gone Smith sat back in his chair, interlaced his fingers in front of him, and smiled at us both like an uncle. His hands were small and thin and he had a ring with a smoky white stone on one little finger.

"Well," he said, "this is really a great pleasure." Very heavy on the really. Then he started with the how-much-you-have-grown-Jenny routine — but in a nice kind of way, the wrinkles at the corners of his eyes bunching up with listening when she tinkled some answer at him. I decided that he was all right — a gentle queer who didn't have to make a spectacle.

He knew Piscino, Jenny's painter, and they talked about him. I kept quiet, but Smith had a way of not letting me get away too much. Somehow he could always think of a question to ask me even when they were talking about somebody I didn't know and didn't give a damn about. His little eyes behind those thick glasses would turn on me and sop up whatever stupid answer I made like it was the most profound thing he had ever heard in his life. But he did most of the talking, holding his hands out in front of him and turning the white ring over and over on his finger.

Finally he told Jenny about the paintings, that he had bought them and all. She didn't say much; she seemed too surprised and happy to say much. She just rubbed the end of her nose with one long finger and looked like a little girl who has been told that she can have an ice cream cone.

"Have you seen her paintings?" Smith said to me.

"Some of them," I said.

"What do you think?" he said, turning his ring.

"About them you mean? What do I think about her paintings?"

He smiled and nodded at me.

"Nothing," I said. "I mean I don't know anything about painting. They're good, I guess. Fine."

Smith gave me a strange look over the tops of his glasses, then quick turned back to Jenny. "I think it is just plain good business," he said to her. "Now I have the first paintings that Jenny Chen ever sold. In twenty years the collectors will be bothering me night and day."

We went in to dinner. The waiter took us to a table that looked out over the golf course and down to the ocean. Jenny sat with her back to the window, the moon over her shoulder making the tops of the waves all silver behind her. I tried to keep from looking at her too much, from noticing too much the velvet swell of her breasts as she leaned forward to listen to Smith's chatter, and I found myself looking out at the ocean, the dark shapes of rocks jutting up out of the silver. But then sometimes he would not let me get away again, he would ask me some question and I would have to come back — then I could feel her eyes on me, watching me in her steady still way. Pretty soon I was clenching my hands under the table to keep them still.

Then all of a sudden he was talking about me. We had been nibbling a while on the things they brought, and all of a sudden he just looks up at me and says, "You have a great gift, Mr. Morse."

I didn't know what he was talking about and said so. Then I watched him put his fork down real slow and lace his fingers in front of him again. There was some game starting, I could feel it.

"Betty told me that I must be delicate about this," he said. "I am going to do my best."

I looked over at Jenny but she was looking at Smith to see

what he was going to say next. My hackles were rising, but he looked over at me with that porcelain smile and I shut up. I knew where the door to leave by was.

"First, I cannot emphasize too much that it was *my* idea, not hers. She merely happened to mention you when she dropped by the gallery yesterday, but then I pestered her until today she brought them by and let me see them. If there is any fault in the matter, it is certainly mine."

"See what?" I said. I knew damn well what, but it was something to say.

"Your drawings," he said. "Your magnificent drawings of the Southwest. You see, I know something about that country — I simply would not let her rest until she brought them to me, and so . . ."

"That's a lot of bullshit," I said. "I know her."

He sighed. Jenny was sitting up straight in her chair like she was about ready to grab me.

"I don't want to argue with you about that," Smith said in a quiet, tired kind of voice. "Let me say my piece and then you can leave if you want. Just let me say it."

He wasn't a bad guy in his way. Anyway I said okay and then he started in with the same quiet voice. They were good he said — he had some six-bit words he used but that's what it amounted to. He said that people should be able to see them, that they should be hung up somewhere for people to see. "You really have no right to hide them away," he said. I started to open my mouth but he saw it and went on fast, twirling the ring around his finger like a merry-go-round.

"Just let me finish," he said. "I have a proposition, a business proposition. Just listen to it and then you can talk or leave or do what you want. All right?" He arched his eyebrows up over his glasses.

"Okay," I said.

"Good. Now this is it: I would like to clear out two big rooms in my gallery for a show of your work. That would be the pencil drawings I have seen together with some others — in pen and ink if possible. Eight of the drawings I have seen I would like to buy myself but I would hang them with the rest for the show. The drawings I have seen should be priced at from fifty to one hundred fifty dollars apiece. You will sell everything you hang — I will guarantee that — and I will take ten percent or, if you prefer, a number of drawings to be agreed upon between us."

He stopped the ring. "Now I am done," he said. "That is my proposition."

I looked at Jenny. Her eyes were round like marbles.

"You can keep it," I said.

He looked straight at me and didn't say anything for a minute. "Is that your last word?" he finally said.

"That's right," I said. "You hang Jenny's pictures up in your gallery. My pictures are my own private business."

Smith sat back in his chair and sighed. "I will hang Jenny's soon enough," he said. "I want yours now. My offer is really quite . . ."

"Sorry," I said.

I looked at Jenny again. She looked stunned now, like somebody had hit her in the forehead with a rubber hammer.

Smith stood up quick. He was smiling again, completely in charge again. "Perhaps we should postpone our dessert until another time," he said. He motioned to the waiter and made a scribbling motion on the palm of his hand with a pointed forefinger. Right away the waiter came with the bill and Smith signed it without looking at the numbers. Then we all got up and went out.

At the door of the dining room Smith held his little hand out to me. "I promised to meet someone here at ten," he said. "It was a very great pleasure to meet you." The same as before, very hard on the very. Then he turned to Jenny and bathed her in smiles and compliments for a few minutes before he looked back at me.

"You will let me know if you change your mind, won't you?"

"Don't hold your breath," I said.

He made one last smile through his porcelain teeth, then turned quick and walked down the hallway.


Jenny sat silent as a stone all the way home. I wasn't in much of a mood for talking myself — it wasn't until we were out of the forest and going fast through the foggy streets of the town that I said: "Those pictures are yours, you know. You can do anything you want with them." She didn't answer at first, just looked straight ahead and let a strange sad little smile settle on her lips — then finally her voice came, soft and small: "Thank you." That was all. In a minute we were pulling into the driveway.

The house was dark. Jenny went upstairs to change her clothes and I got started making a fire. I had just got it going when the phone rang. Jenny called down to say that she would get it upstairs, so I just got a beer from the kitchen and sat down to watch the fire.

She was a long time coming down. Then finally I heard her on the stairs. "That was Mama," she said behind me. "Her aunt has a high fever and she is going to spend the night there." I didn't say anything, and then I heard her walk into the kitchen.

The buzzing started in my brain. Something was going on. Betty was . . . They were . . . But then all of a sudden I just let it pass — there was nothing to do about it, nothing but be ready when the strings started in pulling.

She came back with a big glass of port and slouched down in the other big wicker chair. She had traded her long skirt for those sand-colored pants — that was the only change I could see. Her eyes were blank as she sipped on the port, both hands holding the glass up to her face.

"Tired?" I said.

"No," she said. "I'm fine. I'm happy about my paintings."

"You should be. But you will sell a lot more. You are a real artist now."

She smiled that strange sad little smile again. "Not a bartender," she said.

So that was where it was headed. "No," I said. "Not a bartender." Her eyes on me didn't blink.

"You think that was pretty stupid, don't you?" I said.

"That's your business," she said, quick looking away into the fire.

"I made those pictures for you," I said. "Not to hang in some flit's gallery for old ladies to suck their teeth and coo over. That's something your little mother seems to have a hard time understanding."

She straightened up in the chair. Firelight played over her face and neck as she pulled her long legs up under her and sat on them. "Mama doesn't understand some things," she said in a quiet voice.

A log fell from the fire and I knelt down to fix it. When I stood up again she was watching me, those big round black eyes looking up at me. It was very low, that blue thing she had on — she was so young, so smooth. The blood started going through my head and I quick sat down in the chair again.

"When do you go back to work again?" she said after a minute.

"Monday night."

"Then we have tomorrow — for you to teach me."

"Okay," I said. "If you want. And Sunday too."

"No, not Sunday. I take the plane Sunday at noon. Back to school." She took a sip of port and watched me over the rim of the glass.

"Where's your school?" I said after a minute, to say something.

"Near Phoenix."

"Do you like it?"

"No," she said. Then, when I didn't say anything: "It's all right. I get to paint a lot."

"But you are done in a few months."

"Yes."

"And then it's off to Mexico and that old painter. That will be better."

She was looking into the fire again. "Yes," she said. "I suppose so."

"You don't sound very excited about it."

"It will be all right," she said. "I'm not too crazy about what he does. I'll be able to paint a lot."

"You have to do it yourself," I said. "When you get to a certain point nobody can teach you."

She quick looked up at me. "Who taught you?" she said.

I just snorted and she looked away again. "No one had to teach you," she said.

It was getting too heavy. I stood up and took the empty glass from her loose hand. "I'll get you a little more," I said. She gave me a quick little absent-minded smile and I went to the kitchen.

I turned on the faucet, then looked at my face in the window while the water ran cold. Yes, there was something going on — the air was ringing with it now. I didn't know what it was, where it was leading, where I was being led — but I did know what was going to happen very soon . . . And suddenly that was enough, I would worry about the rest of it afterward. My hand was shaking as I filled a glass with water and, still watching myself in the window, drank it down. Then I got her port and went back to the living room.

She was standing in front of the fire, facing it. I put the glass on the table by her chair, then stood quiet and watched her while the blood pounded in my temples. I could hear the sound of my own breathing over the crackle of the fire.

"Come," she said in a whisper.

I walked over to her and put my hands on her waist. Reaching down, she took them in her own smooth cool hands and, slowly, raised them up to her breasts. I could feel her tremble as she pushed back soft against me.

And she was like a forest in the spring rain . . .

Smith was all teeth. "I am *very* pleased," he said.

Betty stood off to one side, near his desk. "You are a wonder," he said to her. She smiled in a vague kind of way, not looking at him, and touched a black marble statue on his desk with the tips of her fingers.

"I have them right here," I said, holding the folder out to him.

"I *see*. I *see*."

"You said you wanted eight of them, to buy them."

"That's right," he said. "I'll show you which ones." He opened the folder and started through them. I watched Betty — her face was closed as she ran her fingers over the black marble thing.

"Can I take nine?" Smith said. "I'd like this one too." He held up one of the Walpi pictures.

"Sure," I said. "I'll need the money to live on while I finish the others, the ink ones."

"Of course, of course," Smith said. "I am only *too* happy." He laid the nine out on the floor. Mirabel's boy. Santiago drunk. Baca. Brent. Some Navaho ones. "I know Brent myself," he said. "A magnificent and holy woman." I nodded.

Then he was looking down at them again, his hands on his hips, the white ring sticking out. "Nine hundred for the lot," he said after a minute.

"Do you have the money here?"

He quick looked up at me, then over at Betty. She was still with the statue, her fingers resting on it. Her mind was somewhere else.

"Yes," Smith said. "Yes, of course."


"I don't see why you have to go tonight," Betty said. The waitress came with the sandwiches and I looked out the window until she was gone. Betty was looking at me hard. "You can go up on the morning bus with us, put Jenny on the plane, and we'll be back in the city by two o'clock."

"No," I said. "If I take the four o'clock bus I can see Carl tonight and he can start looking for somebody else. Tomorrow I want to find another place, where I can work better. Now that I'm into this I want to get busy. Smith says that the show can be next month if I have the pen and ink things.

She pursed her lips tight over her teeth. "Well, whatever you want," she said. "You seem to be very excited."

"I am," I said. "I am."


Wing was at the desk reading a newspaper. "You not supposed to be back yet," he said. His gold teeth flashed in the light. "Betty come too?"

"No. She'll be back tomorrow. She has to put Jenny on the plane."

"Ah."

"I want to check out in the morning," I said. "I sold some pictures and I need a bigger place now."

"Ah. Okay." He put the newspaper down soft on the desk and watched me start up the stairs. He was still looking at me when I stopped halfway up and turned back toward him.

"Can I keep your suitcase to move with?" I said. "I'll bring it back."

"Yah," he said, a puzzled expression on his wrinkled face. "Yah. Okay."


In the morning I caught the early plane to Phoenix.

*MERLIN* ✛ T hat night . . . she told it. How it, the telling, began I do not remember, but suddenly her voice, that darkly polished voice, was no longer hovering like a moth just beyond the cone of light in which I sat but was pressing in around me, assaulting me with visions of a land, a country I knew only too well: a domain where there were no knights to fight on horses, a realm of dreams and shadowed sacrifices, of conspiracy and dark betrayal. I remember the empty feel of dread lying heavy in my stomach, the metallic taste of terror in my mouth, as her images began to gather and form and, ineluctably, to summon up those others, their elder sisters, which I had tried so hard to cast into the cloudy pit of unremember. I sat huddled in the light, fumbling with some vague and futile struggle, as the voice persisted, insisted, as the images gathered, formed, summoned — until suddenly it (the feel, the taste) was dissipating, dissolving, had dissipated, dissolved, and I was no longer struggling, no longer even wincing as the images rose shadowed against the wall: her images merging, coalescing with mine and then separating again, calling up their own while mine stood silently waiting their turn until, again . . . merging, coalescing . . .

And then it was done — or at least the voice had ceased and there was only the sound of heedless crickets. I lit a cigarette and blew the smoke into the darkness as her images and mine continued their minuet in silence.

"Do you mean that you did not expect it?" I said when, after a long time, the dance was finally done. "Do you mean that you expected her to execute that commission and come out the other end the same as she had gone in?"

I was not sure that she would answer. I was not even sure that I was not alone, that I was not talking with a creature of imagination who, once she had performed the function of bringing my own visions out of their unsealed and unsealable cavern, had departed once more into the shadows.

But the voice came again. "I don't know," it said. "I thought that she could, I thought that she might. She always had a certain . . . remoteness about it."

"Suppose she had, though. Suppose she had been able to turn him around . . . in that way, and then had blithely gone her way again down that path you had carved for her. He wouldn't have gone through with it then, would he? He wouldn't have settled for that, would he? Wasn't it one or the other, wasn't it either lose her and turn him or keep her and let him go on as it was?" My questions seemed to bounce off the face of the darkness.

For a long time there was only the crickets, only that screeching silence. Then, just as I was beginning to think again that it was all imagined, all in my own head: "I don't know. It seemed worth the chance. He might have seen that he could live doing that, he might have . . ."

"But he knew that already," I said. "The man had told him that already before . . ."

"But he had said no. He had to say yes first, to try it first, before he would know. Maybe he would even have kept his word once he gave it."

I sighed into the darkness. "Too many longshots," I said.

"But there was a chance. I thought there was a good chance."

"You bet too much," I said.

"I always bet everything."

I got up to put some more wood in the stove. A blast of orange heat struck my face as I bent down to shove two pieces inside — then I shut the iron door with a clang and, turning, stood up. I could see her faintly now, sitting on the bed with her back against the wall, a rag doll propped up, and as I went back to the table and poured another inch into my glass the voice had begun again, telling now of the long bus ride to the airport, the green rounded hills slipping softly past the window as the girl had tried to explain it, justify it. She had had enough of study now, the girl had said, enough of technique. Now she had to learn to see, to learn to sense where the spark of life hides in a face, where the center of repose lies in a stone, where the rush of motion courses in a leaping animal. He could show her these things now as no one else could, the girl had said — he could lead her to the source and teach her to see . . .

And suddenly, as I sat still and listened to that droning deep voice, that voice of polished teak — suddenly it seemed that her face was drawn, etched, in the darkness into which I stared, but transformed now, boldly transformed by astonishment and frustration and disappointment and simple hate from the smug face of eternal menacing fecundity into another face, a face in which anguished motherhood and outraged womanhood strove together for mastery. And deeply, deeply, I gazed into that face, that strange struggling face, until all at once my mind was asking of it the questions that somehow I could not bring my lips to ask the ever-droning voice, asking . . . and then, just as it seemed about to yield the answers up to me, then it was melting, transforming again into another face: a lighter, once brighter face which, in spite of all its differences, bore that same double aspect, but somehow hardened, settled, beyond that striving into a double set of scars. But, alas, to that grave face not even my mind could put the questions . . .

And then there were only the crickets again. The images faded, vanished, and I sat alone, huddled in my cone of light. I felt a sudden chill — and then there was the whisper of moccasined feet as she came across the floor and, breaking into the cone, stood before me. That face . . .

"Love me tonight, Merlin," she said. "Love me now."


I had told her what it is to be free. She had stood atop the copestone and had surveyed her lands, where knights fight on horses. But the hawks had made her question — and I, her wise man, had told her. There had been no need to mar that bright day by telling her the rest, the difficult part. There is always time on duller days to blur sharp lines. But those days come, and it must at last be reckoned with, the difficult part: the possibility that the very act of choice that seems to distinguish freedom from bondage may itself be compelled, foreordained. For how can we ever truly know whether or not any choice we make — no matter how carefully and consciously considered — is truly "free"? How can we ever truly know whether or not that choice is in reality only a disguised submission to the strongest force? And if we cannot know that, if the act of choice may itself be an empty charade, how can we presume to choose at all?

No, I had not told her that. And yet perhaps I should have — perhaps she should have known it as she stood in that cone of light and looked intently down into my upturned face. Just as on that stormy afternoon six days before, just as then she had come with a need and offered a gift, so now she did the same — and now as then the issue was in her eyes the same: an act of choice was called for. "It is really so easy," she had said that afternoon. "It is really so easy. Keep me or send me away."

Yes, and she would have said that I did choose — for I did speak, I did utter a decision. But when, where, had that decision been made? I had honestly not considered it in the conscious part of my brain; rather I had consciously avoided considering it, had preferred to leave it on the level of torment and self-pity and outrage. I had wailed into the night of the injustice of it — that

I should now be involved in such a thing at all — and yet I had reveled in that very involvement, encouraged it, nourished it, all the while knowing that there would be a cusp, a watershed, that would demand the simple yes or no. And it had come, now it had come.

What must she have seen in my eyes? Not the anguish of decision, no, for the decision spoken then had been made, somewhere, long before; the answer was there, plain and dull and flat as a lead slug. Perhaps then the pain of announcement, the knowledge that by renouncing the gift I would deny the need and throw her back upon herself. Yes, or perhaps even the self-indulgent expression of martyrdom. But no cruelty . . . let there have been no cruelty in my eyes, in my voice . . .

"No, Betty. I am done with that."

I remember her face. It seemed almost to fall in upon itself, to collapse, as she continued looking at me, unmoving, for a long long moment before she turned and, taking her coat from a peg on the wall, walked to the door.

"Good-bye, Merlin Carson," she said out of the darkness.

I did not move — no, not even when I heard the engine start, not even when I heard the crunch of the tires on the gravel.

*CARL BATTAGLIA*  She came in by her-self and sat at the end of the bar. I finished on the phone quick and went over to her. She looked older, smaller.

"I'm back," she said.

I took her hand. "What happened?" I said. "I couldn't find you."

"I didn't want to be found. But I'm back now."

"Sure," I said. "Sure. But what happened? Was it Morse? It was Morse, wasn't it?"

She didn't say anything. Her hand was cold as a fish.

"Where's Jenny? Is she with him?"

"What if she is?" she said in a sharp voice. "I'm back. I'll take two tonight." She pulled her hand away and got up to go.

"I'll kill him," I said to her back as she went out. "If I see him again I'll kill him!"

*JACOB MORSE*  When I came into the hotel, Wing shrank down behind the desk like I was going to hit him or something. "Not here," he said. "She not here."

"Well, where is she?"

He shrugged his shoulders and looked down at his shaking hands. "Maybe working," he said. His face was all wrinkled up like a walnut.

I put his suitcase on the desk and opened it. There was only the folder inside. I took it out and shut the lid again. "Here's your suitcase," I said. "Thanks."

He didn't move to take it. "You welcome," he said in a whisper.


The cab let me out in front of her apartment. I had never been there before, inside I mean. We had walked by it once and she had showed the windows to me way up where it was but I had never been inside. I looked up at the windows now. The lights were on.

It was one of those where you push the button and talk before the door buzzes and you go in. That would be it, I thought to myself, she just wouldn't let me in. But I went ahead and pushed the button anyway. "B. Chen" the little sign by the button said.

Her voice came on right away. When I said it was me she hung up, just like I thought she would. I turned around to go but then the door was buzzing and I turned back and went in, the folder under my arm.

When I got out of the elevator I could see her standing in her doorway at the end of the hall. She was all done up for work and she looked at me cold and hard as I walked toward her. She didn't say anything — just pointed for me to go in, then came in after me and closed the door.

It was all oriental, hanging silk and bamboo screens and brass cymbals and little chicken-scratchy looking paintings on the walls. There were thick rugs with designs on them, and in the fireplace was one of those gas fires with fake logs. I just stood in the middle of the room and looked around — but then she was talking behind me.

"Say it quick," she said. "And then get out. I have somebody coming in half an hour." Her voice was like an icepick. She walked past me and sat down in a chair by the fire. I stayed standing, looking at everything.

"You're really the class whore up here," I said.

She didn't blink. "'Are you going to say what's on your mind or not?" she said, glaring up at me. "I am very busy."

"I'll bet you are," I said. "But yes, yes indeed, I'm going to say what's on my mind — then I'll leave you to John." I walked over to the little low coffee table in front of her chair and laid down the folder, then started to open it.

"Whatever you have in there you can keep," she said.

I didn't answer, just opened the folder and took out the stack of pictures.

"I don't want them," she said. "Put them away."

"You said I should give them to you instead of throwing them away. I'm giving them to you." I started to show her.

"I don't want them," she said, loud now. "If you give them to me they go straight into the fire." Her face glowed with hate.

"Okay," I said, holding them out to her — but then quick she stood up and walked over to the other side of the room. She stood there facing one of the chicken-scratchy pictures for a minute before all of a sudden she whirled around to face me again.

"Where is she?" she said, hissing like a rattlesnake.

"How should I know?" I said. "Probably in bed with something."

"Where is she? She was with you!" It was a whispered shout.

I was not going to holler with her. "She's not with me anymore," I said quiet. "She was with me just long enough to find somebody who could do it better and more often."

Her teeth were clenched, her voice even and without emphasis, as she glared at me across the room. "Oh, you bastard. Oh, how I hate you."

I got up. "Okay, that's enough," I said. "I brought you your precious pictures, now I'm going."

But then she was right in front of me, glowering up at me like a bed of coals. "Like hell you are," she hissed. "Not before you tell me. Where is she?"

I took her by the arms and pushed her hard down into the chair. "Don't get carried away," I said into her face. "I'll tell you what I want to and when." She sat still and I stepped back. "She stayed with me just six days. We had a car and traveled around, saw some friends of mine. Then we were in Taos and there was this hippie bartender with a face like a lizard. She went to get some ice one night and never came back. That's where your sweet Jenny is."

Betty sat still in the chair, her hands tight on the arms. My voice kept on. It should have stopped there but it kept on.

"And so it's all up now, Betty. You just couldn't do it. All that money and encouraging and wishing just wasn't enough. Your little Jenny is no more an artist than I am a tightrope walker. She just doesn't have it, and nothing — no, not all your money and schools, not all your faggot friends who are willing to kid her along — *nothing* will give it to her. She can't see, those big beautiful black eyes just can't see what they have to see, and nothing, *nothing* can change that. But the difference, the difference is that now she knows it — she knows what she isn't and she knows what she is. Too bad that what she is is what you spent all that money and encouraging and wishing to keep her from being."

And still my voice kept on. It should have stopped but it kept on . . .

"And so what do you do now, dear Betty? Your daughter, who you tried so hard to turn into a painter or a lady or both, has broken her brushes and gone off whoring with the gypsies. Me, who you tried to turn into some kind of Michelangelo, I am just the same mean bastard I was before. And where does that leave you, where does the great double backfire leave you? You're not the mother of a cultured lady any more, poor thing. You're not the guiding inspiration of a great artist either, poor thing. Just like the rest of us you are what you are, you are what you have always been: you're just a good journeyman whore . . ."

She had not moved through all of this, had not changed the glazed look on her face. She gripped the arms of her chair by the coffee table and looked straight ahead at a squat green candle burning in a bowl made of soapy-looking white stone.

"Unless," I went on, "unless of course you found that poet you were holding in reserve. Then maybe you can set out on another little fantasy for a while."

All of a sudden she quick looked up at me. At first there was a startled, surprised look on her face — but then that melted into a peaceful reminiscent kind of smile as she lowered her eyes again. "But I *have*," she said in a low voice. "I *have* . . . found him." She was quiet again for a minute, that dreamy look spread all over her face — then quick she looked up at me again with a flinty smirk.

"You are truly an innocent," she said, her voice oily with

contempt now. "Do you really think that your little adventure with Jenny has had such a devastating effect on me? Come on. She has been doing things like that since she was fifteen and will probably be doing them until she is eighty. I am angry, upset, disappointed every time she does it — but she has always returned to what I . . . expect of her. She will come back to me, make no mistake about that.

"And as for you, you really do amuse me. You are the vainest, yes, the *vainest* man I have ever known. Of course I tried to help you, to persuade you just to use what God has given you. Perhaps I tried too hard, perhaps I should have seen the futility of it, that your monumental vanity would not let me succeed no matter how hard I tried. I failed, and I am sorry — but it is for you I am sorry. It is you, not Jenny, who cannot see — it is you who refuse to realize how much more of you there could be if you would only let it happen. But that, as you so dearly love to point out, is your business, your own little closed private business."

She was leaning forward in the chair now, talking up at me with a hardness that I had never seen in her before. Her black eyes had me, held me, like a bug on a pin.

"But you," she went on, "you for some reason insist upon worrying about me. Don't trouble yourself, my friend. If I am just a journeyman whore, as you put it, I am a damn good one — and a rich one too. And yet I am something else on top of that; no matter how much it infuriates you, no matter how much it tempts you to talk of fairy tales and fantasies, I am something else too. If your vanity will not allow you to see that, so be it. There are others who are not so blind . . ."

I sat down in the chair opposite her. The pictures were on the rug by my feet and I picked them up, putting them on the coffee table next to the soapy white bowl with the candle in it. Betty glanced at the top one, then quick got up and stood with her back to the fire. Her face was tense, concentrated, as she went on talking.

"And so you fondly imagine that I was here, back on the job, while you were having your little dalliance in the desert. You may continue to so flatter yourself if you like — but if you had looked for me here you would not have found me. The desert may be lovely in the spring; I assure you that the mountains are breathtaking. For you see I did find the poet, I did indeed find him there . . ."

"That's your business," I said, getting up again. All of a sudden my tongue felt sour in my mouth. She stood there straight by the fire, her face a mixture of triumph and hate and . . . something else as I turned my back on her and headed for the door. I needed to get out of there, into the air.

My hand was on the knob when I heard her voice behind me, quiet and snotty: "You are forgetting your pictures." She should have known better. She should have shut up and let me go.

I stopped and turned around fast. Her eyes were mocking now, mocking me. "Those are yours," I said. "Do what you want with them. Burn them." My voice was too high.

"Well, then," she said in that voice, "if they are mine I do believe I will look at them. Slowly, calmly, she picked them up and, kneeling down on the rug beside the table, started to lay them out on the low marble top. The two Indian faces were there on top, but then she came to the others, the other ten . . .

Her face clouded as she continued to lay them out, one by one. I felt the blood pounding in my throat as I watched her dark narrow hands . . . one by one. Then they were all there on the table, the two faces underneath, the ten of Jenny laid out in two neat rows — and Betty, kneeling, was staring down at them with a wooden face.

That lovely body, so long and smooth and sure — like a lioness in the sun . . .

I remember Betty standing up quick, her arm moving, then the sting of it hitting me, the warm sticky feel of the candle wax in my hair. I went down hard, on all fours, and it was there in front of me on the rug, the soapy white bowl broken into two heavy pieces. Then she was coming, moving past me to the telephone, the door — but I caught her leg and she came down screaming. Her fingernails dug deep into my neck . . . but then I had one of the pieces in my hand and she was screaming, would not stop screaming so I hit her once with it and still she would not stop so I hit her again and she stopped but then I was still hitting her, could not stop hitting her, and I was crying and hitting her . . .

Then there was only my crying — and then it was quiet. I could smell the wax in my hair, sweet and perfumey, as I stood up. The white piece of stone, slippery now, fell out of my hand onto the rug. I did not look down.

The door started banging and I turned around just as Carl came in. He reached in his pocket for the gun and just had it out when I hit him hard in the face. He spun against the wall and dropped it, then slipped down moaning on the rug. I picked up the gun and ran out the door.

The air outside was cool like springwater. I stood on the sidewalk and gulped it in for a minute, then I threw the gun under a car and started in walking. I could feel the wax hardening in my hair as I went.

*RALPH TRESIDDER* ✤ So Ed calls me over to the District and tells me about it, what do I think I can do. Well, I know the old guy a little, have a drink with him now and again at the Grand, so I say I'll go up and give it a try. Not promising anything, don't you see, but I'll give it a try.

He is out back chopping wood when I come up. He has on that red knitted hat he always wears and he is real cheerful, asking me will I have a drink and all. I don't mind if I do, because of it being a special assignment, so we go up on the porch and he brings out the bottle. "Constable," he says — that's how he calls me all the time — "Constable, we are having a glorious autumn. Let us then drink to the glorious autumn." He talks that way sometimes. I never mind. It is kind of interesting to hear him the way he talks sometimes. He has had some education you can tell, crazy as he is.

Pretty soon he's off on some mad story or another — that might even have been the time he told about his teeth, about how they had been hurting him and he was aiming to go down to some dentist in Sacramento and have them all pulled out and then he would bring them home in a paper sack and dump them out on a stump and then get his hammer and pound them all up, just to get even with them for hurting him so long, don't you see. Me

*225*

sitting there laughing until my stomach hurts, him watching me real sly out of the corner of his eye while he jumps all around waving his arms and showing how it would be. I never met anybody could bullshit like him, never in all my days.

Anyway, after a while we have us another drink and I figure it's about time to get down to it. He sits there in his chair still as a stone and listens until I am done.

"When will they start it?" he finally says.

I tell him in the spring. "You probably won't see them at all because they'll be away up there on your north side and they'll be coming up on the road from the other side of the ridge. You might hear them a little but it will only be a month or so. They can put them up in a hurry these days, not like in the old days with wood and all. I remember once working on the raised part of Snow Mountain Ditch, up near the old Terrir Mine . . ."

He sucks on his cigarette while I tell it, then I am done and he is sitting there quiet as an owl again. Finally he up and says real slow, "What if I say no?" Crazy as he is, he isn't nobody's fool, don't you see.

I sit up straight in my chair. "Then the District will have to go to court for it and you might get more if they can scratch it up somewheres. Or you might get less. Anyway, you'll need a lawyer and it will be a lot of trouble and fuss for you."

"No trouble for me," he says, calm as you please. "My son is a lawyer. The court will give me twice what they want to give."

So there it is. I keep quiet.

"But then they won't be able to start on time, right, Constable? Might even have to wait a year."

I nod and keep quiet. He has got us. You can't fool a man who is educated.

"Somebody make a mistake down at the District?"

I nod again. We're done. Ed is going to have to face up to it.

But then the old guy is somewheres else, just staring at the whiskey in his glass. I wait. It doesn't seem to me that it should take that long to decide. I wait some more. He stares at his whiskey some more.

226

Finally I get tired. "Carson?" He gives a little jump and looks over at me, then he smiles a big wide smile.

"Okay," he says.

"Okay?"

"Okay, they can have it," he says.

"At that price?"

"Yeah."

I plaster a grin on my face and stand up. "Are you sure?" I say.

"I'm sure, Constable," he says. "Sit down and have another drink."

I do. I'm not going to argue with him.

# ✠ INTERLUDE

*MERLIN* ✠ **I**t was still dark when Mother woke us. When we were dressed and went into the kitchen, Grandfather and Father and Walter were at the table finishing breakfast. "Hurry up, boys, it's a long ride," Grandfather said. Father went out to the barn to get the Ford. Walter went with him to start milking. We ate in silence while Grandfather sat fiddling with his watch chain.

"Tell Ella that I'll be in next week with some more cherries," Mother said to Grandfather. He grunted at her, then emptied his cup and put it down clattering in the saucer.

"Hurry up, boys, it's a long ride," he said as he got up.

Mother took us out to the car and stuffed some quilts around us in the back seat. She had a bag of cookies for us to eat on the way. When we were all tucked in she went back into the house and brought out a box of cherries. She put it under the seat. "You mind now, boys," she said, "I'll ask Aunt Ella about these cherries. They are for her, not for you."

There was a little gray in the east as we started out the lane. Father and Grandfather sat silent in the front seat while we huddled in our quilts and watched the stars disappearing. We could see a light in Uncle Paul's kitchen as we went by and then headed down the long hill through the cedars. The dark schoolhouse loomed tall and lonely like a deserted castle out in the

*231*

sagebrush, but then we were past it and could see the few flickering lights of St. Joseph off to the north.

The sun was just peering over the mountains when we went through Connor. Father steered through the ruts north of town and we went on up the hill. Jack rabbits standing alongside the road looked at us curiously before they loped away into the sagebrush. We had started on the cookies already.

Grandfather and Father had begun to talk now. We sucked on our cookies and listened. Grandfather was angry. Father was not saying very much.

"I won't stand still for it," Grandfather said. "It's thievery, plain simple thievery. If they think they are going to get away with it they have another think coming."

Father was silent.

"This is how they repay me. After sixty years this is how they say thank you. Well, they won't get away with it. I won't stand still for it." His voice was strong and sharp over the chuckling of the engine. Then there was just the sound of the engine.

"It's just the new people coming," Father finally said. "They all need water and they have to get it from somewhere."

"Let them go and dig a well. If I hadn't put sixty years of my life into this valley there wouldn't *be* any town down there. The damned Indians would still be camping out down there."

Father was silent again for a long time. He was the only one who would even talk to Grandfather when he was angry, but even he didn't want to say very much.

"You know what they will do, don't you?" Father finally said.

"They can please themselves about that," Grandfather said. "I have had enough."

"You don't mean that."

We sucked on our cookies and held our breath as Grandfather turned to look straight at Father. His face was shiny and red. "When did you start telling me what I mean and what I don't mean?" he said in a low furious voice. Father looked straight ahead and did not answer, his hands tight on the big wooden steering wheel.

The sun was warm now. We folded the quilts and put them in a pile between us with the bag of cookies on top. The engine chuckled along hilariously as we watched the cloud of dust whirling behind us like a dust-devil on its side. The sun on the cookies made them warm like they had just come out of the oven.

Grandfather turned around in his seat. "Well, boys, what do you say?" he said, the sun bright on his wrinkled face. We made some smiling murmurings through the cookies and folded our hands on our laps. "You had better save some of those for coming back," Grandfather said as he turned back to the front. Arthur closed the bag and put it under the seat. "Yes, sir." When his hand came back up from under the seat there were five cherries in it. He gave me two and we ate them behind our hands, putting the pits in our pockets.

In about an hour we were coming down the hill into Rowberry. The stores had already opened and there were trucks and wagons parked along the sides of the wide dusty main street unloading things. On the bench in front of the bank old men sat in the sun with their canes and spat into the street. We stopped at the livery stable while Father talked to someone, then started up again and drove up the street to Aunt Ella's house.

She was in the kitchen canning. "They will be fine here," she said. "There won't be any lack of space for them to run in." She pointed out the kitchen window to where the sagebrush stretched all frosty green up to the foot of the mountains. Then Father put the box of cherries on the counter and they began to talk. She had got a letter from one of her sons who had gone to the war. We stood still and listened until she saw us there and shooed us out the door. "Dinner is at one," she said. "Mind you are here."

We went out in back to the treehouse that Arthur and one of Ella's boys, the one who had sent the letter, had built in the cottonwood the summer before. We climbed up and sat on the edge, our feet dangling over the side. Grandfather was still sitting straight and stiff in the car, all alone, and we watched

Aunt Ella and Father come out of the house and walk over to him. After Aunt Ella had kissed Grandfather and they had said a few words Father got in and they drove off down the street. Aunt Ella, hands on her hips, watched until they turned the corner. Then she went back into the house.

"It's a trial," Arthur said after a few silent minutes. "Grampa's going to be in a trial."

"How do you know?" I said.

"I heard them talking yesterday — down by the creek where Grampa was moving those water gates again."

I was quiet for a moment. "What's a trial?" I finally said.

Arthur looked at me with ill-concealed condescension. "It's where they ask you questions to see if you can answer them, and if you can't they put you in jail."

I digested that for a few minutes. There were some big black ants climbing in a line up the trunk of the tree and I watched them carrying things. "Are they going to put Grampa in jail?" I finally asked.

"If he can't answer the questions they are."

"Bullshit," I said.

Arthur looked at me. "You better stop talking like that," he said. "Mama almost heard you yesterday."

I stayed quiet for a while again and watched the ants. He made me mad.

"Well, if you are so smart you just tell me who is going to put our Grampa in jail. Just tell me that, smarty," I said.

"The High Council, that's who."

"Bullshit," I said.

"I'm telling you," Arthur said, "if you don't stop talking like that you are really going to get it. Dad will take you out in the orchard and whale the living daylights out of you."

He took out his new knife and started whittling on a branch. It was just to make me mad, just because he was ten now and could have a knife. I took the two cherry pits out of my pocket and threw them at a bird.

"Who is the High Council?" I said when the bird flew.

He looked at me again with that look on his face, like I was an idiot or something. Then he closed his knife and put it in his pocket. "Well," he said, "do you remember when old Caldwell and the Tanners got into that row about a horse?"

"Yeah."

"And do you remember how they all came to our house and Dad went in the parlor with them for a long time?"

"Yeah."

"Well, do you know what all that was about, why they came to see Dad?"

" 'Course I do. Do you think I'm stupid or something?"

"Why then?" Arthur said, raising his eyebrows like little tents. "Why did they?"

" 'Cause Dad's the Bishop, that's why. Old Caldwell had to keep the horse but the Tanners had to give him five dollars back."

"Okay, okay," Arthur said, looking away again. "I just wanted to see if you knew. Now — suppose instead of old Caldwell it was Dad or one of us that was in a row like that. We couldn't take it to the Bishop, could we?"

" 'Course not. Dad *is* the Bishop."

"So where would we take it?"

He had me there, but I didn't let my face show it. Sometimes he could be so damned pompous. Like now, just looking at me again with that look on his face like he was listening for an answer but didn't really expect to get one.

But I finally had to give up. "Okay, where, if you're so smart?"

"The High Council," he said with an infuriating smile.

I went back to the ants again. Some of them were carrying crumbs and sticks as big as they were. Arthur got out his knife and began stripping long pieces of bark from a branch.

"Well, Dad can't put anyone in jail," I said after a moment.

"Dad isn't the High Council," Arthur said. "He can't have regular trials like them. Besides, we don't have a jail."

After a while we came down from the treehouse and started walking through the sagebrush up toward the mountains.

Arthur said he knew where there was an Indian cave with arrowheads in it. We went along slowly, every now and then flushing some big sage hens and watching them take off into the cedars like huge whirring moths. Arthur said to watch for snakes too; our cousin that was gone to the war had got a big one out here. I walked in back of Arthur so that if anybody was going to step on a snake, it would be him.

We were almost to where the ground started rising steeply up the mountainside when Arthur stopped suddenly. I almost ran into his back. "I've got an idea," he said.

"I thought we already had an idea," I said. "I thought we were going to get some arrowheads."

"I've got a better idea," he said.

"What?"

"Let's go down to the Stake House and listen to the trial."

"You mean Grampa's trial?"

"Yeah," he said. "Let's just go down to the Stake House and listen to Grampa's trial."

It sounded like a lousy idea to me. "I bet you don't even know where that Indian cave is," I said. "You just made it up and now you want to get out of it."

"No," he said with a faraway look on his face. "I know where it is, but we can go there any time. We can't go to the trial any time."

"Well, I'm not going," I said. "You point me the way to the Indian cave and you can go anywhere you want."

Arthur kicked in the dirt with the toe of his shoe. "Well, if that's the way you feel," he said. "If you don't care whether you ever see Grampa again or not . . ."

"Wait a minute. What do you mean by that?" I said.

"Well, if they put him in jail . . ."

"They aren't going to put him in jail. They couldn't. That's just a big load of bullshit."

Arthur just shrugged his shoulders and kept on kicking in the dirt.

We started back toward town, skirting around Aunt Ella's and going down the next street. There was a boy with a bicycle and I wanted to watch but Arthur said we had to hurry. The main street was crowded with horses and wagons and cars now as we ran across and then headed down toward the Stake House.

"Just where is this jail?" I said as we walked in quickstep along the dusty sidestreet. "There's no jail in the Stake House." We had been there to Stake Conference once and had explored the building from top to bottom while Mother and Father and Walter and little Julia listened to the talking.

Arthur was thoughtful. "Well," he said, "you know that little building behind the courthouse?"

"Yeah, but that's the courthouse jail—where they put the miners when they get drunk."

"The High Council gets to use it too," Arthur said. "For special cases." I didn't consider that a very good answer but I kept quiet. We were doing this now and we were almost there.

Our new blue Ford was parked right in front of the Stake House. There were some other cars too, and three buggies. We walked right in the front door like we had some business and looked for somebody to ask.

The place seemed empty. We went into the main meeting room and the chairs were all cleared away over to the side like they were going to have a dance. "Well, there's nobody in here," Arthur said, as if I didn't have any eyes. Then we went on down the hall to where some other little rooms were. Way down at the end we could hear some talking and we went down to the door where it was. We could hear Grandfather's voice, pretty loud.

"Are you just going to walk right in?" I said.

"I guess so."

I watched to see if he could do it. "I dare you," I said.

Just then a voice called at us down the hall. Arthur, looking relieved, turned around. "What are you boys doing?" the voice said.

It was an old man with a broom in one knobby hand, slowly limping down the hall toward us.

"We want to go in," Arthur said.

"You can't," the old man said. "That's a High Council meeting."

"We know. Our grandfather's in there. We just want to go in and listen."

"Well, you can't," the old man said. "Nobody is allowed at a High Council meeting except the High Council."

"Our grandfather's not on the High Council," Arthur said.

"And people that the High Council calls before them."

"Well, we're with our grandfather," Arthur said.

"No, no," the old man said. "There's no kids allowed in there. You get on outside and wait. They will be done pretty soon."

Arthur stood his ground until the old man took his broom and swished it at us. "Go on, get along," he said angrily.

"Our grandfather's expecting us," Arthur said over his shoulder as we went down the hall.

"Git!" the old man said, waving the broom over his head.

We stood in the dust outside the front door. Arthur looked angry, but there was that certain light in his eyes. "It's not fair," he said. "To lock up a man's grandfather and not even let you see the trial." I stayed quiet and waited. I could tell by the way he looked that he wasn't about to give up so easily.

"C'mon," Arthur said after a minute. We started walking around the building toward the back, him in front and me behind  It was going to be dangerous; I could tell there was something dangerous going to happen.

All of a sudden Arthur stopped. I almost ran into his back again. "That's it," he said.

We were at the back of the building, standing knee-deep in sagebrush. Arthur was looking up at a little shed attached to the back wall. The roof of the shed, made of rough cedar shingles, sloped away from the wall — and above it there was a little window, the only one on that side. The window, hinged at the top, was slightly ajar, and if we listened hard we could hear the murmur of voices inside.

I stood still and watched while Arthur walked slowly around

the shed. The low side of the roof was much higher than we could reach and there were no windows to climb on, no gutters, no drainpipes. "There's no way," Arthur finally said. "No way at all."

"Well, maybe if we listen real hard we can hear a little," I said, looking up at his smooth solemn face. He ignored me while his brain ground on.

Then he was walking again to the low side of the shed roof. "Better than nothing," he said.

"What's better than nothing," I said, tagging after him. "What?"

"Listen," he said, "if you get on my shoulders you can get up there." He nodded his head toward the roof. "Then open the window some more so that we can hear. You can watch through the window and tell me what's going on."

"Why don't you get on *my* shoulders?" I said. "Then you can tell me. You're a better describer."

He looked down at me contemptuously. "Have you ever tried to carry me?" He was right; he was twice as big as me.

"Well, can't we hear without opening the window?" I said. "Let's listen real hard." But he was ignoring me again.

"C'mon," he said, turning his back to me and leaning down.

"I don't want to," I said.

"Come on. Don't be such a little chicken."

I climbed up on his back, then stood on his shoulders and held on to the wall as best I could while he slowly straightened up with me. Then I caught the edge of the roof and held on to it until he was standing. The edge came about to my armpits.

"It's too steep," I said. "There's nothing to grab on to. Let me down."

"I'll go on tiptoe and push your legs," Arthur said. "You'll make it. If you fall I'll catch you."

"Let me down," I said.

"C'mon. Just try it once."

I gave a little jump, then slipped down again onto his shoulders. "I mean really try it," Arthur said. "Now, when I count three you jump up as high as you can. At two I'll go on tiptoes and at three you jump. I'll be pushing up on your legs."

I didn't say anything and he started counting. At three I gave the hardest jump I could and was scrambling with my fingernails on the shingles while he pushed up on my legs and feet. Then I was up, lying flat on the shingles and breathing hard.

"Good," Arthur said.

There was a big splinter in my hand. It hurt. "I got a splinter," I said.

"Don't tell me you're going to cry."

"No," I said, turning the tears back.

"Okay. Just pull it out with your teeth," Arthur said. I did. It came out clean and whole.

"Good," Arthur said. "Now shinny up to the window. And be quiet." I did. In a minute I was up to the window, looking in.

There were a lot of people, a lot of men all sitting around a big table. Grandfather was at one end, with Father sitting behind him and a little to one side. At the other end were three men in a row with papers and books in front of them, and along both sides were more men, maybe five or six on each side. One of the men at the other end from Grandfather was talking, and Grandfather was running one hand through his yellowed white hair while he listened.

"What do you see?" Arthur said in a loud whisper. He was over at the side of the shed now, next to the building, where he could see me and the window too.

"A lot of men around a table," I said.

"Is Grampa there?"

I nodded yes.

"Well, what's happening?" He was prancing around on the ground like he had to go to the bathroom or something.

"I don't know."

"Well, listen," Arthur said. "Open up the window a little more. Real slow and just a little bit at first to see if it will stay up by itself. If anyone sees you, climb down quick and jump into the sagebrush. You won't get hurt."

I did what he said. It stayed open by itself. Their voices came out just as if we were in the room with them.

The man at the other end of the table from Grandfather was still talking. "So we will get into the formal proceedings with a reading of the charge. You will get to talk about those other things, Brother Carson, after we have gotten started. Brother Davis, please read the charge."

One of the other men at that end of the table picked up a piece of paper and read from it. " 'We the undersigned citizens and residents of Shambip and St. Joseph precincts and water owners in Shambip Creek do hereby charge Brother Lyman Carson, resident of Shambip precinct, with taking and using more than his portion of water in the above said Shambip Creek and consequently using a portion of our water, which the above said Lyman Carson refuses to give up or restore to the lawful owners.' " The man put the paper back down on the table and folded his hands. Grandfather glowered at him from under bushy white eyebrows.

Then the first man, the middle one of the three at that end of the table, was talking again. "Thank you, Brother Davis. Now, Brother Carson, you have heard the charge. I will ask you to plead to it, guilty or not guilty."

Grandfather raised his fist and brought it down hard on the table. "Not guilty, by Heaven!" Father moved his chair up closer, then he put his hand on Grandfather's sleeve.

"Lyman," the first man said, "I will not tolerate cursing in here. This is a solemn meeting of the High Council and you will conduct yourself accordingly." Grandfather seemed a little chastened. Tugging on the lapel of his coat, he sat back in the chair and was quiet.

"Now," the first man went on, "Brother Carson has heard the charge and has pleaded not guilty to it. We next proceed to the evidence. First is the report of the water master who was appointed at the meeting of the water owners." Then, while Grandfather continued to tug on his lapel, the man went over the report. It was long, all about who had how many acres on what ditch. Arthur had sat down and was leaning against the wall with his chin held in the palms of his hands. I shifted around a little to get more comfortable and he looked up at me to see that I didn't make too much noise. The sun was hot. I watched the flies buzzing around the ceiling of the room.

Then the report was done and the man was talking to Grandfather again. "Now, I should have mentioned this before," he said. "You have the right to ask for the assistance of a member of the Council to help you present your case. I will appoint whomever you choose, Brother Carson, if you wish it."

"I will present my own case," Grandfather said.

"I will even in this instance go outside the Council and appoint your son Bishop Carson."

"I will present my own case," Grandfather said more emphatically.

"Very well," the man said. "Then the remainder of the evidence in support of the charge is simply your refusal to abide by the findings of the duly appointed water master, your threats against Brothers Kincaid and Gowans when they came to fix the water in accordance with the water master's division, and your repeated removal of the gates put in by them. You may proceed to present your case, Brother Carson. You should begin, I would suggest, by indicating why you disagree with the findings of the water master's report."

Everyone sat back while Grandfather squared around in his chair and began in a soft controlled voice. "President Smith, Counselors Green and LeTourneau, members of this Council, I do not accept this report for a very simple reason: I simply do not acknowledge Nephi Gould as a properly appointed water master. I think he was not regularly appointed and I have no confidence in him as water master at all. That is why I will not accept his division of the water."

"And what fault do you find with Brother Gould's appointment?" the man at the other end said. "You were at the meeting which appointed him. About four hundred out of six hundred acres of water was represented at that meeting."

"But I opposed it!" Grandfather's composure was already gone. "Nephi Gould doesn't know water rights from wagon wheels. This report just shows it. I had one share out of eight in that creek in 1857 — and now look at this report!" He pointed with a trembling finger toward the papers at the other end of the table.

"Brother Gould was duly appointed by the meeting," the man said.

"Duly appointed for thievery!" Grandfather was up on his feet now. So was Arthur outside. Father was pulling on Grandfather's sleeve but Grandfather jerked away from him and stood glaring down at the other end of the table. "Do you think those Johnny Newcomers would choose somebody who was going to be fair?"

"Sit down, Lyman," the man said. "There is no need to get excited."

"Don't you 'Lyman' me!" Grandfather roared at him. "I changed your nappy more than once!"

Now Father was on his feet too, holding the old man's arm and talking to him in a low voice that I could not hear. The men along the sides of the table were moving their chairs around on the floor and looking confusedly at one another. Finally Father led Grandfather by the arm back to his chair and sat him down.

"What's happening?" Arthur whispered up at me.

"Nothing," I said.

Then the man was talking again in a soft, soothing kind of voice. "We know how hard this is for you, Brother Carson. We recognize and appreciate your feelings after so many years in this valley, after so much devoted service to this valley and to the church. But I wonder, can you understand how hard it is for us — who have known and respected and loved you all our

*243*

lives — to do what we have to do, what must be done, in spite of those feelings of respect and love and gratefulness. I wonder, can you imagine how it hurts me, personally, to do this." The man looked straight at Grandfather, who sat slouched in the chair, his chin resting on his chest and his eyes cast down. Father's hand still rested lightly on his sleeve.

Everybody sat quiet, waiting for Grandfather to look up, to give some kind of acknowledgement to what the man had said. But the old man did not move, did not stir, did not raise his eyes.

"Very well, I will proceed to give my decision," the man finally said. "My decision is that the charge has been fully sustained by the evidence before this Council, and that Brother Carson's right to water is, as determined by the report and findings of the water master, sixty acres of water in Shambip Creek, which is equal to but not larger than any other water right in the said creek according to the amount of acres. Further, it is my decision that Brother Carson shall pay that portion of the expenses assessed to him which have been or will be incurred in the putting in of water gates on Shambip Creek, including the water master's salary. We will take the vote of the Council."

Still Grandfather had not moved, and he remained with his chin on his chest, eyes downcast, while the Council was polled.

"The decision of the President is unanimously sustained by the Council," the man said when it was done. "There being no further business, this meeting is adjourned."

But then, as everybody began pushing their chairs back from the table, suddenly Grandfather's voice filled the room, echoing against the walls:

"I will not abide by this decision!"

The chairs stopped moving. Slowly, slowly, Grandfather raised his head and looked at them all, one by one. Then he hit the top of the table hard with the flat of his hand as he got up. "I will not abide it!" he bellowed.

Father was at his side again now, but the old man pushed by him and went to the door. When he reached it he turned around and faced them all again. His cheeks were purple with rage, his voice low and choked, as he said, "You tell those boys you send to fix the gates that they better bring their guns with them."

He turned and went out the door, leaving it open behind him. Father made a movement to follow, but then he sat down heavily in his chair again. The man at the other end of the table had his hands over his face and was rubbing his eyes with the fingers of one hand. Nobody said anything.

I watched Father for what seemed a long time, just sitting there looking down at his hands . . . but then slowly, slowly, he was raising his eyes, raising them to the window until, before I could escape, he was looking straight into my face. I could not move, and he did not — we simply looked at one another, his face not surprised or angry or even particularly interested, but just tired, just flat and gray and tired. Then, after an eternal instant, he dropped his eyes again to his folded hands.

"What's happening?" Arthur was saying as I started to crawl backwards down the roof. Then I was going too fast and I slid over the edge and went crashing backwards down into the sagebrush. I lay on my back for a moment looking at the sky and then Arthur was there and I was still alive, Arthur pulling me up, Arthur saying, "What's wrong? Did somebody see you?"

"No," I said.

"Well, let's go then," Arthur said, brushing me off. "It's all over, isn't it?"

"Yes," I said. "All over."

We ran back by shortcuts and were sitting in the treehouse when the Ford came chugging up the little lane and stopped by Aunt Ella's kitchen door. Father left Grandfather sitting straight and stiff in the car while he went into the house, then came out and walked out to us. "Come on, boys," he said without looking at us. "We're going right home."

As we passed the big red brick courthouse on the way out of town Grandfather suddenly turned to Father and pointed at it. "That's where I'm going, Walter," he said in a calm quiet voice.

245

"I'll get some justice there." Father looked straight ahead and didn't answer, but Arthur glanced over at me and nodded wisely.

Father never mentioned it to me — then or ever; not after Grandmother and the church elders had worn the old man down and he stood that day all alone on the hill above the pond and watched the gates being put in for the last time; not after the winter of '18 and its flu epidemic had closed the old man's eyes; not after that horrible spring morning two years later when the great barn that Grandfather had built with nails brought by wagon from the Missouri River disappeared in a boiling cloud of flame and took our brother Walter along with it; not after his, Father's, face had begun to cloud and darken and the new Bishop and his elders would come on Sunday afternoons and go out by the corral with him and talk for hours before they went away shaking their heads; no, not even after we, he and I, had begun that minuet of silent rage which ended with me on my back in the snow that January day and in a fast-moving boxcar the next. But I would have asked him, if he had waited I would have.

He should have waited . . .

# ✠ PART TWO

*(resumed)*

*PETER* ✠ **W**hen the report came I couldn't believe my eyes. It was right there, staring up at me. "Subject received severe concussion from a thrown object immediately previous to homicide and presently complains of visual difficulties. Possible organic damage, suggest electroencephalographic study."

It astonishes me, some of the people they let practice law. I called him up right away. First he didn't remember the case, as if he tries murder cases every day. Then he gets out the file and the report and mutters over them a while before he says: "Oh, I decided there was nothing to that. She threw the murder weapon at him, an alabaster bowl I think it was, and broke it over his head. But five seconds later he had her down and was blending her into the rug with it. That bump on the head couldn't have affected him — except to make him mad, angry you know. I tried it on straight heat of passion and just lost it, that's all. It was a bad case, you know. Sometimes the jury just wants to bring in murder first and there's nothing you can do about it. Whore and pimp cases I call them. Nothing you can do about it."

I went to see Morse. He sat quiet with the telephone while I told him, stroking his cheek with those long fingers. The heavy glasses were gone now and he had sunglasses. I could look at him.

"So it doesn't seem so bad then, is that right?" he said.

"Not so bad as it did," I said. "But don't count on it. They can think of a lot of ways to say no when that's what they want to say."

I took him through it, the part about the bowl. She had been looking at the drawings, the nude sketches of the girl, and all of a sudden she just stood up and threw it at him. "Why did she do it then?" I said. "What made her do it just then?"

He stopped stroking his cheek and was still a moment. "I don't know," he said, smiling broadly in my direction. "Maybe she didn't like the pictures." He hesitated, then abruptly turned off the smile.

"You must have seen the pictures," he said. "Maybe she didn't like them."


Yes, I had seen the pictures. As I walked out to the car, I remembered that morning, the morning that I had gone down to the Hall of Justice to examine the trial exhibits. Perhaps it had been nothing more than morbid curiosity — I recall accusing myself of that as I sat in that little room waiting for the clerk to bring them to me. I didn't really need to see them, not in order to do my job. What properly concerned me was the trial record, the typewritten record of the trial which I had at my apartment — that was where errors of law were going to be found. Yes, and so perhaps it had been just that, just a meddlesome compulsion to see the physical things that had been used, had been present, in an actual murder, where one person physically killed another. And yet, I had told myself, it could be justified, fully justified, on the simple ground of thoroughness. It was my duty to know everything about this case that I could know.

The clerk brought them in a cardboard box. "I hope you didn't have a big breakfast," he said with a smile as he closed the door. I filled and lit my pipe, then opened the box.

The two pieces of the bowl were on top, resting on her blue

silk dress. One of them was still milky white but the other, the larger one, was covered with brownish stains. I picked the pieces up and fitted them together, noticing the green wax remains of the candle that had been burning in the bowl when . . . that night. Then I put down the white piece and held just the larger stained one, tested its weight — before I quickly put it too down on the table.

Underneath the dress were three large manila envelopes, their covers marked with the numbers of the exhibits inside. The first was Morse's confession, the damning statement he had made at the police station after they had found him sitting serenely where he had told them he would be — in the lobby of that dingy Chinatown hotel. The second was what the clerk had been talking about: pictures of Betty, at the apartment and at the morgue. I looked at them all, but quickly, quickly, and put them back in the envelope. He had done such a thorough job of it. I fought off a chill and went to the last envelope. I wanted to be done with it now, to be done with it and out of there.

I remember my wonder, my astonishment, as I opened that third envelope. It was as though there had been a mistake, as though these, the drawings, did not really belong in the box at all. What were these beautiful glowing things doing in the same container with all of that savagery, all of that twisted rage? How could they be reconciled with, accommodated to, the madness of that night? And yet somehow I knew: they were at the center of it, they were its pulsing heart.

I laid them all out on the desk, the two Indian faces above, the ten of the girl below. The faces were old, wise, reflecting at once the weight of age and an ineffable joy in the presence of eternity. One was a man, an old wrinkled man with hair in long rag-wrapped braids that fell down over his chest. The other, a woman, had eyes as still as forest pools. They caught me, tugged at me, begged me to learn their secrets — but I was too impatient, I could not stay. I turned them face down on the desk to free myself from their reproach.

*251*

How can I recall, how can I describe the emotions that flooded through me then? Was it simply the beauty of the girl, the incredible passive elegance of her body? Of course, of course that . . . emotion was there, was present. It could not be otherwise. That long supple smoothness, that tension in repose, that tranquil disdain which she emanated — these affected me, gripped me. But there was something else too, something that was a part of it and yet separate from it, something which seemed to elevate that astonishing animal beauty into a kind of . . . sublimity. Could it be called execution? But no, that implies a mechanical accomplishment, a mindless representation. Rather it was a kind of participation, an involvement with the subject that seemed almost a dance, a soft ballet in which the artist and his subject moved together to create a new entity, a new being. For suddenly it was not only *she* sitting on the broad adobe windowsill and looking placidly out over the garden, not only *she* sprawling carelessly on the unmade bed with a half-peeled orange, not only *she* brushing her hair in the sun — no: it was *woman,* the patient, enduring, fruitful essence itself, the abiding heavy soil of endless regeneration and relentless fecundity . . .

A half-hour must have passed. My body heavy with exhaustion, I picked up the ten drawings and, putting them in the envelope with the two Indian faces, laid the envelope again in the bottom of the box. After the other two envelopes were in I picked up the dress, folded it, and laid it gently on top. Finally I took the two pieces of alabaster, the white and the stained, and put them in. As I closed the lid of the box I could see the blood hardened around the high embroidered collar of the dress.

*JACOB MORSE*  &#10070;   **T**he kid was lighting his pipe. I could hear it over the telephone, the little popping sound he made with his lips each time he sucked in to light it. Then it was quiet while he smoked.

We had been talking about the pictures, going over how she was looking at them when she chucked that thing at me. He had some idea that the hit on the head might have scrambled up my brains for a second and that's when I did it — some idea that they should have gone into that at the trial. It sounded like a crock to me, but he was the lawyer. Then when he was done with that he lit his pipe.

"Is it all gone now, Morse?" the kid said after a minute. "Can you see anything anymore?"

"No," I said. "I mean yes, it's all gone, and no, I can't see anything anymore."

His voice was low and serious all of a sudden. "It must be an agony for you, like a pianist losing his fingers."

"It's not bad," I said. "Kind of restful in fact. Kling is nicer to me too, leads me around soft and gentle like I was his grandmother." I made a smile in his direction.

"But for you, with your . . . ability. It must be terrible, you must feel great frustration."

I finally saw what he was talking about. "You mean the drawing. It's not so bad either. Sometimes I remember something, see something in my mind, and I want to draw it. But then I forget it pretty soon, think of something else, and it's all right again. It's not so bad. People leave me alone."

He was quiet for a minute again. Then: "You take it pretty well. It is really a tragedy . . . to lose such a great gift."

And then all of a sudden my mind was echoing, Betty's voice and the kid's running into each other, bouncing off each other, and then Smith was there too, and the tinkling voice of Jenny — and it was like a swarm, like bees swarming in my head, until it turned off, click, and there was just the kid's voice shouting in the phone. "Morse! Are you all right?"

"Sure," I said. "I just started in thinking of something."

"Well, okay. For a minute you looked like something was wrong."

"No," I said. "Nothing's wrong."

After he was gone Kling came and took me by the arm to the elevator. "What does he look like?" I said when we got back to my cell. "The kid, I mean."

"Like a fucking choir boy," Kling said, slamming the door shut behind me.

*PETER* ✣ **I** took a cab from the office. She was in front, cutting some yellow roses.

"I can't stay too long," I said. "There are some last minute things I have to do."

"Well," she said, putting the roses in the crook of her arm, "you won't have to rush off too quickly, will you? This is a big occasion."

"No. I just want to have an hour or so to review things one last time."

We walked around to the back and up the stairs. I put my briefcase on the buffet in the dining room, then called into the kitchen and asked whether she wanted a drink while she was getting it ready.

"No, thank you," she said. "Make one for yourself. There is ice for you in the study."

I went into the room that she still called the study — the little room off the dining room where Dad used to work nights and weekends. She had never changed it, had never even rearranged the furniture, although it had not been used for anything but an occasional bar for thirty years. His desk was in the same place, dusted and polished and with fresh flowers. The silver-topped inkwell shone like a mirror in its place next to the old picture of the two of them standing by his airplane. Along one wall was the old leatherbound set of Corpus Juris, hopelessly outdated now, and behind his chair by the window his history books and scrapbooks — the ones about Shambip and his grandfather — filled a low bookcase. I went to the other bookcase, the one with glass doors that held his airplane books, and got the martini makings from the top shelf. The ice bucket was there too, like she had said. When the drink was made I took it and sank into the deep leather chair in the corner.

It had only recently occurred to me that Merlin, so far as I knew, had never set foot in this room — never in the twenty-five or more years that he had lived here. The door had always been closed when I was a boy, and it was only after I was seven or so — after that awful birthday of announcement — that Mother would take me in here sometimes in the afternoon to show me Dad's things: his books and pictures, his pipes, the silver-topped crystal inkwell from a French chateau. But never Merlin, never he. It was as if the room did not exist for him, as if the paneled oak door was really just a part of the wall for him — and yet his place at the dining room table, the place where he always sat, was directly across from it, so that he always faced the door when after dinner that distracted look would come over his face and we, Mother and I, would softly excuse ourselves and leave him to his coffee and bourbon. It seemed almost as if the room were forbidden to Merlin, as if he had been excluded from it by some onerous edict. And now, as I sat in the deep leather chair across from my father's desk, suddenly I understood that edict, comprehended its terms: he, Merlin, although he had become my mother's husband, could never become what his brother had been. In a sense he was a proxy, a steward, a surrogate, who although entitled to all of the rights and privileges of his principal, lacked the stature, the substance that was necessary to real dominion — and this room, this small room in which I sat so comfortably, was the badge, the insignia of that lack. It was here that the spirit of my father, of Merlin's elder brother, remained and endured — among the things that were important and dear to him.

256

But no, I thought, perhaps there was nothing to that. For there was that other room, the bleak maid's bedroom next to the kitchen that Mother used to store furniture — I had never seen him in there either, never in all that time . . .

"Peter. I wondered where you were." Mother, her slight but compact figure in the doorway, her old-woman shoes flat on the polished floor.

"Right here," I said. "Next to the booze."

She smiled vaguely at me and then was silent for a moment, looking around the room as if she had not seen it for a long time. Then she was back to me again. "Dinner is ready," she said in a soft voice.

It was of course my dinner, the dinner she always made for me when I came. It had been my favorite meal when I was growing up, and now, because it was easy to make and sure to please, she always made it when I came to eat with her: a big roast beef, slightly overdone, roasted potatoes, pungent dark brown gravy, and a huge green salad with tomatoes and onions and artichoke hearts. I had bought a case of good Pinot Noir to leave here just so that we could have some decent wine with it, and the bottle and a corkscrew were by my place at the table. I sat her down opposite me, in the place that had always been hers, and began to carve the roast.

"You have really set a table tonight," I said. Her best dishes, the English ones that had been her mother's, a lace tablecloth, her best crystal wine glasses, salt dishes with little silver spoons — even those crystal things shaped like a dog's bone to put the carving knife and fork on. It was all her best.

"This is a very special dinner," she said with a soft smile. "My son does not argue his first case before the California Supreme Court every day."

"No. But you shouldn't have reminded me of that. Now I'll start thinking of all the things I still have to do to get ready."

"I won't say another word," she said. "I don't want you to think about that tonight. You will be wonderful."

The food was good, as always — not delicate, but good. I had given up trying to persuade her to make something else for me; I had even given up trying to persuade her to take the roast out of the oven a little earlier. Besides, I rather liked it — perhaps because I had become used to it, had come to associate it with her. Several headwaiters in town would not have forgiven me if they had known, but I rather liked it all the same. As always, I ate immoderately. To please her, I told myself.

I was minding my own business, stuffing myself, when she brought it up. "Would you like to have your father's things, Peter?" she said.

I looked up stupidly from my plate, my face a mask of interrupted gluttony.

"The things in the study," she said. "His desk, the books, everything."

"Well, yes. Sometime I suppose. I hadn't thought about it. Right now they sort of . . . belong here."

"I hadn't thought about it either," she said, "until I saw you in there before dinner. You should have all those things, they should be yours now. Your father would want it, would want you to have them now, when you are almost the age he was . . ."

"I don't know. I have a desk . . . Let me think about it, where to put them. If I had a bigger apartment . . . Anyway, what would you put in there then?"

Her face was impenetrable. "My china," she said. "I need another place for my china."

"Another place? With four empty bedrooms upstairs?"

"I want it downstairs," she said brusquely.

A great uncomfortable silence hung over us for what seemed a long time. She had withdrawn behind a glazed inscrutable expression and I fell to eating again. I knew that my reaction to her suggestion had disappointed her, but I didn't know what else to say. Perhaps some day there would be a wife and a house and a place for all that, but not now, not now. The place for it now was . . .

"Are you really going to keep this place now, Mother? To live

258

here, I mean?" I heard my voice speaking it, there was no way to retrieve it.

"Of course," she said, looking curiously at me.

Why couldn't I stop? There was no need to go on. But I went on. "But Mother, five huge bedrooms. The taxes on this place alone would pay for a penthouse apartment downtown. You could be nearer me, we could see more of each other, go out to dinner . . ."

The glaze on her face had deepened, hardened. I sat still — watching her, waiting. We had not mentioned his name yet — in fact we had not mentioned it since that evening five months ago in my apartment when I came back from the cabin to find her ironing in front of the television set — but it continued to hover over us like a great moth. For that had been her justification, her excuse, before: that they were two, that in spite of his peripatetic habits they were still somehow a man and wife and needed a bigger place — her justification to me even though he would have laughed at it, scorned it. But now he was gone, there could be no doubt about it. It was a year now, and he had not budged from that cabin, had not written a single letter. The only way I knew he was alive at all was that he cashed the checks every month, regular as a clock. But he would not come back now, that was clear — and so . . .

"This is my house," Mother said. Her voice was choked, wavering. "I can afford to live here. My things are here. I will stay here."

It was enough. Something had driven me to go this far, but I was not going to twist the knife. I backed off as gracefully as I could. "That's all right too, Mother," I said. "Anyway, the subway will be done in a year or so and you can come downtown in five minutes. We will see as much as we can stand of one another then."

It was like river ice breaking up in the spring. Her face had softened already as she stood up and went to the kitchen for the coffee, and when she came back, the pot in her hand, it was as if nothing untoward had been spoken all evening.

"Where is the pie?" I said as she poured into my cup.

"Just be patient. I only have two hands."


I had two pieces of pie, the traditional cherry pie, while she watched and sipped her coffee. Then, while I was pouring some cognac for myself: "Peter?"

"Yes."

"I know you don't want to talk about it, Peter; you said you didn't. But can't you just tell me something about the case, the one you are going to argue tomorrow? It's your first one, after all, and . . . well, couldn't you tell me something that I could understand?" Her face was completely relaxed again now, soft and open and beautiful.

"Why don't you come down and listen?" I said. "It's open to the public. You could just . . ."

"No, no. That would make you nervous. Just tell me something about it."

"It wouldn't make me any more nervous than I'm going to be anyway. Besides, this isn't really the first. I have argued six cases before the Court of Appeal already."

Her eyebrows were arched with attention. "But that's not the same," she said. "This is the Supreme Court."

"Yes. This is the Supreme Court."

"Well, you can tell me that anyway. Why is this case in the Supreme Court and the others were just in the Court of Appeal?"

"This is a murder case," I said. "A case involving the death penalty."

Her eyes clouded as a confused look spread over her face. "Oh," she said. "But I suppose someone has to argue those cases too," she added after a moment.

"Yes. Someone."

She was silent again, as if she didn't know what to ask next but considered herself somehow committed to ask something. "Well, did he do it?" she finally said with some effort. "Did he kill someone?"

"Definitely."

"Then what are you arguing to them about? If he is guilty what is there to argue about?"

I smiled patiently. "Many things. Whether he should be allowed to show that he didn't have the kind of evil intent that is required for murder of the most serious kind — that, for instance."

She still looked uneasy, perplexed. "That is too hard for me to understand," she said.

I smiled again. It is always such a problem, explaining it. I took a sip of cognac and started to light my pipe.

"I can't imagine it," she said suddenly. "I just can't imagine how someone could actually kill someone else. It seems almost . . . blasphemous, or maybe sacrilegious is the word I mean. Lewd."

"They do it all the time, Mother. Dozens, maybe a hundred, every year in this city alone."

She shuddered. "I can't imagine it. I just can't imagine what would make a person do that. I just can't imagine what kind of a person could do that."

I had heard it so often, from so many people — people who like every one of us have been within a whisper of murder themselves at some time, if the instrument had only been there . . .

"I'll show you," I said. "I'll show you what kind of a person. Just an ordinary man . . ."

I got up and went over to my briefcase. The newspaper picture was there, stuck down in the bottom: sandy hair standing up, deep-set eyes without glasses then. I smoothed out the wrinkles and put it on the table in front of her. She sat perfectly still, her hands flat on the table on either side of the picture.

"Just an ordinary man," I said. "And yet, like most ordinary men, not so ordinary in everything. It turns out that he is an artist, a considerable one it seems to me. He has these gigantic hands, would make two of mine, but somehow he can take a pencil and make some of the most wonderful drawings I have ever seen, astonishing some of them. Or he *used* to be able to do that, because in the struggle that preceded the homicide he was hit on the head . . ."

And as I, who had so strongly alleged disinclination to talk about the case, went prattling on like a millrace, she sat stony still, her hands still flat on the table but the one with the emerald moving, twitching a little now and then. Finally I ran down and there was silence — just the two of us looking down at the wrinkled piece of newspaper lying on the great round table.

"Who did he kill?" she finally said in a voice that seemed to come from far away. My mind was suddenly troubled by a memory, a fleeting recall — but I could not capture it and then it was gone, dissolved.

"Just a prostitute."

"Just a prostitute," she repeated in a strange flat voice.

She was quiet a moment, her hands still resting flat, palms down, on each side of the picture. Then, slowly, she stood up. Her face seemed . . . empty.

"It is late," she said. "You have to review your notes."

"You're right. You look tired too."

"I am tired," she said. "Suddenly I am very tired."

*CLARISSA*  A dark man whom I will recognize. Every day, every morning when I lay them out he is there. For a year now, more than a year. Every morning.

And I do — oh, yes, I do indeed recognize him . . .

Is there no end, Arthur? Is there no limit to your vengeance?

*JACOB MORSE*  **I** would lie on my bunk while Tolliver, sitting on a stool in the corridor, would read them to me — spelling out the words he didn't know. "You really want me to read some more of this?" he would say. "It's a pile of horseshit." "Come back and try some more tomorrow," I would say, taking the book back through the bars.

This poet—the Indians have had people like him since the beginning of time. *Cacique* — that's the Spanish word for them. *Cacique.* Usually it's an old man, thin and stringy and tough. When the time comes they take him down into the kiva and give him a jar of water that he's not supposed to drink from. No food, no water — but every day the elders of the pueblo come and wash his feet. Four days . . . and when the four days are done the elders go down and get him, bring him out into the sun. Then everyone is there with presents, they pile them around him in heaps — jewelry, food, animals, rugs, everything. Because it is for them that he does it, for all of them: he is their stand-in, their substitute. It is his job, his profession — he is a professional penitent.

And this poet, is he an old man too? Is he thin and stringy and tough? I would like to know. I would really like to know.

*PETER* ✦ **I** never eat breakfast before a court appearance; it doesn't agree with me.

At the court building I got a Hershey with almonds from the blind lady in the lobby and went back out on the front stairs to eat it. Cars were lined up to get into the garage under the square, and people with briefcases and newspapers were streaming into the building like distracted ants. It was going to be a hot smoggy day — already the dome of City Hall was swathed in yellow haze.

When the Hershey was done I stuffed the wrapper into my pocket and went inside again. Surprisingly, I got an empty elevator. I went inside, pushed the button marked "4," and was watching the door move silently closed when suddenly there was a big briefcase in front of the electric eye. The door stopped, then opened again to admit a trim, bright, smiling man. I was noticing the perfect tailoring of his expensive suit when he looked me straight in the face and said, "How are you?" I said, "Fine," and he said, "Good," and then, "It's going to be a hot day." Then we were at the fourth floor and he insisted that I precede him out of the elevator. I had no idea who he was, but there were some bailiffs talking in the lobby connecting the judges' chambers with the courtroom and I saw them look up as he approached them.

"Good morning, Chief," they said as he passed them and disappeared through the door marked "Chambers." The Chief Justice. I hoped that he would be as friendly later in the morning.

There was no one in the courtroom but a few attorneys. I didn't know any of them so I sat down behind the rail and waited for something to happen. The massive golden state seal floated like a harvest moon on the blue draped wall behind the bench, the long elevated table behind which the judges would sit. Beneath the seal seven huge blue high-backed chairs loomed up like so many waves about to break . . .

And indeed they would, indeed they could, break — and with a crash. I had seen another fellow from my office demolished in this room by questions from the bench, had watched him strangle on his words as the merciless questions pinned him to the wall like a wriggling insect. But I had seen other arguments that day too, skillful presentations during which the judges sat silent in their soft chairs like so many purring cats. I hoped that mine would be like that, I fervently hoped it.

Now there were more attorneys and the court clerk had come in to tell us how much time we would have and ask if we wanted to reserve some of our time for rebuttal. He was a brisk business-like man who talked too fast, but there was a certain vague kindliness about him. I was sure that he liked to garden and drove an older car than he could afford. I asked for thirty minutes to open and ten for rebuttal. He smiled gently. "How about twenty and five?"

The deputy attorney general was there too — Garibaldi, the one who would argue for the state. I knew him only from his briefs, which were good, and his voice on the telephone, which was nasal and annoying. We shook hands and said that we were happy to meet each other. When he smiled his eyes twinkled behind horn-rimmed glasses and he drew up the corners of his mouth and pursed his lips as if to say that he had some great surprises in store for me.

The courtroom was filling now. Over on the right-hand side of the spectators' section I could see the judges' law clerks, all sitting together like members of a college fraternity chapter at national convention. They were a bunch of smug bastards, whispering amongst themselves so that they would not divulge any inside information. The legend was that these were the people who really decided the cases. I doubted it. My hunch was that the judges let them believe it in order to keep them happy. Over on the other side of the courtroom was a gang of students from the law school down the street. Sprinkled among the men and boys were a dozen or so of those flinty-brained women who had begun to infiltrate the profession. Two of them, one shaped like a hatchet and the other like a pear, were whispering together and pointing at an attorney who was sitting inside the rail near me. He was young, or maybe ageless, and he had a cadre of boy lieutenants who constantly consulted with him and supplied him with little-known facts. I remembered that he was to argue the first case, the one immediately before mine.

Then the courtroom was full, overflowing into standing room, and the chief bailiff, an incredibly square and powerful-looking Negro, was banging his gavel. "Please rise," he shouted, and then as the members of the court filed in through a door behind the bench, he went on with his "Oyez, oyez, oyez, the honorable Supreme Court of the State of California, sitting *en banc . . .*" and so forth. When the seven judges had settled into their thrones the square bailiff said, "Be seated, please," and it was time for business.

I had seen them, the seven members of the court, only once before — when they had eviscerated my colleague two years previously — and I remembered none of them immediately. Someone at the office had made me a chart showing how they would line up behind the bench so that I could address them by name, and I pulled it out of my pocket so that I could attach the names to the faces. The Chief Justice I recognized from the elevator; as the clerk called out the list of cases to be argued he looked out over the assembly as if he were scanning the horizon from the bridge of a battleship. To the right of the Chief Justice, and to my left as I faced him, were Mulvey, Singer, and Fox. The first, sitting immediately next to the Chief Justice, was a broad but sinewy old man whose smooth round head was innocent of hair save for two snowy tufted eyebrows, which sprang out from behind thick, almost opaque spectacles. He seemed to be dozing already — his satiny pate lay placidly against the high back of the chair and the glasses made it difficult to tell whether his eyes were open or not. Singer, sitting next to the old man, sat up in his chair like a long-necked squirrel and twitched his nose, obviously anxious to get into the fray. At the end, Fox stroked his long chin with one hand and read something on the bench in front of him.

On the other side of the Chief Justice, his left and my right, were Perth, Berliner, and Fitzgerald. Perth I almost remembered — both because he had worked my friend over pretty badly and because he was not easily forgotten. He was like a great jowly bullfrog sitting on a rock and waiting to flick out his tongue. His body had been broken by some disease, and his ponderous gray-maned head seemed to be withdrawn somewhat into his chest as he sat forward in the high-backed chair and rested his arms on the bench. The visual impression was reinforced by the aural one, for even now as the clerk read out the calendar Perth would occasionally whisper something to Berliner on his left in a hoarse croaking voice that could be heard all over the room. Berliner, round-faced and alert, listened to his elder brother with a broad pleasant smile. Finally, on the other end sat Fitzgerald, a cherubic Irishman with a perpetual expression of incredible candor on his rosy face.

When the clerk had finished calling the calendar the Chief Justice announced the first case. The lawyer sitting near me, the one whom the girls had been discussing with such interest, rose with one of his youthful assistants and, going to the counsel table, sat down on one side of the lectern. When the two opposing lawyers had seated themselves on the other side the Chief

Justice spoke the name of the first lawyer. He rose and went to the lectern, his long sensitive hands empty of books or papers. I glanced over at the larval lady lawyers, the hatchet and the pear. Their eyes were rapt with anticipation.

As it turned out, their attention was well justified. The case had to do with school financing, an attack on the constitutional validity of the age-old system based on the real property tax, and the lawyer was a consummate artist — articulate without being glib or arrogant, perfectly in command of the facts and the law. I noticed that the judges sometimes called him "Professor" when addressing him, and within ten minutes they were content to be students, putting an occasional question for no apparent purpose other than to hear him say in a different way what they so much wanted to hear. Fitzgerald, the leprechaun on the right-hand side of the bench, was taking copious notes. Singer, his eyes round with admiration, craned his long neck to avoid missing even a syllable. Even Perth, crouching over the bench like a specter, was content to lay that great maned head in the palms of his hands and silently watch the confident gestures of the phenomenon. Only Mulvey was proof against the spell — his smooth head continued to repose against the back of the chair; his eyeless face, glowing like polished pink marble in the light, was completely without expression.

When it was over I expected to hear cheering and applause. Instead, however, there was only that excited murmur which is reserved for churches and courtrooms. The law students were elated; the two girls smiled vaguely into space with the misty eyes of ecstasy.

The object of this commotion and adulation sat down in his chair with a look of reserved assurance on his intense features as the other lawyer, the lawyer for the state, came gravely to the lectern. He, the state lawyer, anticipated a difficult time; he was not disappointed. The judges, Singer and Fitzgerald leading the attack, confronted him with statistics and precedents with which he could not or would not deal. Fitzgerald especially seemed to

269

derive an almost malicious pleasure in dragging him back to the inescapable issues and rubbing his nose in them. "Now Mr. Johnson," he would say, his face bathed in that radiance of ingenuous candor, "you must not answer my question by asking me one of your own."

Finally the state lawyer crept back to his chair and the Chief Justice asked the "Professor" whether he wished to proceed with the rebuttal for which he had reserved time. The lawyer stood and, exuding respectful self-confidence, said, "Mr. Chief Justice, I know that the court has several other significant matters on its calendar this morning which will require much time and attention. I have fully stated our position and will therefore waive rebuttal." Then, amid whispers of approval exchanged among the smiling judges, he and his minions swept triumphantly from the courtroom.

My involvement in this masterful performance was cut short by the sudden realization that I was next. I gathered up my papers and made my way to the seat on the right-hand side of the lectern — hoping that some of the skill of the now departed "Professor" would be communicated to me through his chair. However, the hubbub in the courtroom did not die down immediately. I turned in the chair to see the spectators moving down the aisles and out the door. The two girls were talking together as they went out, the hatchet gesturing forcefully to the pear. I turned again toward the judges' bench. They were now sitting calmly, waiting while the bailiffs shepherded out the last of the spectators who wanted to go. When finally it was quiet again I looked back over my shoulder. The only people sitting in the spectators' section were two of the judges' law clerks — one in a wheelchair and the other, slouching in the chair beside him, a wistful-looking fellow in a drooping bow tie.

"People against Morse," the Chief Justice said, his voice sounding different in the empty room.

I got up and went to the lectern, my notes clutched in one damp hand. Fitzgerald was looking down at me intently; the others, excepting the inscrutable Mulvey, were reading. My legs were a little shaky, but I steadied them by leaning forward against the lectern.

"If the court please," I began with the timeworn rubric, "if the court please, I am Peter Carson and I represent the defendant Jacob Morse. Defendant was convicted by a jury of murder in the first degree. The same jury fixed the penalty at death. This, his automatic appeal from the ensuing judgment of conviction, is now before this honorable court. The facts are quite simple. During the evening of April 21, 1970, defendant Morse went to the apartment of . . ."

"We know the facts, Counsel. And we know the law." It was Perth, his great croaking voice coming out at me like distant thunder. "Just answer this question for us: Was this trial reduced to a farce or sham — those are the words of the *Hermion* case — was this trial reduced to a farce or sham by trial counsel's failure to look into the effect of the blow on defendant's head which he received immediately prior to the homicide?"

I held on tighter to the lectern and cleared my throat. My careful notes for an ordered presentation were beginning to look worthless already.

"I would answer that in two ways, Mr. Justice Perth," I said in a voice that I wished was steadier.

"One will be sufficient, Counsel. Yes or no."

I felt a little anger rising. If he would only let me get started. "Well, then yes," I said.

"Why?" came the rasping voice.

"First, I would quote from the same *Hermion* case to the effect that whenever trial counsel fails to make factual investigations sufficient to enable him to make informed decisions on his client's behalf, and that failure results in withdrawing a crucial defense from the case, then the defendant has not been given the assistance to which he is constitutionally entitled. Now, in this case trial counsel did not follow up the information in the psychiatrist's report to the effect that defendant had suffered a blow on the head immediately prior to the killing which might have caused brain damage — a blow which as it turns out has apparently rendered the defendant totally and permanently blind . . ."

"But Counsel . . ." Now it was Berliner, interrupting. A high voice, flat as a sheet of tin. "We have the doctor's report — the one you submitted to us stating that he is blind *now*. But that is irrelevant, isn't it? Whether he is blind *now* doesn't concern us at all, does it? It is the effect that the blow might have had prior to the murder. Your crucial defense that you say trial counsel might have developed is diminished capacity to commit the crime of murder — but that is diminished capacity *at the time of the murder,* not diminished capacity at some later time."

Suddenly it was better. The questions were coming hard, but I had the answers. I stood back from the lectern. "That is perfectly correct, Mr. Justice Berliner, perfectly correct. The only reason I mention the blindness is this: The psychiatrist's report — the one that trial counsel had before him — mentioned that the defendant complained of visual difficulties, visual difficulties which continued to increase up to the present state of total blindless. That report also indicated that the blow on the head might well have been responsible for those visual difficulties, and it recommended an electroencephalographic study in order to determine whether there was any organic brain damage as a result of the blow. I submit that any competent trial counsel, in view of these factors—*one,* a blow on the head prior to the murder; *two,* very serious aftereffects; and *three,* a recommendation by a court-appointed psychiatrist that a brain wave be taken to determine whether the blow had resulted in organic brain damage — I submit that any competent trial counsel would have had the brain wave taken to see whether its results could be the basis of a defense based on diminished capacity to harbor the intent necessary for murder. Therefore — and this is the other side of that coin — I urge that the failure to have the test taken in these circumstances deprived defendant Morse of the effective assistance of counsel which the Constitution says that he must have."

They had been listening. Now, as I ended, no question broke the silence. "Go on, Mr. Carson," the Chief Justice said in a soft voice.

"Yes, your honor," I said as I tried to find a place in my notes where I could pick up the thread. I had just found it when the smooth gentle voice of Fox came from over on the left.

"Tell me this, Counsel. We have language in many cases to the effect that a defendant cannot complain of inadequate counsel when his lawyer makes a 'tactical or strategic decision' which results in the exclusion of one defense or another. We also have language — and I think this was the point of Justice Berliner's question — that when such a decision is made it makes no difference whether, with the benefit of hindsight, it turned out to be wise or unwise . . . "

"But . . ."

"Please let me finish, Counsel. Now, in this case the lawyer has a psychiatrist's report which says — as defendant himself says in his confession — that defendant was hit on the head with the murder weapon immediately before the killing. It suggests an electroencephalogram in view of that and also in view of some visual difficulties which the defendant is experiencing. Now, it turns out that the blow was very serious, that the defendant ultimately becomes blind as a result of it — but the lawyer doesn't know that then. All he knows is that the defendant was hit on the head right before he killed the victim. Now, my question is this: Can't the lawyer, knowing only what he does, make a 'tactical or strategic decision' right there? Can't he decide that the interval between the blow and the killing was so small, so short that the effect, in terms of motivation or intent, was negligible? Now, Counsel, you may answer."

I had been tugging and pulling at the lectern, yearning to say something. The words rushed out now. "Your question was whether the lawyer could make a tactical decision that the blow was so soon before the killing that it had only a negligible effect. No, no, he can't make that decision! No! That's a medical decision, not a legal one, not a tactical one! What are his qualifications to make that decision? None! It is the doctor, after he takes the brain wave, who can say whether or not defendant's mental condition was affected in that moment of time between the blow and the killing. The lawyer is not qualified to make that decision at all!"

Fox was not convinced. "I don't think you understand me, Counsel. Couldn't the lawyer legitimately decide that *whatever* a brain wave might show, the interval was to short to have any realistic effect?"

My mouth was open, but it was Perth's voice that came rumbling out. It was not directed at me this time, however. The old man's hands gripped the front of the bench and he had pulled himself to a half-standing position so that he could see around the other judges to Fox. "How could he do that?" the voice croaked. "What if the test showed that the hit on the head scrambled his brains like an omelette?"

Fox reddened. He was about to say something in return when the crisp voice of the Chief Justice cut in. "What about this, Mr. Carson? What about this? Say the lawyer has all of these things in the psychiatrist's report — the blow on the head, concussion, visual difficulties, and all that. And say there might, there just might be a diminished capacity defense in there if he has the brain wave done. But look at the rest of the case. The obvious line of defense is that it, the killing, was done in the heat of passion — that because she hit him on the head with the alabaster bowl he became so suddenly enraged that he struck her with it and killed her. That would be manslaughter, not murder — right, Mr. Carson?"

"Right," I said.

"And that would seem to be the most obvious line of defense in a case like this, wouldn't you say? The defendant might be very happy to get off with manslaughter. Right?"

"Right," I said. I knew where he was headed.

"So here is this lawyer. He has a case designed for a heat-of-passion defense. He has the possibility of a diminished capacity defense too, just the merest possibility. But here he makes a decision, a *tactical* decision. He decides that rather than confuse the jury with a lot of psychiatrists and difficult instructions on diminished capacity, rather than do that he will try it straight and clean on the heat-of-passion approach. Can't he do that? Isn't that a permissible tactical decision?"

"No," I said. My mouth was open to say why when the soothing voice of Fitzgerald came from my right.

"Let me see if I can guess why you say that," the voice said. I looked over at his round cherubic face with its halo of wispy red hair. "Can I try to guess?"

"Yes, sir," I said. "My pleasure." They laughed, Perth's rumble echoing around the room. Even Garibaldi, sitting primly on the other side of the lectern, laughed. Too loudly, I thought.

"Well, thank you, Mr. Carson," Fitzgerald said. "You are too kind. Now, just tell me what you think of this answer. The lawyer can't make that decision, the decision to forego a possible diminished capacity defense and concentrate on heat of passion, because he doesn't know enough yet. If he did it after he got the brain wave, well that might be fine. But he does it *before.* That brain wave might show that diminished capacity was far and away the best defense, that his brains were scrambled like an omelette, as my learned brother Perth so eloquently puts it — and he would want to pursue that line of defense then. Or the test might show that there was nothing to it. But he will never know that, one way or the other, unless he has the test done. Until he does that he just hasn't reached the point where he can make a tactical decision which preserves the defendant's right to the effective assistance of counsel. Now, Mr. Carson, what do you think of that answer?"

"I couldn't have said it better myself," I said. Fitzgerald gave me a bright broad smile as the croaking thunder of Perth's laughter filled the room once more.

"Well," said the Chief Justice, still smiling, "your time is up, Mr. Carson. I'm sorry if we didn't let you say any of the things you had prepared. But let us hear now from the attorney general."

I sat down happy as Garibaldi got up, then watched as Fitzgerald and Perth and Singer pursued him mercilessly for twenty minutes. His calmness under fire was astonishing, but they gave him no rest. Throughout it all I watched Berliner. I thought that the Chief Justice would vote against me, along with Mulvey and Fox, and the other three for me. Berliner was the man in the middle — but his round intelligent face said nothing, nothing at all.

I had five minutes for rebuttal. When Garibaldi sat down, his hair not even mussed from the encounter, I stood up again. I did not want to belabor the "Professor's" approach, but I thought that I could get away with something. "If the court has any questions," I said, "I will be happy to answer them. But otherwise I will rest on my briefs and my opening remarks."

"As well as those of Justice Fitzgerald," the incredible voice of Perth added.

I gathered my papers together as the chuckling died away. "Thank you, gentlemen," the Chief Justice said. "A very instructive argument." I had already turned away from the counsel table and was headed toward the door when the voice of Berliner, flat as tin, came from behind me.

"May I ask you just one question, Mr. Carson?"

I stopped, then turned back toward the bench. "Yes," I said. "Of course."

"If you had tried this case, Mr. Carson, would you have had the brain wave taken?"

"Yes, sir," I said — but the note of uncertainty was there for everyone to hear.

*ELWIN KLING*  The warden called me in and gave me the message to take over to him.

He was asleep. I rattled the door until he woke up, then I read it to him. He sat on the edge of his bunk and scratched his head. There was smiling all over his face.

"I didn't expect it so soon," he said. "The kid said it might take six months."

"Sometimes they hurry," I said.

He just smiled at the other wall, his dark glasses shining in the light.

"But now you must be all broken up, Ellie," he said. "I know how much you were looking forward to walking me down to the smokehouse."

"I'll get over it," I said.

"Sure you will, Ellie. Sure you will."

He was still laughing when I went out.

*JACOB MORSE*  W hen they had proc-
essed me in again at San Francisco they took me to a little room
and he was there. He had been just a voice on the telephone —
now he was a hand too, a small soft hand without rings.

I sat and smoked while he talked. His voice seemed rounder,
fuller than it had before. He talked about the new trial mostly
— the lawyer who would do it, the doctors who would come to
see me. I listened as well as I could. I still couldn't quite believe
it.

Then he was done with that and was lighting his pipe, making
that little popping sound with his lips after he sucked in each
time. The smell of the smoke surprised me.

"What do you think are my chances this time?" I said when he
was done lighting it and there was just the quiet sucking sound
of his smoking.

"I don't know," he said. "The doctors might find something."

"But what if they don't? I don't think they will."

"That still doesn't mean that this jury will say what the other
one did."

"You mean they could even let me go?"

"A jury can do just about anything it wants," he said.

I was quiet a minute, sopping that up. "But I did kill her, you
know," I finally said. "They couldn't just ignore that."

278

"No," he said. "They couldn't just ignore it. But they might think that you have been punished enough already."

"What?"

"You are blind this time," he said.

"That's right, I'm blind. That's right," I said. And then I was laughing.


I heard him getting up to leave. "Wait," I said, putting my hand on the rough tweed of his coat sleeve. "You'll come back, won't you? I mean you aren't going to just turn me over to this other lawyer, this trial man, you call him?"

He didn't say anything right away. Then: "No. If you like I'll come back to see you. But just to . . . just to visit. The trial will be his business, I won't have anything to say about it. Like I said before, trials are his specialty."

"Okay. But you'll come back anyway, just to visit?"

"If you like," he said.

"Next week?"

"If you like."

I was quiet for a minute, listening to him suck on his pipe. "I've gotten used to talking to you," I finally said. Then after a second I added, "Peter."

In the silence he seemed to have gone away. I was about to say something again when his voice came low and soft. "What do they call you?" it said.

"Jay," I said. "My friends call me Jay."

Again he didn't say anything for a second, like he was thinking it over. Then: "I'll see you next week then, Jay."

"Okay," I said. "Right. I'll see you then . . . Peter."

I felt the small soft hand in mine again, then it was gone and there was only the sound of his footsteps dissolving down the corridor.

## *CLARISSA*

"You seem to spend a lot of time down there," I said. "I mean since you are not actually doing the trial."

"I am on the record as one of his lawyers. He wanted it that way. Besides, it is good for me to be there while the trial is going on. He is more comfortable, less frightened."

He finished cutting the roast and laid the knife carefully on the crystal holder. I looked into his face while he put the potatoes on our plates. Something had happened to him in the last year — he seemed less . . . young. His face was not quite as smooth, his eyes were softer, more tolerant. He had formed a nasty habit though — always stroking his cheek with one finger. Arthur used to do the same thing, or almost the same. And yet Merlin never did . . .

"It seems to make a big difference to him," Peter went on as he opened the wine. "With his blindness, you know. If he can feel someone near him, someone he knows — well, it makes him feel less isolated."

"Yes," I said. "That must be terrible."

Then there was just the clicking of knife and fork as he began to eat. I continued to watch him, to look at the lines in his strong forehead as he chewed. He would soon be a man — at thirty he might perhaps be a man.

"What do you two talk about?" I said. "I mean when you used to go to the jail to see him before the trial."

"Oh, lots of things," Peter mumbled through an enormous mouthful of food. "Experiences we have had, what we think about various things. He hasn't had much education, but he is one of those people who knows a lot anyway."

I did not answer. "Your food is getting cold, Mother," he said after a minute. I took a sip of wine and began to pick at my potatoes. The gravy was cold.

"The gravy is cold now," I said. "Don't you want me to warm it up?"

"I just want you to eat," he said, pouring himself another glass of wine. He had become a very forceful person, Peter had. I cut a piece of meat and pushed it around in the gravy.

"So you go to the trial every day, then?" I said.

"I have so far," he said. "But I will have to miss tomorrow — which is too bad because he is going to testify. There is a meeting. I did everything I could to get out of it but I couldn't. That's the breaks sometimes. I told Morse, though, and he said he would be all right."

"Yes, I am sure he will be all right," I said, getting up to warm the gravy.


I called a cab for two o'clock. A half-hour later I was standing in the blowing fog in front of the new courthouse, looking up at those stark gray sides. I held my coat closed around my neck and listened a moment to the wild flapping of the flags before I started up the gray stone steps. Pigeons were huddled in a corner of the doorway eating bread crumbs that someone had left for them.

The halls inside were crowded with desperate-looking people; I could feel their empty eyes on me as I looked for someone to tell me the way to the right courtroom. Then there was a lovely young policewoman — she took me to the elevator and then told me where to go when I got off. As I was waiting for the elevator a Negro woman with two young children and one in her arms came up and stood beside me. One of the children, a boy of about five with a cap of curly black hair, did not take his eyes off me until the elevator came. Then we all got in, they and I. When the car stopped at the third floor and I got out alone, I felt as if I had been released from a cage. I was so afraid . . .

I walked down the hall to the courtroom and went inside through the swinging doors. There were only a few people in the audience and I was able to sit alone in the back row. I could see him, the back of his large head, at one of the tables just inside the rail. The lawyer, Peter's friend, was questioning a doctor who was in the witness box, and some reporters in the front row were busily writing on their pads. The people in the jury box seemed so intent, so concerned, as the doctor, a young Arabian-looking man, answered the questions — but then the other lawyer, the district attorney, made an objection in a loud metallic voice and everything stopped while the lawyers talked to the judge. The doctor looked impatient; as they argued back and forth at the judge's bench he tapped the ends of his fingers on the rail of the witness box.

"But your honor," the district attorney was saying, "is this a murder trial or a workmen's compensation hearing? Defendant's present condition, which Counsel insists upon parading before the jury, is simply irrelevant to the issues in this case. What brought about that condition is equally irrelevant. If Counsel is going to put on medical evidence he *must* limit it to the matter for which such evidence has been admitted — defendant's mental condition at the time of the killing. All of this other is simply a brazen attempt to appeal to the sympathies of the jury!" The district attorney was shouting now, his voice whining with frustration. Peter's friend was smiling — he did not answer.

"Yes, Mr. Sigmund," the judge finally said with a stern smile, "I must warn you again about that . . ."

Finally the doctor was done. As he walked past me and out

the door his face was tight with anger. "We will call the defendant Jacob Morse," Peter's friend said then.

I watched his, Morse's, back as he stood up, his long gangling arms hanging at his sides. Then the lawyer came and, taking him by the hand, led him past the jury to the witness box. He sat down slowly, gingerly, and then, as the oath was spoken to him, turned his blank face toward the jury. His hand covered the Bible like a great sycamore leaf . . .

Can I really say that I recognized him? No, no more than I can say that I recognized that face in the picture that Peter put before me on the table that evening last March. I simply knew. Whether it was likely that thirty years would have transformed that cap of fine yellow hair into these sparse gray-blond strands, whether it was reasonable to assume that time would have so broadened and strengthened his jaw — these things did not even occur to me. I simply knew. I would not have been more sure if those dead globes of unknown color had suddenly become again the bright green eyes which had watched me so carefully . . . that night so long ago. I would not have been less sure if he had hidden from me those enormous hands which had fondled mine so gently . . . that night . . . so long ago. Fingernails like fluted shale . . .

And as he began it, his high voice forming those hesitant but inevitable sentences, I found that I was not really listening, not really listening at all. Instead, that voice became an accompaniment to my own thoughts — a backdrop against which my mind thrust visions of a time long before that which the voice described, a time in which the voice itself had lived, had participated in an event (no: an occurrence, rather) which had doubtless been too insignificant to it to have left any trace in present memory. And yes, as the occasional word or phrase thrust itself out of the backdrop to jar those images, a strange correspondence began to assert itself, suggest itself, a vague relation beyond the mere sharing of a common character between that time and this, his time and mine. Was it simply the ambience of motive and intrigue, commission and betrayal? Was it . . . And yes, suddenly I found myself thinking of Merlin, but in a way that I so rarely thought of him — thinking that if he knew it all, and if he were here, listening, he, *he* could describe it, that correspondence, that strange relation . . .

But then, then the voice had died away, the calm high voice telling it, and the lawyer, Peter's friend, was walking slowly back to his seat at the table. I watched the district attorney rise and move toward the witness box, then listened as his hard metallic voice began to whine questions, meaningless questions. I got up to go, moving down the row of upholstered seats toward the aisle. A girl, a tall beautiful oriental girl in a smooth camel's hair suit, was sitting placidly in the aisle seat now, and I noticed her graceful fingers, covered with rings of turquoise and silver, as I moved past her and went out the door.

It was five o'clock when the cab left me in front of my house. There was just enough time before dinner to change the flowers in Arthur's study.

**JACOB MORSE**  **D**ust devils whirling around the foot of the cross . . .

He is like a crumpled rag doll, hooded head hanging limp against his chest, hump pressed tight against the splintery wood, black arms like an owl on a barn door. Dust devils . . .

Baca comes out of the morada, reaches up with the flint knife. "Blood and water!" a hoarse voice bawls. "Blood and water!" I turn to look . . . it is Betty, her head covered with a black shawl, in her hand the squat green candle, burning evenly in spite of the wind. "Blood and water!"

Dust devils . . .

Now another woman with her — young, blond, fragile. I almost recognize her . . . no, no, I do not recognize her. I watch while she and Betty weep in one another's arms, the wind making dust devils around their feet . . .

"O God! I die!"

The wind blows away the last of the cracked scream as Baca and the others come with their picks and shovels. Betty and the other woman moan and bawl as the men dig, as they take the cross down and lay it on the frozen ground, as Baca takes his knife to cut the ropes. The wind howls, the women . . .

*And then all at once it is quiet. There is no wind, no sobbing, no sound at all as Mirabel, smiling, goes to the head of the cross and slowly, carefully, takes off the hood.*

*Under the crown of wild roses . . . my face.*

*MERLIN*  When I opened the mail-box the envelope with the check was there. I stuffed it in my pocket and headed back along the ridge trail. It was a luminous autumn day.

When I reached the top of the ridge I went down to where the trail goes through the bulldozer cut now. I sat in the sun on the stack of railroad ties and looked down at the water moving smooth and swift in the new cement ditch. There was a big dry root near my foot. I threw it down. It hit with a splash, went under for a moment, then bobbed up ten feet further down, spinning in the current like a lazy country windmill.

I lit a cigarette, then took out the envelope and opened it. It was the check — but the letter was there too. *What you will surely consider a strange request. Acquitted by jury at second trial. Artist. Tragedy. Loss. Gift. Longtime admirer. Great ambition to meet. See your way clear. Understand completely if you.*

I folded the letter up again and put it in my pocket with the check. Far down the ditch the root was still there, still spinning in the current like a country windmill. Then it went into the covered portion and was gone.

# ✦ Part Three

*A little onward lend thy guiding hand*
*To these dark steps, a little further on . . .*
— SAMSON AGONISTES

*1 NOVEMBER 1971*

*PETER* ✠ W here are we now?" he
said.

"Just coming into Sacramento."

"I thought so. I can smell the river."

He sat over beside the open window and breathed deeply,
those huge hands folded in his lap like a pair of sleeping cats. In
the stiff new clothes he looked like a middle-aged sailor on leave.

"Now you are really free," I said. "When you smell that, you
know that you are really free." He said nothing, but the smile
on his face as he sat back in the seat was answer enough.

We went through Sacramento on the new elevated freeway,
then came down and began the long gentle climb toward the
mountains. The air was full of autumn. The heat of Indian
summer had gone and all of the poplars stood golden yellow
along the lanes. Even the sky looked different — higher, deeper,
bluer . . .

"You never told me what he actually said, in the letter, I
mean." We had been silent a long time, rolling along through
the drab suburbs northeast of town, and the question startled
me. I looked over at his face, so gravely calm.

"You mean Merlin? His letter?"

"Yes . . . Merlin."

"Well," I said, "he just said to come on ahead. He said it in
his own way, of course, but that's what he said."

"What do you mean, his own way?"

"Well, he clowns, he always clowns. You will see what I mean."

"Yes," Morse said. "I guess I will."

The road began to climb more steeply as we neared Auburn and the turnoff. The hills looked dry as tinder, the oaks like clouds of green against the gold. Far up ahead, seeming to rest on the hills like a great humped fogbank, the blue mountains rose into the bluer sky . . .

"Why do you call him Merlin?"

"What?" Again his voice had jarred me out of a reverie.

"Your father," he said. "Why do you call him Merlin, by his first name I mean?"

"Because he's not really my father," I said. "He's my step-father. I just say he's my father because it's . . . simpler."

"Oh." Morse raised one hand to his face and ran a finger across his cheek.

"My father was killed in the war."

"Oh," he said. "But you're not . . . you must have been just a baby."

"Yes. Merlin has been as much of a father as I've had."

He was quiet a moment. "The way you say that," he finally said, "it doesn't sound like he has been very much . . . of a father."

"No," I said. "Not much."

In the silence it seemed that there was something more to say. "How about *your* father?" I said after a moment. "Did you know your father?"

"I met him a few times," he said with a smile that seemed to register tenderness and amusement at the same time.

"A few times?"

"We didn't see him too often."

"Was he away a lot, then?"

"Yes, a lot," he said, still with that same smile. Then, after a moment: "My father was the best counterfeiter in Kansas, but he didn't know how to choose his friends."

And as we turned off the freeway and headed north into the pine hills he began to talk about his father, a reluctant farmer whose graphic genius had combined with a monumental credulity to earn him lodging at the expense of the federal government for most of his adult life. He, "the best counterfeiter in Kansas," had somehow managed to come home from the war, the first one, with a military airplane which he kept in the barn and cranked up only during the dark of the moon in order to ferry whiskey to Chicago for a local bootlegger. Morse, as he told of the miraculous exploits that grew out of this enterprising sideline, became almost giddy. I chuckled along with him, finally watching out of the corner of my eye as he raised one enormous hand to simulate the flight of the ill-fated craft as it descended, full of white lightning but empty of gas, into the forbidding waters of Lake Michigan. Then, as the description of his father's damp outrage overcame him, he took off the dark glasses and tears of laughter began to stream down his pale cheeks. "He got two bottles of the stuff out before it went down, before it sank," he gasped. "When the fishermen found him next morning, bobbing up and down in his yellow lifebelts, they thought he was dead . . . but he was only dead drunk!" Morse threw his head back and crowed like a rooster.

I drove silently while it subsided, while he dabbed at his naked eyes with a handkerchief, put on the dark glasses, and finally folded his hands again in his lap.

"Well," he said after a few minutes, "at least they can still cry."

Before long we were dropping down the long hill to the crossing, the tall grave pines casting mottled shadows on the once again calm and inscrutable face beside me. At the bottom we turned to go over the bridge. The river was low, just as it had been before, and clear as gin — but now the rusty cars were gone and there were picnickers, two couples in bathing suits on the small gravel beach downstream from the bridge. As we turned and started up the dry north side of the canyon I saw one of the girls wade out into the water, her hair blowing behind her like a yellow silk scarf in the gentle afternoon wind . . .

Merlin, his red stocking cap firmly in place, was fishing. I saw him stand up as we drove into the clearing, and he was already walking toward us, his rod in one hand and the carton of worms in the other, when we stopped in front of the cabin. "He is coming up to meet us," I said to Morse as I got out of the car. He, Morse, got out the other side and stood with his hand on the door handle while I walked a few steps toward the approaching fisherman. He looked the same, in all ways the same.

"Any luck?" I said, holding out my hand.

He tucked the carton of worms into his armpit and took my hand. *"Pas une plume,"* he said, his face a serene smiling mask.

"Did you bait your hook?"

"Not today," he said. "I thought I would save some for you."

We walked over to Morse and I introduced them. There was a strange intentness in Merlin's eyes as he looked up into that smiling blind face — but that was soon and predictably displaced by an expression of bemused wonderment as he grasped the four bony fingers that Morse held out to him. I found myself grinning slyly as they stood there in silence, Merlin looking down at their clasped hands, the great and the small, and Morse smiling vacantly over the top of the red stocking cap — but then Merlin had withdrawn his hand and was breaking the silence in his customary manner: "Well, gentlemen, shall we repair to my humble porch for a little medication? Peter's gout has been acting up again I know, and if I am not mistaken, Mr. Morse, I perceive some symptoms of chronic rumbling appendix in your own noble carriage . . ."

We walked to the porch, and after I had installed Morse in one of the chairs (there were three now I noticed, a sign of preparation) and sat in another myself, Merlin disappeared behind the burlap.

"Do you see what I mean now?" I said to Morse.

"Yes," he said, leaning back in his chair. "I see what you mean."

We sat in smiling silence as, inside, Merlin commenced his crashing search for the wherewithal. Then, just as I was becoming convinced that he had been surprised by a bear, Merlin erupted through the burlap with the bottle and glasses. He had taken off his cap and his pate shone pale in the fading light.

"Mr. Morse, how do you take it? In pills or injections?"

"Just neat, thank you," Morse said.

"For which you will flourish." Merlin pushed a glass in his direction, then poured about two inches in each of the three. I put the glass in Morse's hand and he took it down to hold in his lap. Merlin said something that sounded like "Chin, chin," and we all drank, Morse returning the glass to his lap again.

Merlin coughed. "Ah," he said, "the clouds are beginning to disperse already, those in my brain I mean. New vistas beckon, new discoveries in the wilderness of the human spirit." He took another drink. This time he did not cough. "In plain fact," he went on immediately, "in plain fact — and if you will forgive my omission of customary inquiries concerning your journey, which I am sure was delightful — I would like to open this meeting by relating to you a certain occurrence . . ." He leaned forward and put his hand on my knee, then took it quickly away again. "And you, Mr. Morse, if you will forgive me the same inquiries . . ." He glanced up at Morse, who was nodding yes and smiling broadly, then looked out again over the clearing.

"Well, gentlemen, it is simply this — a matter of absolutely no consequence, but yet one which I am all eagerness to impart. It concerns the noble mule, a creature which next to the rat and the praying mantis must surely be reckoned among the most gracious and intelligent in all of God's creation." Merlin rubbed the top of his head with the palm of his hand and went for a cigarette. "Well then — not to bore you with prologue — it happens that hardly eight hours ago, yes, this very morning, I had two other distinguished visitors at these premises. One was a brave rustic who from time to time provides me with fresh meat, in and out of season, in return for an occasional sonnet. The other was his faithful companion, a dainty Jenny mule with a nose as soft and white as dandelion fluff. These, gentlemen, are the characters." He took a long deliberate drink from his glass. "Well then, as soon as the provisions had been unloaded and secured I bade these two join me on this very porch for some small liquid to keep our voices clear. The rustic freely assented but the mule, pleading a vow of abstinence all too common in her species, declined the invitation and, there being much grass in the place, commenced to browse thereupon, occasionally scratching her hinder parts against yonder tree in an altogether fetching manner." Merlin blew out a cloud of smoke and pointed to the scraggy pine near the corner of the porch.

"Now then," he went on, "this is what transpired at that point. The good rustic and I, seated calmly on this porch and clutching our respective cups of cheer, were discussing something significant — the traditional patterns of Limoges china I believe it was — when what should rend the air but . . . what? Have you guessed it? Yes, the most magnificently musical *fart* that has ever blessed these wrinkled ears! We, the woodsman and I, both sat in wonder as it began in the low resonating tones of the register and then, building to its sputtering crescendo, ended in a gaseous peal of heartbreakingly exquisite tone and pitch. The very shingles, gentlemen, nay, the very rafters were set to trembling! Then, as we gazed in stupefaction upon her, the mule — for indeed, the musician was she — snorted from her snowy nostrils by way of coda and commenced to rub herself upon the tree. It was an astonishing performance — brilliant, marvelous, splendid, breathtaking, awe-inspiring . . . my impoverished vocabulary lacks all means for suitable encomium. I can say this, however: that we, the virtuous pathfinder and myself, observed a respectful silence and communed with our own thoughts for a full minute until its redolent memory had cleared from the air."

Merlin looked at us, from one to the other, a smile of impish triumph all over his face. He had Morse in his pocket, chuckling down into his lap like someone had been tickling him with a feather. I was smiling myself as Merlin turned brusquely away from us and carefully filled the glasses again. "Not a history of great consequence, I freely admit," he said as he poured. "And certainly not an invocation worthy of opening a convention of this importance — but nevertheless something which I had promised myself to share with you . . . with you both." He put down the bottle with a thump and sat back in his chair again.

Morse was still chuckling over on the other side. "Well, what do you say, Mr. Morse?" Merlin said after a moment. "Have you had any acquaintance with mules in your long life?"

"Yes, sir," Morse said in a breathless voice. "Some."

"I thought so. I can sense these things. But tell me this: Did any of those mules ever produce a fart of the splendor and dimension which I have related to you?"

"Yes, sir, some," Morse said, starting up again.

"Well," Merlin said, turning to me, "there you have it my boy, absolutely impeachable corroboration. Can you dare to disbelieve me now?"

"It appears I am prevented," I said.

"Yes," Merlin said, looking away.


After an hour or so had passed, laden with similar business, we adjourned to make dinner. While Merlin went out for more wood I set Morse up at the table with his glass. He asked me to describe the room to him; I did my best. Everything was about the same as before — the narrow brass bed against the wall, the bookcase filled with newspapers, the brightly swept floor. But now there was a picture — on the wall over the bed. It was El Greco's John the Baptist, a good print in a wooden frame. Even more surprising, there was a book, an actual book sitting on the top of the bookcase. I walked over quickly and picked it up. It was heavy, stoutly bound in buckram — the 1949 edition of the Farmer's Almanac. A broomstraw marked the compilation of the world's lowest altitudes.

Merlin came in with an armload of wood and dropped it rattling into the box beside the stove. Then he set about his fire, kneeling down and peering through little iron doorways, prodding with a long black poker. Morse sat with his hands folded on the table, silently enjoying the sound of Merlin's awkward labors. Several minutes passed before Morse said, "Can I call you Merlin?"

Merlin turned and looked at him quickly, then went back to his stove. "To be sure," he said, opening another little door and probing inside with his poker.

"With a name like that it doesn't seem right to call you by your last name."

"This is true," Merlin said, slamming the door and turning the little chrome handle. "That name has always been a problem — people expect too much of me, like magic, for instance."

Morse chuckled down at his folded hands.

"And what is your name, your Christian name?" Merlin said, still involved with his stove.

"Jacob."

Merlin turned, a smile lighting up his face. "That's right, I remember now. People must expect too much of you too."

"Yes," Morse said. "Sometimes they do. But they call me Jay, not Jacob."

Merlin was radiant. "But you must let me call you Jacob — you will let me do that."

"Sure," Morse said. "You bet."

"And tell me this, Jacob: Did you have a brother?"

Morse looked a bit confused. "Yes," he said. "One."

"Ah yes," Merlin said. "And did you take him by the heel?"

"What?"

"Nothing," Merlin said, turning back to his stove. "Nothing."

Morse raised one hand to his face and ran a finger across his cheek. "What did you say?"

"It was nothing," Merlin repeated. Then after a moment he added: "I have often thought that my own name should have been Jacob. Jacob Carson — has a nice ring to it. Can't you see it engraved on a leatherbound edition of my collected works?"

"Sure," Morse said with uncertainty. "You bet."

Merlin, silent, began to stuff newspapers into the stove.

Throughout this little exchange I had sat on the bed, uneasily listening as I turned the pages of the Farmer's Almanac. Something was going on with them, something that I did not understand. They seemed to have some bond, some connection — and yet at the same time there was a certain vague . . . hostility between them. Perhaps it was simply Merlin feeling him out, finding out how best to dominate him — yes, perhaps it was just that . . . but there seemed to be something else too, something . . . And now, as the fire began its soft roaring and Merlin assembled the dinner makings on the sinkboard, they were at it again . . .

"But that was a long time ago," Merlin was saying. "When I was Peter's age — a very long time ago."

"Where?" Morse said. "In what cities?"

"Oh, New York — twice there. Philadelphia. Bangor, Maine. And Chicago, one very bad siege in Chicago. I still remember the sergeant checking me out, a big mick with those little cobwebs of red veins in front of his ears — looking at me very stern, *very* stern indeed, and saying in his best fatherly voice: 'You shouldn't do this, Merlin. You are a brilliant man.'" Merlin laughed out loud and hit the sinkboard with the flat of his hand.

Morse, his hands folded on the table, smiled down at them. "I spent some time in Chicago — Cook County, I mean — when I was a kid. Pretty bad place."

"I don't remember too much about it — even what jail it was. There were some big orange spiders in the cell with me I remember, but that doesn't mean too much because there were snakes and scorpions and tigers too — and one big scaly dragon with a yellow spotted tongue and a long tail with barbs on it.

And a man who came twice a day with a bucket of acid he poured all over the floor so that I couldn't get down from my bunk."

"It wasn't quite that bad when I was there," Morse said.

"You probably had the misfortune to go in sober."

For a moment there was silence — or rather only the sound of the fire and of Merlin peeling the potatoes. Then:

"Peter, you ought to spend some time in jail." I looked up from the book. It was Merlin — he didn't turn around, just kept on with the potatoes. "It would do wonders for your character."

"What's wrong with my character?" I said.

"Oh, it's just fine, what there is of it," Merlin said, still with his back to me. "But it needs expansion. It lacks that certain richness which only a few nights in the slammer can provide."

"Go to hell," I said.

"No really, Peter, seriously. Just take our Jacob here, you have a living example right before your eyes. I imagine that Jacob was stealing from his mother's purse when he was five and molesting little girls in the neighborhood by the time he was ten. From there he doubtless graduated to grand theft auto and then went on straight to the top." Morse was sitting now with a quiet but alert smile on his face — he had unfolded his hands again and had commenced that rubbing of his cheek with one long finger. "For all of this," Merlin went on, "our Jacob has paid in the heavy coin of confinement. Who knows how many nights he has spent on those narrow hard bunks? But behold the result!" Now Merlin whirled around and pointed at Morse's now grinning face with the potato peeler. "Those nights of fertile contemplation have brought forth a man full of sympathy and tolerance, those days in the Philistine yoke have yielded up a man deeply sensitive to the woes of the afflicted. It is this kind of richness to which you should aspire, my boy, this kind of resonance which you should seek to infuse into your brittle timbers!" He ended by plunging the peeler into a potato and holding it aloft like a torch.

My mouth was open to say something but Morse was already

talking. "You should listen to your . . . you should listen to Merlin, Peter. But don't let his kind words for me make you ignore his own good points. Jail is good, but you don't want to forget whiskey. You will have to drink more if you want to amount to anything . . ."

"Nobly spoken!" Merlin, armed now with an upraised colander, resumed the podium. "Brother Jacob, if I could only express to you . . . if I could only tell of the countless times when I have sat down with this ungrateful whelp, a bottle of nectar between us, and found myself, an elderly gentleman, assigned to the laboring oar. Is it any wonder, is it any wonder I ask you, that there now sits before us this quivering mass of irresolution, pitifully fingering his soiled copy of the Farmer's Almanac?"

"No, no wonder," Morse was saying.

"You two make me sick," I said through a weary smile.

"Well," Merlin said, "if you are going to get sick please go outside to do it — and bring me an armload of wood while you are about it."

I accepted the invitation. Merlin would go on blustering like that all night if Morse continued to encourage him. The least I could do was escape now and then. I went out and stood on the porch under a sky brilliant with stars. A gentle wind moved stealthily through the willows behind the shrill symphony of frogs and crickets; somewhere, an owl called . . .

Somehow, I thought, somehow Merlin was a little easier for me to take this time. Perhaps it was Morse — the fact that he acted as some kind of a buffer between us, something that Merlin had to bounce off of before he could get to me. But, whatever it was, the visit had been almost pleasant so far. I had been able to do something that had never been possible before — to simply let him entertain me. Always before I had resisted it; yes, even as I had outwardly cooperated, played my part, always there had been something in me that would not allow me to submit to it, accept it, enjoy it for what it was. But now, this time, so far, it was different. That vague sense of duty had disappeared, that feeling of adjunct-ness, and in its place there was some new confidence, some new . . . wholeness. Yes, perhaps it was Morse . . .

I went down off the porch and around to the back for the wood. The bathroom window was open and I could hear the sound of them talking as I picked up the stove lengths with one hand and piled them on my arm. Morse's voice, that high but resonant voice which was now so familiar to me, drifted out and then withdrew again behind the sustained chirruping of the frogs. Then Merlin's, lower and more rough, more splintered by the assaults of whiskey and tobacco, rose up for an instant and I caught the single word "everything," spoken loud, just as a light gust of wind slammed the window. I could hear Merlin's footsteps, coming to lock it, as I topped off the load of wood and headed back around to the front.

They were silent, Merlin cooking the steaks, when I came in. I put the wood in the box, then went over and sat across from Morse at the table. His expression was vaguely troubled, his lips faintly pursed as if he had wanted to say something but had forgotten what it was. I poured some more whiskey into his glass and he made a feeble smile in my direction.

"Have you ever thought of trying some sculpture, Jay?" I said after a moment. "With clay, I mean. You could, you know — feel the shapes."

"No, I hadn't thought of it," he said. "I might try it."

"I mean as much as you talk about not missing it, it would be nice to have some . . . outlet, you know, when you do get the urge."

"I don't know," he said. "I've never tried it. With these big things . . ." He held up his hands, palms toward me. The six-inch fingers, each with a girth larger than my thumb, were like great blunt chimneys.

"They seem to have done all right with a tiny wooden pencil," I said. "They didn't have any trouble with that."

Merlin was putting the food on the table now — a huge

platter of venison steaks, some boiled potatoes and string beans. "You will recall," he put in, "that the biblical Jacob was a considerable sheepman. I will hazard that somewhere along the line the family interests turned from sheep to cows — yes, that our Jacob's forebears were not unacquainted with cows."

I looked up at him, annoyed that he had interrupted. "What?" I said.

"His hands, our Jacob's hands," Merlin said with a grin as he sat down. "Only generation upon generation of methodical teat-pulling could produce such fearsome hooks."

"No," Morse said. "No cows that I know of."

"You search your pedigree," Merlin said as he dished out the food. We were all silent a moment, inhaling the heady smell of the meat, before Merlin added: "Anyway, we'll get you some clay tomorrow. I know where there is a fat vein of it."

It was after dinner, when we were down to coffee and whiskey again, that I mentioned the print on the wall. No, it was not just innocent curiosity. He had had a year and a half now to finish that masterpiece which was to justify to posterity this extended alpine retreat. His agent, Reimer, had given up asking me about it by now, but I wanted to know anyway — to find some vindication for my oft-expressed opinion that he had not written a blessed word. Besides, there was something else. If he would just talk about it, which I had no doubt that he would, then Morse would have an opportunity to observe the grand poetic mind in full creative flight. That, after all, was why we had come.

Merlin looked up at the print as if he had forgotten that it was there. "It's a self-portrait," he said after a moment. "Just some dime store paints, a piece of old canvas, a chip of mirror . . . Not a bad likeness, wouldn't you say?"

"Not at all," I said. "Maybe you can read us the poem

tonight — the long one that you were writing about it last year. I'm sure that Jay would like to . . ."

Morse, his long face bright under the gas lamp, looked expectant, wary almost.

"That *is* too bad," Merlin said. "I just sent it away last week."

"What a shame." There was only the smallest trace of scorn in my voice. I didn't want to quarrel, I just wanted to know — for myself.

"But I can tell you about some changes, some new insights into the characters," Merlin said serenely as he looked over at me. "A poem is never really done."

"Good," I said. "We'll have to settle for that. But first you have to tell Jay how it was last year."

"You tell it," Merlin said. "You can remember it." He took out a cigarette and leaned back in his chair.

I told what I could remember. Merlin sat watching me with a calm approving smile — the teacher listening to the recitation of his prodigy — and Morse, his brow wrinkled with listening, leaned forward over folded hands as I first went through the Bible story and then explained what I could remember of Merlin's alterations and embellishments. "And so you see Herodias — Merlin's Herodias — is not seeking vengeance for those bad things the Baptist said about her when he was baptizing. No, she is after his skin because he told her to go to hell when she tried to seduce him. And Salome . . ."

When it was done I looked over at Merlin. "That's all I can remember," I said to him. He leaned forward in the chair and, putting out his cigarette, looked into Morse's now impassive face a moment before he turned back to me.

"That's good," he said. "Perfect. And that is just how I had it planned, projected, when you were here last fall. But then as I wrote it out, as it took shape, it seemed to me that there were some . . . gaps, something not quite right in the motivation of the characters." He took a sip of coffee before he went on. "Take Salome, for instance. She seems like such a tool, like an automaton whom her mother directs by remote control. Is she really that simple? Isn't there another dimension to her that we might have missed, overlooked?" He glanced up at us, looking intently from one face to the other.

"I mean think of this," Merlin went on. "Antipas has offered her half of his kingdom — *half*. Doesn't that mean, couldn't that mean that he is offering to make her his queen? Maybe he has grown a little weary of Herodias, of her everlasting ambition for him, her perpetual pushing to get him into projects that he really doesn't want to undertake. Because Antipas is in many ways a very simple man, you see, a man who wants just to be let alone — the kingdom he has is enough for him. It is Herodias who wants to expand the borders, Herodias who involves him in those little intrigues that she loves so well, Herodias who never seems to tire of trying to make him something besides what he is. And so perhaps, perhaps . . . but, whatever the reason, it seems to me that that is the offer he is making to Salome. And if that is so, then — think of it — is Salome so uncomplicated, so devoted, that she is not in the least tempted to accept? She, herself, certainly has no reason to get the crazy old Baptist bumped off — that's all her mother's idea. And so maybe, just maybe . . . Anyway, I wonder about it. After all, that is how Herodias herself got to be queen, by displacing another. Why not she? Why not Salome too? Of course, it is her own mother she would have to displace . . . but you must understand that this was long ago, when people had less conscience about such things."

Merlin sat back in his chair and looked at us again, from one to the other. "What do you think, Jacob?" he said after a moment. "Doesn't that seem possible to you?"

I glanced over at Morse. He was smiling, smiling more broadly than I thought the question or the whole silly exercise warranted. "Yes," he said. "It just might be possible."

"Good," said Merlin, leaning forward in his chair again and taking a long swallow from his glass. "I think it might too. And so suppose, just suppose this then: that Salome, instead of asking for the head of the Baptist like she has been commissioned to do, instead of that she takes Antipas up on his offer and bumps Herodias out of the queen's chair. Bump — new queen. But wait a minute; knowing Salome, I would be willing to bet that she wouldn't last in that queen business for very long — those receptions and formal dinners, all of that pomp and circumstance. No, it wouldn't be long before she'd be out with the shepherd boys again. What does she want with a decrepit old king anyway? She'd rather roll in the hay with the rustics. And then that would be that." Merlin scratched his bald head and looked at Morse again. "What do you say, Jacob? Have I got it right so far?"

Morse, looking faintly troubled now, rubbed his cheek with a long forefinger. "Sounds pretty good so far," he said in a low voice. "It makes sense."

"Good, good," Merlin said. "But now it gets harder. Salome's gone, Antipas has no queen. But what about Herodias? He might as well take her back, mightn't he?" His glasses flashing in the light, Merlin turned from Morse to me. "What do you think, Peter?"

"I think you have finally lost your mind," I said. "What's the sense of all this? If you don't stay fairly close to the Bible story it just all falls apart."

"Oh, it's just a fundamental question of motivation," Merlin said. "Just a matter of getting to know the characters well enough — so that when you put them together they seem to act by themselves. Otherwise the author always seems to be intruding, always seems to be bullying the characters into doing something they don't want to do."

"That's great," I said. "But then why hang the name of Bible characters on them? If you have your own characters, let them have their own names."

"You may have something there," Merlin said with a broad grin. "But sometimes it is . . . amusing to find out how historical characters would have acted if they had been more true to themselves. Names don't matter."

"Bullshit."

"Okay, bullshit," Merlin said. "But you bought a ticket and now you have to play. You're the one who got me into this; now you have to help me out of it." He regarded me gravely while he scratched his dome again.

I looked over at Morse. "What do you think, Jay?" I said. "Isn't this the silliest damn thing you have ever heard? You are really getting some insights into the mind of the poet."

"It is an interesting game," said Morse, smiling vaguely. "You learn about people."

I looked back at Merlin. He still had that same serious look on his face. It was two against one again. "Okay," I finally said. "Give me my question again."

Now Merlin smiled. "Herodias," he said. "Is Antipas going to take her back?"

"Of course not," I said. "He's sick and tired of her, her and her cunning schemes. It's too much effort just to keep up with her, let alone stay half a step ahead."

"Precisely," Merlin said archly.

"Besides," I went on, getting into the spirit of it, "besides, he probably knows by now that she was down in the prison with the Baptist."

"How would he know that?" Merlin said quickly.

"Lots of ways. Your leering jailer down there, he might have told. Or Salome. Or even the Baptist himself, during one of those afternoon sessions he and Antipas used to have. Lots of ways."

"Even Herodias herself maybe?"

"Sure. I wouldn't put it past her. The way you've made her, she would probably just up and tell him after Salome had taken off — just to twist the knife a little."

"To make him jealous."

"Sure," I said.

"But he wouldn't be jealous, would he?" said Merlin, taking it up again. "How could he be jealous of a grizzled old bird like the Baptist? No . . . but angry, he would be angry anyway. This is just the last straw — her having made such a spectacle of herself. Every scullery maid and pastry cook knows about it, they titter about it in the hallways: how the queen tried to entice the crazy old Peraean and he had told her to tend to her knitting. It's too much, just too much. But what should he do with her?"

"Send her packing," I said. "Just like he did with the other one, the King of Arabia's daughter."

Merlin scratched his head and took another long swallow of whiskey. "He could do that, I suppose," he said. "Or he could put her away in the cooler with the Baptist — in separate cells, of course. But there is one thing he has to do before he does any of those things . . ." Merlin looked at both of us again, from one to the other. Morse was still and sober, seemed almost to be holding his breath. I didn't have the answer.

"Well," Merlin said after a moment, "well, it's just this: before he gets shed of her he's certainly not going to pass up the opportunity to tell her what an ass she's been. I can just hear him burning her ears, can't you? But wait a minute: she's not the kind to just sit there and take it; she'll listen to just so much of his pious homily before bang! she'll sit up straight and start giving it right back. And who knows what might happen then? What she might do, what he might do . . ."

Merlin's voice faded away. He looked down into his whiskey and was still for a long moment — then his face came up and he was looking at Morse, still still Morse, gazing intently into that expressionless face for a brief instant before, slowly, he lowered his eyes again to the glowing amber spark in his whiskey glass. He was pretty drunk now; he had reached the point of soliloquy.

"But then . . . then she will be gone. He, Antipas, will be alone. But wait — alone? No, not really — for we must not forget the Baptist. Has he finally gone really insane now, does he beat his grizzled head against the cold stones of the prison and curse that God or Demon, who knows which, that allowed him to think for a moment that he was the Promised One and yet, that dream withdrawn, did not allow him to be a man? For yes, yes, perhaps we have oversimplified him too, have failed to grasp his essential dimension. Perhaps we are sadly mistaken when we see in that moment of abnegation only the predictable reaction of religious fervor and devotion to a bold and undisguised act of temptation. It is too easy, all too easy to forget that at that moment, at that very moment of temptation as well as during the several days preceding it, the Baptist had been locked in mortal struggle with himself, with the feelings of disappointment and disillusion — yea, even of deception — which had overcome him when his disciples had returned to Machaerus with the news: Yes, they had seen the Christ — yes, it was really He. For to him, to the Baptist, this meant no, he, the Baptist, was not He. The dream that he had dared, the dream that he had cherished even while denying the possibility to his followers — that had become like dust in his hands, dust in the form of the almost apologetic admonition of Jesus to take no offense. Yes, he was after all only a man, a man in prison. But yet a man, yet really a man? Would all those years, all those years wherein the outward ministry of precursor masked the inward dream of avatar, all those years secretly practicing for divinity — would they allow him to be a man? For he did, you see — he did want to be a man. If he could not be God, he would be a man . . .

"And then, then, in the midst of this roiling agony of doubt, the test had come, had appeared as if it had been ordered — the moment of perfume and clicking palms . . . and it seemed that he was watching himself, standing back and watching, curiously wondering which way he would jump . . . when suddenly, as he watched, those gaunt muscles tensed, tightened . . . and he jumped — no, not forward into the unknown, into the labyrinths of the flesh which his conscious mind had determined upon in preference to the continuation as less than God along the path he had followed as God — no, not forward but back, back, pulled back by those responses which were so deeply cut, so thoroughly ingrained, that they would not brook contradiction by mere conscious choice. For he was tired, you see. He was old and he was tired . . ."

Merlin was silent, lost in contemplation of his whiskey. There was only the sound of a dripping water faucet against the shrill background of cricket music as I filled my pipe again. Morse, his hands folded on the table in front of him again, seemed made of stone.

"But all that is passed now," Merlin finally resumed, still staring down at his glass. "Herodias — the meddlesome bane of one man, the abnegated tempter of another — she is gone now, disappeared, evaporated, as if she never had existed. And they, the two old men, remain. Should they meet now? Should Herod Antipas go as Herodias did into the Baptist's prison, should he confront him there?"

Merlin looked up at me, a strange look of entreaty spread over his face. Behind the lenses of his glasses his eyes seemed damp, out of focus. "Should he, Peter?"

"I don't know," I said, surprised by the sound of my own voice. "I suppose he should."

"I suppose he should," Merlin repeated. He glanced quickly over at Morse's blank face, then back at me. "I suppose they should . . . But tell me this, Peter: tell me what will happen, what should happen then. I am confused; you must help me with this . . . with this one point."

He continued to gaze at me with those damp pleading eyes while I sat silent, thinking. "Well," I said after a moment, "well, like you said, the king should go to him, like Herodias did, rather than have him come to the king. He's still in prison, he can't go anywhere — and besides, that makes it symmetrical."

"Symmetrical," Merlin repeated, still looking at me.

"And then he should find the Baptist there in his cell, like she did, and they should talk . . . I don't know, they might become friends . . ."

"They might, they might indeed," Merlin said.

"And then after they had talked a while, well then Antipas might just take him out of the cell and then the two of them would just walk together down . . ."

"Wait," Merlin said. "Wait. Doesn't something else have to happen now? Even supposing they are friends, doesn't one of them have to . . ."

"Why?" I said. "It's all over. She is gone. Everyone is gone. It's just them, just the two of them walking down the corridor and then out into the courtyard, out into the sun."

Merlin sat up straight in his chair, smiling bemusedly, and rubbed the top of his bald head with the palm of his hand. "And that's it?" he said. "That's all there is to it?"

"That's it," I said.

With an abrupt turn of his head Merlin looked over at Morse, who was sitting still and silent, his face blank and impenetrable, just as he had been for the last ten mniutes. "What do you think, Jacob?" Merlin said. "Has Peter got it right, just to leave it there?"

At first it seemed that Morse had not heard — for a moment his expression remained the same, but then slowly, imperceptibly, a faint and wary smile came to his lips. Then his voice, strangely hushed:

"Yes, I think so. It sounds right to me, Merlin."

Merlin drained his glass, then put it down hard on the table. "I don't know," he said, getting up. "There seems to be something lacking."


The morning was bright and clear. I left them on the porch after breakfast and went down to the stream with my gear. There was a decent hatch going on and I walked downstream past Merlin's hole and several hundred yards beyond it, watching the rise. Finally I came to the end of a good stretch and sat down on the bank to rig up. They were coming up for a small black

*311*

fly, a midge of some kind. I found one in my fly box that looked like it, a tiny thing on a number twenty hook, and tied it on. Then I lit my pipe while the fly dressing dried. Across the stream by the edge of the forest a young doe was feeding by herself, her head deep in the high grass.

After a few minutes I stood up and started to work back upstream. The fish were small and I released three before I found a decent one. He was under some overhanging willows and I had to cast sidearm in order to reach him. After a few mangled attempts I finally got it right and the tiny fly came riding down over him, floating high and sassy. The fish took it softly and then, when he felt the hook, headed down toward the roots of the trees. I turned him before he made it, and then he came up to see if he could shake it out in the air. He was an acrobat, but it wasn't about to come out. Before long I had him in the net — about thirteen inches long and bright as a beggar's smile.

There were more small ones as I worked on up. I tried to keep the fly away from them, but two or three I had to bring in and release. They were spirited little villains; I promised to meet them another day when they were grown. Then, on the far side of a flat-topped rock, I got into another good one. This time, though, he got into the roots before I could turn him and I brought back only half my leader.

I waded to the bank to put on a new leader and fly. Now I was just at the foot of the riffles leading up to Merlin's hole. I could see a big fish working methodically just where the riffles flattened out into the pool.

As I sat on the bank and took a new leader out of my vest it all came flooding back: that morning, that fish. My rage . . . I could almost feel it returning, that numbing incredulous fury as the great fish had gone churning down the feeder ditch and into the stream again — as I had looked helplessly down at his boots in the grass. It had been almost as if he did not want me to touch the fish, to soil it with my fingers. After all, it was his fish, his to keep or release as he wished — there was no need to . . . humiliate me. I would not have soiled it . . .

When the fly dressing was dry I stood up and waded carefully into the bottom of the stretch of riffles. The fish was still working, calmly and deliberately sucking the tiny flies under as they passed over him. My line hissed in the windless air as I worked it out, then dropped the fly three feet up from his nose. I held my breath while it moved down toward him . . . then disappeared in a soft swirl as, softly, he took it.

As soon as he felt the sting the great fish turned and bored down into the bowels of the pool like a runaway locomotive. It was impossible to turn him without breaking the leader, so I just kept a steady persistent pressure on him as he went deeper and deeper. If there were roots where he was headed, well that would be the end of it. But then suddenly he was not moving, not diving any more — he was on the bottom, sulking there and gathering his strength. After a few minutes of waiting I increased the pressure on him, but still he would not move. Finally I eased up on him a little and, taking my knife from the pocket of my vest, tapped several times on the butt of the rod with it. The fish seemed to shake his head — then suddenly the line was slack and he was exploding through the surface like a Polaris missile. I quickly brought in some line and then watched him walk all over the top of the pool, twisting and turning and pirouetting in the sun — until finally he turned and went down again, hard and deep.

He had grown an inch or two.

I kept the pressure on. After a few minutes he came up again — not to the surface this time but just beneath it, running first to the head of the pool and then, as I succeeded in turning him, returning almost to my feet. There he lay in the shallow water for a moment glowering up at me around his broad black forehead as, gills working frantically, he considered his next move — then all at once he was off, running again to the head of the pool. I eased out the line after him, gradually increasing the pressure until I turned him back again just where the upper riffles began. Once more he came back, over against the far bank this time — but now he was fading. I coaxed him over into the shallow water, talking to him in a soothing low voice. He was not watching me this time, only thrashing weakly as I bent down with the net. Then I had him.

I splashed up onto the bank and dumped him in the grass. He thrashed a few more times and then lay still, the great gills moving slowly in and out in the suffocating air. He was very dark, the maroon spots along his sides blending into the dusky black-green of his back. His calm eyes were as big as dimes.

"Well, fish, we meet again," I said as I sat down in the grass beside him.

Across the river the young doe was still feeding unconcernedly along the edge of the forest, her smooth brown flanks glistening in the sun. She raised her head and looked at me curiously, then buried her head in the grass again. I watched her for several minutes before I stood up and, slipping a forefinger into one great scarlet gill-slit, carried the fish to the stream and threw him in, end over end.

I could hear Merlin's hoarse laughter as I walked back through the willows. They were still on the porch, the coffee pot and whiskey bottle on the table between them, and as I waded through the damp meadow I could see Morse, his face bright in the morning sun, raise one hand high above his head in some gesture while Merlin pounded on the table and roared. When I got closer I could see the two Indian pictures, which Morse had presented to him at breakfast, lying on Merlin's bony knees.

"Our Jacob was telling me about this worthy," Merlin said through tears, holding up one of the pictures as I came up. "What a knave, what a varlet . . ." He collapsed in laughter again.

"Well, anyway, just to finish it," Morse said with a broad open smile, "anyway, from in front of his hogan he could see the dust of anybody coming up the road about half an hour before they got there, and he could tell from the speed whether it was a wagon or a truck. When it was a truck he knew it had to be the Indian agent because nobody else came to see him in a truck. So up he gets and drives the horses, ten or fifteen of them sometimes, into the cave — and then he covers the front of it over with brush and when the agent gets there he is sitting in front of the hogan shucking his puny corn. Well, the agent, he sees enough horseshit for a regiment but . . ."

I left them crowing and wiping their eyes while I went inside to clean the fish. The breakfast dishes were still on the table so I did them too, piling them upside-down on the sinkboard to drain. It was going to be a warm day. Out of the window by the sink I could see a hawk hanging still in the air over the far edge of the clearing. He stayed there a long time, just moving his wings a little now and then, before he let the rising currents take him back and up and over the ridge — out of sight.

I went over to Merlin's bookcase to get a newspaper to wrap the fish in. In one corner there were some old ones with faded front pages. I pulled out one of them, opened it up, then took out some inside pages and went back to the sink. I was just about to wet the pages under the tap when I saw the article — with a little red mark beside it. It was about the trial, the first trial. I took the pages back to the bookcase and slipped them into the newspaper. Then I sat down on the bed and, taking the little pile with the faded front pages, began to go through them one by one, looking for the little red marks. It was pretty complete, right down to the acquittal a few weeks ago in some recent editions at the bottom of the pile.

I sat still on the bed, my mind full of strange, half-formed questions. I was flattered that he should take such an interest in the case. Why, he had even gone to the trouble of finding the articles about the first trial, long before I had told him about it or had anything to do with it. Yes, they were all there, every article. I could just picture him going through his old newspapers to find those early articles, putting them all in order so that he could read it — from cover to cover. And yet, and yet, what were those questions, those vague feelings that so roughly jostled that satisfaction? Was there, could there be some other reason for his interest, some reason other than . . . parental concern? Yes, that day a year ago he had said that he was interested in . . . perhaps the case had caught his artistic fancy, perhaps he had an article in mind, a book, a poem. That must be it, certainly that was it. And yet . . .

Merlin's rough laughter came again through the burlap, then died away into the stillness as I put the little pile of newspapers back into the bookcase.

When I went out they were sitting silently in their chairs, both smiling vaguely out over the meadow. "What's wrong?" I said. "Did you two run out of back-country humor?" Merlin looked up at me slyly, taking a sip from the ubiquitous glass.

"Just resting, my boy," he said. "Just catching our breath. I expect that you have about a dozen good fish for us all cleaned and in the refrigerator."

"No," I said. "Just one."

"You jest."

"No. All the big ones got away."

"You are losing your touch," Merlin said.

"Could be," I said.

The sun came in long slanting shafts through the solemn pines as we made our way up the trail, our boots sending out sudden puffs of dust as fine as ground graphite. The biscuit-dry woods, littered with fallen cones, pleaded for an early rain to geld the menace of fire that hovered like a grim presence in the parched afternoon air. A forlorn caravan we made — in front, Merlin's stocking cap bobbing along like an apple in a barrel; behind, me leading Morse by one great loose hand like an awkward burro. A forlorn caravan through an anxious forest.

Morse had insisted upon coming along. He needed the exercise, he had said — he needed to smell and feel and hear the forest, the air, the stones. I had opposed it, even resorting to oblique suggestions that it would take twice as long if he came. Merlin, although noncommittal at first, had ended by taking Morse's side. If he was going to be a sculptor, Merlin had said, he ought to go where it was, to touch it in the ground where it had grown, to take it out with his own hands. For yes, this was the expedition to gather Morse his clay.

Merlin ranged ahead like an eager puppy, stopping every now and then to catch his breath and wait for us. "This is perfect for me," he said when he stopped the first time by the water tank — before we headed up the trail toward the ridge. "I don't often get the chance to be in front." We, Morse and I, came deliberately and steadily after him, our shuffling feet leaving a low cloud of dust which settled on the granite boulders alongside the trail. Every now and then I would tell him about a narrow place or a rock, but otherwise we were silent, wrapped in the concentration required by our yoked advance.

After we had gone about half an hour the trail became steeper and the woods thinned out into rocky slopes covered with tinder-dry grass. Soon we came around a bend in the trail to find Merlin sitting on a rock with a cigarette and his pocket flask. Beside him was a tiny spring of water coming out from between two massive boulders and trickling down into a small rock basin. "I thought you might want to wash your hands before the going gets tough," Merlin said. I helped Morse take a drink and then, when I had him settled on the rock with Merlin, bent down and put my whole face in the clear water. It was very cold — the end of my nose was numb when, after a long drink, I straightened up. Taking out my handkerchief, I wetted it in the spring and then knotted it cowboy-style around my neck.

"Now, if you look right up there you can see the new ditch,"

Merlin said, handing the flask to me. I took a short burning sip and gave it back to him. Through the trees where he was pointing, but high up on the hillside, I saw the new cement wall of a water canal — the one Merlin had essentially donated the right-of-way for. I sat on the rock and listened while he told us about it — how it was made and how long it took. When that was finally done he took another drag from his flask and then pointed again, higher up.

"Now your clay, Jacob, is on the other side of it, way up high, right above it in a cut they made with the bulldozers. You can see it, Peter — that big red scar." I saw it. "We have to get on the other side of the ditch to get there, but there is a place where we can go under it, where it is up on pillars, and then the path goes right on up to the cut — and then out the other side and up the top of the ridge. Comes out by that big outcropping of boulders . . ." Merlin's face sobered, darkened for an instant — but then he was smiling again, his hand on Morse's shoulder.

"What I mean, Jacob, is that we're almost there," he said.

We slid down off the rock and started out again, me in front this time and Merlin leading Morse. In five minutes I had left them far behind. I stopped on a promontory and looked down over the forest below and, off to the left, Merlin's clearing like a small blemish on the great green face of it. The cabin was hidden but I could see the line of willows where the stream was. Far beyond the clearing, in the distance, some rough stony bluffs rose into the sky — and beyond them were the high mountains, blue in the afternoon haze. The tiny black speck of an airplane moved slowly along the crest of the peaks.

Merlin and Morse came around a corner two switchbacks below me. The obvious proverb came to mind as I watched their halting progress, Merlin's small lean body seeming sometimes to be almost pushed along by the gangling figure that he purported to lead. An unlikely pair, I thought, a strange and unlikely pair. At times, at moments, they seemed so alike — as if they were brothers, brothers long separated who had been brought together

318

by some outrageous coincidence. But in other ways they were so utterly dissimilar. Merlin seemed, had always seemed, so wholly impotent — too dazed by his self-generated cloud of words to take a positive step in any direction at all. Morse, on the other hand, was the image of potency, a set trap — his blindness, far from removing that impression, actually seemed to heighten it. And yet perhaps, perhaps that kind of difference could be found in brothers too — I would not know. It might just be that dissimilar traits between brothers could be really complementary, each filling some lack, some need, in the other. I would not know. Brotherhood — that was something I knew nothing about. But there was one thing, one difference, which I could not dismiss so easily — which I could not accomodate within any concept of friendship or brotherhood that I knew about. That was simply, again, that strange unstated hostility that lay between them, separating them and yet seeming in some way to bind them together. In spite of their alliances, their agreements, it was always there, always silently there, like a tension demanding resolution. It was almost as if they had had an argument, long ago, an argument that had been interrupted and that they were now waiting to resume, each having thought of more reasons to justify his position during the forced intermission. Strangest of all, I could not dispel the feeling that the argument could not proceed, could not be resumed, without me. Was it that I was needed as an interlocutor, a medium through which their thoughts had to pass? Yes, perhaps it was that — but there was something else too, some more . . . direct involvement. Sometimes it even seemed that I . . . that I was myself at issue.

They came around the corner toward me. Something was wrong with Merlin — his face was pale, almost white, and the sweat was pouring in rivers down his cheeks.

"Are you all right?" I said, walking down to meet them.

"Well, I wouldn't go that far," Merlin said, giving Morse to me as he slumped down on a rock. "A man of my age does not undertake an expedition of this nature without suffering some vascular distress. Besides, my throat is like a dry crust," he said as he brought out his flask.

I sat Morse down on another rock, watching Merlin out of the corner of my eye. His hands did not shake as he brought the flask up to drink, but it seemed that it took some effort to keep them steady.

"Are you sure you're all right?" I said. "You're white as a sheet."

"You must learn to avoid trite similes," Merlin said. He wiped his forehead with his handkerchief and moved to sit down on the ground, his back against the rock. He began to look better as his nostrum took effect.

"Well, you should stop and rest more often," I said. "I'd rather not carry you down."

"I'm light," he said. "Just a sack of old bones. Why, a big strapping lout like you . . ."

I looked away from that stubborn insolent face. Through all of this Morse had been sitting on his rock, breathing easily in the sun. When after a moment it became clear that I was not going to engage Merlin again on the subject of his health, he asked in a quiet voice if I would describe the view from where we were. I did my best, telling him where the clearing was, describing the rocky bluffs and the distant peaks. He listened placidly, one great hand holding the wrist of the other in a loose grip as the sun reflected off his broad smooth forehead. Then I was done and Merlin was stirring, struggling up from his seat on the ground. "Let's go," he said. "We'll be there in ten minutes."

We set out again, Merlin resuming the lead with apparently renewed energy. Before long we had reached the canal, or the "ditch," as Merlin called it. It was huge, the slightly convex concrete walls rising what looked like twenty feet from the ground. Merlin led us along beside it for some distance, then down a little hill into a dip where the whole thing was raised up off the ground on massive concrete trestles. There was no need to stoop our heads as we went under, listening in vain for the sound of the water above us, and then we were on the other, the uphill, side of it and on a path that angled up the hillside. Soon we were level with the top of the canal and we could see the water moving along fast and smooth. Just "downstream" from us the whole thing was covered, big flat concrete slabs laid on top to make a roof that cleared the surface of the water by only about a foot.

I asked Merlin about it — why the part of the canal "up-stream" from where we stood was not covered like the rest of it. "I don't know," he said. "They started down below and just came up to here. Maybe they ran out of money." He turned abruptly and led the way up the path.

In a few minutes we were all standing on the wide flat shelf of the cut. There were still bulldozer tracks where they had sheared into the rocky hillside with their blades, and there was one part that was compacted as if a crane or something like that had been stationed there. At the far end I could see where the path picked up again to go to the top of the ridge. I left Morse with Merlin and walked over to the edge. The canal was about fifty feet below us, its near wall nestled against the almost vertical hillside, and it extended up around the corner like a silver serpent in the afternoon sun. I wondered where all that water could be going, what desert it was causing to flower. Merlin would not know; that was the sort of thing that Merlin would not know . . .

When I turned around the two of them were over against the sheared hillside. Merlin had Morse's big hand in his and was guiding it, forcing it, into a diagonal crevice between two boulders which had been left embedded in the sheared wall. A small trickle of water dripped from the bottom of the crevice and disappeared into the dirt at their feet. I stood silently watching while Morse, his hand half hidden in the crack, probed and strained — and then brought out a dripping handful of fine yellow clay.

Merlin was ecstatic, childlike, as he went hopping to Morse's side. "Is it good? Is it good?"

*321*

"I don't know," Morse said, smiling broadly while he squeezed and kneaded the clay until it pushed out from between his fingers. "There are a few little rocks in it."

"We can wash it, strain those out," Merlin said excitedly. "You see how these two rocks . . ." Merlin, forgetting for a moment that he was talking to a blind man, commenced to point and gesture as he propounded his theory concerning the genesis of the vein — that the constant dripping of the water had done it, deposited it. "The best should be down here near the bottom of the crack," he said, drawing Morse by the hand again to direct his mining. "Dig it out, Jacob!" he crowed as Morse began to probe in the crevice again with those enormous fingers. "Oh, do dig it out!"

I continued to stand silently watching them. Soon Merlin was holding a ball of clay the size of a softball, working new pieces into it as Morse produced them. They, both of them, were radiant — like two small boys. Morse worked with amazing energy, a wide grin on his face, while Merlin, the receptacle, continued to cheer him on. "This vein is endless!" he would cry when a new handful appeared. "Endless!"

Yes, and as I stood there dumbly witnessing that joyous excavation, suddenly it seemed that that other thing, that vague voiceless hostility, had evaporated, disappeared — it, whatever it was, could not penetrate the joy of this moment, could not infect it. They, Merlin and Jacob — suddenly they were children, innocent as the sun . . .

But moments end, as do veins of clay. "It's just rocks now," Morse was saying. "No good. How much do we have?"

"More than we can carry," Merlin said, his face still glowing with excitement. "Let's work it up a little. That's sculptor talk, Jacob — you have to learn the lingo too. Work it up. Work it up. Let's get busy and work it up!"

Over near the edge above the canal there was a pile of seven or eight railroad ties, something to do with the crane or whatever it was that had been there. Merlin, his red stocking cap pitched at a jaunty angle, led us over to them and we sat down. He broke the ball of clay — as big as a melon now — into three pieces and gave us each one. "You too, lawyer," he said to me. "Get those silky hands going and work it up!"

And so we sat, we three, all on one tie like birds on a fence, kneading and probing the spongy yellow stuff like so many baker's apprentices. Merlin, still in the grip of that strange rapture, chattered like a jay while I watched our hands working — the great and powerful yet gentle hands of Morse, the nervous birdlike hands of Merlin, and my own hands, soft and refined but so utterly nondescript. They spoke so much about us, those hands, so much that words could only hint at — the strange ambivalence of crushing and caressing that was Morse, the reckless but ineffectual energy of Merlin, the patrician formlessness of Peter. We three.

"And so you see," Merlin was saying, "although we do know for a fact what Brigham Young said when he gazed out over that blooming Utah valley, we have no reliable account of what he was doing at the time. 'This is the place.' Well, that is very grand and fine — but for all we know he may have been having his back scratched by one of his wives. Or he might even . . ."

And as I looked from the grinning enigma of Morse's face, glowing bright in the dying sun, to the impish features of Merlin, and then out toward the blue mirage of peaks in the distance — all at once the chattering drone of that tireless voice had withdrawn into the background, the periphery, and I was bathed in a wonderful calm sense of well-being. It was not really so bad, this life that had been served up to me. The vacuum that I had carried around inside me for so long, that emptiness which neither a constructed image of the dead nor its reluctant proxy could be made to fill — suddenly that seemed gone; no, not filled — gone. And yet somehow it was not just that either, not just the removal of an emptiness — for it all seemed so . . . necessary now, so essential to the working out of it. Yes, even the rage, even that too. For suddenly it seemed that without that, all of

it, I could not have become . . . could not have been becoming
. . . could not have found myself perched on a railroad tie between Merlin's senseless but now somehow comforting prattle
and the blind smiling silence of that man whom chance or fate
was attaching, had attached to me, linked to me. ("Yes, Jacob,
Peter may just be right. They might just walk out into the sun,
each of them too surprised to be happy yet, too surprised that it
has worked out that way — when it could have worked out so
many ways. It's bad drama, of course, but it has a certain dig-
nity . . .") No, without it all we could not have been . . . we
three, without it all those blue peaks could not have seemed so
far, so vast . . .

I heard the lump of clay fall heavily to the ground, then
looked up to see Merlin standing, facing me. His arms were
folded in front of him and he seemed to be squeezing himself,
squeezing his chest and gasping for air. His face had become
pale slate; the sweat was springing from his forehead as he held
out his hand to me.

"Peter."

I jumped toward him, but already he was crumpling, stumbling
backwards, and I was just able to grab the sleeve of his old flannel
shirt before he went over the edge — but then I had lost my
balance and the water of the canal was flashing in my eyes and
we were falling, beginning to fall . . . then stopped, hanging in
the air, a great hand tight on my ankle, a high voice saying,
"Let him go," just as the sleeve began to tear and I watched
Merlin's limp form tumble down the bluff and come to rest
against the wall of the canal with a dull thump. His red cap,
which had come off during the fall, floated lazily down and, land-
ing upright in the canal, went speeding away in the current.

Grunting and tugging, Morse pulled me up until I was lying
on my stomach with just my face over the edge. Down below,
crumpled against the wall like a broken doll, Merlin lay perfectly
still. I could hear the sound of Morse's heavy breathing behind

324

me as I watched the red cap turning gently in the current, far down . . . until it shot under the low cement roof and was gone.


The sun was gone when we started down. Merlin's body over my shoulder, Morse holding one dead hand, we descended into the gathering darkness. We did not stop, not even at the spring.

He was right. Just a sack of old bones.

# ✤ Coda

2 NOVEMBER 1972

*CLARISSA* ✣ The chrysanthemums — this year they simply take my breath away. Never have I seen them so bright, so strong and wonderful. When I bring them into the house, great heaps of yellow and white and rust and red and gold, it is like carrying a treasure in my arms. When I put them out in their vases, upstairs and down, my rooms glow . . .

I must ask Peter to dinner again soon. He . . . they have been back from New Mexico for two weeks now and I have hardly heard from him at all. I suppose he has gone back to work — he can't really be serious about taking more time off to finish that silly scrap of a poem he found in Merlin's cupboard. I don't know where he got the idea that he could do something like that. He has never done anything like that . . .

Someone is laughing.

Let them laugh. Let them tell their everlasting stories to one another and laugh until they cry . . .

Yes, this year they are so bright and strong and wonderful — it is just like gathering up jewels, like carrying a treasure into my rooms. They simply do take my breath away.

And the rust looks so much better in Arthur's study. The white was too cold . . .

# ✤ APPENDIX

It is a stubborn unyielding land, a land
Standing stiff against time. In those days it was
Very much as it is.

                    The holy river rose clear
And cold from the snowy side of Hermon, tumbled
Gaily down the oleandered glades
Of pagan Dan, then softly flowed through Huleh's
Storked lagoons and down again to rest
For a time in Gennesaret. There it lay flat
Among the gentle Galilean hills
Of oak and terebinth and measured fields
And, decked in splendid shades, sapphires and jades,
Reflected from the east the red and ochre
Cliffs of Hippos and Gadara — but only
A moment before it plunged into the dreadful
Ghor, a shifting gash whose wastes of slippery
Ashgray marl bordered hanging tropic
Forests born of Hermon's flood; there,
Amid acacia and calamus, lived
The lion and the boar, the useful asp,
The creeping monitor. And still it fell,
Twisting down that gaping wound below
The roses of recumbent Jericho

Until, a quarter-mile beneath the seas,
It reached the lowest land that sun can strike,
Slipped into those oily pewter waters
And was gone, was lost.
                              The Dead Sea,
It could bear no other name.  Then
As now it squatted on the low cheek
Of the scalded earth like a great pool of lead:
Heavy fishless waters lying flat
Beneath the bright blue haze that marks
The sun's extraction; stark shores, lined
With reeking beds of saltwort and purslane and spurge,
Standing naked save for isolated
Clumps of feathered tamarisk where small
Streams enter doomed from the east;
Static air, heavy with the tang of
Mineral decay — empty of birds yet filled
With boiling clouds of insects  . . .
                              And here the holy
Man of Qumran gazed in solitary wonder
Over waters which had covered Sodom
And Gomorrah — which once were like a garden,
Even as the garden of the Lord.